SKALSINGER

CHRONICLES OF ALGARTH #2

L.A. WEBSTER

First paperback edition September 2021

Book design by Katya Dibb
katdibb.wixsite.com/design-cat
Images from Shutterstock.

ISBN 978-0-6487175-4-6 (paperback)
ISBN 978-0-6487175-3-9 (ebook)

Published by Gateshaper Books
www.lynwebster.com

For Meg, who loves fantasy.
I hope this story brings you joy.

For we do not wrestle against flesh and blood, but against the rulers, against the authorities, against the cosmic powers over this present darkness, against the spiritual forces of evil in the heavenly places.

Paul, *The Letter to the Ephesians*

I will not say: do not weep; for not all tears are evil.

J.R.R. Tolkien, *The Return of the King*

ONE

Cahira

For weeks now, nightmares had stalked her sleep. They crouched, sly and dangerous as wild cats, poised to spring the moment she closed her eyes. Their terrible claws slashed and ripped at her very being, gripped her by the throat and refused to let go. Tearing free of them took all of her will and most of her strength.

She clutched at any excuse to stay up late, fighting sleep until sheer exhaustion pulled her under. When morning came, she parted sticky eyes to find herself curled in a tight ball, mewling and drenched in sweat, with new terrors fresh in her mind and her energy drained before the day had even begun.

From the first moment, she knew this dream was different. Perhaps the clue was in the flames flickering and dancing in the fireplace, defying the cold, black night that pressed against the windows, or the golden lamp light bathing the faces of the relaxed, chattering crowd. Whatever the reason, a surge of gladness broke over her. She drew all the brightness and warmth around her like a soft blanket, and let herself sink deeper.

She looked down to see she was standing on a low stage. A thrill ran through her. She recognised this dream. It was one she hadn't experienced for a long time. She thirsted for what was coming next, but she wouldn't hurry it. There was nothing like these few precious seconds, when pre-performance nerves burned away and a sweet energy thrummed through her, begging to be released. When she could bear to wait no longer, she set it free.

A melody without words, low and sweet, flowed from her lips. The tavern settled to stillness. Faces lifted towards her, bright with expectation.

And there he was, seated in the front, smiling up at her through the yellow thatch of his beard. His hooded brown eyes crinkled at the corners in the way she loved so much.

He never seemed to tire of hearing her, or of sharing her with an audience. He didn't complain when people clustered round her afterward, each demanding their few seconds of contact with the Skalsinger. And although she did her best to satisfy those who paid to hear her, it was only his approval she truly needed. Her love. Her husband. Her Bram.

He winked at her, acknowledging that she had the crowd in the palm of her hand, and she began to weave in the words. She'd chosen a simple folk song, one that this audience of farmers and foresters would recognise: a tale of two children lost in the woods, scared and lonely, but comforted by the creatures they met along their way.

She threw a glance upward, to the image forming in the air above her head. Hazy at first, it quickly solidified. The colours deepened. Trees with shaggy, red-brown trunks soared into a cloudless sky. At their roots, moss-covered rocks emerged from a thick carpet of emerald ferns. The children appeared, walking hand in hand in the verdant shade.

Gasps reached her from several points in the room. There were always some who'd never heard a Skalsinger before, or at least not one who controlled both music and images so precisely. She was handling three voices now—the girl, her brother, and a blackbird calling from a branch—and the song was almost a palpable thing to her.

Tavern and audience fell away as she gave herself wholly to the performance. She was the sigh of the wind in the trees, the distant gurgle of a stream, the wail of a lost and lonely child, the trill of a glossy blackbird singing its heart out. It lasted forever, and it lasted no time at all. Then it was over, and she was back.

Cutting through the enthusiastic applause, she heard Bram's deep voice. "Cahira!"

She sent an affectionate smile in his direction, but he was no longer there. And yet he was still calling her name from somewhere nearby, the sound growing louder with every repetition. A jolt of fear shot through her. Her eyes scanned the room in a panic, but saw only strangers. Where was he? And why was he shouting at her?

"Cahira! We have to go."

Cahira sat bolt upright in the sagging armchair, her heart pounding. Brutal reality crashed over her. Bram was dead—killed months ago. He would never speak her name again, never smile up at her as she sang. This waking was more terrible than any nightmare. It threatened to crush her.

"Cah? Are you in there?"

She sprang to her feet, dashing the wetness from her eyes. Niall poked his head into the doorway of the herders' hut. His sharp, narrow features were nothing like Bram's generous ones. The neat black hair, the precise lines of moustache and beard, couldn't have been more different from her husband's unruly blond masses. Just for a moment, she hated him for that, and most of all for still being here when Bram was gone forever.

"There you are," he said. "The weather's closing in again. Time to go." As if sensing something, he took a step into the room and peered harder at her. "Were you asleep?"

She swallowed and schooled her voice to as normal a tone as she could manage. "I sat down for a rest. I must have drifted off."

"You're exhausted. But the storm's coming on fast, and I want to get the horses out of the valley before it breaks. Can you make it?" He had that anxious frown on his face again, the one that made her want to shake him. Did he think she was a child? A feeble old woman? She could do anything he could.

But before she could tell him so, a cold gust blasted through the unglazed window opening, raising goosebumps on her arms. The scents of moisture and dust told her he was right about the storm, and the horses. She suppressed her irritation and strove to banish the last remnants of the dream from her thoughts. That life was gone. Thinking about it only made things worse. She had to focus all her energy on finding Adric now.

They were halfway out of the valley, on foot and leading the horses, when the first heavy drops fell. In seconds, the rain was pounding on the black clay all around, turning it treacherous.

"Stand clear," Niall shouted above the downpour.

Cahira stepped away. Niall slapped the rumps of both horses. "Up, up!"

Blackbird and Sienna gathered their hind legs and plunged up the hill, greasy black clods flying from their hooves. Cahira hunched down and ducked her head to avoid being spattered in the face. By the time the barrage stopped, the horses were out of sight. Cahira and Niall followed.

Uncountable minutes later, Cahira's boots shot from under her for at least the third time. She thrust out her hands as she went down, barely saving her face from the slimy mud. The rest of her was already beyond saving. Drenched, freezing, and filthy from neck to toe, she thumped the soggy ground with a fist. She didn't need this, on top of everything else.

But she'd rather lie here on this cursed slope forever than utter a single complaint to Niall. Of course, he'd noticed her latest fall and was already sliding the short distance back down to her. The infuriating look of concern was back on his face, and she could just imagine his eager offer to take her home, where she should have stayed in the first place. Not that he would say that last part, but he'd be thinking it.

He'd wanted to go in search of Adric alone, leaving her safely behind in her parents' house. But safety was overrated, even if it came with hot baths, clean sheets, and shelter from the rain. Finding Bram's missing twin was her responsibility, no one else's. Certainly not Niall's.

Disdaining the outstretched hand, she raked long, sopping wet strings of hair out of her eyes, and used the sparse tufts of grass poking out of the mire to haul herself the rest of the way upward on hands and knees. When she reached the top, she flopped onto her side, gasping for air.

Niall leaned over her. "It's no good, Cah. Even if that carter was right, and Adric joined the cattle drive, they're all gone now. I checked every hut. No trace of anyone, and not a single cow in the whole valley." He squinted upwards. "And no sign of this rain stopping, either. We'll follow the first signpost we see, get to the nearest town as fast as we can." Again, he held out a slim, muddy hand. "Come on. At least we'll sleep in real beds tonight."

Cahira stood, without his help, and sloshed through the long grass towards the mares. A tiny part of her felt bad about the way she was behaving. But ever since Bram's death, Niall had been treating her like a piece of brittle porcelain, and it set her teeth on edge.

Where was the friend she'd known since childhood, the one who was never lost for a witty comment, usually at someone else's expense? Even during those terrible weeks when they'd all been outlawed and fleeing, knowing that only a miracle could keep them safe from the authorities for long, Niall's tendency to treat the world and its inhabitants as a kind of joke created for his own amusement had lifted her spirits so many times.

She desperately wanted that Niall back again. More than that, she needed him. Because even though the miracle had happened, Bram hadn't lived to see it. He'd died protecting a foolish, headstrong young man named Kelan, a boy they'd only just met.

And then, when Cahira hadn't believed things could get any worse, Adric had disappeared without a word. That was two months ago, and she didn't even know if he was dead or alive.

Meanwhile, her best friend had turned into a humourless stranger. He spoke to her in the same careful, patient, oh-so-calm voice he used when he was gentling a particularly flighty horse. It was insulting, and she didn't know how much more of it she could take. Maybe this entire trip had been a terrible mistake. Adric could be anywhere, even back home by now.

She hunched down in the saddle, soaked to the skin, her thoughts as dark and dreary as the ragged-edged clouds dropping more water onto her bowed head. She had endured perhaps five miserable reaches of this when Niall, who was riding in front, pulled Sienna up.

Cahira reined Blackbird in. "What is it?"

"Wait." He was peering down a narrow track that branched off the road. Cahira followed his gaze, but couldn't see anything that might have caught his attention. There wasn't even a signpost. He turned to her with a look of triumph on his face. "Briar."

Cahira caught her breath. "Where?"

"Not far, about a reach to the west."

Cahira's gloom fled. Niall was too strong a Beast Speaker to be mistaken about this. They'd found Adric's horse.

"Is Adric with him?"

"I can't tell." There was a hint of the old, familiar Niall in the crooked grin he sent her way. "Let's go find out."

Cahira slid from the saddle and dashed into the stable, ignoring Niall's shouted warning to wait. Only a few stalls were occupied, and she recognised Briar immediately. The chestnut gelding raised his head at her approach and nickered in greeting.

A rush of happiness filled Cahira as she stroked his neck. "Hello, boy. How did you get here, then?" Briar nudged her enthusiastically, almost pushing her off her feet. Cahira surprised herself by laughing.

Niall appeared at her side. "There's a big house not far away, but I can't see anyone outside. You stay with Briar, and I'll find out if Adric's there. But be ready to ride if there's any trouble."

Cahira just looked at him.

He huffed out a breath and threw up his hands in surrender. "All right. We'll both go."

She gave the gelding one last pat, and they headed for the house. It was a long, low building of grey stone, with a slate roof and no decoration of any kind on the facade. It looked grim on this rainy afternoon, but smoke was coiling from the chimneys. Someone was home.

Cahira mounted the steps leading to the large wooden door and worked the iron knocker energetically. After the booming echoes had died away, there came the clunk of a bolt sliding aside. The door swung inward to reveal a young girl in a long-sleeved dress, almost the same hazelnut shade as her neatly pulled-back hair.

Solemn russet eyes examined them briefly. Then the girl inclined her head in greeting. "Welcome, travellers, to Mirhome, a House of Aal. Are you seeking hospitality?"

The words were strangely formal for a youngster, and she held her slight body taut, with her hands folded in her sleeves. She regarded them gravely as she waited for their answer.

"No, we just have a few questions about a horse in your stable," Niall said.

"It's my brother-in-law's horse," Cahira said, impatient with this beating around the bush. "Adric Gelt. Is he here?"

"There are no guests staying at the moment, but you are welcome to enter. One of the sisters may be able to help you."

They followed their guide down the hallway and into a large room with a brightly burning fire.

"Sisters?" Niall asked.

The girl halted and turned, her movements neat and contained. "There are twelve Aalden living here. I will inform the Elder of your arrival." She pattered away, closing the door behind her.

They waited with their backs to the fireplace, rubbing the feeling back into their chilled hands. As the welcome heat penetrated Cahira's body, she felt her muscles relax. She rolled her shoulders. It was wonderful to be warm again, and on the way to being dry.

The door opened to admit a tall, square-shouldered woman in a long cream robe. Her iron-grey hair was shaped close to her head, framing a strong brown face. Energy seemed to radiate from her as she strode across the room and offered a firm hand to each of them. "Welcome to Mirhome. I am Meril, the Elder here." Her voice was a pleasant alto.

"I'm Cahira Gelt and this is Niall Crawley."

"I'm pleased to meet you both. Novice Perna, whom you've already met, will bring us some tea soon. If you're warm enough now, come sit with me and tell me what brought you to our House."

When they were all seated in the well-stuffed armchairs, Cahira burst into speech. "My brother-in-law, Adric Gelt, is missing. Niall sensed his horse in your stable. Is he here?"

Meril glanced at Niall. "You're a Beast Speaker, Master Crawley?"

He inclined his head.

"Is Adric here?" Cahira insisted, aware she was raising her voice and not caring. She clutched the arms of the chair tightly, hoping against hope that the girl who'd let them in had been mistaken, and Adric was at Mirhome after all.

But the woman shook her head. "I'm deeply sorry, but no. We haven't seen your brother-in-law. I know the horse you mean, a chestnut gelding. Two of our sisters found him wandering on the road, almost a week ago now. They couldn't identify his owner, so they brought him here. You're welcome to take him with you when you leave."

Cahira slumped against the back of the chair. They were too late again. And something bad must have happened to separate Adric from his horse. She hadn't been able to protect Bram, even though she'd been right there in the same room. How was she going to bring his twin home safely if she didn't even know where he was?

"Where exactly was Briar found?" Niall asked.

"On the Mirston road, just north of the town. The sisters were on their way to the market there. They asked questions when they arrived, but no one had reported a missing horse. I wish we could be more help."

Niall shot a glance towards Cahira. She stared back in silence, leaving the rest of the talking to him. It was all pointless, anyway. Another dead end.

"How far is Mirston from here?" Niall asked.

"Only about three reaches. I can give you directions."

"Thank you. We were looking for somewhere to stay tonight anyway, and the sight of Briar might jog someone's memory, even after a week."

"I do hope so. But the day is almost over and the weather is worsening. Why not spend the night here, and set out again tomorrow? We always have several rooms prepared for guests."

Again, Niall looked questioningly at Cahira. She turned her eyes towards the fire, unable to bring herself to care either way.

"Thank you, Elder," she heard Niall say. "We'll stay the night."

TWO

A pale sun broke through the fog as they saddled up the next morning. Impatient to get moving, Cahira took the lead, nudging Blackbird along the muddy, uneven track as fast as she dared. She berated herself as she rode. She should have insisted they set out again as soon as they knew Adric wasn't at Mirhome. But she'd been tired and cold and discouraged, and when Meril had offered warmth and a soft bed, she hadn't been able to muster the will to refuse. That had been a mistake. Adric was already at least a week ahead of them, and it was a bad sign that he hadn't come looking for his horse in all that time.

At last Blackbird reached the point where the track joined the Mirston road. On the firmer surface, Cahira leaned forward and pushed the startled mare to a gallop, ignoring the shout that rang out behind her. She knew Niall couldn't keep up with her while he had Briar on the lead rope, but she told herself it made sense for her to go on ahead. By the time he caught up with her in Mirston, she might already have found out something more about Adric, saving them valuable time. Niall wouldn't approve of them separating, but that was just too bad.

Without warning, Blackbird slackened her pace. Cahira pressed her heels harder. The mare shook her head and ignored her. There was no hitch in her gait to suggest she'd gone lame, but she settled into an easy trot and refused to speed up again.

Baffled, Cahira stood in the stirrups and scanned the surroundings. "What's going on, girl? Can you see something?"

The growing sunshine had thinned the fog to little more than translucent wisps. The road ahead was broad and straight. Nothing moved on it, or in the cleared fields on either side. The only sounds were her own breathing and the clopping of Blackbird's hooves. The mare didn't seem alarmed or jittery. Her ears pricked, swivelling back towards Niall and the other horses.

Suddenly Cahira knew exactly what had happened, and rage consumed her. She reined in with shaking hands and waited until he pulled up beside her.

"You did it," she said, low and hard.

"Yes." His eyes held no trace of either warmth or apology. His mouth was a thin, taut line under the narrow black arc of moustache.

Cahira's jaw set as hard as rock. She spat out a single word: "Why?"

"I'm not letting you go off alone," he said flatly.

"Not *letting* me?"

He glared back without a trace of apology. "No."

"That's not your decision to make!"

"I've made it."

"Let her go!"

"No."

She wanted to hit him. But that wouldn't make Blackbird move any faster. Instead, she swung a leg over the saddle and slid to the ground. "Fine. I'll walk to Mirston."

"Then we'll walk together. But you're not leaving me behind. You might not care what happens to you anymore, but I do. What's the point of searching all over the place for Adric if you die before you find him?"

She gaped at him. "What?"

"Have you seen yourself lately? No, of course you haven't. No mirrors on the road, right? But I can see you. You get thinner and paler every day. The circles under your eyes are blacker than my boots. You're having nightmares, aren't you? And now you want to ride into an unknown town alone with no idea what you'll find there. Are you hoping to die? Is that it? Do you want to join your precious Bram?" His mouth twisted in what looked like contempt.

"How dare you? He was your friend—"

"Yes, he was my friend, and your husband. And he's gone." His eyes were hard as stones. "He's gone, Cahira, and nothing is going to bring him back. Not this obsessive search for Adric, not ignoring your own health, not putting yourself in danger, nothing."

"You don't understand anything!"

"I understand this is no way to grieve. It isn't what Bram would have wanted—"

"Don't you dare say his name again!"

"Does it upset you? Have you even let yourself shed a tear for him, your beloved husband?"

"It's none of your business!"

All the fight abruptly seemed to go out of him. He sighed and shook his head. "You're wrong. It is my business. You're my oldest friend and I can't stand seeing you like this." For the first time in all the years she'd known him, she heard an entreating tone enter his voice. "Give this up, Cahira, please. Adric is a grown man. He can take care of himself." She almost had to strain to hear the last few words. "Come home with me."

The tremor in his voice both appalled and freshly enraged her. He wasn't angry at all. He was scared for her, and that was so much worse. He didn't believe she could do this. More hot words rushed to her throat, but this time she squashed them down. Arguing with him would only waste more time.

"I'm not going home until I find Adric," she said with finality. She turned her back on him and mounted up again.

She hauled Blackbird's head around, breathing a quick apology when the mare snorted at the rough handling. Then she waited, staring straight ahead, not even bothering to give her mount the signal to move off. Let him do it, if he was so determined to be in charge. After a few moments, the mare began walking. She shifted to a trot and from there to a moderate canter. If he thought this counted as some sort of peace offering, he could think again. This fight wasn't over, just postponed.

The road slowly rolled away beneath her as Blackbird's smooth gait ate up the reaches towards Mirston, with the other horses following close behind. Cahira's nerves screamed in vain for more speed. If something terrible happened to Adric because of Niall's insufferable interference, she would never forgive him.

Her anger had cooled only a little by the time they entered the town, and the dark grey buildings did nothing to improve her mood. The fog had gone without a trace, but not even the bright sunlight could relieve the bleakness of this place. It was all hard, unfriendly stone, with no trees or gardens, no brightly painted signs or shop window displays. The few people on the street were clad in black, brown, or grey. It was as if the town had gone into some sort of mourning. Niall, in his habitual blacks, fitted right in, but Cahira was wearing her favourite deep blue, and she sensed the stares.

They stopped at the first tavern sign they saw. Stark black lettering on a grey background proclaimed they'd arrived at The Black Bull. The interior was as dim as a cave after the bright daylight, and Cahira halted inside the doorway to let her eyes adjust. Niall stepped around her without a word. His booted feet rapped loudly in the silence as he headed for the young man who was wiping down the bar set against one wall. He'd taken control again, and she had no intention of trailing after him. She'd find someone of her own to question.

An old man slumped forward on a stool at the other end of the counter, grey head nodding low over his tankard despite the early hour. Not a promising source of information. She scanned the room for other patrons, but the tables and chairs were empty. She ground her teeth and stomped over to join Niall.

The barman was shaking his shaggy blond head with a look of regret. "I don't know what else to tell you, sir. As I said, I haven't heard of any horse missing, nor any man, neither. And we get to know most of what goes on in town sooner or later."

"Is there another tavern here, or an inn?" Niall asked.

"Well, there's the new tavern, not that it's much of a tavern at all, not to my mind. There's no ale there, not a drop, nor any other liquor, but folks can stop in for a meal, and there's a big group that meets there most nights. I suppose someone might've seen your man."

"Where is it?" Cahira put in.

"The other side of town, Mistress, last building on the western road. The Virtuous Man. You'll see the sign."

Niall laid a coin on the bar. "Thanks."

"Thank you, sir." He pocketed the coin, then leaned closer and lowered his voice, glancing sideways at Cahira. "But if the lady wants to go with you, she should change her clothes first."

Cahira stared at him, offended. There was nothing wrong with her clothes.

His beardless cheeks reddened. "Begging your pardon, Mistress, it's just that some of them that meets in that place don't approve of ladies putting themselves forward, wearing what they calls vain finery, meaning bright colours and such." His blush deepened. "I wouldn't want you to feel uncomfortable, ma'am."

No one had ever called Cahira ma'am before. It disarmed her. Close up, she could see that he was even younger than she'd thought, barely out of his teens, or maybe still in them. He was blinking unhappily at her. She changed what she'd been about to say. "Thank you for the warning."

They stepped away from the bar and talked it over. Much as Cahira hated the idea of relying on Niall for anything right now, from what the barman had said, it was possible that he might have more success getting information in this other tavern than she would, her being a "lady" and all, and possibly a source of disapproval. But the worst thing was that they'd have to wait until tonight to find out. If only they'd come straight here from Mirhome yesterday, they might have the answers by now! Instead, they had a whole dreary day to fill in. It was going to be torture.

They arranged rooms for the night and went upstairs to stow their belongings. After a few moments' struggle with herself, Cahira changed out of her blue and into a more subdued grey. There was no point in antagonising people who might be able to help them, no matter how stupid their ideas were. The only important thing was to find Adric. Changing her clothes was a small price to pay.

Niall insisted on seeing the stables next. When he'd satisfied himself they were adequate, the two of them explored the town, taking Briar with them in hopes of jogging someone's memory. When the sun finally lowered to the horizon, Cahira was ready to drop, too. Mirston wasn't a big place, and they'd traced and retraced every street and lane-way, speaking to anyone they saw, with no result. It was as if Adric had never been here at all. Perhaps he hadn't, and Briar had simply wandered near the town from somewhere else. It had been another wasted day, and Cahira couldn't make herself believe that tonight would be any different.

She hadn't forgotten what Niall had done on the way here, not at all. She just lacked the energy to argue about it right now. But she made herself a promise: as soon as she knew Adric was safe, she and Master Crawley were going to have it out once and for all.

Despite the lack of ale, The Virtuous Man was crowded. There was no bar counter here. Serving girls moved between the tables, bringing food and drinks to the patrons. There weren't many spaces left, but Cahira spotted a tiny table with two chairs tucked away in a corner. Despite the number of people, the room was strangely quiet. No one was speaking above a whisper. Even the young girl who approached them for their order murmured so softly that her words were barely audible.

It didn't feel like any tavern Cahira had ever been in, and she'd visited dozens with Bram. They'd done a lot of travelling together after their marriage, working and seeing more of Algarth at the same time. Some tavern owners had even let them stay for free because of the extra custom Cahira's singing brought. After every performance, Bram always said the same thing: "Beautiful." Just that one word, but with his face so full of love and pride that it made her whole being fizz with happiness. And she'd sung for him too, as they rode alongside or lay in bed at night. He'd hold her in his arms and she'd sing ballads that told of lovers from long ago, as dreamy images filled the room and the music wrapped them both in its embrace.

Cahira gulped and wiped the sudden moisture from her eyes before it could overflow and drip onto the table. Wallowing in grief wouldn't help her find Adric, and she had to find him, whatever it took. It was the only thing she could still do for Bram. Clenching her hands until her nails bit into her palms, she regained control before Niall noticed anything amiss.

Their drinks arrived. Even in her current state of mind, Cahira couldn't help but be amused by the sour look on her companion's face as he contemplated his tankard. Cahira tried the dark red juice and found it a little tart but acceptable. She was just wondering how they might approach someone to ask about Adric when the loud squeal of a chair being pushed back drew her attention to the far end of the room.

A man was rising to his feet, and all conversation ceased as his dark gaze swept the room. He was physically imposing, tall and broad-chested. His brown hair and beard were long and unkempt, woven through with strands of grey, and his leathery face looked more used to scowling than smiling. Cahira disliked him on sight. As if he sensed her hostility, his eyes alighted on her. She lifted her chin and stared back. When his gaze finally moved on, she wondered why she'd felt such a need to assert herself, when he had done nothing but look at her.

He held out his hands and spoke in a slow, deep voice. "Fellow Seekers and visitors, welcome. We seek the way of purity. Virtue is all."

Voices echoed him, murmuring softly, "Virtue is all."

The back of Cahira's neck prickled. She raised her eyebrows at Niall, who grimaced back.

"My name is Bred Berek," the speaker went on. "I was born and raised right here in Mirston, like my father and his father before him. My parents were good people, sincere people. They taught me the differ-ence between right and wrong, and they were proud when I joined the Warrant Guards in Eorna. They believed, as I did, that being a Guard was a high calling, a worthwhile ambition. I am glad they passed away before they could learn the truth.

"My friends, I tell you, as I walked the streets of our capital city in the course of my duty, I saw much that disturbed me. Evil, vanity and frivolity were everywhere. Women, painted and dressed to inflame men's passions and the envy of others, brazenly flaunted themselves. Drunken men gambled away their money in dens of vice, and attacked each other in tavern brawls."

There was a lot more in this vein. He spoke in exhaustive detail of the shocking things he'd seen everywhere in the city, even among the Warrant Guards themselves.

Cahira caught herself tapping her fingernails on the table and clasped her hands together before anyone noticed. Would the man never get to the point? She hadn't come here for a speech. She wanted him to sit down so she could start asking her questions. Across the table, Niall's expression was openly contemptuous, but the other patrons were lapping it up, murmuring in agreement and disapproval in all the right places.

Cahira's attention wandered again, and she jumped at the sudden sound of Berek banging a fist on his table. "I did not stand idly by! I sent a report to Commander Renn himself. Do you know what reply I received?" The fist slammed down again. "None! The message was obvious. The corruption had risen to the highest level, the level of the Council of Six itself!"

Shocked murmurs swelled and subsided.

"And so I came home, disillusioned and sick at heart, but determined to bring the light of virtue back to the people of Algarth. I came home to you, and you received me. Day by day our numbers grow."

Nods and smiles from the audience. Berek's voice grew hoarse with emotion. "Thank you, my friends, for giving me hope. Together, we will change Algarth. We will bring virtue back to our nation." He bowed his head, as if overcome by their support.

Cahira wasn't buying any of it. She'd associated with singers, musicians, and actors for years at the Academy, and she recognised a performance when she saw one. She glanced across at Niall, who sent a sardonic smile her way, no more fooled than she was.

Berek raised his head again. "Many of you have your own stories to tell. We will hear some of them tonight. But first, I notice we have some visitors." Alarmingly, he stretched out a hand towards the table where Cahira and Niall were sitting. "Have you come to hear the truth, friends? Have you come to forsake your vain and corrupt lives?"

Cahira's heart beat faster as the attention of the crowd focused on them. She didn't like this at all. The quietness, which had already been strange and unsettling, now felt almost threatening. Why had Berek singled them out for questioning? And what would happen if he and the others didn't like their answers?

She was still debating the best way to reply when Niall beat her to it. "Actually, *friend*, we haven't come to forsake anything. But we are seeking truth, so perhaps you can be of help to us." His well-bred drawl sounded as carefree as if he was drinking with friends and someone else was buying. Cahira gave herself a mental shake and sat up straighter. If Niall could put on a brave face in this bizarre situation, so could she.

"We're looking for information about a man who may have passed through here recently, name of Adric Gelt," Niall went on. "Big fellow, blond hair and beard, good with a bow? Ring any bells?"

A low hum of disapproval, and Berek's face froze. He clearly wasn't used to being addressed so flippantly, and he didn't like it. But he held up his hands to silence the crowd and forced a smile. "Certainly, friend, we will help you if we can. Why are you seeking this man?"

"He's my brother-in-law," Cahira said. She wouldn't let Niall do all the talking.

"Then you must be Mistress Cahira Gelt." Berek's teeth gleamed out from his dense beard in a wolfish smile at her stunned expression. "Yes, I met your brother, nine days ago. He told me about you, and your shared loss." His face turned solemn again. "He was in a sorry state when our paths first crossed, a young man lost in darkness and vice, in desperate need of guidance. I provided that guidance, and although no other here has met him yet, he has already joined us." He spread his arms wide as if to encompass everyone in the room, and there was a soft patter of applause.

Cahira couldn't think of a single thing to say to this.

"So where is he?" Niall demanded.

Berek's eyes remained on Cahira as he replied. "At Virtue Farm, half a day's ride from here. We are building a unique community there, a place of morality and restoration. I return tomorrow. You are most welcome to join me and see for yourselves."

"Thank you, we'd love to," Cahira said, resolutely ignoring the hard stare from across the table.

When they'd extricated themselves from The Virtuous Man and were on the way back to their own tavern, Niall tried to talk to her.

"Later," she said firmly, and lengthened her stride. She'd found her lead to Adric at last, and no one was going to stop her from following it.

Entering The Black Bull was like stepping into a different world. The air was full of the scent of roasting meat and the yeasty tang of ale. A man was playing a flute, its pure tone rising high above the clamour of voices and the clatter of tankards and dishes. Nearby, a group of young-sters were dancing to the music with more enthusiasm than skill. There was the same lack of colour in the people's clothing that Cahira had noticed before, but it wasn't stopping anyone from enjoying themselves.

They were almost at the stairs when a loud bang reached their ears. A girl in a brown dress was standing in the centre of the room, repeatedly thumping a metal tankard on a table top. For such a slightly built person, she seemed to have a powerful arm. The noise died down as the patrons crowded around her, clearly hoping something entertaining was about to happen. A couple of beery voices cheered.

The girl stopped her hammering. "You should all be ashamed of yourselves!" she shouted. "Do you think Aal is pleased with this behaviour?"

Cahira stared in dismay. It was Perna, the novice from Mirhome. What was she doing here? Most of the customers just seemed confused by her words, and one or two chuckled good-naturedly. But a few were looking ugly, especially a bald, black-bearded man only a few strides behind Perna. He was scowling fiercely and swaying where he stood. Drunk and angry: a poor combination. Someone had to rescue the silly girl before she got hurt. Cahira turned to Niall, but he was already halfway across the room.

The drunken man staggered forward and stretched out a beefy arm. Niall was making slow progress, elbowing aside the people standing gawking at Perna.

The novice continued berating the crowd, oblivious to the danger. "Go home to your families. Ask for Aal's forgiveness for your drunkenness, and—" She broke off with her mouth open as the big man's hand landed on her shoulder.

Niall reached them, grabbed Perna around the waist without breaking stride and lifted her off her feet, swinging her out of the man's grip and putting his own body between them. He spoke loudly, in a jovial tone. "Come on, young Perna, you've had enough excitement for one night. Let's get you to your room." Perna was struggling in his grasp, but Niall's lips kept moving as he added something under his breath to her. Whatever it was, it seemed to work. The girl's resistance subsided, although her small face was like thunder.

Niall raised his voice again, addressing the crowd with a knowing smile. "I'm afraid she's had a bit too much to drink." He winked, inviting the onlookers to join in his amusement. "She's not used to it, and her mother would want me to make sure she doesn't come to any harm." The good-natured patrons made way for them, nodding and smiling knowingly. The bearded man had vanished.

Cahira led Niall and the reluctant novice upstairs to her room, which was the larger of the two. As soon as the door shut behind them, Perna backed away from Niall, her face blotched red with fury. "How dare you touch me!"

Niall carefully resettled his rumpled cloak around his shoulders. "I just saved you from a beating, or possibly something worse. You're welcome, by the way."

"What are you talking about?" Perna snapped. She turned on Cahira. "What does he mean, a beating? Is that meant to be some kind of joke?"

"No joke," Cahira said. This girl was starting to annoy her. "There was a man standing behind you, very big and very drunk, and not happy at all with what you were saying. He already had a hand on you when Niall reached you. And I don't think he intended to give you a friendly pat on the shoulder."

The fiery colour drained from Perna's face, leaving it chalky, and Cahira relented. The novice was very young and she must have led a sheltered life at Mirhome among all those women. "Here, sit down before you faint." She eased the girl down beside her on the bed. "Look, Perna, you can't just yell at people like that, especially if they've been drinking. They don't like it. What were you thinking?"

Perna pouted. "I was trying to show them the error of their ways. At first, I wasn't going to come in at all, to a place like this, where men drink and fight and look at women." Her mouth twisted in distaste. "But it was cold and dark and I had nowhere to stay, and suddenly I saw the truth. Aal did not want me to run away from evil, but to confront it, as a test of my purity and dedication." She stuck out her lower lip defiantly. "I knew I had to be brave, and I was."

Good grief, Cahira thought. For a moment, she couldn't trust herself to speak, and she didn't dare glance Niall's way, in case he took it as encouragement to comment. She was sure that anything he might say would be less than helpful.

A more normal colour had returned to Perna's cheeks. She sat with her back straight, smoothing the skirt of her dress and shaking her head gently. "I was foolish to let you frighten me. Aal would never have allowed any harm to come to me." She sent an imperious stare in Niall's direction. "Even so, I suppose I should thank you. You were trying to help me, although it was unnecessary." She folded her hands in her lap and granted him a condescending smile.

I think I liked her better when she was yelling, Cahira thought.

Niall bowed low. "It was my pleasure to serve you, Mistress Perna." He raised his eyes to meet hers, his face almost glowing with earnestness. Cahira sighed inwardly.

Perna's cheeks reddened slightly again. "But you should not have picked me up like that," she said severely. "It was not proper. And you lied, too. You said you were looking after me for my mother."

"I believe I said that your mother would want me to make sure you didn't come to any harm. And although I've never met your mother, I am convinced she would want that."

"Well, you said that I had too much to drink. That was definitely a lie."

"Not at all. You were shouting and waving an empty tankard around. Naturally, I assumed you had emptied it, and become a bit overwrought as a result." He shook his head sorrowfully. "I must say, you seem determined to mistake my intentions. It's rather hurtful."

A vertical line had appeared between Perna's straight brows. She frowned at Niall with her head on one side, as if he was a puzzle she was trying to work out.

Cahira was fed up with both of them. This wasn't the time for Niall to be amusing himself. Eventually, even Perna would realise he was making fun of her. And then the haranguing would resume. She jumped in before either of them could say any more. "The important thing is, we're all safe now, and we should go to bed." She skewered Niall with a glance. "We have an early start tomorrow, remember?"

"I don't trust that man, or his Seekers of Virtue either." Niall's levity had fallen away. "They're too quiet. Anyone that quiet has something to hide."

"Well, if you feel that way, you don't have to come," Cahira told him sweetly.

"Don't be stupid. Of course I'm going if you are."

"Are you talking about Master Berek of Virtue Farm?" Perna piped up.

"Do you know him?" Cahira asked, hoping to get some useful information.

"Only by reputation. But I intend to join his community."

"I thought you were training to become an Aaldan."

Perna shifted uncomfortably. "Oh, I was, and I will complete my training, someday. But right now, I am on my way to Virtue Farm. Is that where you are going?"

Cahira nodded.

"Does the Elder know you're here on your own?" Niall broke in.

Perna stood and drew herself up to her full, diminutive height. "I am twenty-two years old and I do not need Elder Meril's permission to go anywhere." Despite the defiance in the words, her voice shook a little.

Could she really be twenty-two? Cahira had been thinking she was about sixteen. But whatever her age, she didn't seem to have much experience of the world. "Perna, don't you think it would be better to go back to Mirhome?"

Perna switched her glare to Cahira. "No."

"But do you even know anyone at this farm?"

The novice folded her arms. "I do not need your permission, either. And I will not return to Mirhome, whatever you say."

Her stubbornness gave Cahira no choice. She couldn't let this naive girl try to make her own way to the farm; anything could happen to her on the road. She sighed and bowed to the inevitable. "Well, you'd better come with us tomorrow, then. It'll be safer than travelling on your own, and we have a spare horse."

"None of us should go." Niall rounded on Cahira. "How do we know Berek's even met Adric? Are we supposed to take his word for it? The entire story could be a trap to lure us to a deserted place and rob us. Or worse."

Perna's russet eyes burned into his. "I have heard only good of Master Berek. Everyone says he is an upright man, with firm principles. He would never stoop to lying or thieving."

"Naturally not." Niall waved a hand extravagantly. "Perish the thought. I'm sure that every hair of his beard is holy." He snapped his fingers. "Of course. That's why he never washes it. I did wonder when I first saw him."

Perna's voice turned high and shrill. "My mother always said that those with questionable morals cannot recognise virtue in others. I see that it is true. And—"

Cahira had heard enough. "Stop it!" Two surprised faces turned towards her. "Do you think I want to sit here all night, listening to you two sniping at each other?" She gave Niall a level look. "Yes, it could be a trap. But Berek seems to have a lot of followers, and if he wanted to harm us, he could probably arrange for it to happen right here, without needing to lure us anywhere. It's worth the risk, anyway, and I'm going."

"I will come with you." Perna's small mouth pursed as tight as a drawstring bag. "I am sure no harm will come to either of us. And now, I would like to go to bed. Good night, Mistress Gelt, and Aal keep you." She pointedly said nothing at all to Niall as she swept from the room.

Niall sat down beside Cahira and let his breath out with a whoosh. His sardonic mood seemed to have evaporated, replaced by weariness. "That girl is going to be the death of me. And you want to spend even more time with her."

Exhaustion had washed away most of Cahira's anger. "Leave her alone, Niall. I know she's annoying, but you're just making it worse by stirring her up. I don't want to take her with us, and I'd love to send her back to Mirhome. But you heard her, she won't go. She's determined to set out tomorrow, with or without us, and it wouldn't be safe for her to travel on her own. You know it wouldn't. We don't have a choice."

"And do you think she'll be any safer when she gets there? What if she finds they're not as virtuous as she thinks and starts banging tankards again?"

"I'll have a word with her about being more tactful."

Niall snorted. "Good luck with that." He looked at Cahira's face and sighed ruefully. Then his mouth turned up just the tiniest bit in the corners. "Oh well, I suppose I can always sweep her off her feet again if she gets into any more trouble."

"You'd better be careful it doesn't become a habit, or she might develop feelings for you." Her own lips quirked up a little at the thought. "Other than loathing, I mean. You cut quite the heroic figure back there, you know. You lifted her and swing her around as if she didn't weigh a thing."

"Well, she hardly does. She's all skin and bone under those layers of clothing. It was like picking up a bird. An angry, screeching bird."

"What did you say to her, anyway? She was struggling against you, and then she just stopped."

"I told her if she didn't calm down, I'd send word to Elder Meril that she'd been so drunk she passed out."

"Niall!"

He shrugged. "It worked."

Fighting the urge to smile, Cahira watched the scene replay in her mind. "That man, the one that tried to grab her? The way he reached out, it didn't seem like he was just some random drunk who happened to be there. It looked more, I don't know, deliberate."

Niall looked questioningly at her, but she found she couldn't explain the feeling any more clearly. "Oh, maybe I'm just imagining things. You should go. We both need to get some sleep. Breakfast before sunrise, remember."

At the door, Niall suddenly wheeled around and tried one more time. "Cah, listen. Are you really sure about this? I mean about meeting Berek?"

And then, as she stirred herself to answer him yet again: "No, just wait a minute. Do you really believe that Adric, of all people, would ever want to be a 'Seeker of Virtue'? They're against drinking, shouting and wearing bright colours, three of his favourite things. Why would he join Berek's creepy little club?"

"I have no idea," Cahira sighed. "But I'm going to find out."

"You mean we are," he said, and left the room before she could reply.

THREE

Despite Blackbird's warm body beneath her, Cahira shivered as they waited at the crossroads. She was back in blue again. She didn't care how much Berek might disapprove; her blue cloak was the warmest, and she had no intention of suffering just to appease him. She'd put a long brown skirt over her riding trousers, and that was enough of a concession. Winter was only a few weeks away, and frost lay thick on the ground. As the horses stamped and snorted, their breath ascended in clouds.

Perched on top of Briar, Perna was bundled up in layers of brown wool, with only her small pink-cheeked face showing. Niall glowered from Sienna's back, his blacks stark against the whiteness all around. He wasn't happy about this trip, but he'd refused to let her go alone, so it was his own fault.

Berek emerged from the fog and joined them. The rising sun struck sparks from the frost as they rode away, but soon thick clouds rolled in, swallowing most of the light. Cahira pushed away the thought that it was some sort of omen.

After a long cold ride past whitened fields separated by dark belts of evergreen trees, they drew up at a pair of closed gates with "Virtue Farm" painted on a sign. A faint shadow behind the fresh lettering suggested the place had once had a different name. Berek raised a hand in greeting to the two men stationed in front of the gateposts. One of them came forward and swung open the gates, and they all passed through. Cahira couldn't help noticing both men were wearing swords: the farm entrance was guarded. To keep people out or to keep them in? She suppressed a shiver born of more than the weather.

Around the first bend of the driveway, a building of straw-coloured stone came into view. It was three storeys tall, with wings coming forward on both sides, and its imposing bulk loomed around them as they entered the forecourt and dismounted. Berek led them to a spacious room on the ground floor and ensconced himself behind a large polished desk. He gestured them to take the hard, upright chairs in front of him, and started without preamble.

"Have you ever wondered about the purpose of life? We are born, we live, we die, and others take our place. All the work, all the ambitions and achievements, all for nothing in the end." He leaned forward and pierced Cahira with his dark fanatic's eyes. "So why are we here at all?"

"Personally," Niall said in his most infuriating drawl, "I've always thought that drinking as much good ale as possible is as noble a purpose as any."

Cahira shot him a sour look, but he only quirked an eyebrow at her, unrepentant.

"The purpose of life is to serve Aal," Perna said. She folded her arms, as if there was nothing further to say.

Ignoring Niall's remark, Berek nodded solemnly to Perna. "Certainly, that is a noble purpose, my dear. But how should we go about it?"

"We must keep ourselves pure by shunning vice: drinking, gambling, violence, greed, vanity, and all immorality." Perna rattled off the list as if she'd memorised it. Perhaps she had.

Niall snorted, but Berek was nodding again. "You will discover the purity you seek here. I do not tolerate drinking, gambling or the men fighting among themselves. We live simple, disciplined lives. Would you like to stay and see for yourself?"

"I would," Perna said, her face glowing.

"And you, Mistress Gelt?"

Cahira had already had enough of Berek's rhetoric. She pushed herself to her feet. "Before we decide anything, I want to see Adric."

"Of course." If she'd disappointed him, he didn't show it. "The third cohort should be on the training ground this morning."

"Cohort?" Niall's voice was sharp.

"We must keep the body strong if it is to resist temptation. We have grown so numerous that we have divided the men into three groups for physical training."

He led them from the rear of the house across a square courtyard, along a paved path, and through a long cobblestone yard lined with stables. At the far end, the ground dropped abruptly away. Sounds reached them as they drew closer: the scrunching of feet on gravel, a deep shouting voice, and a repeated clacking Cahira couldn't identify. Halting beside Berek on the brink, she peered down a set of wide steps onto a fenced area where perhaps fifty men milled around, their feet raising clouds of dust.

They were fighting in pairs with staves and wooden swords, following the directions of a man in a red cloak who was striding back and forth between them. His swirling scarlet garment stood out like a bloodstain. The air was filled with the thwack of weapons, grunts of exertion, and occasional cries of pain from the fighters. Between the obscuring dust and the constant movement, it was impossible to tell if Adric was down there.

The red-cloaked man bellowed a final command to the combatants. They lowered their weapons and stood at attention. The dust settled, except for an occasional flurry whipped up by the freshening wind.

Beside Cahira, Berek's deep voice boomed out. "Commander Ruston, a word please."

The red-cloaked man barked a dismissal, and the fighters headed for a row of barrels lined up along one fence. Cahira strained her eyes as she followed Berek down the steps, but still couldn't identify Adric among the crowd. When they reached level ground, the waiting man slammed one meaty fist to his chest in salute.

Berek nodded in acknowledgement. "How are they coming along, Ruston?"

"Most of 'em are untrained sir, never even held a weapon before, but they're gettin' there." His bullfrog voice seemed to come from a long way down in his barrel chest. "Another few weeks, they'll be up with the others."

Now that they were all on the same level, Cahira saw that Ruston wasn't as tall as she had first thought—only about Niall's height—but his legs were like tree trunks and his bare arms bulged with corded muscle. A red fuzz of hair covered a head shaped like a small boulder.

"I have every confidence in you, Commander," Berek said. "But now, we wish to speak to one of your men, Adric Gelt. This lady is his sister-in-law."

Ruston's pale blue eyes stared at Cahira's body in a way that brought her hackles up. Then he turned his head and bellowed to the men sitting on the ground passing ladles around. "Adric Gelt! On the double!"

Cahira's heart lurched as a figure sprang up in response: tall and square-shouldered, topped with a thatch of blond hair. She'd forgotten how alike the brothers were at a distance. For a moment, it was as if Bram himself was coming towards her. But this was Adric, not Bram, even though he didn't look like himself in that dull brown tunic and pants.

By the time he reached them, he was scowling. "What are you doing here?"

Cahira froze, and then her own temper blazed up in a rush of words. "What do you mean, what am I doing here? I came to find you. You disappeared without a word. I was worried about you. We've been searching for weeks."

Adric's scowl deepened. "Of all the stupid—"

Berek interrupted. "Perhaps you would be more comfortable having this conversation in private. I suggest we all return to the house."

Adric stared grimly ahead the whole way back, refusing to even look at Cahira. Anger and worry warred inside her. Why was he acting like this? He'd been very bitter after Bram's death, but even in his darkest moments, he'd never directed his temper towards her. And after so long on the road, ignoring the discomfort, pushing down the grief, hoping only to find him safe, she deserved better. Anger had won out over anxiety by the time Berek showed them into the same room and left, saying he'd be back after they'd talked.

Cahira stepped up to Adric. "What's wrong with you?"

"Nothing," he rumbled to the floor. "I'm fine."

"Well, you don't seem fine to me. Tell me the truth. What are you doing here?"

This time, he didn't even bother to answer.

"Adric!"

"You know, Adric," Niall drawled from behind her, "I never took you for the religious type. Shows how wrong you can be about someone. Although, now I think about it, I recall one evening in Gadara, when you got down on your knees to beg that old tavern keeper for just one more drink before bed. I suppose that was a kind of praying."

Where Cahira's demands had failed, Niall's taunting did the trick. Adric's head snapped up. "Sneer all you want. But tell me, *Master* Crawley, what did you do after those Guards murdered Bram? *Nothing.* And what have you been doing since then? *Nothing.* Well, I'm doing something. So, you can just push off and let me get on with it."

"But *what* are you doing?" Cahira pleaded with him. "And what does it have to do with Bram's death?"

He gazed at her with an expression she couldn't read. His lips parted and she thought he was going to answer, but then his mouth hardened and he turned his head away.

Cahira planted herself in front of him again, staring up into his face, forcing him to look at her. His expression was like stone, but she could be just as stubborn. She felt like shaking him, but she took a deep breath and spoke calmly and reasonably. "Adric, help me understand. You just disappeared, and you never sent word about where you were. The thought of losing you, as well as Bram…" To her horror, her voice broke on the last word. Water welled in her eyes, threatening to spill over.

Adric's expression wavered. He'd never been able to withstand her tears, even when they were children. She had got her own way more than once by knowing that, although she hadn't done it deliberately this time.

"Well," he said gruffly, "things were bad for a while, but that's over now." He took her hands in his big ones and stared earnestly down at her. "You don't have to worry about me anymore, Cah, honestly. I'm fine. Go home."

Cahira stared up at him, and doubts crept in. Was she making a fool of herself? Adric was a grown man. He had the right to make his own decisions, even if they were mistakes. But the thought of leaving him here felt wrong, like singing out of tune.

"Aal's teeth, just trust me, will you?" Adric burst out when she didn't reply. "I know what I'm doing."

The brash confidence suddenly reminded Cahira of the fearless boy he'd been, always the leader of their best adventures. And the expert in getting the three of them into trouble with their elders. Not that Adric had ever cared about that.

There was a tap on the door and the unwelcome Berek came back in, followed by a young girl carrying a tray. "Mistress Gelt, you must be hungry after our journey. I am returning to the dining hall, but I thought the four of you might like to eat in here. We only take a light meal at midday, but the bread is fresh and I think you will like our cheese. And then, perhaps, Adric might show you around our community?"

Cahira nodded. A tour, without Berek around, would give her a chance to question Adric some more. Maybe then, her uneasiness would go away.

"Excellent. Enjoy your meal. I just need a word with Adric outside."

As the girl set out the food on a low table, Cahira suddenly realised that she'd forgotten all about Perna. The novice had come in with them and was sitting quietly on a chair in the corner with her head bowed and her hands folded in her lap, as if their interactions had nothing to do with her. Either she was being tactful for once, or she really didn't care. It was hard to tell.

"I suppose we're all going on this jolly tour, then," Niall said after the serving girl had left.

Cahira kept her voice low so Perna wouldn't hear. "I think we should. I don't care what Adric said, I have a bad feeling about this place." She turned to the novice and raised her voice to normal volume. "Do you want to come, Perna?"

Perna looked up. "Of course. It should be very interesting to see how a truly moral community lives."

"But you lived in a House of Aal," Cahira said. "Isn't that a moral community?"

Perna paused, as if choosing her words with care. "Elder Meril is a very good woman, I am sure, but she does not always seem quite as…as dedicated to Aal's service as I had expected when I came there. And the others follow her example."

"What do you mean?" Niall looked delighted at the idea of some secret scandal.

"Everything at Mirhome is so…so *comfortable.*" She pursed her mouth as if the word tasted sour. "Warm fires, and soft beds, frivolous chatter at the table, and always so much food."

The smile still hovered around Niall's lips. "And that's bad?"

Perna frowned fiercely at him, her hesitation gone. "The desires of the body are not important. Suffering and self-denial bring us closer to Aal."

"Do you really think so? Most of the suffering people I've met haven't been very interested in religion at all, unless they're cursing Aal for their situation."

"First, one must have the desire to be holy," snapped Perna, her expression saying clearly that Niall would never meet the qualification.

Adric returned after lunch to show them around the farm, as Berek had promised. Safely away from the house, Cahira tried again to get her stubborn brother-in-law to see reason, but he refused to answer her questions, always turning the conversation back to Virtue Farm and the community there. Giving up for the moment, she started to pay attention to the tour. Maybe she'd get a clue about why Adric was so keen to stay.

They visited stables, workshops, and sites where new buildings were being erected. Then they went out into the windblown fields to watch late fruits and nuts being harvested from the orchards. Adric explained that all the men could be called on for any task that benefited the community.

"What about the women?" Cahira asked, realising she had seen none apart from the serving girl who'd brought their lunch.

Adric shrugged. "Probably working inside. You know, looking after the children and cleaning, stuff like that."

"What if a woman has a skal of, say, Metal Shaping?" Niall said in his most innocent voice. "Surely she should use it. For the good of the community, you know."

Perna nodded in agreement. "Elder Meril says that Aal gives us skals so we might use them to help others. If we do not, we deny who Aal made us to be." She paused, and her didactic tone softened. "She was training me as a Folk Healer." She sounded almost wistful.

"Um, I guess so," Adric said, clearly not very interested. "But you have to come and see the new grain store. It's really impressive."

They ended the tour hours later in a barn-sized timber building that had been split into a kitchen and communal dining hall. And there Cahira found the women. About a dozen were working in the steamy kitchen, others were bringing out food and drinks, but most sat at the long tables with the men, many with children beside them.

The meal was roasted meat, fresh vegetables, and newly baked bread, followed by platters of fruit and nuts. Despite her substantial breakfast at the tavern, and the bread and cheese at lunch, Cahira piled her plate, as did Niall and Adric. Perna hardly ate anything, only taking a piece of bread and a few late autumn berries. Remembering what Niall had said about the novice being 'all skin and bones', Cahira tried to persuade her to eat more, but Perna silently shook her head.

Despite the clatter of cutlery on plates, the room was quiet for a place where hundreds of people were gathered. There was plenty of talk around the tables, but it was all conducted in a near whisper, like the meeting in The Virtuous Man. Even Adric lowered his normally loud voice, as he boasted that he'd probably shot the deer they were eating. "We mostly kill our own stock animals for meat, but hunting is good shooting practice, so archers go out regularly too."

"Practice for what?" Niall asked, but two men sitting nearby frowned him into silence. His expression said that he was only postponing the question, not letting it go. After the meal, as people were leaving, he pulled Cahira into a shadowed corner and whispered urgently to her.

"The more I see of this place, the less I like it. For one thing, it's a much bigger community than we thought. There must be hundreds of men here, all being trained to fight." He raised a brow. "By a *Commander*, if you please. And what does Adric mean by *good shooting* practice? What are they practising for?"

"I don't know," she hissed back. "But they were only using wooden swords, not real ones. Maybe it's just physical fitness, like Berek said."

Niall glanced around and lowered his voice even further. "Did you notice that new building near the grain store that Adric very deliberately didn't show us inside? The door was open a crack, and I got a quick look. It was full of weapons, Cah. Real ones: swords and spears. This isn't just a crazy religious community. Berek is raising a personal army here."

Cahira gaped at him. "But why?"

Niall shrugged. "It could just be some local power play. But remember back in the tavern when he said the Seekers were going to change all of Algarth? What if he's planning something big?"

"Like what?"

"Like overthrowing the Council. It's not as though Algarth has any kind of army. Only the Warrant Guards, and they're spread all over the island. If he attacks Eorna, his men could outnumber the garrison."

"Adric would never be a part of that!"

"I'm not so sure, Cah. He was furious with the Council and the Warrant Guards after Bram's death. What if Berek took advantage of that to recruit him?"

"No, I'll never believe it," Cahira whispered fiercely. "Berek's tricked him somehow." She gripped his arm. "We can't leave him here."

"We can hardly drag him away by force, and I don't think he's going to agree to come with us." He held up a hand. "I know you think he isn't part of the plot, but we can't be sure. We have to get word to Logen and the Council about the danger they're in."

She bit her lip, trying to think. He was right. As the new acting Chairman of the Council, Logen needed to know. But she wasn't leaving without Adric. The solution finally occurred to her. "You could go."

He shook his head. "Not without you. But we could both return to Mirston."

"I told you—"

"Just temporarily. The barman in The Bull didn't seem very impressed with Berek and his crew. We'll pay him to send someone to Eorna with a message, then come straight back here for Adric. I'd be happier if someone outside this place knew we were here, anyway."

"And what if Berek won't let us back onto the farm afterwards? No, I have to stay."

"It's too dangerous!"

"Look, I'll tell Berek I'm impressed and thinking about joining. That should keep me safe enough, and I can get more information, too."

"What're you two whispering about?" Adric's voice from close behind made Cahira jump. She turned to see Perna and Berek right beside him. How long had they been lurking there, and how much had they heard?

Cahira trotted out the story she'd suggested to Niall. It was hard to tell if Berek believed her, but he showed no outward sign of suspicion. Adric, on the other hand, didn't look happy at all—he probably knew her too well to be fooled—but at least he said nothing.

And then, just when she had it all sorted out, Niall announced he was staying too. Unable to argue with him in front of Berek and Adric, she settled for a black look in his direction, which he blandly ignored.

So they were both stuck here, and no one was going to Mirston to get a message to Logen. Why couldn't Niall just trust her to look after herself for once? Did he think she was like the Seeker women, content to stay in the background, only useful for cooking, cleaning and child-rearing?

Berek seemed pleased, however, and offered a bed in the stable block to Niall and one in a building shared by some of the other single girls to Perna. He called over a couple of youngsters to show them the way. After they left—Niall with an anxious backward look, which Cahira in her turn ignored—Berek himself led the way to a bedroom on the top floor of the main house. It was small, containing only a bed and a chair.

A single window looked west over the fields. Suddenly uneasy, Cahira protested that she didn't need a room of her own when the other two had to share.

"Adric is a valued member of our community, and so his sister-in-law is an honoured guest," Berek said complacently.

This was hardly convincing. Adric was a new recruit probably only one among many. But she had little choice other than to accept it and thank Berek with as much grace as she could. She expected him to leave then, but he just remained standing between her and the door, stroking his tangled black beard and staring at her in silence. His eyes didn't drop below her face, but she felt as uncomfortable as if they were roaming over every inch of her. She felt herself reddening and turned hastily away, cursing herself for her inability to hide her unease in his presence.

At that moment, he spoke again, and his words were the last thing she expected to hear. "Perhaps you would consider singing for us this evening? We have few entertainers here. It would be an uplifting experience for everyone."

For a moment, she was too surprised to answer. But she couldn't afford to do anything that might make him suspicious, not if she wanted to help Adric and keep herself and Niall safe. Heart sinking, she mumbled a polite agreement without turning around. Berek said he would be back in an hour to escort her to the meeting hall, and then left her alone with her thoughts, which were not happy ones.

Why, oh why, hadn't she said she was too tired, or even feeling ill? Because she was an idiot who had let that odious man fluster her, that's why. And now nausea really was rising at the thought of performing here, where the people were so serious and only spoke in whispers.

She distractedly raked a hand through her hair, but her fingers stuck in the first tangle. She tried to pick it apart, but it was no use. If she was going to look presentable tonight, she needed a comb. She bent to her pack, doubts gnawing at her. What had Berek meant by 'uplifting?' How could she know which songs these people would enjoy, and which might offend them?

And what about the fact she was a woman? The women of this community stayed in the background. How would the men react to her drawing attention to herself, in the way Skalsinging always did? But Berek himself had asked her, so it must be permitted. Nevertheless, she felt queasy. The leader of the Seekers didn't strike her as someone who was keen on entertainment. Just the opposite, in fact. Could it be some kind of trap?

Still crouched over the pack, she drew a deep breath. She couldn't do anything about it now. She'd just have to get through tonight somehow. And she'd stay on her guard for any sign of danger.

Straightening up with the comb in her hand, she hauled the dark mass of her hair forward over one shoulder and examined the ends. The tangles were even worse than she'd feared. This was going to be a tedious, painstaking job. She sighed and lifted the comb, only to find her hand falling back to her side. She was so tired. Too tired to think of a song, or even to face the thought of combing her hair. She needed to rest, just for a few minutes.

She lay down on the bed. Outside the window, the sun had finally broken free of the thick clouds that had been obscuring it all day. It lay low on the horizon, piercing the room with long rays of golden light. She hadn't slept well for a long time, apart from that one night in Mirhome.

Closing her eyes and enjoying the last warmth of the setting sun on her cheek, she consciously softened and relaxed her body, one section at a time, beginning with her feet and moving up. It was a ritual she'd learned as a student, to allow her to rest on the night before a big performance. She'd never needed it when Bram was with her, and she'd almost forgotten all about it. As she released the tension in her head and face, she pictured all her anxious thoughts as a mass of threads twisted in a tight ball behind her forehead. She willed them to gently separate and spread out one by one, floating further and further away, until they disappeared entirely, leaving only a calm, still emptiness behind.

A tiny fragment of music teased lightly at the edge of her drowsy consciousness. Recognising it, she let it come. It wasn't part of her

Skalsinging repertoire, but an ancient lullaby, one her mother had sung to her when she was just a tiny girl, scared of the darkness in the corners of her room and what might be hiding there. The familiar melody spoke of comfort and safety and love. It spoke of home. Cradled by the song and the memories, she breathed deeply and sank into sleep.

FOUR

For a few seconds after the knocking woke her, Cahira lay where she was, her thoughts hazy with sleep. Then Berek's unwelcome voice from outside the door brought everything rushing back. "Mistress Gelt? It's time to go."

Heart pounding, she sprang to her feet and stood trembling. She had to sing, and she had nothing prepared.

Her mind was still in a whirl as she trailed downstairs and followed him into a large room filled with people. They mounted a low stage and the quiet murmuring of the crowd died away. Hands clenched by her sides, Cahira desperately tried to think, but the silent rows of spectators were eerily distracting. Children were sitting on the floor in the front, along with a sprinkling of adults with smaller ones on their laps. Not even the youngest child was making a sound. Behind them were ranks of occupied chairs, and more people stood against the walls. And every one of them stared curiously at Cahira.

She'd never been this nervous in front of an audience before. Just as she felt herself truly beginning to panic, Berek spoke. It seemed that he didn't have to follow the whispering rule. His deep voice boomed out over the heads of the seated people and echoed back from the rear wall. "My friends, we have a rare treat tonight. A gifted Skalsinger, Mistress Gelt, has agreed to perform for us. I am sure we will find it enlightening and uplifting."

There was a soft pattering of applause as he descended from the stage, leaving her standing alone on trembling legs. She swallowed twice, to no avail. Her mouth was dry, her mind blank. Memory was her secondary skal, a very useful one for a singer, but it seemed to have deserted her now. She couldn't recall a single line or musical phrase. Her eyes scanned the audience, hoping to alight on Niall or Adric, or even Perna, but couldn't locate any of them. Her throat tightened.

A piercing whistle rang out, shocking in the quietness. Necks craned towards the back of the room, where a slim figure in black was rising to his feet. Relief flooded Cahira. She wasn't alone. He grinned at her and put his fingers between his lips again. The second whistle was even louder.

Bless you, Niall, she thought, and nodded at him. He flicked his fingers in a carefree little wave, then sat down composedly. The faces that turned back to Cahira were stiff with disapproval. But now she was ready for them.

On the heels of Niall's whistle, a song had come to her. An old ballad, sung from the points of view of a farmer and his wife, celebrating their joy in their work and living on the land. It had been one of the earliest works she'd learned in her apprenticeship. She'd moved far beyond this kind of simple song, but if it didn't show off her skill, at least there was nothing in it that could cause offence, even to the Seekers of Virtue.

She began with the rough, resonant voice of the farmer, singing his tale of ploughing and sowing, the notes as rich and deep as the newly turned earth. Above her head, the images formed, at first misty, then solidifying. There were a few murmurs and some soft gasps from the crowd.

She switched to the farmer's wife, who sang of feeding the chickens, milking the cow, and cooking the breakfast. Her voice was higher, lighter, filled with the joy of the early morning and the new sun rising, and her images were all gold and pale pink like the dawn.

In the next verse, the two voices blended as they expressed the contentment of their life together. The pictures came thick and fast, showing harvest picnics with good friends, spring dances and cosy winters around the fire. It was an idealised version of living on the land, ignoring the hardships and disappointments that farmers often faced, but it had been one of Cahira's favourites, and she was suddenly glad to be revisiting it. The Seekers seemed to appreciate it, too. There were smiles and nods and even a few tapping feet.

As she ended, the applause came quickly, and with it another song flowed into Cahira's mind: the journey of a river from the mountains to the sea. It began lightly, with runs of notes that sparkled and danced like tiny streams rippling over rocks. The melody swelled as the tributaries merged into a torrent, which rushed along a stony bed before spilling noisily over a cliff into a still pool. Other voices—the calls of birds, the drone of insects, the clop of horses, and the lowing of cows in fields—joined in as the river wended its way between widely spaced banks, the song of the water now deeper and slower. It passed through towns, and Cahira wove in the sounds of industry and human revelry, always with the voice of the river flowing steadily underneath.

It was a very technical song, that she'd chosen for her third-year exam-ination. Thousands of hours of practice had polished the harmonies and sharpened the images beyond anything she'd attempted at the Academy before. It had impressed the examiners enough to gain her the status of Master, an almost unknown achievement after only twelve months as a journeyman. At twenty-one years of age she had attained a level of expertise that few Skalsingers reached in their lifetimes. She'd been proud, but also a little embarrassed, and she'd never used the honorific. *Master Skalsinger Gelt* was a name suited to someone much older than she was, and several shades more pompous than she ever intended to be.

The Seeker community seemed pleased with the river song too, and Cahira suddenly found she was enjoying herself. She'd missed this more than she'd known. Not only the singing itself, but also the way the music connected her with an audience. She ended with the haunting sound of gulls, and was rewarded with a rush of applause. Elated, she decided to give them one more song.

She was considering a humorous little ditty about a frog who wanted to be a bird, usually a favourite with any children present, when a different melody nudged at the edge of her mind. What was it? She hummed it softly, and recognition came.

It was the account of a real battle, fought more than a hundred years ago. Two noblemen had both claimed ownership of a valley that formed the boundary between their estates. It had been an ugly encounter, the victor losing almost as many men as his enemy, and the song wasn't a favourite. But it had taken hold of her now, and she couldn't think of another. The audience was gazing up at her expectantly. With a mental shrug, she began.

Immediately, she sensed that something had changed. As the images formed above her, she felt the emotions she was describing even more vividly than usual. She tasted the black bitterness of one Earl as he accused the other of theft, and her heart thrilled in response to the marching song of his soldiers on their way to war.

> *Stout-hearted and strong, to battle we go*
> *Full wrathful and righteous, we face down the foe*
> *Their numbers we deem not, their doom is at hand*
> *For greatness, for glory, for lord and for land!*
>
> *Rise brother, and ready your sword and your spear*
> *Our vigour and valour will freeze them in fear*
> *Strike swifter than lightning, stand stalwart as stone*
> *Unyielding as adamant, unbending as bone*
>
> *Our cause and our courage burn bright as the sun*
> *Come blade, blood and slaughter, this day will be won!*

As the stirring rhythm beat from her throat, Cahira was suddenly—shockingly—transported to another place. Agonised cries and the deafening clash of weapons assaulted her ears. Her nostrils filled with the scents of blood, metal, and fear. Rooted to the spot, the hairs standing up on the back of her neck, she swung her head wildly, desperate to find a way of escape.

And then her breath caught, not in dread but in wonder. For Bram was there, only a few strides away. His face was in profile to her, his gaze fixed on the front rank of the enemy, who were clad in blue Warrant Guard shirts. His hand gripped his half-raised sword awkwardly, as though he didn't know what to do with it, but he was here and he was whole.

Cahira's knees almost buckled in relief. He wasn't dead! Why had she been thinking he was dead? He was in terrible danger, but he was alive.

But before she could take a single step towards him, the enemy surged into motion. A huge Guard ran straight at her, blade raised high. Her tongue cleaved to the roof of her mouth. She couldn't utter a sound. She tried to back away, but there was nowhere to go. The fighters of her own side pressed in behind her, cutting off any chance of escape. The Guard's thumping strides ate up the ground between them. Her hands were empty of any weapon. She was defenceless, about to die.

And then Bram's broad shoulders appeared in front of her, his body blocking the enemy's way. Sunlight flashed off metal as their blades met with a shattering screech. Then Bram grunted, low and deep. Horrifically—unbelievably—he tilted forward. He was falling. Cahira strained to reach him, to grab his tunic, but she couldn't move a single step.

He toppled face down in the mud and lay unmoving, with a hideous scarlet stain blooming between his shoulder blades. She knew at once that he was dead. The Guard stood astride Bram's lifeless body and lifted his bloody blade again. His lips pulled back from his blackened teeth in a monstrous grin as he headed towards her once more.

White-hot fury took possession of Cahira, sweeping away every trace of fear or doubt. Sound throbbed in her throat, demanding to be released: an ugly, buzzing melody, composed of rage and the need for vengeance. She had sung it once before, on that terrible day when she had lost Bram the first time.

The first time? A shock like icy water hit her. Bram had died at Fortune Creek months ago. How could he be lying dead in the mud in front of her? It must be a trick of her mind. She'd been singing about a battle and somehow she'd become caught in her own song. None of this was real. She wasn't on a battlefield, and there was no Guard coming at her with death in his eyes. *Wake up, wake up!* she screamed inside her head.

Everything turned to smoke and swirled away. She swayed and almost fell, but recovered herself with an enormous effort and stayed upright. The audience was clapping again, and much louder this time. She must have finished the song. Still trembling in reaction to what had happened, she searched the faces, but they appeared untroubled. Whatever had been going on in her head, no one else had noticed anything wrong. More than that, they were showing more animation than she had yet seen in this place.

A round-cheeked matron in a white bonnet smiled widely at her, eyes shining. A tall, grey-haired woman with an intelligent face, standing against the side wall, caught Cahira's eye and dipped her head in a gesture of respect. Niall was on his feet again, grinning and applauding. And he wasn't the only one. That last song had roused the usually placid Seekers in a way that scared Cahira even more, if that was possible.

They were still clapping. She bowed her head as if acknowledging them, but really in order to hide her expression. She'd never heard of anything like this happening to a Skalsinger before. Was she losing her mind? She wanted to flee the stage and bolt back to her room, but they might take that as some sort of insult. No matter what had happened, she had to be careful.

The audience finally quietened. Berek returned to her side. Cahira heard his voice booming, but she was in no state to comprehend anything he was saying.

She stayed there, frozen in place, until she noticed people filing out. Avoiding Berek, who was too busy being congratulated on her performance to notice her, she slipped out the side door and made her way to her bedroom, keeping a tight rein on her emotions. The journey seemed interminable, but finally she closed the door behind her and sank down on the bed. Her teeth were chattering and her hands were shaking as if with deadly cold.

She missed Bram so much. Reliving his death like that had been terrible, unspeakable. And the images wouldn't leave her mind, taunting her until she burst into shuddering sobs. Afraid someone would hear, she grabbed the pillow and pressed it to her mouth to muffle the sound. She rocked backwards and forwards in silent anguish.

Why had she picked that song? From now on, she'd stick with farmers and rivers and frogs who wanted to fly. The rocking slowed as she thought about that. After what had happened tonight, did she really want to sing again?

Yes, she answered herself fiercely, surprised by her own vehemence. *I do*. She wouldn't let the music go, wouldn't allow fear to beat her down. There was nothing wrong with her mind. She was tired, and grieving, and the stupid battle song had struck too close to home, that was all.

She was a Skalsinger, so she'd sing. She'd choose music that lightened hearts and celebrated life and joy, even though the latter had departed from her forever. Or maybe because of that. She'd honour Bram, by performing the kinds of songs he'd loved best.

Gradually her sobs quietened. The images faded from her mind, and she found a measure of peace. She replaced the pillow and stretched out on the bed, and her hand went to the pocket where the sky stone was safely tucked away as always. She lifted it out and turned it over in her fingers, remembering.

Bram had wanted to give her a gift for their first anniversary, and they'd found a street market in an unfamiliar village. The first stall was piled high with parchments and scrolls, even a few leather-bound books. But right at the front lay a row of polished stones, all different sizes, shapes and colours. The old stallholder said a charm had been Shaped into each one. If the owner lost their stone, they could always find it again.

Bram picked up a small sapphire-coloured oval, not a true gemstone, but bright and clear, with no flaws or intrusions, and held it out to Cahira. "It's how I see you. Like the summer sky on a cloudless day. We could have it set in a necklace."

Cahira laughed and tapped a different one. Three-sided, with rounded corners, and as long as her thumb. "I think this is more me." It was a dark, moody blue with grey and black streaks running across it like storm clouds. She'd been joking, but as she held it in her hand, it seemed to warm in her grasp, as if it felt at home there.

Bram looked doubtful. "Are you sure?"

She nodded, and he bought it for her. He wanted to have it strung on a chain for her to wear, but that didn't feel right to her. She liked it the way it was. Every day from then on, the sky stone had lain nestled in her pocket.

The old woman had told the truth: the stone was Charmed. If Cahira sang a particular sequence of three notes, it glowed so she could see it in her mind as well as with her eyes. She breathed them softly now, and they brought other memories of Bram with them, warming her but also sharpening the pain of her loss. Tears threatened again.

After a few moments, she couldn't bear it anymore, and resolutely tucked the past away with the stone. It was Adric she should be thinking about. Bram had gone beyond her help, but his twin still needed saving, and she wouldn't fail him.

FIVE

Cahira woke early, with a plan of action already unfolding in her mind. First, she'd go to the kitchen and offer her help to the women preparing breakfast. They must hear a lot of conversations as they moved around the tables, and probably knew as much about what was going on here as anyone. And women talked together as they worked, sharing stories, getting to know each other. She'd use her skal of Memory to tuck every detail safely away for whenever she or Niall could get a message to Logen.

Then she'd find Adric again. Despite her failure yesterday, a night's sleep had renewed her confidence. She would persuade him to leave with her, even if she had to lie and tell him it would only be temporary. Deceiving him would be a small price to pay for his safety. And once away from this place and Berek's influence, she and Niall would make him see sense.

She left the warm bed and stood at the window, impatiently combing through the rat-nest of her hair. Even the sight of another grey-shrouded day outside didn't dampen her spirits.

The kitchen women welcomed her without fuss. They chattered freely as they prepared food and scrubbed down the long tables in the dining hall. She learned that they were mostly country girls without families, or whose parents couldn't support them. They'd made their way to the city hoping to discover a better life. But all they'd found in Eorna was poverty and danger.

Bett, a short, sturdy blond seventeen-year-old, had a crippled arm. When she caught Cahira looking at it, she explained without any sign of embarrassment. A man had twisted it until the bone snapped, calling her filthy names the whole time. All because she'd refused to give him 'a bit of fun' in an alley. She'd been fifteen. With no money to pay a Healer, the bone had set crooked. The arm had no strength in it, and it still gave her pain. But there wasn't a trace of self-pity on her round, pink-cheeked face as she used her good arm to show Cahira how to knead bread dough.

Mara, the middle-aged woman who was in charge, had terrible burn scars. She kept pulling her long hair forward on one side to cover them. But as she rolled balls of pastry into thin sheets, the brown tresses swung back and forth, revealing shiny pink patches. The skin around them had wrinkled and bunched together, dragging down her lower eyelid and the side of her mouth.

Bett whispered that Mara had worked as a kitchen maid for a rich family. One morning she'd been too slow in her work, and the cook, hungover and in a foul temper, had struck her with a ladle of boiling fat. The housekeeper had believed the cook's account that the accident had been caused by Mara's clumsiness, and had turned her out.

With nowhere to go and in too much agony to look for work, Mara slept on the streets and begged food from passers-by. Even when the worst of her burns had healed, no one would employ her. A single glimpse of her face, and they moved away in disgust. Here in the kitchen, though, the other women deferred to her.

"She's a good cook an' she knows about medicines an' such," Bett said. "Her mother was a Healer, taught her all kinds o' things about herbs. We don't have no female Healer at the farm, but Mara helps us when she can."

The others didn't have physical scars, but Cahira learned they'd all been desperate in one way or another when a group of Berek's Seekers had come into the city. They'd stood on street corners, giving out food to anyone who needed it, and talking about a better life, in a safe place where everyone was welcome. These women had taken the chance, and they didn't seem to regret it. But what would happen to them if Berek really was planning sedition? She had to find out more, for them as much as for Adric.

She helped to serve breakfast in the dining hall, and took the opportunity for a quick low-voiced conversation with Niall, who wasn't his normal dapper self. He was bleary-eyed and unshaven, but he listened intelligently enough when she told him her plan for the day. He agreed to spend the morning pumping the stable-hands for information and then meet her in her room after lunch to compare notes. She moved on before he could start pressing her again to leave as soon as possible.

After they'd cleared away the meal, the talkative Bett picked up a large empty basket and disappeared into the storeroom adjoining the kitchen. Cahira grabbed a second container and followed.

"Bett," she said quietly, as soon as they were alone, "what do you think of Berek?"

"Oh, he's no worse lookin' than most men, I s'pose, but he's a bit old for me." She sent a sly glance in Cahira's direction. "An' for you too, I reckon."

Cahira felt a blush mounting her cheeks. "No, I don't mean as a man, but, well, as a leader."

Bett stopped transferring apples to her basket as she thought about it. "I dunno really… He talks a lot, likes the sound o' his own voice, I'd say." She frowned, as if she didn't understand exactly what Cahira wanted from her.

Cahira pressed harder. "It's just that he told me he's going to change Algarth. Do you know what he meant?"

"Well, he's always speakin' about *purity*, an' *discipline*. Maybe he wants everyone to live like we do here." Bett snorted out a laugh. "Not that we're all as pure as he thinks."

"What do you mean?"

Bett leaned closer and lowered her voice. "The boys an' girls sleep in diff'rent buildings. But there's ways, if you look hard enough for 'em. An' some folks look pretty hard."

Cahira was learning some surprising things about the community this morning, even if they weren't what she really wanted to know. "You mean you…"

Bett shook her head vigorously and snorted again, this time apparently in derision. "Not me, I'm not int'rested in all that stuff. I'm just waitin' for my skal to come in, an' then I'm leavin' to get a proper job. Ma was a Scriber before the fever took her, an' you don't need no two hands for that. So I can't be saddled with a baby, can I? Some o' the others—boy mad, they are. Always sneakin' out to visit their latest *love*." She snorted a third time and went back to the apples.

"But what if they get caught?"

Bett shrugged. "Chucked out I s'pose. But none o' us would give 'em away, an' the boys ain't goin' to say nothin', so—" She shot Cahira a look of wide-eyed alarm. "You won't tell? They don't have nowhere else to go."

"I won't say a word, I promise."

Bett threw her strong arm around Cahira's shoulders and squeezed. "I knew you was a good 'un."

Other than a growing fondness for Bett, Cahira felt she hadn't gained much from her time with the women. She wondered if Niall was having more success in the stables.

SIX

Niall

Niall was having a trying morning. Actually, his bad luck had begun last night. The man sleeping in the next bed snored like the rumbling of thunder, refusing to wake despite increasingly frequent kicks and cursing from his roommates. As a result, Niall had presented himself for work in the stable block with gritty eyes and a brain less agile than usual.

The stable boss had looked him up and down, taking in the neatly cropped head, the thin line of hair that ran along his jawline and arched into a narrow moustache above his lips, the closely woven black shirt and trousers and the fine leather boots. At least Niall had left his expensive sword and scabbard behind, hidden beneath his mattress.

After his inspection of Niall's person, the old man's mouth twisted. He spat sideways on the ground. "Bit of a dandy, ain't you, for this kind o' work? Be you a noble then, or just a rogue, gotten rich by takin' advantage o' poor folk?" He hacked and spat again. "Not that there's much diff'rence 'atween the two."

There was no good answer to that, so Niall said nothing, merely giving the man his most innocuous smile.

The scowl didn't change, unless it deepened a little. "Well, they say as you're a Beast Speaker, but we don't have no call for one o' them here. We got thirty horses, and it ain't their heads that need dealing with, it's th' other end, and what comes out of it." His face cracked into a leer, and he cackled at his own joke. "Not afraid t' get those nice clean hands dirty, I hope?"

Niall kept his own smile nailed in place, but his head was still thick from lack of sleep, and his patience with this idiot was wearing thin. He hadn't mucked out a stable since he was a boy, and it hadn't exactly been his favourite activity even then, but it would give him a chance to check on Sienna and the other two horses. Besides, Cahira was expecting him to pick up information from the stable hands. Hopefully they'd be more amenable to his charm than their boss.

But first he needed some quiet time to gather his thoughts and restore some of his wits. If he had to shovel muck to get it, so be it. "Not at all, lead me to it."

After a few more insulting remarks, the old stableman finally seemed to tire of Niall's lack of response. He stumped across the yard into a smaller stable, pointed out a pitchfork and a two-wheeled cart near the doorway, grinned evilly, and left.

The stable was empty of horses and clearly hadn't been cleaned out for some time. Even with the door wide open, the stink was overwhelming in the enclosed stalls. After half an hour of pitching soiled straw into the cart and emptying it onto the manure pile behind the building, Niall's nose and eyes were running, his stomach was churning, and his hands were beginning to blister.

So yes, so far it had been a trying morning. But at least the exercise, or perhaps the fumes, had cleared his head a bit. It was time to do something more useful and hopefully less odorous. He would set out in search of someone to talk to, man or beast.

He'd only just stepped into the yard when the scream of a maddened horse stopped him in his tracks. He twisted round to locate the source. It was coming from a stable further along. He took off, with the animal's cries filling his ears and its pain and terror pounding in his brain.

Skidding to a halt inside the right doorway, he tried to take in the scene in front of him, but the dimness of the stable and the thundering in his head were making it hard to concentrate. Then a huge shape loomed up, stark and black against the general greyness, and his vision snapped into focus. He saw the rearing horse, the human figure, the long cruel whip, and he lunged forward to grab the upraised arm.

The bald man spun around with a curse, but Niall twisted the weapon out of his grip, drawing a satisfying howl of pain. Predictably, his opponent's other hand came up in a fist. Niall blocked the blow and drove the thick butt of the whip into the man's face. The stableman grunted and staggered backwards, blood already gushing from a nose that was almost certainly broken. Recovering his balance for a moment, he stood dripping gore and staring at Niall in hatred. Then his eyes widened as if in surprise. He swayed. The eyes rolled back. An instant later, he was stretched out flat, still breathing but unconscious.

Niall dropped the foul whip and turned to the black stallion, trapped in its stall. Its front hooves had dropped to the straw, but its eyes were wild. It tossed its massive head, spattering the walls with scarlet-flecked foam. Its hooves began drumming. Any second now it would try to break out through the thick wooden gate that barred its way. He had to calm it down before it hurt itself badly.

Hush now, he thought, *no need for that. I'm here, you're safe.*

The stallion's agitated movements gradually stilled. It stood trembling, its drenched flanks heaving as it noisily sucked in air.

There, that's it. That's it. Hush now.

The big liquid eyes turned curiously towards him. Blood oozed from the dark stripes where the whip had already cut into its neck. Forcing down his rage so the horse wouldn't sense it and be spooked again, Niall stepped up and reached out a hand to unfasten the gate.

His fingers had only just touched the latch when someone grabbed his upper arms from behind and jerked him backwards.

"What the hell do you think you're doing with that vicious devil?" a voice growled in his ear. He struggled to free himself while sending more calming thoughts to the stallion, but he couldn't break away or even twist around.

To make matters worse, the bald man he'd thought safely unconscious stirred and groaned, then clambered slowly to his feet. Blood trickled from his nose, and his expression was murderous.

Niall strove harder against the vice-like hands that held him, to no avail.

"What's going on?" his captor demanded, but no one answered him.

The other man moved in a slow, deliberate way to position himself squarely in front of Niall. He briefly turned away to spit a gout of blood onto the straw. The burning gaze that returned to Niall's face told him this would be bad. He braced himself. But instead of attacking immediately, the man ran a hand over his bare head and then took several long paces back.

Striving to keep the edgy stallion calm, Niall opened his mouth to plead with his captor to release him, to give him a fair chance in this fight, but the words remained unspoken.

The bald man clenched his fists, lowered his head, and exploded into action. Pumping his arms as he ran, he covered the short distance at frightening speed and barrelled headfirst into Niall.

It was like being hit in the stomach by a battering ram. All the air emptied out of Niall in a single gasp. His legs buckled, and he sagged against the other man. His lungs heaved desperately for a breath that wouldn't come. The word grew dim and blurred. From far away, he heard the horse scream in fury.

No, no, don't...

He couldn't hold the thought together. The stable had disappeared from view. In its place yawned a hazy grey tunnel, surrounded by a flickering blackness. Something unidentifiable was travelling towards him from the other end. It grew rapidly until it filled his vision.

And then, nothing.

SEVEN

Cahira

Cahira had hoped to catch up with Adric at breakfast time, but if he'd been in the dining room at all, he'd slipped away without her noticing. When she finally tracked him down, he was alone and stacking hay in a shed. She grabbed his arm and pulled him deeper into the shadows, out of sight of any casual passer-by.

Despite what Niall had said about the need to be careful, the direct approach was usually best with Adric. He didn't understand subtlety. Still holding onto him, she planted her feet and stared up into his face. "I know Berek is planning an attack. Are you crazy? What are you doing with these people?"

He looked as shocked as if she'd hit him with the pitchfork that was leaning against the wall. "How do you know about that?"

"Niall saw the weapons. Are you trying to get yourself killed?"

He groaned. "You don't understand."

She let go of his arm and took a step back. "Then help me understand. Why have you joined Berek's religious army?"

An internal struggle played itself out on his face while she waited with folded arms. Then he plopped down on a bale and huffed out a gusty breath. "All right, I'll tell you."

Cahira sat down next to him while he gathered his thoughts.

Finally he spoke. "It's not about religion."

"Then what?"

He turned his face away. "It's my fault Bram died."

Cahira was nonplussed. "How could it be your fault?"

"He was my brother, and I knew he couldn't look after himself in a fight. That's why I went with you when Tarn outlawed the Greenhaelen. To protect him. Protect you both." Still not looking at her, he bowed his shaggy head. "And I failed. I couldn't face you. I had to get away."

She'd never imagined he felt like this. "Where did you go?"

"All over, finding any work I could. Drinking the money away at night." He gripped his knees with his broad hands. "Pretty soon there was more drinking than working."

He lifted his head, his gaze going past her towards the open doorway. He stared for a while as if lost in thought, then went on slowly, choosing his words in a way that was so unlike him that Cahira knew he wasn't telling her the whole truth. "That's how Berek found me: passed out after a drunken fight, and not the first one. He brought me here, sobered me up, and listened to my story. He made me see that I didn't need to drown my guilt; I needed to make sure that what happened to Bram wouldn't happen to someone else's brother or husband. He said that Bram's murder was only a symptom of everything that's wrong with Algarth."

"What do you mean? The Warrant Guards killed Bram because they thought he was a Greenhaelan terrorist. They were just following bad orders."

"And who gave the orders? How did a man like Tarn get to be in charge in the first place? They're all the same. Oren, the Guards, the Council, all of them." His voice had risen loud enough to be heard from outside.

Alarmed, she tried to calm him down. "Not Logen, and he's the acting Chairman now."

"He's just another politician like all the others. I heard they've promoted Oren to commander. The same man who tried to arrest us. Promoted him!" He almost shouted the last two words.

Fearful someone would come to investigate the noise, Cahira laid a warning hand on his arm and flicked her own gaze to the doorway. Was that a figure whisking out of sight? A spy who'd listened to their conversation and was now running straight to Berek with the news?

She had to convince Adric he was wrong, and she had to do it now. She gripped his hands tightly and spoke as forcefully as she could without raising her voice. "You're talking about a civil war; do you realise that? People will die, maybe hundreds of them. And they won't all be guilty. Come to Eorna, talk to Logen. He's an honest man, he'll listen."

Adric stared miserably at her for a second, his mouth working. Then he pulled his hands away. "You don't understand," he said again. He stood up. "Don't follow me." He walked straight out the door, leaving her staring after him in astonishment.

Adric had always been stubborn once he got an idea into his head, but this was insane. He might be going to Berek right now to tell him everything she'd said. She had to warn Niall. Poking her head carefully outside and seeing no one, she emerged and sprinted for the stables.

Several heads turned as she ran into the yard. She skidded to a stop in front of the first door she came to and called out Niall's name. There was no answer. She moved on. In the third stable, an old man accosted her. He stood in her way, hands on hips, scowling as his hard eyes raked her up and down. "Who the hell are you, girlie, and what're you doin' screechin' like that in my stables?"

Knowing in her gut that she'd be in danger with this man if she showed any fear or uncertainty at all, Cahira worked to control her expression. Her skin crawled as she heard more men entering behind her, but she resisted the urge to turn around.

Taking her cue from the way Great-Aunt Alys, the terror of her childhood, had spoken to anyone she considered beneath her, Cahira drew herself up to her full height and lifted her chin imperiously. Fixing a withering gaze on the old man, she let him have it, including the aristocratic title she had inherited from her mother but never normally used.

"My name is *Lady* Cahira Gelt, and I am a guest of Master Berek. I sent my horseman, Niall Crawley, to work here in the stables today. Inform him I wish to see him immediately."

The shuffling behind her died away. The old man hesitated, visibly weighing her words. "A dandy in fancy black clothes, is he?"

"Niall does dress in black, yes." She held his gaze, saying nothing more.

His sallow cheeks flushed, and his resentful eyes dropped in surrender. "He's workin' across the way." He gestured curtly to someone behind her. "Stable Four. Show 'er."

"Thank you." Cahira followed her new guide, with her head high and her back arrow-straight. Triumph thrilled through her. Was this how her great-aunt felt when others wilted before her?

The man led her into a small stable that was clearly empty. She turned on him. "Where is he?"

He gaped at her and shrugged, as if to say it was nothing to do with him. She drew herself up again. "Well, I intend to find him. And you are going to help me. Come along." She swept out without looking back. To her great satisfaction, she heard him plodding behind. *Thank you, Aunt Alys.*

They searched two other stables, and then found themselves in another that also seemed empty at first glance. There was no answer when she called, but as her eyes adjusted to the dimness, she saw a horse at the far end: a big black stallion. She headed towards him. But the closer she came, the more agitated he grew. He laid his ears back flat and showed the whites of his eyes. When she reached his stall, he snorted and tossed his head at her. Dried blood steaked his neck.

The stableman suddenly cursed and darted into the adjoining stall. Cahira followed, letting out a strangled cry as she saw the figure lying on his back. He was still, and his eyes were closed.

"Niall!" Heedless of the filthy straw, she knelt beside him. A purple bruise stained his cheek, and a line of dark blood trailed from one side of his mouth. His skin was a stark, terrifying grey. She desperately looked for the rise and fall of his chest, but couldn't tell if the slight movement was real or just her imagination. She whipped her head around. "Get a Healer!" The stableman ran out.

"Niall," she whispered, tears falling down her cheeks. "Don't be dead. Please, don't be dead." She tried to find a pulse in his neck, but didn't even know if she was doing it right. Why wasn't she a Folk Healer? What use was singing, anyway? Her skal hadn't saved Bram, had it? And now she couldn't do anything to help Niall, either. He might already be dead for all she knew. Guilt squatted like a lump of stone in her rib cage, growing heavier and heavier, until she could barely breathe. *I'm so sorry, Niall, it's all my fault. We should never have come here.*

A figure dropped down beside her. Turning her head, she slowly recognised Perna. The novice was peering down intently at Niall. She felt his neck and leaned forward to lay one ear on his chest. Straightening up, she placed her hands on either side of his skull and closed her eyes. Was some colour returning to Niall's face? For an instant, Cahira thought so, but the next moment she couldn't be sure.

Perna removed her hands and sat back on her heels. "He has had a blow to the chest, and some of his ribs are broken. That is why his breathing is so shallow. I can speed the Healing there, but it is not the major problem. Someone hit him hard in the face, and he struck the back of his head on the wall as he fell. I think his brain is bleeding inside, and that is beyond my knowledge and skill." She met Cahira's eyes. "I am sorry."

With an enormous effort, Cahira forced her voice past the immense weight in her chest. It came out weak and breathy, like a stranger's. "Then we need a stronger Folk Healer."

She turned to the stableman, who had returned and was leaning uselessly against the wall. "Get Berek," she ordered. *"Now!"*

They carried Niall into the main house and laid him on a bed. Berek introduced the cloaked woman already waiting in the room as Mistress Hellin, a Healer who'd been visiting the farm to learn more about the Seeker community.

The woman pushed back her hood to reveal a fall of hair, dark grey shot through with pure white, hanging almost to her waist. Cahira recognised her now. She was the one who'd been standing against the wall last night, nodding to her after she'd finished singing.

The Healer stepped forward. "Call me Fadra, please." Her voice was deep, with a pleasant, almost musical tone. Cahira took the proffered hand, meeting brown eyes set in a tanned face that was only slightly lined, despite the colour of her hair.

"I'll do my very best for your friend," Fadra said.

"Thank you," Cahira replied faintly.

Fadra laid long, capable-looking hands along either side of Niall's head. Closing her eyes, she became nearly as still as her patient. Cahira stared at the unmoving form on the bed, alert for any change. Was his breathing growing deeper? After a moment, she was sure of it. His chest lifted and fell, the movement becoming more pronounced with each intake of air. And now some colour was coming back to his grey cheeks. Cahira drew in a deep breath of her own. Whatever the Healer was doing, it was helping.

After several long minutes, Fadra withdrew her hands. Her eyes seemed to hold both intelligence and compassion as she regarded Cahira.

"How is he?" Cahira burst out.

"He is no longer in immediate danger, but he needs rest and time."

"Perna said his brain might be bleeding."

The Healer directed an approving smile towards the novice. "She was correct. I've stopped the bleeding for now, but he will have to be watched closely in case it begins again. I believe that your friend will wake eventually, but I am afraid some damage has been done that is beyond my ability to Heal."

"What kind of damage?"

"To his memory. We won't know how much of it he has lost until he regains consciousness, but you should prepare yourself."

Cahira's stomach tightened. Memories made you who you were. Niall might wake up a different person. Even if he survived, she could still lose him.

The fear must have shown on her face, because Fadra leaned over and patted her hand gently as it lay on the bed between them. Her voice was gentle. "Now, now. It is not as bad as all that. Your friend is lucky you found him when you did. You saved his life. And even lost memories sometimes return on their own, given time." She pressed Cahira's hand and smiled at her. "So, we will hope for the best for him, you and I, yes?"

Cahira nodded, unable to speak but grateful for the kindness.

With a few formal expressions of sympathy, Berek took his leave, followed shortly by Perna.

The Healer straightened up from the bed and removed her cloak. "You should go, too. I have more work to do here, but you have had a shock and you need to rest." She held up a hand to forestall Cahira's protest. "I promise to send for you if there's any change."

Cahira shook her head. "Thank you, but I'm staying."

Fadra frowned at her as if she was about to insist, but then seemed to sense that Cahira wouldn't budge on this. "Very well, but you should at least sit down. I don't wish for a second patient."

Berek and Perna took their leave. For most of the time they simply sat, one on either side of the bed, watching Niall and saying nothing. At intervals, Fadra laid her hands on Niall's head again and closed her eyes, as if praying.

Cahira wished she could pray—anything that might make her feel useful—but she'd never had much to do with religion, and didn't know what to say. Besides, she couldn't really believe anyone was listening. But the minutes dragged, and she had nothing to lose by trying.

Fadra's head was bent over Niall again. It was as good a time as any. Cahira closed her own eyes. *Excuse me, Aal, if you're there. Please help Niall. I know he makes jokes about you sometimes, but he's a good man underneath.*

She was painfully aware that it wasn't an eloquent prayer. She tried to think of something better, but she had no idea if she was even doing it right. Maybe you had to perform a ritual or say some special words before Aal would listen to you. Perna would know. Perhaps she was praying for Niall, too. She didn't like him much, but she might consider it her duty. And surely Aal would listen to Perna, who spent all her time trying to please the god, and even aspired to be an Aaldan someday.

Assuming, of course, that Aal was real. No miracle had arrived to save Bram, had it? And if anyone deserved to live, it was Bramley Gelt, a gentle man who had never intentionally done harm in his life. He'd been a believer too, praying every morning and night. And despite all that, he'd died violently at the order of evil men. Either Aal didn't care about any of them, or the god was simply a figment of the imagination, as she'd always suspected.

Her thoughts were going around in circles. She gave up the effort and just sat there, watching Fadra work, as the time slowly wore away.

She must have dropped into a doze. When she woke, three words were echoing in her tired mind. *Help him. Please.*

It wasn't exactly a prayer, because she didn't expect an answer. But she silently sent it out anyway, and found some comfort in the act itself. Enough to hold back the worst of the despair, at least for now.

EIGHT

Niall slept away the whole afternoon and night, and most of the day after. He looked well enough and his colour was good: he just wouldn't wake up.

Cahira had gone to her own bed when she couldn't keep her eyes open any longer, but true sleep had eluded her, and she'd soon returned. She was beginning to hate that bare little room, where nothing changed, and the only sound was Niall's soft, steady breathing.

Anonymous women entered at intervals, bringing food and offering to take a turn at the bedside if she wanted a break. Cahira recognised their kind intentions, but feelings of gratitude were beyond her. More than once, she snapped at them. Perna came twice and prayed silently. Fadra was there for much of the time, but she seemed able to conserve her strength, resting peacefully in her chair in between tending to Niall. Where the others only irritated, Fadra's calm presence brought Cahira some small comfort. Adric didn't appear even once.

In the late afternoon of the second day, while Fadra was absent, Berek himself turned up again. Cahira asked him if Adric had been told about Niall's injuries.

He shook his head. "I'm afraid we have no way of getting a message to him."

She stared at him in alarm. "What do you mean? Where is he?"

"In Eorna. He should have arrived there last night."

Cahira leapt to her feet. "I don't believe you! Adric wouldn't have gone like that, without a word to me."

Berek looked taken aback at her vehemence, but rallied quickly, stepping forward to close the gap she'd deliberately left between them. "My dear, I assure you I'm telling you the truth. Even though Adric has only recently joined us, he takes his role as a Seeker of Virtue very seriously. When he heard that a group was planning to bring food and aid to the unfortunates in the city, he volunteered immediately. They will be there at least a week, perhaps longer."

He must be lying. Adric wouldn't have left without saying anything. But a small, hateful voice inside reminded her he'd done exactly that, after Bram's death. And he hadn't been happy to see her here. In fact, he'd practically run from her after she'd cornered him in the hay shed. A horrible, sinking feeling assailed her. By tackling him, she'd made things worse. She'd driven him away.

Berek's self-satisfied tones interrupted the turmoil of her thoughts. "I trust we will continue to enjoy the pleasure of your company until he returns. And perhaps you might sing for us again?" His smile showed too many teeth, as if he wanted to eat her.

Cahira stared blankly at him. The man must be mad.

But even the blockhead Berek seemed to sense he'd made a misstep. "Well, well, I will give you time to think it over. And if you need anything, anything at all, just send for me." After bestowing another disturbing smile, he moved to the door and let himself out.

A shudder ran through Cahira. There was no mistaking the way he'd looked at her this time. He wanted her to stay for reasons that had nothing to do with virtue. She suddenly needed to escape the stifling atmosphere of this room and breathe some fresh air. When the next volunteer came in, Cahira accepted her offer to sit with Niall and headed outside.

She followed a path that wound down to the lower fields. The westering sun hung beneath slate-blue clouds, splashing intense gold against trees and buildings and lighting up each grass stalk and seed head along the way. There was a nip in the air, signalling the approach of winter, but when the view opened up, that otherworldly light turned the ordinary pasture spread out below Cahira into a gilded carpet. The sight made her pause and forget her cold fingers, but not even such beauty could keep anxiety at bay for long.

When would she be able to escape from this place? She couldn't leave Niall—that was out of the question—but he still showed no sign of waking up. And Adric would be away for at least a week, according to Berek. Her heart sank at the thought of staying here all that time, never knowing when the Seeker leader might decide to try something more than words and creepy smiles.

If only she could go right now, taking Niall with her. But how? She'd need a cart or carriage, impossible to organise without Berek's approval. And the last thing she wanted was to feel as though she owed him anything. Not that he was likely to agree anyway, judging by the way he'd leered at her. The bright afternoon seemed to dim. Whether she was inside or outside, she was trapped here until Niall woke up. Even so, she couldn't bear the thought of going back to him just yet.

Craving a friendly face, she turned and headed for the kitchen. She was in luck. The first person she saw was Bett, bent over with her sleeves rolled up, kneading dough with the hand of her good arm and the elbow of the other.

Bett straightened up as Cahira approached, pushing wayward strands of damp blond hair off her forehead. Her fingers left tiny spots of flour in their wake, like white freckles on her flushed skin. "Cahira! I heard about your friend. Is he any better?"

The genuine concern in her voice was very warming, and Cahira found herself describing Niall's condition and her fears for him. Bett made sympathetic noises and squeezed Cahira's shoulder. When she turned back to her work, Cahira stayed and watched, finding comfort in the steady rhythm of the kneading.

As soon as she'd worked the dough to her satisfaction, Bett set it in a bowl to rise and wiped her hands on her apron. "Can I ask you somethin'?"

"Anything."

"I was there when you sang the other night. I've never seen nothin' like it, the pictures in the air an' all the voices. How'd you do that?"

Cahira shrugged. "It's my skal."

"But did you have to learn it?"

"Not at first. It just happened. One day I was singing in my room, and out it came, two voices at once. My mother heard me and said I was a Skalsinger. But after that I spent three years studying at the Academy in Eorna, and that's when the images started too."

"Well, I hope my skal comes in soon. I've had enough of workin' in this kitchen." Bett began on a second lump of dough, giving it a few hard thumps to relieve her feelings. "Singin's pretty good, but I'd rather be a Scriber like my Ma."

Cahira hoped Bett would get her wish. Scribing—making words appear on paper or parchment without quill or ink—was an uncommon skal, and strong Scribers were in high demand. Bett could earn a decent living anywhere on Algarth, and her crooked arm wouldn't matter a bit. Not that she let it hold her back, even here. But Bett deserved a better future than she'd have with the Seekers. And that thought reminded Cahira of someone else she should check on.

She reluctantly took her leave and went in search of Perna. She couldn't seem to shake her sense of responsibility for the ex-novice, and she wanted to reassure herself that she was all right. Or maybe she was just looking for an excuse to put off going back to that bed where Niall was lying so still.

On her last visit to the sick room, Perna had mentioned she was working in the laundry. After a moment's thought, Cahira recalled passing it on Adric's tour, and headed in that direction.

As she hauled the heavy door open, steam puffed out in a dense cloud. She stepped backwards with sweat already prickling across her scalp, and tried to peer through the thick white fog. Sloshing and a dull, rhythmic thumping reached her ears.

"Perna?" she called over the noise. "Are you in there?"

The small brown figure materialised in front of her with a suddenness that made her jump. Without a word, Perna pushed the door closed, shutting sound, heat and moisture inside. Cahira drew in a lungful of cool air, fanning her hot cheeks. Perna's own face was as red and shiny as a holly berry, and her hair had escaped from its bonds and was curling in wet tendrils over her forehead and ears. Ignoring the water trickling into her eyes and off the tip of her nose, she stood with her hands primly folded, waiting for Cahira to speak.

Why did Perna feel such a need to control herself, even standing there scarlet-faced and dripping? Was it her Aaldan training? But Elder Meril hadn't behaved this way at all.

The ex-novice was still waiting. Cahira pulled herself together, remembering why she'd come. "Um, how are you, Perna?"

"I am well, Mistress Gelt. And you?"

So much for that topic. She supposed she'd have to take Perna's word for it she was okay. But now Cahira had an opportunity to test the truthfulness of what Berek had told her.

"I'm fine, Perna, but I'm a bit worried about Adric. He seems to have gone away." She drew a breath. "Have you heard anything from the other girls about where he might be?"

Perna's face resumed its familiar expression of disapproval. "I do not listen to gossip, but some of them think that Master Berek sent him to Eorna. They were complaining that 'such a strong and handsome man' had to go away so soon." Disdain rang in her voice.

"Did they say how long he'll be gone?"

"No. I do not even know if it is true. Idle chatter is seldom reliable."

Apparently Perna was less than impressed with the young women of her 'truly moral' community. Hopefully, she was disappointed enough to want to run straight back to the safety of Mirhome.

"So, have you found what you wanted here? Do you think you'll stay?"

For a moment, Perna looked almost uncomfortable. She opened and closed her mouth, as if fumbling for the right words. Her cheeks, which had resumed their normal colour, flushed again. When she spoke, her voice was higher than usual. "Yes, I am remaining here for now. It is true that not everyone has the high moral standards I had hoped to find. But with Berek's firm leadership, I am sure that will change." Her eyes dropped.

She wasn't telling the truth, or not all of it. There was something else keeping her here. Could it be that she'd found a 'strong and handsome' man of her own? It would explain her discomfort and reticence on the subject, and the way her cheeks were glowing. Suddenly Cahira was sure she was right. *I wonder if he feels the same about her, whoever he is?*

It was hard to imagine any man being drawn to Perna's stiff and prickly personality. Still, love was a strange thing. No one would have predicted that Cahira and Bram would ever become a couple—he so steady and quiet, she with her emotions always swinging up and down. He'd loved nothing better than time alone with her, whereas crowds excited and energised her. And yet, they'd come together. Perhaps even Perna, with her strict code of propriety, was some young man's ideal woman.

The thought tickled Cahira enough that she felt ready to go back to Niall. She wished she could share Perna's news with him. He'd be amused. She left Perna to get on with her laundry duty and returned to the house in the gathering dusk.

Fadra was there, bending over Niall with her hands on his head and her face hidden by her long hair. The sight made Cahira feel peaceful. Fadra straightened up to greet her with a smile. "Our patient is doing well. I have no fears about leaving him in your care, and Perna's."

Cahira's peace shattered. "You're leaving?" she repeated, hoping she'd somehow misunderstood.

Fadra spread her hands in apology. "I'm sorry, Cahira, but I must return home. I've already stayed here longer than I planned, and there are things that need my attention."

"But—when are you going?"

"First thing tomorrow morning."

Panicked words rushed to Cahira's lips: *Please don't go. I'm scared to be here alone.* She suppressed them. She wasn't a child, and Fadra didn't owe her anything. It was she who was indebted to Fadra. She had no right to ask for anything more. But that didn't stop a sick, hollow feeling lodging in her stomach.

Fadra touched her shoulder, as if she understood what Cahira hadn't said. "I hoped Niall would wake before I had to leave. But my home isn't far, less than a day's journey. If anything happens and you need me, just ask Berek to send someone. I'll come. I promise."

"Thank you for everything you've done." Cahira threw her arms around the older woman and hugged her tightly. When she stepped back, she ducked her head so Fadra wouldn't see the tears.

"You're most welcome," Fadra said. "I'll look in again before I go, just in case our friend decides he's had enough of sleeping."

After Fadra had left, Cahira sat down, staring bleakly at Niall. *It's all very well for you, lying there so peacefully. No problems, no fears, no decisions to make. No Berek, getting all creepy and suggestive.*

Bitterness bloomed within her at the unfairness of it all. Even Niall's calm expression and the steady rise and fall of his chest seemed to mock her. Fighting a sudden desire to slap his smug face, she reached forward and shook him roughly by the shoulder instead.

There was a catch in his breathing. Cahira's pulse beat a tattoo against her temples as she held her own breath, willing him to open his eyes. An eternity later, he gave a kind of hiccough, and the air whooshed back out of him. After that, his breathing steadied again. His chest lifted and fell as before. His eyelids hadn't even flickered. It was as if nothing had happened at all.

Sick with anger and disappointment, Cahira beat her fists uselessly on the bed. *Wake up, curse you*, she wailed in silence. *Wake up.*

The lamps had been lit, and someone had brought a meal to Cahira. She hadn't eaten any of it. She was still pushing the pieces of food around her plate when the door opened and Fadra came back in.

The Healer surveyed her and frowned in disapproval. "Cahira, you look exhausted." She took off her cloak and sat down. "I've had a thought. I can't extend my visit here, but if you agree, I can take Niall home with me. It's not far, and I'm sure the trip won't do him any harm now that he's stable. I have people there I trust, who'd be happy to care for him."

Cahira's hope swelled, then collapsed as she realised she couldn't accept. "That's so generous. Thank you. But he's my responsibility. I can't abandon him."

But Fadra was already shaking her head. "Of course not. I meant both of you. Would you like to come and stay with me for a while?"

Relief and gratitude flooded Cahira's whole being. It was the answer to everything. Too full of emotion to speak, she smiled through her tears and nodded in agreement.

NINE

Things moved quickly next morning. At the news that Cahira wasn't staying after all, Berek's complexion darkened and he scowled into his tangled beard. Cahira was grateful for Fadra's presence in the conversation. In the face of the Healer's matter-of-fact statements, Berek dropped his burning eyes and mumbled gruffly that he hoped Cahira might return for another visit soon. And that was that.

Cahira made a point of finding Bett in the kitchen before they left, and Bett surprised her by hugging her fiercely. Hopefully, the girl would be safe here, but there wasn't anything Cahira could do for her right now.

Perna was in the dining hall, picking at a mostly empty plate. Cahira's news didn't seem to affect her either way. She repeated her intention to stay, and added that when Adric returned, she would tell him where Cahira and Niall had gone. Her sudden blush confirmed Cahira's suspicion that Perna was staying for a more personal reason than she was willing to admit.

Less than an hour later, feeling more like herself in her tunic and riding trousers—no need for the dull brown skirt now—Cahira stood beside Blackbird and Sienna, watching as men carried Niall from the house and laid him on a pallet in the single-horsed cart Fadra had organised.

Sienna's head lifted and she snuffled as she caught her owner's scent. She lunged forward, dragging Cahira and Blackbird with her, and bent her elegant neck to nose at Niall's chest. When he didn't respond, she snorted and pushed harder.

Cahira tugged on the lead rope. "It's all right, girl, he's just sleeping. Come away now."

With a final snort, the mare backed up a few steps. Cahira stowed her pack in the cart, fastened Sienna to Blackbird's saddle, and sprang up. It was good to be riding again, and even better to be leaving this place.

Fadra was already mounted, and Cahira recognised the black stallion that had been in the stable with Niall. He was standing calmly under the saddle, betraying no trace of his former distress. Cahira had grown up around horses—her family owned some of the best breeding stock in Algarth—and even she had never seen a finer stallion. He must be worth a fortune. She wondered where he'd been bred and how a humble Folk Healer had come to own him.

Just as they were about to set off, a high-pitched cry broke the silence. A compact figure tore around the corner of the house, with brown skirts swirling and unbound hair streaming out behind her. She skidded to a stop and gasped out: "I changed me mind, I'm comin' too." Without waiting for a response, she clambered up over the back of the cart and crouched down in the tray, squeezing as far into one corner as she could. This was a whole different Perna, her eyes wide with fear and all composure gone.

"What's wrong?" Cahira asked, seeing no reason for this alarm.

"Nuffin'—I mean, nothing. I just changed my mind." Her gaze darted about like that of a trapped animal. "Can we go?"

Cahira glanced towards Fadra, who merely raised her eyebrows, leaving the decision up to her. Cahira was keen to get away as soon as they could, and Perna clearly wasn't getting off the cart voluntarily. Anyway, what harm could it do to take the girl with them? She'd be safer with Fadra and Cahira than here at the farm. "It's okay with me."

Fadra gave the order and they set off along the winding drive. But as they drew near to the closed gates, a sudden uneasiness swept through Cahira. What if Berek's agreement had just been an act? He'd wanted her to stay, and it didn't seem to be in his nature to give way so easily. She watched the guards closely as they opened the gates, and turned her head to keep them in sight as she rode through in the cart's wake. But they made no move to accost her, merely swinging the gates shut behind her and resuming their places. The tension in her back eased slightly. *I'm imagining things. It will be better once we're on the road.*

Yet even when they were safely on their way, she couldn't shake the feeling that she was being watched. She scanned the sunlit way ahead and the dark shade beneath the trees on either side: no one was in sight. Blackbird picked up on her uneasiness and fidgeted, dancing sideways a few steps. If Cahira didn't calm her down, Sienna would start, too. She permitted herself a final long look all around, then resolutely faced forward again. There was nothing wrong. It was just nerves, probably brought on by worrying about Adric and Niall.

Blackbird settled down into a steady walk as the road took them west, winding lazily between farms and small copses of maple and birch. The morning was bright, with high, thin clouds streaking a pale blue sky. A chill, capricious breeze plucked the last few leaves from their branches, twirling them in the air before letting them drift to the ground. In a week it would be winter. Hopefully Fadra's house had stout walls and generous fireplaces.

To dispel her edginess, Cahira began to hum an autumn song. It was a favourite of her mother, who loved this in-between season of icy mornings and golden days, of storms and blue skies, of fruitfulness and decay. She matched the tempo to Blackbird's gait and sang softly:

> *Now is the warmth of summer gone,*
> *The restless, wandering geese are flown*
> *To southern shores so far away.*
> *Yet here my heart dwells; here I'll stay.*

> *The days grow short and when they're done,*
> *The chill of night cuts to the bone,*
> *As high above the cold stars ride.*
> *Yet here my heart dwells; here I'll bide.*

They burst without warning from the trees: big men on big horses crowding around her, separating her from the others. It was all she could do to keep her seat as Blackbird plunged and kicked. She looked for a way out, but there was nowhere to go. She heard Perna scream. The horses pressed in even closer. Men shouted, and hooves clattered on the road.

Sienna's lead rope snapped tight, pinning her leg, and she cried out with the pain. The rope suddenly released; someone must have cut it. Sienna had disappeared behind the wall of men and horses. Hemmed in too tightly to move, Blackbird stopped bucking and stood trembling in place, her ears laid flat.

A bald-headed rider, bearded and scowling, reached across Cahira to snatch the reins. She pushed at his arm, but it was like trying to shift a tree. He grabbed both her wrists in an enormous hand, squeezing hard enough to wring another cry from her. Almost as furious as she was scared, she struggled against his grip. His hairy arm was in her face now, crushing her nose, mashing her top lip against her teeth, smothering her. He was too strong to fight. There was only one thing she could do.

She reared her head back, took a deep breath, and bit him as hard as she could in the fleshy part just above his elbow. He yelled and tried to pull away, but she clamped her jaw down harder. His sour stench was in her nose, and her mouth was full of his disgusting skin and hair. Tasting blood, she swallowed convulsively and fought against the almost overwhelming urge to gag. She still couldn't breathe. She held on.

Out of the corner of her eye, she saw his other arm lift and knew what was coming, but there was no time to avoid the blow. The fist smashed down on the top of her skull like a hammer, punching her teeth deeper. He yelled again. She was going to pass out at any second, but at least she'd hurt him, maybe badly. There was some satisfaction in that.

A second blow slammed into the centre of her forehead, snapping her head back. Her jaws sprang apart as sharp agony shot down her spine. She sucked in a single gulp of air before nausea rolled through her, vile and unstoppable. Her neck bent forward again, and she vomited onto the saddle.

"Bitch! The bitch bit me!" Threats and cursing seared the air above her. Gasping between spasms, desperately trying not to choke on her own vomit, she waited helplessly for the final blow: the one that would kill her.

But it never fell. When her aching stomach was empty and the world had stopped spinning, she raised her head, fighting for every breath, to find Blackbird still hemmed in tightly on all sides. But a different rider was holding the reins now. He was young and he was grinning all over his face. She hated him.

"She's a game wench, I'll give her that," he said to someone on her other side.

"The bitch needs to be taught some respect. We'll take her, too." That was the bald one, the man she'd bitten. She was pleased to see he was clutching his arm tightly. She hoped her teeth had gone right down to the bone. And that the wound would get infected. He was glaring at her with his little piggy eyes. She glared back, realising that she'd seen him somewhere before. He must have been at the farm. She should have listened to her instincts, been ready for an attack. Berek wouldn't let her go so easily.

Without warning, a pair of arms snaked around her from behind, staying well clear of her teeth. They pulled her out of the saddle and dumped her on the ground. She staggered, grabbing the stirrup leather to stay upright. Her pounding head spun again. She closed her eyes and took in deep, gasping breaths. She could do nothing except fight the pain and nausea, as her hands were jerked in front of her and her wrists were tied together with coarse rope. Where were Fadra and Perna? And Niall, had they hurt him?

"Put them in the cart." It was the big man again, the familiar one.

"There's someone lying in here, Dostig. A dandy all in black. What'll we do with him?"

Cahira waited fearfully for the answer.

"Is he dead?"

"No, he's breathing, but he won't wake up. I hit him a couple of times, to be sure he wasn't fooling."

"Dump him out, he's no use to us. And hurry up."

Sagging in relief, Cahira felt herself lifted again and dropped hard onto the floor of the cart. Trying to ignore the thundering pain in her head, she struggled to sit up and see what was happening. After several tries, she managed it, bracing her back against the rough wooden side.

With more room to move, and unencumbered by the weight of a rider, Blackbird was bucking and kicking again. Several attackers hastily backed their mounts out of reach of her hooves. Taking advantage of the opening, the panicked mare whirled and bolted for the trees. Cahira bit her lip, terrified the dangling reins would catch on the underbrush and bring her down. But Blackbird kept going and soon disappeared from sight between the closely spaced trunks.

Sienna was nowhere to be seen; she must have escaped earlier. Presumably Niall was now lying in the dirt behind them as Dostig had ordered, but riders blocked Cahira's view of the road in that direction. Blackbird, Sienna and Niall: she'd lost them all. With a sob in her throat, she turned her attention to her immediate surroundings.

Fadra had been bound and dumped in the cart soon after Cahira. Perna huddled beside her, hands also tied, her whole body shaking. Cahira shuffled sideways until their shoulders touched. "It'll be okay, Perna. We'll get out of this." She wished she believed her own words.

The vehicle jolted into motion. They were still travelling in the same direction they'd been heading before the ambush, with their attackers split in front and behind. Cahira counted eight of them.

Fadra inclined her head to indicate the riders. "Who do you think they are?" She kept her voice down, but she didn't sound frightened, just thoughtful.

"Aren't they from Virtue Farm?" Cahira asked in surprise.

"I don't believe so. If Berek wanted to harm us, he could have done it before we left. Why take the risk of doing it on the open road where anyone could see?"

That made sense, Cahira thought. But if not Berek, then who? "They called the leader Dostig," she said. "I've seen him before, but I can't remember where."

Fadra leaned back and sent a hard stare towards the leading riders. "They look like common bandits to me, just vermin looking for a ransom."

"He's not a bandit." Perna's head was bent, and her voice was barely above a whisper.

"Perna," Cahira asked gently, "do you know this Dostig?"

Perna nodded, keeping her face concealed.

"Who is he?"

Perna's reply was almost too low to hear. "He's my father."

"It's all my fault," Perna said suddenly.

After her revelation, she'd retreated into a miserable silence, resisting all Cahira's efforts to persuade her to say more.

Cahira had turned her attention to her bonds, noting that Fadra was doing the same. But no matter how they pulled and twisted, the ropes around their wrists wouldn't budge. They were stuck here. Finally giving up, Cahira had leaned against the side and watched the countryside slide by, trying not to think about what might happen to them when the cart stopped.

But now Perna had broken her silence. "I should never have run away. This is a punishment."

"You mean they're taking us to Mirhome?" Cahira was almost giddy with relief.

"No, not Mirhome. That's where I ran away to, from my home and my father." Tears spilled from Perna's eyes again. She sniffed. "And then I saw him at the farm early this morning and I ran away again. Why did I try to defy him?"

With her small face all tear-stained and blotchy, she looked even younger than before. Cahira felt the urge to give her a hug, but all she could do was bump gently against her.

"Fathers don't always know what's best," she said, thinking of her own, who hadn't wanted her to go after Adric at all. But it had been the right thing to do, and the mess she was in now didn't change that.

Perna's eyes widened, as if Cahira had said something shocking. "It's not my place to judge if he knows best, only to obey him. But I—I just couldn't…"

Cahira's empty stomach churned again. She pictured frail little Perna and that huge, brutal man and suddenly didn't want to know any more.

But Perna was already going on. "I should have been stronger. If I had, Aal would have blessed the marriage and everything would have been all right." Despite the tremble in her voice, her words relieved Cahira. Perna had run away from an arranged marriage; that was much better than what she'd been imagining. Arranged marriages weren't common any more, but they still happened and they could lead to happiness if the parents chose well.

"Who did he want you to marry?"

"An ungodly man called Nathan, who owns the tavern in our village. My father spent a lot of money drinking and gambling there and he can't pay it back. He said if I hadn't found anyone else to marry me at twenty-two years old, I never would, and it was my duty to accept Nathan and settle the debt. He went on and on at me. I know I should want to help him." Perna gulped and sniffed again. "But N—Nathan's about fifty, and he s—smells. He's already had two wives. And I would have to w—work in the tavern, and let him…" She broke down completely, sobbing noisily and shuddering against Cahira's shoulder.

Passionate anger flooded Cahira. To force a naïve young woman to marry a man thirty years older just to pay off a debt was shocking. No, more than that: it was evil. She glared at Dostig's back.

As if he felt the heat of her stare, he turned around briefly in the saddle. He was frowning, and the expression gave Cahira the clue to his identity she'd been looking for: Dostig was the man who'd tried to grab Perna in The Black Bull, the one they'd thought was just a belligerent drunk. After he'd sobered up, he must have found out his daughter was at Virtue Farm and come after her. But he hadn't come alone.

"Perna, do you know who all these others are?"

"No, I've never seen them before."

"Could they be Berek's men?"

"I don't think so. When I saw my father this morning, he was talking to Berek, but it looked like they were arguing. I didn't stay to listen, I was too scared." Perna took a deep breath. "I was a coward. And now you're in trouble too. When we stop, I'll tell my father that I'll marry Nathan if he lets you go."

Cahira was shaking her head before Perna finished. "No, you won't. None of this is your fault. We'll find another way."

Fadra has been listening to the conversation in silence until now. "Perna, are you sure these men aren't friends with your father?"

"I'm sure. Our village is small, I know everyone there."

"Then he's probably paying them. And from what you say about his debts, he can't be paying them much. Which means they might be open to a better offer. I have funds at my home. If we can persuade one of them to listen to us, I could try to make a deal."

Cahira was full of admiration for such clear thinking. "My parents are wealthy, they'd help too. It's a good idea, Fadra."

Perna bowed her head for a moment in thought. When she lifted it again, there was a new determination on her tear-streaked face. "No. This is my fault and I won't allow my weakness to cost you more than it already has." There was no sign of shakiness in her voice now. "I was stupid. Stupid and wicked to believe I could make up for my disobedience by becoming an Aaldan. I am going home." Her face was closed, her expression set. Even her speech had reverted to its previous formality. The old Perna was back, hard and certain of her convictions, unreachable.

Fadra tried anyway. "Perna, what kind of god is this Aal, to want you to be miserable?" she asked gently. "Why would you obey such a being?"

Before Perna could answer, the cart jerked to a stop. They were on a short piece of road between two bends. The scattered groups of trees had become solid walls of greenery on both sides.

"Spread out!" Dostig barked. The riders formed a wide circle around their captives. Their hands gripped the hilts of their swords as they faced outwards.

Cahira craned her head in every direction, but couldn't see any reason for the alarm.

"Get down," Fadra said. "If there's going to be a fight, we don't want to be hit by accident."

She had a point, but Cahira couldn't bear the thought of not being able to see. She compromised by wriggling down until her eyes were just above the slatted side of the cart. The top of her head was exposed, and it wasn't a pleasant feeling, but she couldn't help that. Fadra and Perna were lying flat on the boards, looking up at her.

A figure came around the forward bend. He was on foot, but barely, wavering from one side of the road to the other. He was so short that at first she thought he was a young boy. But as he drew closer, she made out a long grey beard. He wore ragged working clothes, and he was either drunk or addled in his mind. His arms waved wildly, and he alternately mumbled and shouted, but she couldn't make out any words. The riders relaxed and took their hands off their swords. One of them made a coarse joke and his companion laughed.

The stranger looked up at the sound, as if noticing for the first time that he wasn't alone. He broke into a shambling run, heading for Dostig. His windmilling arms must have startled the big man's horse, which snorted and jumped backwards. Dostig swore as he fought for control of the animal. The old man stopped a few paces away and peered up from underneath his battered hat.

Dostig got the horse back under control. "Move, you idiot!"

The tramp stared upwards, his slight body swaying.

The other riders came forward to support their leader. Fear for the old man froze Cahira. They would trample the frail figure down if he didn't obey.

A small, frightened sound drew her attention to Perna, who was looking up at her with wide eyes. "Don't worry," Cahira whispered. "It's not an attack, just an old man."

The other women sat up to see for themselves. Fadra spoke urgently. "No one's watching us. We can slip off the back and disappear."

She was right: this might be their only chance to get away. All the men were distracted, including the one on the driver's seat, but that probably wouldn't last long. They had to try now. Cahira nodded and shuffled to the rear of the cart as quietly as she could. Unfastening the tailgate would make too much noise, but it was low enough to scramble over, even with her hands tied like this. She would fall onto the road, and that would hurt, but better a few bruises than staying here.

"I do not want to escape," said a clear, soft voice from behind her. "I told you. I am going home." Cahira groaned softly at the girl's stubbornness. But she couldn't afford the time to argue; she had Niall to think about. The men had left him unconscious on the road, where anything could happen. She had to get back to him.

Fadra joined her, then turned to make one last appeal to Perna. "Don't be foolish," she hissed. "You are throwing your life away. And for what? A father who only thinks of himself and a god who doesn't want you to be happy. You're young. You could be so much more than this. Come and see for yourself."

Perna just shook her head, her expression mulish.

"If we're going, we need to go now," Cahira said tightly. Fadra shot one last look at Perna, then nodded.

Cahira got to her knees and checked to make sure their captors were still focused on the old man. He was shouting up at Dostig in apparent delight: "Dobbo, my old friend, I never thought I'd see you again! Let's get a drink!"

Cahira took a deep breath, tucked her chin to her chest, and rolled up and over the tailgate. There was a brief sensation of weightlessness before she slammed into the ground, shoulder first. The side of her head hit next, and then her hip. The explosive bursts of pain were as bad as she'd expected, but adrenaline pushed her to her feet. She heard Fadra drop beside her. The older woman sprang up like an acrobat, impressing Cahira again. They waited a moment, in case Perna had changed her mind, and then they ran.

They headed straight back along the road, using the cart for cover. At the first bend, they made a break for the trees. No alarm was raised as they ducked under the closest branches and began scrambling through the thick undergrowth. The trees here were mostly pine, with a tangled understory of blackberry bushes. They'd lost most of their leaves, but none of their vicious thorns.

Cahira led the way, avoiding the prickly mounds where she could, but there was very little open ground. She was glad she was wearing trousers and not a dress. Fadra wasn't so lucky. Her long cloak and robe kept catching and having to be tugged free. Not a simple thing with her hands still bound in front of her. But each time Cahira glanced back at her, the older woman just nodded at her to keep going, her lips set in determination.

As they forged deeper into the wood, the light levels fell and the air cooled noticeably. The brambles became sparser, their canes elongated, the gaps between them wider. And then Cahira came upon a track beaten into the moist black soil, narrow but distinct, stretching out of her view in both directions.

After a few seconds, Fadra caught up with her. "Well done, Cahira, that's a welcome sight. I've had enough of thorn bushes for a while."

Cahira peered back the way they'd come. "I don't think anyone followed us."

"I'm sure you're right. And now, can you reach inside my cloak? There's a scabbard strapped against my ribs on the left side."

It was the last thing Cahira had expected the older woman to say. But she'd begun to trust that the Healer knew what she was doing. She lifted her tied hands and stepped close. After some fiddly manoeuvring, her fingers found the leather sheath and unfastened the flap. Obeying Fadra's instructions, she carefully drew out the short knife.

Gripping the hilt in both hands, she sawed at the rope around Fadra's wrists. Twice she dropped the blade and had to get down on her knees in the dirt to retrieve it. But finally the strands parted.

Fadra rubbed her arms, then took the knife and freed Cahira. She tucked the sharp little weapon away. "Now we go back for our unconscious friend, yes?"

"Are you sure?" Of course Cahira intended to do exactly that, but after everything that had happened, she'd half-expected Fadra would want nothing more than to continue on her way home.

Fadra smiled at her. "We can't just leave him on the road, can we? Not after we've spent so much time looking after him already."

"Thank you." Cahira felt ridiculously relieved. If anything had happened to Niall while he was lying helpless—no, she wouldn't think about that. Niall would be fine. Even so, she was very glad that Fadra was coming with her.

They turned eastward, the going much easier now that their hands were free and they had a clear track to follow. The sun had disappeared behind a mass of steely cloud and the air felt heavy, as if a storm were on the way. And it was cold. Rain would be bad enough, Cahira thought. She only hoped those darkening clouds weren't holding the first winter snow.

TEN

Niall

Niall couldn't understand why the roof was so far above him, and so grey and blurry. He couldn't even make out any beams. What was holding it up? The question occupied his mind until it occurred to him that he might see better if he wasn't lying down.

Struggling upright, he let out a hoarse cry and clutched his throbbing head. Eyelids clenched shut against the stabbing pain, he tried to remember if he had been drinking last night. But no—he'd been at Virtue Farm. Not a drop of alcohol in the whole place. And now a memory assailed him: a stable and something coming fast towards his face. They had knocked him out. That accounted for the discomfort and confusion, and the lack of a roof. Someone had found him unconscious and carried him outside. Satisfaction at solving the puzzle dissolved as another spike of agony hammered into his skull.

He gingerly cracked his eyelids open just a slit: grey sky, trees, dirt. No sign of a building. He winced as his fingers explored his pounding head. There was a large lump on the back, tender to the touch. A brief survey of the rest of his person uncovered a few more sore spots, especially along his right cheekbone, which by the feel of it must be blooming with an impressive bruise. But he wasn't bleeding anywhere and nothing seemed to be broken. His mouth was as dry as dust, but the dizziness was fading. Even the thudding in his skull had diminished. Things were looking up.

He got to his feet and scanned his surroundings properly. He was in the middle of an empty road. The only moving objects in view were a few birds flying across the overcast sky. He ran a thumb along his jawline, thinking. Why dump him all the way out here? Had they believed him dead? But then why not bury him? His imagination shied away from exploring that thought any further.

Perhaps robbery rather than murder had been their aim. He clapped a hand to his belt and swore. His knives were gone. And his sword was in the loft at the farm. At least he still had his boots and the little dagger in its hidden sheath.

Whatever had happened after he'd been attacked, he had to find his way back and make sure Cahira was all right. He concentrated and reached out for Sienna, turning slowly in a circle and trying to ignore the renewed thundering in his temples. There she was, and not too far away. She didn't seem to be confined, but her thoughts were skittish, swirling with a combination of fear and anger.

Niall kept a tight rein on his own emotions as he soothed her. *There, girl, steady sweetheart. Here I am. Come get me.* The burst of joy that flooded his mind warmed him and humbled him at the same time.

But regret gnawed as he waited by the side of the road. He should never have let Cahira talk him into letting her stay, not after they'd discovered how dangerous Berek was. He should have dragged her off with him then and there. Anything could have happened to her while he'd been gone.

Sienna began to panic in response to his rising tension. He clamped down hard on his mind, pushing all thoughts of Cahira away, thinking only of his lovely bay mare and how glad he'd be to see her. She settled again. She was very close and travelling fast. Not long now.

ELEVEN

Cahira

They emerged from the woods and headed west along the road, searching for Niall. Cahira kept glancing sideways at Fadra, concerned the older woman might need to rest after their exertions. But if anything, it was Fadra who pushed the pace. Once or twice she smiled at Cahira and made an encouraging remark, but the remainder of the time her face was set in grim lines. At last Cahira asked her outright what was troubling her.

Fadra stopped walking. "I didn't want to worry you, but those men weren't gentle when they rolled Niall onto the road, and one of them had already hit him before that. I'm concerned that they might have started another bleed in his brain."

It was as though all the air had been sucked out of their surroundings.

Fadra gripped her shoulder. "Cahira! You have to be strong for Niall. Come on, breathe."

Cahira was light-headed and sick to her stomach, but Fadra was right; they had no time to waste. "I'm okay."

"Good girl." Fadra let her go and strode off so fast that Cahira had to jog a few steps to catch up.

Surely Niall couldn't be far now. Maybe just past this curve, although it was hard to tell one stretch of the road from another.

But Niall wasn't around the next bend, or the two after that. It was only when the trees thinned out and finally gave way to unbroken farmlands that Cahira accepted the awful truth. They'd passed the site of the ambush. Niall was no longer on the road. And they had no way of knowing where he'd gone. Weakness came over her, and she dropped to her knees in the short grass.

Things went hazy after that. She was aware of Fadra putting a small bottle to her lips and telling her to drink. The liquid tasted bitter, but she swallowed it obediently. She didn't seem to have any will of her own, now that she'd messed everything up so badly. She'd lost them all. Adric, Niall, the horses. She hadn't even been able to protect little Perna, on her stubborn way to a miserable marriage. Niall had been right. She should have stayed at home like he wanted.

And she was so tired. At Fadra's gentle urging, she lay down on her side and drew up her knees. She needed to sleep; things always looked better in the morning. But it was already morning, wasn't it? The problem was too difficult to work out, the thought too slippery to hold onto. Her eyes closed.

She woke with her own cry ringing in her ears. She was being bumped up and down, and her injured shoulder was throbbing. She stared around wildly.

"It's all right. You're all right." It was Fadra, sitting next to her.

For a horrible moment, Cahira thought that the escape had been a dream and they were still Dostig's prisoners. But her hands weren't tied, and the sides of this vehicle were higher than those of the farm cart. She levered herself up on one elbow and rubbed her smarting shoulder. "Where are we?"

"I didn't arrive home when I was expected, so two of my students came to look for me." Fadra nodded towards the young man and woman sitting on the driving bench. "You were so deeply asleep that we couldn't wake you."

"We have to go back for Niall."

"We don't know where he is, Cahira."

"Then we have to find him!"

"We will, I promise, but first we need to look after you. How long is it since you ate a proper meal?"

"It doesn't matter—"

"Or slept for more than a few hours?"

Cahira shook her head impatiently.

"Cahira, you're exhausted. You can't go on like this." Cahira opened her mouth to keep arguing, but Fadra added, "And the weather is turning bad. I want to be under cover before the storm breaks."

Cahira glanced upwards to a mass of clouds the deep purple colour of bruises. An icy gust slapped her hair across her face. She shivered and hunched her shoulders, lowering her eyes again and trying to work out how far they'd come. The road was featureless and empty ahead and behind. But Fadra's black stallion was trotting on a lead rope beside them.

"Your horse!"

"Yes, he found us soon after the wagon arrived. I think he was on his way home."

The young man twisted around. "It's going to snow."

"How much further?" Fadra asked.

"Not far, but I don't like the look of this sky. It'll be a bad one."

"Pick up the pace."

The young woman flicked the reins, and the horses responded so quickly that Cahira had to grab onto the top rail to save herself from sliding backwards.

It was a nightmare journey. The wind buffeted harder and harder, and no matter how tightly Cahira pulled her clothing around her, it couldn't keep out the icy air. Her warm blue cloak was gone, left behind with everything else in her pack when she'd escaped over the back of the cart. The livid sky pressed on her as the driver urged the horses to even greater speed. The rutted road tossed the wagon violently up and down.

By the time they slowed down to turn onto a grassy track, the first fat drops were spattering her head and shoulders. Her hands had clamped to the rail like claws, and the skin over her knuckles looked bloodless, as bleached as bone. She couldn't feel her fingers at all.

The drops became a downpour, plastering her clothing to her body. Freezing water ran across the boards around her. Even though it could only be mid-afternoon, the light was almost gone. Through the grey curtain of the rain, she could just make out the trunks of trees passing on both sides as the wagon wove its slow way between them. The wind grew to a gale, whipping the branches and sending wet twigs and fir needles flying past her head. She hunched down lower and closed her eyes. After an eternity, the wagon bumped to a stop.

"Come on," Fadra shouted.

They had reached an area of tumbled rocks that sloped up a short distance before fading into grey nothingness. No house was in sight. Cahira prised her fingers from the rail and stiffly followed Fadra down from the wagon.

Seemingly indefatigable, Fadra forged ahead through the storm. Stumbling behind on shaky legs, Cahira found herself on a narrow, beaten track that curved upwards between the rocks. She slipped once—on a scattering of loose stones that rolled beneath her boots— but someone held her up until she gained her feet again. The afternoon darkened further, until she had to concentrate on every step.

As she laboured to keep moving, a small patch of deep black appeared up ahead, noticeable even through the obscuring rain. It grew as she approached, until it filled her vision. The deluge slackened for a moment, long enough for her to recognise the yawning mouth of a cave. Fadra had already disappeared inside.

Wind and water cut off instantly as Cahira stepped into the shelter of the cavern. She clawed away the strands of wet hair hanging in front of her eyes, and stood there dripping, striving to see through the velvety darkness.

A sharp sound made her jump. An instant later she recognised the familiar scrape of metal on flint. A spark flared and a faint yellow smudge appeared, followed by another, and then many more. Someone was lighting candles—two long rows of them, one on each side of the cave. The flames stretched higher, casting a golden glow all around. Cahira almost forgot her weariness at the wonders revealed by the growing light.

She'd thought she knew as much as she wanted to about caves. In stories and songs, they were always sinister places, dark haunts of dangerous beasts and violent fugitives, cramped and dirty and ugly. But this cave was nothing like that.

Deeply pleated curtains of stone, the colour of thick cream, clothed the walls. High above, translucent veils, exquisitely draped and folded, glowed peach and amber and rosy pink. Row upon row of white icicles hung from the roof. In some places, their twins ascended from the floor to meet them, like reflections in a pool. It was altogether strange and utterly lovely, both at the same time.

Cahira no longer cared that she was wet and freezing and that her hair was plastered flat to her head. All her anxiety about Niall, Adric, and Perna was swept away. She stared, her mind empty of thought but filled with awe, until Fadra's voice broke the silence. The surrounding stone added even more resonance to her musical tone. Cahira concentrated, sure that Fadra must be uttering some profound thought, some wise words that would be worthy of such a setting. But in fact what the Healer said was, "Ferdy, a fire, and quickly. Elise, she'll need some warm, dry clothes."

Cahira woke from the spell the cave had cast on her, to find herself shivering violently. Fadra was facing two youngsters who seemed to be in their teens. The red-haired boy ran off, and the girl came towards Cahira with a welcoming smile on her fine-featured face. Her long ash-blond hair was pulled up into a high ponytail on the crown of her head, giving her the look of a crested bird. "Hi, I'm Elise." She pursed her lips. "You're taller than me, but I think some of my clothes will fit you. Close enough for now, anyway." She tucked her hand companionably under Cahira's arm and led her unresisting to the back of the cavern and into a wide, candle-lit passageway.

They made several turns, passing the mouths of other passages and the entrances to what looked like smaller caves. Elise stopped before one of the latter and pulled aside a curtain hanging across the doorway with a theatrical flourish, setting her high ponytail swinging. "Welcome to my room." She tugged Cahira inside, kicking away pieces of clothing and sheets of parchment to make space for them to stand. "Sorry about the mess. Here." She gathered up an armful of cloth and thrust it out. "See if these will do."

But now that Cahira had stopped moving, she couldn't seem to start again. Just staying upright was taking all her concentration.

"They're clean, I promise," Elise said, sounding offended.

Cahira made a mighty effort and grasped the offerings with hands that felt like they belonged to someone else. "Thank you." Her voice came out breathy and hoarse.

Elise's face was wreathed in smiles again. "I'll be outside." She ducked back into the passage, twitching the curtain across behind her.

Cahira forced her stiff fingers to drag off her sodden boots, then her trousers and tunic. It seemed to take forever. Her entire body shaking, she struggled into what Elise had given her: thick tights, a woollen dress, a long jacket trimmed with fur and soft sheepskin slippers. Everything fit her well enough, except for the slippers, which were tight. She pulled them onto her frozen feet, anyway. Feeling like a sleepwalker, she joined Elise outside.

The girl took one look at her and quickly slipped an arm around her waist. "Put your hand on my shoulder. Okay, off we go, slow and steady. That's it."

Not far beyond Elise's room, the passage widened into a large circular space, furnished with armchairs and rugs. Heat radiated from a pile of logs burning in a hearth carved directly into the rock wall. Most of the chairs were already occupied, but Elise guided Cahira to an empty one close to the fire and eased her down.

"Feeling better?"

Turning her head slowly, Cahira recognised Fadra sitting next to her, also dressed in fresh, dry clothing. Too tired to speak, she managed a nod.

"They'll bring us some food soon. Rest now."

Cahira closed her eyes and sank back. The heat was fierce on her face, but her hands and feet were aching with cold. She wondered if she would ever feel truly warm again.

She woke to find herself lying on a yielding surface, wrapped in softness, facing a smaller fire which had burned down almost to coals. A bell was ringing. It hurt her head, and she wished it would stop.

Elise was at her side as soon as she stirred, telling her she was in the bedroom Fadra had assigned to her and it was breakfast time. Cahira was blessedly warm and too drowsy to be hungry, but Elise, who seemed to have appointed herself as chief carer, coaxed her to eat some of the thick soup and dark bread she'd brought.

Cahira slept again. This time, she woke in a panic, convinced her body was on fire. She had to find water to douse herself before she burned up. She jerked upright, flinging off the smothering covers, and swung her feet to the floor. She clutched her head and choked out a hoarse scream. A knife was piercing her brain, stabbing over and over.

She could never remember clearly what happened after that. She thought Elise was there, and later Fadra, but their faces were distorted and strange. They swam in and out of view and then vanished completely, replaced by blinding whiteness and biting cold.

A figure appeared in the distance. It was small but clear, and Cahira knew it at once. Adric was trudging across a snowy landscape, moving further and further away from her. She had to catch up to him.

But she was standing in a deep hollow, buried up to her waist in powdery snow. When she shouted to him to come back for her, the drifts muffled her voice to almost nothing.

Perhaps he heard her anyway, because he stopped and turned. He took a step towards her, and whiteness enveloped his knees, then his thighs. He twisted around, trying to return the way he'd come, but to no avail. He was stuck, and still sinking. There was no one else in sight. If she didn't reach him, he would freeze to death.

But struggling only caused her to flounder deeper into her hole. Soon she was buried up to her chin, unable to move or make a sound. She could do nothing but watch in agony as Adric sank deeper and deeper, until the snow closed over his head and he was gone, swallowed up without a trace. She would be next. She stared at the spot where he had disappeared, and waited for the end.

An acrid odour filled her nostrils. She tasted bitterness on her tongue. A voice just on the edge of hearing spoke words she couldn't understand.

The snow vanished. Darkness lay spread out before her, pierced by a myriad points of light. They swirled in dizzy patterns, and she closed her eyes.

The next thing she knew she was running across cracked, parched dirt under a cruel sun. A long way ahead of her, a man dressed in black stood under the eaves of a tinder-dry woodland. Fire abruptly kindled behind him, blooming among the dead branches like a poisonous scarlet flower. The flames spread, roaring and crackling towards him, but Niall didn't seem to notice.

She cried a warning to him, stretching out her hands and weeping as she ran, knowing it was already too late.

The merciless fire engulfed him and moved on, leaving behind only a small pile of black ash and the echo of a tortured shriek, both swept away an instant later by the hot wind.

She screamed until her throat was raw and her breath was gone.

Dense fog descended, blotting out everything. She thought she heard Fadra's low, soothing voice somewhere nearby, but the words were unintelligible and the Healer was nowhere to be seen.

Abandoned and numb, drained of hope, Cahira wandered aimlessly, trapped for eternity in a grey realm of nothingness between ice and flame.

TWELVE

Niall

Niall vaulted onto Sienna's warm back and turned his attention to deciding which way to go. The road ran east to west. Where was the farm from here? He focused first on Blackbird and then on Briar, trying to sense their distance and direction, but couldn't find either of them. He pushed, and the pounding in his head increased to an unbearable level, forcing him to break off. Sienna had come from the east, so he'd try that way.

And it seemed that the luck was with him. Even sooner than he'd hoped, the closed gates of the farm came into view. Not bothering to slow down, he set Sienna at them. She soared over, leaving the two guards gaping in her wake, and cantered up the winding drive to the house.

Cahira wasn't in her bedroom. He'd half expected that, but every trace of her presence was gone too. He hurtled downstairs and flung open the door of Berek's office, letting it bang loudly against the wall. "What've you done with her?"

Berek's head jerked up from his desk. His dark-bearded face wore a startled expression that immediately changed to a black scowl. He stabbed the point of the pen he was holding in Niall's direction as if he'd like to skewer him on it. "What do you mean by bursting in here?"

Niall's skull was being hammered on an anvil, but he was going to get some answers. "Where's Cahira?"

Berek's scowl deepened. "Isn't she with you?"

"What?" The idiot wasn't making any sense.

"Sit down, Master Crawley." When Niall didn't move, Berek sighed and put the pen down carefully in the inkwell. He'd been working on some kind of map. He slid it into a drawer under the desk and wiped his hands on a piece of cloth. "I will forgive this intrusion because you are clearly upset and still unwell. Sit down."

Niall sat. To be honest, it was a relief to be off his feet.

Berek steepled his fingers together on the desk. "About three hours ago, Mistress Gelt and a fellow guest—Mistress Fadra Hellin—left here in the company of two of my men. They took you with them, in the back of a farm cart. You had been unconscious for two days."

"Two days?"

"You were attacked, Master Crawley. In my stables, I'm sorry to say. You have been under Fadra's care ever since. She is a skilled Folk Healer who happened to be visiting us, fortunately for you."

Niall peered into Berek's face, searching for a sign the villain was lying, but found none. "Where were they going?"

"To Fadra's home. This is very concerning, Master Crawley. Why have you returned alone?"

There was no point in holding anything back. Niall explained the little he knew.

Afterwards, Berek sat in silence for so long that Niall's temper boiled over again. "Well, what are you going to do about it?"

Berek glared. "I'll thank you not to use that tone with me."

With an enormous effort, Niall grabbed onto the tattered shreds of his patience. Finding Cahira was all that mattered now, and Berek could help with that. "I apologise, Master Berek. You understand, I'm not quite myself after my ordeal."

Berek harrumphed, only partly mollified. "I will send out a search party at once."

"Adric should be part of it." Cahira wouldn't thank him if he missed this chance to get Adric away from the farm.

But Berek shook his head. "He isn't here."

"You've lost him too?" Despite his best intentions, Niall's voice vibrated with anger.

Another glare. "*I* have lost no one. Adric is in Eorna. He left the same day you were hurt."

Niall wasn't inclined to trust Berek's word for this, but he had to accept it for now. "What about Perna, the young girl who was with us?"

"I believe she also travelled with Fadra. And now, if there are no more questions, I have a search to organise." Berek stood abruptly, clearly at the end of his patience.

Niall left him. He wanted to drink a few gallons of water to tame his headache and then fetch Sienna's saddle and bridle. Bareback riding was all very well, but it grew wearing after the first hour or so, and he could be out until dark, or even longer.

The search party set off half an hour later, with Niall in the lead. They soon came across one of the men who'd been driving the cart. He was trudging along the road, heading for the farm. His cheeks flushed brick-red in embarrassment as he told his story. Niall, by contrast, felt the blood drain from his own face as he listened.

An ambush, and the three women captured. But the man insisted he'd seen two of them slip over the back of the cart before the bandits—blaming him for the escape—had knocked him on the head and left him behind. In answer to Niall's barked question, he confirmed that the one with the long dark hair—the Skalsinger—had been one of the women who got away.

That was something, but where had Cahira gone next? To this Fadra Hellin's house, wherever that was? No one seemed to know, except that it was west of the farm. They scoured the road for more than a reach past the ambush site in that direction, going deep into the flanking fields and woods. But they found no sign of another person or any dwelling.

It was only the middle of the afternoon when the rapidly fading light and freezing rain drove them all back to the farm, with Niall cursing the whole way. He stumped up the stairs to the room above the stables, fully determined to set out again at dawn.

It was a good thing no one tried to talk to him. His temper felt as ready to explode as his clanging head.

Next morning, his headache was gone but the rain was still falling. Niall took stock of his assets. He had Sienna, of course. But his pack with the spare clothing and other necessities for the road was no longer in the room. Presumably, Cahira had taken it in the cart. The sword wasn't beneath the mattress where he'd hidden it, either. No way to know if it was in the hands of Berek's merry little band of rebels, or the bandits on the road. The pair of long daggers, likewise. He supposed he was lucky that no one had thought it necessary to undress him when he'd been unconscious. He would have really hated to lose these boots.

And there was at least a chance that they'd left him something else. He pulled the small dagger from his boot and knelt down beside the hearth. He used the point of the weapon to prise up the broken piece of flagstone sufficiently to wriggle his fingers underneath, and lifted it out. And then he grinned for the first time since he'd woken on the road.

Thank Aal he hadn't trusted Berek's Seekers to be Virtuous enough to refrain from stealing his money, and had made the effort to scrape the hollow in the dirt beneath the hearth that first night. He tucked the heavy purse into his tunic. Things were looking up.

It was still early when he rode away. The rain was pelting down and the world was grey. No one at the farm had admitted to knowing exactly where this Fadra woman's house lay, except somewhere to the west, so west he went.

The thought that he should be heading east instead, to warn Logen about Berek's plans, scratched at his brain. He rejected it. Berek could wait. There'd been no sign at the farm that he was ready to make his move yet. Anyway, it was just a theory, based on nothing but a shed full of weapons. Perhaps Berek had confiscated them from his followers, and had no intention of attacking Eorna at all. Niall wasn't about to abandon

Cahira on such flimsy evidence. With these and other arguments, he convinced himself that he was doing the right thing, rather than the only thing he could bear to do.

It must have been around midday when he entered a tiny village, no more than a cluster of neglected-looking houses and a small tavern. Time for a break from this cursed weather, and perhaps a chance to hear some news. A stable lay behind the tavern, not fancy but clean enough and in good repair. For the promise of two bronze pennies, the stable boy agreed to rub Sienna down and give her some hay.

The inside of the tavern was warm and dry, but once you'd said that, you'd said everything. It was dark and dingy and smelled worse than the stable. The barman was the only other human being in the place, a lanky, grey-haired man wearing a bad-tempered expression on his unshaven face. He replied to Niall's request for beer with a brief grunt.

The drink was as thin and sour as the man who grudgingly poured it out. At least it was cheap. Trying to look as though he was enjoying it, Niall thawed himself out in front of the fire and sought to draw the fellow into conversation. "I've never been to this village before. What's it called?"

"Hem."

"Nice place to live?"

The man didn't dignify that with an answer.

Niall drank in silence for a while, then tried again. "I'm looking for some friends of mine. They might have passed through here yesterday. Two women, probably on foot?"

"Haven't seen 'em."

"Where does the western road lead to?"

"Welsea."

"I don't think I've been there either. On the coast, isn't it?"

"Yup." The man moved off. Sparkling conversationalist.

The door banged open and four men clumped in, shaking off the rain and calling for beer in loud rural voices. The barman served them and exited through a door in the back of the room. He returned carrying a big pot, which he hung on a hook over the fire. Niall peered inside.

The soup looked as pale and watery as the beer, and it had too many grey lumps of turnip floating in it for his liking.

The men had gathered at a corner table with their drinks. He sauntered over. "Good day to you, friends. Filthy weather."

"Weather's always filthy. If it's not droughting, it's flooding." The voice sounded more resigned than bitter, and the expression on the round face was friendly enough.

Niall pulled up a rickety chair and joined them. "Very true, very true," he said. "It's a hard world, all right."

An older man narrowed his eyes. "Don't look like it's been too hard on you, young fella. That cloak cost a pretty penny, I'll warrant."

"Ah, don't let appearances fool you, friend. I've had nothing but bad luck lately. First, I was kicked by a horse and almost died, and now my friends have disappeared." He spoke lightly, trying to win them over, but then realised that it was true. Apart from the hidden purse, his luck seemed to have deserted him. He drank gloomily.

"Now Nathan over there is the lucky one," the original speaker said. He raised his voice to reach the barman. "I said you've been having some rare luck, Nathan. Getting married tomorrow, aren't you?" He turned with a wink to Niall. "The bride was so overcome with the honour that she ran away, but she's back home now."

The other three laughed coarsely as the barman's scowl deepened. The comedian raised his tankard. "A toast to Nathan."

One of the others added, "And to Perna, Aal help her." Another burst of laughter greeted this witticism.

Niall almost dropped his own tankard. He stared at the speaker in sheer disbelief as the others drank the toast. It must be a different Perna. The coincidence would be too great. Unless his luck was finally changing after all.

"Perna?" he asked, as casually as he could manage.

"Aye. Dostig Braden's daughter. Plain little thing. Ran off to join the Aalden, if you can believe it."

"Dostig brought her back though," put in the first speaker. "He's not a man to stand for any nonsense like that. He fetched her yesterday and arranged the marriage for tomorrow." He glanced slyly across the room at Nathan. "Before she can run away again."

Niall's head was reeling. Perna was here. Cahira might have followed her, hoping to help her escape from this marriage. It was just the kind of crazy thing she'd do. And if it hadn't been for the rain, he would have ridden straight through this god-forsaken place and never known.

"Did anyone come with her?" He heard the over-eager note in his voice and cleared his throat before continuing. "I mean, any woman friend to help her get ready for the wedding?"

"No, just her."

Even if Cahira wasn't here, Perna might know something. Cahira could have talked to her, told her where she was going. He schooled his face to a nonchalance he didn't feel. "Her father must be relieved to have her back. What does he do?"

"Blacksmith."

Niall thought fast. "That's lucky. My horse has gone lame. I think she might have a loose shoe. Where would I find the forge?"

"Other end of the village, just on the bend."

Now that he had some information, he was desperate to act on it, but it would be wiser to stay here a little longer. No man in his right mind would be in a hurry to leave the warm tavern in this weather. He couldn't afford to raise any suspicions. He sat back and sipped slowly at the disgusting beer as if he was savouring the finest ale in Algarth. Just a few more minutes and he could go.

The barman began ladling the soup into rough wooden bowls. He brought five of them to the table on a tray. Apparently, there was no need to order. And nothing else on the menu, not even bread to dip in the soup.

Niall drank his portion of slop as fast as he could, trying not to grimace at the taste. Then he took leave of his new friends, paid the barman and left.

Sienna was dry and happy to see him, but not so pleased about going back out into the rain. Still, her obvious misery would give credence to his story of her lameness. He led her down the road to the forge.

Inside, a mountain of a man wearing a leather apron was nodding on a stool. He stirred blearily as they entered, and a shock of recognition ran through Niall. The blacksmith was the angry drunk who'd tried to grab Perna back in Mirston. That incident suddenly made complete sense.

Perna's father wasn't looking his best today, either. Possibly he hadn't done so for years. Purple veins crisscrossed his nose and cheeks above the unwholesome tangle of beard, and drops of greasy sweat beaded his fleshy, pink scalp. His enormous hands were nursing a battered tankard. A tapped barrel sat beside him. He showed no sign that he recognised Niall, not surprising considering the unfocused look in his eyes and the way he was swaying on his stool.

Niall plastered on his most charming smile. "Master Braden, they told me at the tavern that I'd find you here." He trotted out the story of Sienna's lameness.

The mountain heaved himself up and shambled over to the mare. He lifted the foot and gave the bottom of the hoof a few taps with his hammer. "Shoe's sound enough." The words were slurred. "Prob'ly jus' picked up a stone. Gone now." He lowered the foot and straightened up with a grunt.

"Thank you. That's a great relief." Niall smiled again. "I'm told that your daughter is getting married tomorrow. Congratulations."

Dostig made his way back to his stool without replying.

Niall chattered on. "May I express my good wishes to the bride?"

The blacksmith stared at him out of eyes that resembled dull black pebbles. He didn't reply.

Niall was trying to think of a next move when a soft sound drew his attention to the back of the forge. Perna stood there, framed in the open doorway, white-faced and gaping at him. The plate she was carrying dropped to the wooden floor and shattered.

Startled into alertness, the drunken smith left his seat, shaking a meaty fist. "Stupid girl!"

"I—I'm sorry, Father. I'll get you some more." She turned and fled.

Niall spoke loudly to draw Dostig's attention. "I must be going too, Master Braden. What do I owe you for your time?"

Dostig muttered something and sank back onto his stool, reaching for the tankard with one hand and waving Niall away with the other.

As soon as he was outside and out of the blacksmith's sight, Niall tore around to the back of the forge, telling Sienna to follow. A tiny house stood a short distance away. It was in a sorry state—practically falling down—and Niall had no trouble believing it belonged to the drunken blacksmith.

He headed for the door that was sagging open, hanging lopsidedly by one hinge. He'd almost reached it when a small brown missile shot through the doorway and ran straight into him. He lurched back but stayed upright, grabbing her by the shoulders to halt her flight.

"Take me away." Perna scrabbled at his chest, panic written all over her face. "Take me away now!"

He gripped her shoulders tighter. "Perna, listen to me! Is Cahira with you?"

"No! She got away. We have to go now!" Her voice had risen to a shriek.

Niall didn't hesitate any longer. He boosted the girl onto Sienna's back and leapt up behind her. As they rounded the corner of the forge, a bellow sounded. Waving an iron poker, Dostig closed the distance between them faster than Niall would have believed possible.

Niall urged Sienna on, but the rain had turned the ground into a mire. The mare's near forefoot sank into soft mud up to the hock. She lurched and came to a shivering halt, stuck. The smith was almost on them. He let out a hair-raising roar and raised the poker. Niall slid to the ground and slapped Sienna hard on the rump. *Go!*

Sienna pulled herself free of the sucking mud just in time. The poker connected with nothing but air, its momentum turning Dostig halfway around. But the mare only went forward a few steps before stopping again, reluctant to leave Niall behind. And now Dostig had reset himself. Ignoring Niall, he forged through the mud towards the horse, swinging the weapon back in a low arc, his intention hideously clear. He was going to break Sienna's leg so she couldn't carry Perna away.

Without a second's thought, Niall barrelled straight at the blacksmith. It was like hitting a wall. With his head ringing from the impact, he grabbed the arm holding the poker and put all his strength into deflecting the blow. He knew he couldn't win against this man mountain; his only goal was to give Sienna and Perna enough time to escape to safety.

Sternly commanding the mare to flee, he gritted his teeth and found a more secure grip, just above the blacksmith's elbow. Dostig roared again, but this time it was a shout of pain rather than triumph: he had some kind of injury there. Niall dug his fingers in, and was rewarded by a louder bellow. Dostig began flailing at him with the other fist. Certain that he was going to die here, Niall hung on and dug even harder.

The bellow changed to a high-pitched yell, and the poker abruptly dropped to the ground. Niall let go of the arm, ducked beneath the next blow, and snatched up the heavy iron rod in both hands. Without hesitation, he swung it with all his might at one massive knee. He heard a crunch and a scream, then the smith crumpled.

Niall left him writhing there and ploughed through the mud, calling Sienna. Despite his command, she hadn't gone far. She appeared around the corner of the stable and came towards him, tossing her head. He stroked her neck to calm her and vaulted up behind Perna again, his brain working at lightning speed as he directed the mare onto the road.

Someone might have heard that last scream. Dostig was in no state to ride after them, but others would be—chiefly Nathan, who was about to lose his bride for the second time. Niall needed to buy himself some time to get away.

He reached out to any horses nearby, finding four, and gave them all the same instruction: *run!* If they were unrestrained, they'd take off immediately, as far and as fast as they could. If they were tied up or in enclosed stalls, they'd flee as soon as they were released. Anyone in Hem who wanted to chase after Perna now would have to do it on foot.

They cleared the village without incident and headed west towards Welsea. There was a chance Cahira had gone that way. But it was time to stop searching blindly and use his brain. The first necessity was to buy clothing and provisions, and a sword. He'd been lucky in the fight with Dostig, and he couldn't depend on that again. Welsea was the closest town big enough to provide what he needed. There would be inns there too, and it should be safe to stay for one night. He'd made the command to the horses as strong as he could, and he was confident they would evade recapture at least that long.

He'd have a bath and a shave and a decent meal, and make Perna tell him exactly what had happened and everything Cahira or this Fadra had said. And tomorrow he would set out again to find Cahira, properly equipped and determined to succeed no matter how long it took.

Despite the still-falling rain, the road surface was hard-packed and in good repair. He pushed Sienna to a canter, then a gallop. The sooner they got to Welsea, the better. Finding Perna was proof that his luck had turned, no doubt about it, and he meant to take advantage of it before it swung back.

It was almost dark when they pulled up outside The Leaping Fish, having already bought what they could in the market behind the wharves of Welsea before it closed down for the day. The plain but solid-looking building hunched low beneath its overhanging tile roof, as if trying to ward off the rain. Slivers of warm yellow light escaped from narrow gaps between the shutters, and noise spilled out when Niall pushed open the door.

A fleshy, clean-shaven man bustled up, rubbing his plump hands. "Welcome, travellers. What can we do for you?"

"Two rooms for the night, and a hot meal," Niall said. "And stabling for my horse."

The man's answering nod set his jowls quivering. "Certainly, certainly. We are very full right now, but I'm sure we can squeeze you in. You and your…sister?" Insinuation flavoured the pause as the man directed a knowing look towards Perna.

"Cousin," Niall answered flatly.

"Of course, of course. Right this way."

The inn must be a lot more profitable than it had looked from the outside, judging by the price the innkeeper quoted for the rooms and stabling, but Niall decided against going back out into the weather to look for somewhere cheaper. Perna was shuddering violently from the cold and wet, and he himself wasn't feeling his best. He left Perna at her door, having instructed the innkeeper to arrange hot baths for both of them.

Niall's room was pleasantly luxurious. A generous fireplace stretched along one wall—the fire already lit—and a bed wide enough for three sleepers was set against another. Plump white pillows sat invitingly on top of the thick mattress, and the blankets looked clean and soft. The waxed wood of a tall wardrobe and a round table with two chairs glowed in the light of the wall lamps. And in one corner, glory of glories, an oval tub stood on four feet carved like bear paws.

He'd only just taken it all in when a maid entered with a bucket, a cake of soap and a towel. A cloud of steam puffed up from the cascade she poured into the tub. She left without a word, but returned in a few minutes, staggering a little under the weight of two more brimming buckets.

"Thank you," Niall said, and meant it.

"Do you desire anything else, sir?" She glanced up at him from beneath her lashes in as open an invitation as he'd ever received.

"No, no, just the bath, thanks."

As the door closed behind her, he wondered how costly a yes would have been. Not that he'd felt tempted, at any price. That would make him too much like his father, and no encounter, however pleasant, was worth that. Dismissing the unpalatable thought, he stripped off his clinging clothes and stepped in. Fragrant steam enveloped him as he picked up the soap and set to work.

An hour later, freshly shaved and dressed in the new clothing he'd bought at the market, he knocked on Perna's door.

"Who is it?" She sounded nervous.

"It's me, Niall."

Her face was flushed pink from the heat of her own bath, except along one cheekbone, where a purple-black bruise stood out. He should have broken both Dostig's kneecaps, not just one. She caught him staring and hid her face. At the clothing stall, she'd chosen a plain, undyed dress and hooded over-tunic. Niall had insisted on adding a warm fur cloak and slippers, as well as a pair of sturdy boots. Inside all those clothes, with her head bowed, she looked smaller and younger than ever.

They dined in a private room downstairs, closed off from the main drinking area. The food was good, and even Perna ate a halfway decent amount for once. The ale was some of the best Niall had tasted, rivalling Bella's tavern in Eorna. Perna accepted only water. After meeting Dostig, Niall could understand why she was so set against drinking, and he resolved not to tease her about it again.

They talked amiably for once, at least at first. Perna seemed willing to speak about the ambush now that she wasn't in Hem any more. But she had little to tell him that he hadn't already heard. She didn't know where Cahira and Fadra intended to go after their escape from the cart. She hazarded a guess they might have continued on to Fadra's house, where they had been heading before the attack.

"But you don't know for sure?"

"No."

"Or exactly where it is?"

She shook her head.

It was a huge disappointment, but if this Fadra was as kind as Perna claimed, perhaps Cahira was safe with her for now. And yet he was uneasy. How could he trust the judgement of a naive girl like Perna? After all, she'd insisted that the snake Berek was a good man, hadn't she?

And so he kept pressing her for more information, and Perna grew at first tearful, then stubborn, and finally angry. "I hate you! You only saved me because you thought I knew something! Well, I don't, so you can just go away and leave me here. You don't care about me, anyway. No one does." She leapt to her feet and fired her final shot. "You're a wicked man, and Aal will punish you!"

It was a childish outburst, and for that very reason it silenced Niall completely. He was being a brute, as bad as that worthless father of hers. He started to apologise, but she threw him a black look and fled up the stairs. Slumping back in his chair, he heard her door slam.

After another drink, any pleasure ruined by the taste of guilt, he left the table to retire in his turn. But as he climbed the well-lit steps and ran his hand along the carved and polished banister, remorse gave way to puzzlement. Welsea was a big place, but it was essentially a fishing town. In his experience, fishing towns weren't wealthy and they didn't attract rich travellers. Their inns tended to be rundown and flea-bitten. Yet the quality of the fittings and the hospitality at The Leaping Fish matched any establishment in the richest quarter of Eorna. He couldn't work it out.

Back in his own room, after checking that Perna's door was locked and turning the key in his own, he thought about tomorrow. He wasn't certain that Nathan would come after Perna, but it would be wise to assume the worst. Niall's job was to find Cahira, but he could hardly leave Perna here on her own. She'd have to come with him. Which meant he needed to make up the quarrel with her, and also find her a horse of her own. He hadn't replaced his sword or daggers yet, either. The weapon sellers had already closed up by the time he'd arrived at the market.

Lying on his back in the soft bed, he ticked the list off on his fingers: early breakfast, apology to Perna, a reliable horse, a decent sword and two good knives. The little dagger lay under his pillow next to his money purse; even sturdy locks could be picked, and he had no reason to trust anyone here.

THIRTEEN

Niall set out along the broad walkway that ran through the centre of the marketplace, scanning the tightly packed stalls beneath their colourful awnings. He was on foot, with Sienna close beside him, while a silent Perna trailed behind. He'd managed to placate her over breakfast, at least enough to persuade her to come with him. He'd even restrained himself from commenting on how little she ate.

The clouds had fled overnight, giving way to a cold but bright morning. The gabbling of dozens of voices surrounded him, talking, shouting, arguing, and haggling. He drew level with a stall holder who was loudly boasting the virtues of his swords and knives, but the metal was of inferior quality and Niall moved on.

He was keeping a fine thread of his attention attached to Sienna's mind so he'd have warning if anything disturbed her. He glanced back at Perna, who was concentrating on holding up the skirt of her new dress to avoid the water that lay in the hollows of the paving stones. Real paving stones, not cobbles. Another sign that this town was doing very well.

The weapons on the next stall looked more promising. After a thorough inspection and some vigorous bargaining, Niall secured a medium-length sword with a thick leather scabbard. The hilt was a plain crosspiece with no decoration, but the balance was excellent and the fine patterning of the blade told him it would hold a keen edge and resist shattering.

Buckling his purchase onto his belt, he turned to see Perna fingering a small dagger with a carved bone handle. He hadn't considered supplying her with the means to defend herself, but it wasn't a bad idea. She demurred and hastily withdrew her hand from the weapon. But when he bought it, and a delicately tooled little scabbard, she accepted the gifts without a word and began shrugging off her pack.

"Wait," Niall said. "Put it in your pocket. If you ever need it, you'll want it close."

She frowned at him doubtfully, but did as he instructed.

He also purchased two long knives to replace the ones he'd lost and tucked them into his belt. Feeling better now he was adequately armed, he sent out a roaming thought and discovered a large group of horses not too far away. Hopefully, he'd located a dealer with beasts for sale. After a quick word of explanation to Perna, he led the way out of the market.

They were halfway down a long, straight alley when Niall thought he heard footfalls following along behind. He stopped and turned, sensing rather than seeing a rapid whisk of movement as if someone had just ducked into a doorway. Hand on the hilt of the new sword, he kept going, every sense on the alert. He saw nothing else to disturb him, but the feeling of being spied upon grew. Had Nathan tracked them down already? Or was it a thief, hoping to prey on two customers as they left the market? Niall whispered a warning to Perna before boosting her up onto Sienna and sliding the sword silently out from its scabbard.

He followed behind the mare, walking backwards with the weapon at the ready, eyes scanning for any movement. Checking again on the location of the horses, he directed Sienna to the end of the alley and around the corner, seeking the fastest way to his destination.

The next street was narrower and crooked, switching back on itself between buildings as lopsided and uneven as a row of broken teeth. Not liking the number of potential hiding places, Niall urged Sienna to pick up the pace. They'd almost reached the far end when a head appeared briefly about twenty spans behind them before ducking out of sight. Niall hadn't been imagining things. Someone was following them.

Without hesitation, he swung himself up behind Perna and pushed Sienna to a canter, steering her around the next corner and then another, searching for a safer route. But they had entered a maze with no obvious way out. The laneways twisted and turned like a bunch of snakes. Increasingly decrepit buildings sagged against each other and leaned drunkenly overhead, their looming shadows cutting off most of the light.

Every street looked the same. If Niall hadn't had his skal to guide him, he would have been completely lost. He pushed a nervous Sienna towards the group of horses as fast as she could go without risking a broken leg on the uneven cobbles. His blood pounded in his ears and the hairs stood up on the back of his neck. He didn't like to think what might happen if they hit a dead end.

But his luck held. They emerged from the dark tangle of the maze into a grid of straight streets lined with houses that were modest but in better repair, and finally entered a large sunlit square with a sizeable stable at the far end.

The merchant had several horses of adequate quality for sale. Niall chose a neat bay mare with one white sock, and added a used but well-made saddle and bridle. Perna said little, but she seemed happy with his choice, stroking Dulcina's velvety nose as Niall completed the transaction and asked the dealer for directions to the main road out of town.

Their route this time took them along well-maintained ways flanked by prosperous-looking houses and businesses. The streets were wide, but grew more and more crowded with people and vehicles as they progressed. Finally, they dismounted and lead the horses, threading their way through the press.

The crowds and the noise seemed to make Perna uneasy. She kept twisting around, trying to see in every direction at once. Dulcina picked up on her anxiety and tossed her own head, jerking the reigns. Niall reached out with calming thoughts, but he couldn't do the same for Perna.

He stopped. "What's wrong?"

"I don't feel safe."

"We'll be out of town soon."

She bit her lip and nodded. Niall tried to speed up a little, but in this dense crowd it was impossible. Perna's face grew white and set. Her eyes were enormous. It was the look of a horse about to bolt.

The entrance to a lane opened on their left. It ran straight and fortunately seemed to be empty of people. Niall gestured. "This way."

Halfway along the lane, he stopped to see how Perna was doing. "Better?"

Some of the colour had returned to her cheeks. "Yes. Thank you."

"We'll have to go back out there, it's our road out of town. But we can wait a few minutes."

She nodded, putting up a trembling hand to stroke Dulcina.

A movement, spotted from the corner of his eye, jerked Niall's head around. The silhouettes of two large men blocked the entry to the lane. A shout rang out from the opposite direction: "Halt! Let's see your hands!"

As Niall was already standing still, he concluded he wasn't dealing with the smartest of criminals here. But it didn't take brains to attack someone, just a weapon and the willingness to use it. He raised his hands and slowly turned back, careful not to make any sudden moves.

The speaker was striding towards them: black trousers, blue tunic, the telltale yellow badge on his chest. Niall relaxed slightly.

The Warrant Guard reached them. "Trying to avoid the toll, were we?"

Niall blinked. "Toll?"

"Don't be smart with me. I saw you leave the road. Thinking you'd get out of town without paying your dues."

Niall shook his head. "Not at all, Master Guard. I wasn't aware of any toll. I'm sure we can discuss this like reasonable men—"

The Guard sneered. "We'll *discuss* it at the garrison. Hand over the sword. And the knives. Slowly."

The other two Guards had reached them now. All three were gripping thick staves in a way that told Niall they were used to using them. If he'd been alone, he might have risked trying to escape anyway, but with Perna here it was out of the question. He regretfully unbuckled the newly purchased sword and handed it over, then the knives. One man grabbed the reins of the horses and led them away. Niall sternly instructed Sienna to behave, motioned Perna to walk in front of him, and followed. Their other two captors brought up the rear.

They avoided the main road, taking side streets that emptied of people as soon as they appeared. The townsfolk seemed to have a lot of respect for authority here in Welsea. At least Niall hoped it was respect. But he was getting an uneasy feeling about all this. He'd never heard of a toll for leaving a town.

After a few more turns, they emerged onto a broad road leading upwards, looping backwards and forwards as it climbed. After several of these traverses, with no destination in sight, he began to suspect these 'Guards' were just robbers wearing fake uniforms, taking them to some high, lonely spot where they could be relieved of their valuables and thrown over the edge into the sea. But then he caught the first glimpse of massive walls up ahead. They were heading for Welsea Garrison after all. It was larger than he'd expected, and held a commanding position on the headland above the harbour, like the one in Eorna.

As soon as they passed through the gates into the marshalling yard, the horses were led away. Niall's instinctive protest almost earned him a cudgelling. Defeated for the moment, he told Sienna to go calmly. She hesitated, and he felt her strong desire to lash out. He reinforced the command. She tossed her head once, then capitulated. Dulcina didn't seem concerned at the turn of events, and followed the other mare willingly.

Accompanied by the same three Guards, Niall and Perna crossed the yard and entered a large building set into a corner of the enclosing wall. They passed through a room where four off-duty Guards were drinking and throwing dice, then down a corridor lined with barred cells.

One Guard relieved them of their packs and another searched Niall, finding his purse and taking it too. The search wasn't thorough enough to discover the boot dagger, which was a minor comfort. They didn't bother searching Perna. The Guards locked them in adjoining cells and left. Apparently, the 'discussion' was to be postponed.

Niall went forward to the bars. "Perna?"

No answer. He raised his voice and tried again, the sound echoing off the stone and metal. She must have heard that.

He detected movement in the next cell, and then her trembling reply reached him. "Yes?"

"We'll get out of here, I promise."

She surprised him. "Of course we will! Putting us in gaol is unjust, and we have every right to escape." He'd mistaken the shakiness in her voice for fear, but it had been anger. That was probably better.

"Any idea how?" he asked.

Before she could answer, a new Guard appeared. Unlike the others, who had tended towards the hulking, he was small and wiry. He moved down the corridor with a deliberate swagger. As he approached their cells, Niall saw that his badge was edged in red. A sergeant. Perhaps they could sort this out by talking. Niall was good at talking.

The sergeant's narrow, pointed face wore a pleased expression as he halted outside Niall's cell. "Well, well, what do we have here?"

Niall groaned inwardly. His confidence in his ability to talk his way out of the situation took a nosedive. He despised smug, self-satisfied officials even more than the ordinary kind, and found it hard not to let them see it.

Even the man's voice was annoying: high and nasal. "One, two little spies, both caught in the net."

Spies? Niall was taken aback. "There's been some sort of mistake, Sergeant—"

"Yes, and you made it, Master Crawley. Did you really think you could enter my town undetected?" He shook his head slowly from side to side, a maddening little smirk turning up the corners of his mouth.

Niall was dumbfounded.

Unfortunately, Perna seemed to have plenty to say. "How dare you detain us like this? I demand you release us immediately! The wrath of Aal will fall on you for this injustice—"

"I'm not speaking to you yet, my girl." The sergeant's superior smile transformed into something else entirely. "Your turn will come, no need to be impatient."

Niall's fingers itched to retrieve his boot dagger, but this wasn't the time. He forced himself to speak calmly. "Sergeant, I assure you we're not spies. We simply—"

The man held up a hand. The broad band of a gold signet ring gleamed on the little finger: an expensive trinket for a Guard. "Don't bother denying it. We've been warned about you. But no one told us you'd have a young companion with you. A bonus, you might say."

Niall thought fast. If he was right about the kind of weasel this sergeant was, he would be susceptible to two things: flattery and money. "I see you run a tight ship here in Welsea, Sergeant. Very smart work to find us so quickly. But we're both reasonable men, and surely we can come to some sort of agreement. Your men will have told you they took a purse from me. I have much greater funds at my disposal. At my *complete* disposal, you understand." He paused to let his meaning sink in. But the words didn't make the impression he'd hoped for.

"Oh, there's no rush, Master Crawley. We'll have your money, never fear, with or without your cooperation. And all the information in your possession, too. Sit tight for now. I'll be back."

When Niall was sure the sergeant was out of earshot, he spoke to Perna. "Look, it might be a good idea to be a bit more tactful. We're in these people's power. No point in antagonising them."

"I won't be silent. It's an outrage—"

"I know, but you don't have to keep telling them that."

She huffed, but subsided. Niall didn't delude himself that he'd convinced her.

After a few moments, Perna spoke up again. "Aal will show us a way out."

No point in arguing with her about that either, but Niall wasn't going to hang his hopes on supernatural help. Bribery hadn't worked, but that had only been the first move in the game. He had his wits and a knife. He'd wriggled out of worse situations with less. He lowered himself to a seated position on the hard, thin pallet, leaned back against the wall, and began to think.

FOURTEEN

Cahira

The fever nightmares had been terrifying, but it was just as bad to be in her right mind again. She'd lost close to two days, with no idea what had happened to Niall or Adric in all that time.

Fadra was adamant. "Cahira, you almost died. The drenching you had in the storm, on top of your already weakened state… well, no matter. You're out of danger now, but you're still in no condition to go anywhere."

"You're lucky Fadra was here to help you," Elise said. She was changing the sweat-soaked bedding while Cahira sat on a chair in the cave room that Fadra had promised would be hers for as long as she stayed. "I've never seen her work so hard on anyone. She had to brew a special medicine and everything." Elise plumped up the pillow with a vigorous shaking. "You should be grateful."

"Oh, I am," Cahira said hastily. "It's just…"

"You want to go after your friend," Fadra soothed. "I understand. But even if you were strong enough, it's impossible right now."

"Impossible? Why?"

"You can't hear it this far into the caves, but it's been raining ever since we arrived. Last night, the stream we forded burst its banks. It's flowing too fast and deep for anyone to cross."

"But…"

Fadra gave her a level gaze. "See for yourself. Elise will show you the way."

By the time they reached the entrance cave—and even walking that short distance took a ridiculous amount of effort—Cahira had almost persuaded herself that Fadra was exaggerating. It couldn't be that bad.

But the Healer had spoken nothing but the truth. The rain was falling in sheets, enshrouding the world in misty grey. Cahira could just make out a dim green wash of forest in the middle distance and a hint of purple hills on the horizon. But directly below the ledge on which she stood, the land was drowned.

The narrow stream lined with trees had vanished. Turbulent brown water, topped with dirty foam, churned between vertical black trunks. Rafts made of logs and branches, jammed with unidentifiable debris, tossed on the torrent. It would be madness to try to cross it on horseback, or even in a boat. She was trapped here until the water fell.

A clanging arose from deeper in the cave system, echoing off the stone.

"That's the noon bell," Elise said. "Lunch time. We can't see the sun from inside the caves, so Fadra came up with this. The bells are rung every three hours: one for waking, two for mid-morning, three for noon, four for mid-afternoon, and five for dinner." She sounded proud of the system. Cahira briefly wondered how the bell ringers knew what hour it was, but realised she didn't care. She didn't want any lunch, either.

She left Elise at the turning of the passage leading to the dining hall and shuffled along to her room, hugging the walls for support. When she finally arrived, she was clammy, breathless, and shaking. She closed the curtain, climbed into bed, and turned her face to the smooth stone wall.

The waking bell roused her the next morning, but she had no reason to get up. Niall was probably dead by now, just like Bram. And Adric was committed to Berek's cult. It would have been better if the fever had taken her in her sleep.

Because only in sleep had she found any relief, at least until the nightmares had returned to taunt her. She'd bolted upright, heart hammering, the echo of her own shriek ringing in her ears. It had taken a long time for exhaustion to reclaim her, but then she'd fallen deep down into the welcoming nothingness: free of pain, free of anxiety, free of everything. Waking was nothing but a bitter disappointment. She rolled onto her other side and pulled the blanket over her head.

Fadra came sometime during the morning and told Cahira that this feeling of despair wasn't unusual after such an illness. She said it would pass and that, meanwhile, she would visit every few hours. Cahira wished she wouldn't, but didn't feel able to say so.

Elise brought food and tried to cheer her up by chattering about the happenings in the cave community. When Cahira refused to eat, Elise said she'd be back later with lunch and wouldn't take no for an answer again.

They weren't going to leave her alone until she got up. So when she heard the noon bell, she dragged herself from her warm blankets and made her slow way to the dining hall.

She was slumped in a chair by the fire, listlessly toying with some soup, when her hand froze in place. The contents of the spoon slid unheeded into the bowl.

She'd already noticed that sound behaved strangely in the caves. More than once this morning she'd been startled out of her dozing by the voices of strangers talking right next to her, only to open her eyes and find herself alone. The vibrations were bouncing off the ever-present rock and travelling along the passageways to her room. So it didn't surprise her to discern up a human voice when no one was in sight. But this person wasn't speaking.

She put down the bowl and spoon and lifted her head, tilting it this way and that in an effort to hear better. She hadn't been mistaken. Somewhere in the caves, someone was singing.

He had a high voice for a man, a tenor or even countertenor. His tone was very pure, piercing cleanly through the echoes generated by the surrounding stone. She didn't recognise the song. With no awareness of having made a conscious decision, she found herself rising to her feet.

She lost the thread more than once in the maze of tunnels, and was forced to retrace her steps and try another way. But the volume steadily increased until she was able to move with confidence. It was an extraordinary voice. She wanted to know who it belonged to. She tracked it down to a narrow, out-of-the way corridor, and then to a small, curtained doorway at the end. The song finished as she approached. It didn't matter. She'd found him.

Unexpected shyness came over her at the thought of announcing her presence. She was a stranger here. What would he think of her just turning up outside his door? But her curiosity wouldn't allow her to leave without at least a glimpse. Peering furtively through the gap between curtain and wall, she stared in confusion at the sole occupant of the room.

How could the slight figure with the freckle-covered face and springy curls of red hair be the singer she'd heard? He was scarcely out of childhood, twelve years old at the most. She must have made a mistake. Then he opened his mouth, and the sound that poured out put all her doubts to flight. *Not a countertenor*, she marvelled, *a supremely talented boy soprano*. Yet even that didn't feel quite right. His tone was too rich, too mature.

She made an involuntary movement, twitching the curtain. He broke off, his startled gaze going straight to the doorway. Having no choice, Cahira gently pulled the curtain aside.

The boy stared wide-eyed at the strange woman standing outside his room. "Can—can I help you?"

"I heard you singing—"

"I'm sorry, was it too loud? Fadra says I have to keep practicing, but I didn't mean to disturb anyone. I'll be quieter, I promise."

"No, no, it wasn't—you didn't—" Cahira pulled herself together. She was supposed to be the adult here. "I mean, it was wonderful."

He blushed a bright strawberry red under the freckles. "Fadra says I'm getting better. But I still can't do more than two voices at a time—"

"You're a *Skalsinger*?" she interrupted in shock. He was so young!

"Sure." He was trying for nonchalance, but he couldn't hide the pride in his voice. "Want to hear?"

"I'd love to." Gazing into that eager face, she couldn't have said anything else. Besides, it was true.

The room contained only one chair. She settled herself on it and waited. But now that he had an audience, the boy seemed overcome by embarrassment. He opened his mouth, closed it again. His cheeks reddened even more.

"What's your favourite song?" Cahira asked gently.

"Froggy Bird."

"That's a good one. Would you sing it for me?"

He started with a wobble, but soon gained confidence. That high, pure voice was a perfect instrument to depict the birds, laughing merrily at the frog who wanted to fly. But he could also deepen and roughen it just enough to be convincing as the frog.

And yes, incredibly, he was a Skalsinger. He alternated between the two voices for most of the song, but performed the final chorus as a flawless duet. A faint, smudgy image had even taken shape above his head by the end. Completely charmed, Cahira couldn't help herself: she jumped up and hugged him. He froze in surprise, standing stiff and awkward. She stepped back, offering an immediate apology. But nothing could have kept the smile off her face or the delight out of her voice. "That was amazing! How old are you?"

"Fourteen." Older than she'd guessed, but still incredibly young to have manifested a skal at all, let alone one as developed as this. It was fascinating.

The slightly alarmed expression told her she was staring at him again, and grinning like an idiot, too. If she wasn't careful, she'd frighten him off completely. She sat back down and took a deep breath. "I'm Cahira. What's your name?"

"Ferdy."

"Well, Ferdy, I've never heard of a fourteen-year-old Skalsinger before. How long have you had the skal?"

"Only half a year. I was performing in the market square with my troupe, and a second voice just came out."

She'd been eighteen when something similar had happened to her. And her tutors had called her precocious!

"Do you have a teacher?"

He nodded. "There aren't any other Skalsingers here, but Fadra's helping me. She's training all of us, so we can learn how to use our skals better."

Cahira had wondered about the origins of this community, but she hadn't considered it might be a place of learning. "So, it's like Eorna Academy?"

"I guess so. I've never been there. But Aidan says Fadra's better than any stuffy old teacher at the Academy, anyway."

"Aidan?"

"He's a Metal Shaper. He made all the candle holders and lamps. He says he could barely Shape a horseshoe before he came here. Now he reckons he could make the finest sword anyone could wish for. *I* wish he'd make one for me, but he says I'm too young." He rolled his eyes at the foolishness of adults.

Cahira still didn't quite understand. "But Fadra isn't a Shaper, is she?"

He shook his head. "No, but she's really smart. She has things she calls *experiments*, and she uses them to help all of us—Healers, Shapers, anyone. She's amazing."

"It sounds like you're happy here."

"I am, mostly. Some days I miss my troupe, though. They took me in when I was a baby, taught me to perform. But none of them are Skalsingers, so when Fadra heard me and said she'd teach me for free, they told me to go with her. I know I'm lucky to be here. I just wish I had someone to sing with sometimes."

A cue, if she'd ever heard one. Her lungs still ached a bit, but she could probably manage it. And the truth was, she was itching to try. She hadn't joined her voice to another's for years, not since her student days. She hadn't even known she missed it until now. More than that, she hungered for it. "How about me?"

His face lit up. "You'll sing with me?"

"I'd love to. I'm a Skalsinger, like you."

His eyes widened, but then he ducked his head, suddenly bashful. "Are you sure? I'm not very good yet, even though I pray to Aal about it every day."

Prayer was all very well, and probably a comfort to a boy far from home, but practice would be more effective. Cahira nodded. "I'm sure. I'll take the frog, and you be the birds."

She started, and he joined in when his turn came. The simple story played out above their heads in bright, whimsical pictures as their voices intermingled, separated, twined together again. Cahira felt ridiculously happy. But she noticed that each time Ferdy glanced up at the images, he stuttered a little. They'd have to work on that.

She slept dreamlessly, and was already up and dressed when she heard someone shuffling around on the other side of her door curtain. "Hello? Who's there?"

"Um, it's me. I mean, it's Ferdy."

She stepped across to the doorway and put her hand to the curtain, feeling the first stirrings of curiosity about it. How did you hang a curtain in a cave? The answer lay in two perfectly curved iron hooks. They jutted from the stone about an arm's reach above her head, cradling a long wooden rod. Rings, sewn into the top of the thick fabric, slid along the rod as she pulled the curtain aside. It was an ingenious arrangement, well-made and elegant, like the lighting in the passageways and the system of bells.

Ferdy was carrying a lantern, the candle inside shielded by panels of clear glass set in a metal frame. Another indication that this cave-dwelling community had surprisingly sophisticated resources. He shifted from one foot to the other. "You said we could start lessons today."

She had said that, hadn't she? She'd enjoyed singing with him so much that the offer had just slipped out. But today she wasn't sure that it was such a good idea. She wouldn't be staying here long, maybe only a day or two more, until the water dropped enough to allow travel again. Should she really start mentoring a young Skalsinger? How much progress could he make in such a short time?

When she didn't answer immediately, his face fell. He looked like a puppy that had been promised a walk and then been left behind. "You did mean it?"

"Well, yes, but—"

"That's great! I'm going to work real hard, you'll see."

Cahira was still doubtful, but now she realised the true source of her hesitation. He had so much faith in her, she'd hate to fail at this and disappoint him. "You know I'm not a teacher."

"But you're a Skalsinger and you've been to the Academy, right?"

"Well, yes."

"Then you can teach me what they taught you."

She supposed he was right. And it was only for a day or so. Besides, if she was honest with herself, she was dying to sing with him again. "Let's go look for somewhere to have these lessons then."

A grin split his freckled face. "I already thought of that. I've been up for hours and I've found the perfect place. Come on."

He trotted along, confidently taking turns to the right and left. Cahira was breathing hard—she was still far from her normal level of fitness—when he halted at the foot of a short flight of stairs. The steps were uneven, and their edges were rounded and blurred. Rather than being cut, it looked as if the stone had flowed like liquid before solidifying into this form. And now Cahira saw why they needed the lantern. To this point, their way had been lit by the candles that lined the main tunnels, but the low opening at the top of the steps was dark.

Holding the light out in front of him, Ferdy climbed the stairs, ducked his head and squeezed inside. Cahira, being taller, had to stoop lower. For half a dozen steps, she could see very little except Ferdy's bent silhouette. But then he straightened up and strode ahead, with the lantern held high.

Cahira stretched her own spine thankfully before following, noting that the air on her skin felt neither warm nor cold. The candle flame burned strongly, the sphere of light revealing part of a large chamber, bare of furniture or other evidence anyone had been using it. The floor was free of debris, but webbed with cracks, ranging from the finest hairlines to deep-looking fissures as wide as her hand.

She knew even before she opened her mouth. Ferdy might be young and inexperienced, but his Skalsinger instincts were sound. This chamber would both cradle the music and reflect it, adding resonance and depth to anything they sang. More than that, it felt right. It welcomed her. It had been waiting for her. No, that was fanciful. It was just a cave. But a cave she longed to fill with music. And with light.

"We need more candles."

"I know," Ferdy said. "There's lots in the storeroom. I just wanted to show you first and see what you thought."

"I think it's great."

He grinned in relief. "Right? I couldn't believe no one was using it. I guess they don't know it's here."

"That makes it ours then, at least for today. Go and get the candles, and we'll start training."

As he turned away, she added, "Leave the lantern with me."

He handed it over and ducked out.

Cahira explored the chamber, playing the light along the walls and up as high as it would reach. There were no delicate translucent veils or frozen pillars here. The stone was rough and almost featureless, a dull grey-brown with none of the fantastic shapes and colours she'd admired in the entrance cave. Here and there, tiny specks of a glittering mineral winked out at her, but that was all.

She hummed as she moved along, enjoying the way the walls picked up and magnified even this subdued sound, murmuring it back to her in a friendly fashion. She experimented with snatches of songs in different keys, and then changed to scales. No matter how she varied the pitch, the tempo, the volume, the cavern carolled it back. It was enchanting.

All too soon, Ferdy returned with an armful of wooden staves, each with a fat candle bound to one end. Together they rammed them into the deeper and wider cracks in the floor, forming a rough circle. Ferdy used the smaller candle from the lantern to ignite the wicks.

Soon the two of them stood in a wide pool of light. Multiple shadows streamed outward in every direction, growing larger and larger until they merged completely into the greater darkness at the base of the walls. Cahira took a moment to let it all soak in: the silence, the golden glow, the feeling of being in a place set apart from the ordinary world.

It was nothing like the bland classrooms at the Academy, deliberately designed to provide the students with as little distraction from the lessons as possible. But it was a classroom, nevertheless. She had promised.

She took a deep breath, let it out and turned to Ferdy, trying to sound as if she knew what she was doing. "We'll start with Master Robart's Scale, I think."

"What's that?"

"Just repeat each note after me. You'll get the hang of it."

And so they began.

FIFTEEN

When Cahira returned to her room to rest, she found Elise waiting outside the curtain to tell her that Fadra wanted to see her right away. Even as she thanked the girl for delivering the message, Cahira couldn't help feeling slightly nervous.

Fadra hadn't summoned her this way before. And although the Folk Healer had been nothing but kindness itself, she was also unmistakably the ruler of this settlement. They all deferred to her. If Fadra decided that Cahira had done something wrong—like using an empty cavern for singing lessons without asking permission first—no one here would stand up for her.

In consequence, her heart was beating faster than usual as she stopped in front of the only proper wooden door she'd seen in the caves so far. It fitted tightly inside its frame, probably as a precaution against any contagious illness escaping to infect the rest of the community. Elise had told her that Fadra treated patients here. Cahira raised her hand to knock.

"Come in, Cahira."

She pulled open the heavy door and entered the large chamber. It took a moment for her eyes to adjust to the abrupt change in lighting. Dozens of bowl-shaped lamps, of a kind she'd never seen before, hung on chains from the roof, spilling brightness into every corner. After days surrounded by the soft glow of candles, and especially after her experience in the singing cave, the white glare felt harsh, almost threatening.

She shook her head to dispel her overactive imagination as Fadra came to meet her.

"Cahira! I was concerned when you missed lunch. Are you feeling well?" Fadra touched her gently on the shoulder with one hand and stared into her eyes. "Never mind, I can see you are." She stepped back. "Come over to the fire and eat something. You must be starving."

The small round table was already set with twin platters of cold meat and cheese, along with sliced late tomatoes and bread and butter. Fadra poured a fragrant pale green tea into pottery cups, and Cahira discovered she was as hungry as Fadra had said. How much time had she spent singing with Ferdy, anyway? She hadn't even noticed the noon bells ringing.

The Healer waved away her thanks for the food and told her to start. "I always have extra brought here. If I'm looking after a patient, I often forget to leave the room for meals."

They ate and drank for a while, talking of inconsequential things. Then Fadra leaned back with her elegant hands wrapped around her teacup and fixed dark eyes on Cahira. "And now, what was it that caused you to forget about lunch today?"

Cahira stopped dead with a piece of bread halfway to her mouth. This friendly meal by the fire had dissolved her earlier apprehension. Now the nerves came flooding back twice as strong. She set the bread down, her own gaze firmly directed towards her plate, and tried to think of the best way to explain what she'd been doing.

"I was with Ferdy," she said at last. "We were singing." It sounded as weak as she'd feared it would. "I mean, we were Skalsinging. He's a Skalsinger." As if Fadra didn't know that already.

"Yes, he's very talented. As are you."

"We—that is Ferdy—found a cavern." She glanced up, but couldn't tell anything from Fadra's bland expression. "No one was using it." That sounded defensive. She had to pull herself together. She plunged ahead, speaking as fast as she could to get it over with. "Ferdy asked me to give him some training, and the cavern has really good acoustics. We lost track of the time. I hope it was okay. We borrowed some candles." *Stole, more like.*

But Fadra didn't seem to care about the candles. She took Cahira's hands. "But that's wonderful. Do you need anything else?"

"You don't mind us using the space?"

"Of course not. Cahira, do you know what I'm aiming to do here?"

Cahira wasn't sure how much she should reveal of what Ferdy had told her. "You're a Healer."

"Yes, but I'm trying to become a stronger one. More knowledgeable, more effective. Every patient I treat is helping me do that. Come and have a look."

She led Cahira to a bench set against the back wall. It was covered with books, papers, and scrolls. "I'm writing down everything I do, and all my results." She picked up a page. "This is a list of ingredients for a medicine to help with fevers when willow bark isn't effective. It's not quite right yet, but I'm close."

She put the paper down and moved to a second bench, longer and sturdier than the first. It held rows of vessels of different sizes. Some were made of pottery, their necks sealed with cloth and wax, their contents hidden from view. But others were of thin, blown glass with wooden stoppers, allowing Cahira to see inside. All these contained liquids, their colours varying from a yellow that was almost clear, through deeper tones of green and brown, to delicate pinks and winy reds. Patches of the same shades stained the surface of the bench, along with areas of powdery white and dull black, as if the wood had been scorched first by frost and then by fire.

"Don't touch!" Fadra spoke sharply. Cahira drew her hand back from the tall jar, feeling like a child caught stealing a honey cake.

"Some of these are very strong. They can be dangerous if you handle them without gloves."

"Did you make them all?"

"Yes, with Elise's aid. She has a knack for this sort of work."

"Is there anything here that might help Niall?"

Fadra was silent for a moment. "I'm not sure. Perhaps, with a little more time."

"Then we have to find him and bring him here!"

Fadra shook her head. "The water has begun to go down, but the ground is still too soft. Even a horse would get stuck, let alone a wagon. And I'm told it's going to snow heavily tonight. I'm sorry, Cahira, you'll have to wait a bit longer."

Cahira gritted her teeth. She'd done nothing but wait. And pity herself, of course.

"May I ask you a favour?" Fadra said.

Cahira wasn't feeling very generous right now, but she was hardly in a position to deny Fadra anything. She was living in Fadra's home, eating Fadra's food and expecting Fadra to provide transport once the ground dried up. Not even the clothes on her back were her own. Most of all, she was depending on Fadra to Heal Niall once she found him. Swallowing past the sudden lump in her throat, she nodded.

"Ferdy seems to have taken to you. Would you keep training him, as long as you're here with us? My goal isn't only to become a better Healer, but to enhance the skals of everyone in this community. I believe Ferdy could learn a lot from you."

Relieved that Fadra hadn't asked for something more difficult, Cahira nodded again. "Of course I will."

"Thank you. It might help pass the time for you, too."

It might, at that.

As Cahira returned to the corridor, she pushed away the little tingle of excitement she'd felt at the thought of continuing Ferdy's lessons. It didn't matter that she enjoyed singing with him. She was only staying because she had no choice. As soon as the road was safe, she was going after Niall. Skalsinging with Ferdy was a way to occupy herself until then and make up some of the debt she owed Fadra. That was all.

She'd just entered her room when she heard the first scream. She was on her way out again before the echoes had died. The meal with Fadra seemed to have done her good, and she moved easily, bodily weakness forgotten. She skidded to a stop at the intersection, uncertain of her direction, until a second scream galvanised her back into action.

Strangers emerged from rooms and hallways as she raced along, everyone heading for the source of the terrible sounds.

The screams were coming from the entrance cave. Rounding the last turn, accompanied by half a dozen other runners, Cahira stopped short in confusion. Halfway across the floor of the huge cavern stood an enormous swaying figure, its shaggy outline silhouetted against the bright daylight outside.

The screaming had ceased, but a low, continuous growl was emanating from the occupant of the cavern. It could almost have been a very tall man in a bulky fur cloak, but the proportions were all wrong. The head was too big and too round, the arms too short. And it was wider than any man she'd ever seen.

Suddenly everything snapped into focus, and she knew what she was looking at. Not a man, but an animal, standing upright on its hind legs, broad shoulders hunched as it swung that enormous head one way and then the other.

It was a bear.

It couldn't be—no bear sighting had been reported in Algarth for decades—but it was. It must have been living in the caves, unobserved, and been forced out when Fadra and the others arrived. And now that winter was almost here, it wanted to move back in.

Cahira wondered what it would take to drive it out again, even if anyone was willing to risk harming the rare creature. They had to retreat to a safe distance and make some kind of plan. But as she was edging backwards and gesturing for her companions to do the same, she noticed something that rooted her to the spot and sent a fresh fear cascading through her.

On the floor in front of the bear, almost concealed by its shadow, a tiny, crumpled figure lay—a child in a red and white dress. The screams must have been hers. She wasn't making a sound now. She wasn't moving, either. The grey faces around Cahira reflected the same shock and horror she felt. This couldn't be happening.

A low moan emerged from the girl. One arm moved slightly. She was alive. But the bear's agitation was increasing. It lifted its head higher, pointing its snout to the roof, and roared. The sound was awful, but even worse was the sight of that gaping mouth: the red tongue mottled with black, the long yellow teeth curving to wicked points. It roared again, then dropped to all fours and stretched its nose towards the tightly curled child lying at its feet.

Cahira was shaking with terror, but she couldn't stand there and watch the girl be ripped apart. No one else was moving. It was up to her. She scanned the floor nearby for a stone large enough to cause some damage, or at least discourage the creature, but there was nothing bigger than a pebble.

The bear was nosing at the girl now. Its growling rumbled through the cave. The hairs lifted on the back of Cahira's neck, even as she automatically echoed the sound under her breath. Maybe she had a weapon after all.

Still mimicking the bear, she increased the volume. The animal heard her. Its head swung up, its tiny black eyes sought her out. She didn't care. She wasn't scared now; she was angry. And the anger told her exactly what to do. She wove the growling into a song without words, an anthem of rage against any creature, human or beast, that would harm the helpless.

Soon she couldn't tell if she was singing the song or if it was singing itself through her. It echoed and grew, aided by the stone that surrounded her. She could see the bear rising on its hind feet again, its red mouth opening wide, but its feeble roaring was consumed, overpowered, by the waves of sound that poured from Cahira's throat. They filled the space, crammed into it. Tone upon tone rolled out to the walls and rebounded, discords multiplying as the notes slammed into each other, ugly, but full of power.

A jagged bolt of white lightning ripped across the space between the bear's upraised head and the roof, leaving a stark negative image on the back of Cahira's eyes as it vanished. Still singing, she blinked a few times to clear her vision and saw the animal drop to all fours, shaking its head.

A second flash, and the bear retreated a step. Not enough. She increased the volume again. Flash after flash lit up the cavern, until all she could see were black spots swimming in a sea of blasted white. She clenched her eyes shut and kept going. Even through her eyelids, the world flared white and black. The sound was appalling.

The bear must have gone by now. She could stop.

Except she couldn't. She wasn't in control any more. The song had taken over, and it wouldn't be silenced. It battered at her from inside and out like a wild animal itself, fighting to survive. Her throat was raw. Her heart was about to burst. She was going to die here, deafened and blinded by her own terrible song.

Would she see Bram then? Would he gather her up and wrap her in his arms? Or would he look at her—as he had never done in life—with disappointment and condemnation? She was using her gift, the ability that he had called beautiful, to create something ugly, a weapon born of fear and fury. Bram wouldn't even recognise her.

She had to stop. She fumbled in her pocket for the stone, the solid proof of Bram's love, and gripped it hard. She pictured her husband: the smile on his face, his foot tapping, his warm brown eyes happy and proud, seeing only her. And an idea came to her.

This had all started because of her fear and anger towards the bear. The song reflected that. She couldn't stop singing, but what if she could change the feelings and so change the song?

She clutched the stone even tighter and desperately conjured up a memory: singing to Bram on their wedding night, singing their song. It had been her very first composition and it had come, whole and complete, on the day before the wedding. It returned to her now, to her mind and her heart and her voice: slow and gentle but with as much power in its own way as the one that had called the lightning.

The flashing stopped. The sound died away. She felt moisture course down her cheeks and warm arms go around her. A low voice was calling her name. She let the song trail off and opened her eyes.

The arms holding her weren't Bram's. The voice calling her wasn't his. It was Fadra, cradling Cahira like a child and saying her name over and over, calling her back.

Cahira wept, hardly knowing if her tears were born of grief or thankfulness. Maybe both.

SIXTEEN

Niall

On the third night of their imprisonment, a loud clanging from the empty cell next to him startled Niall out of sleep.

"Inside," snapped a gruff voice.

The sounds of a scuffle were followed by a grunt of pain. The cell door banged shut again. Heavy footsteps retreated.

Niall sat up. This was the first even mildly interesting thing to happen since they'd been here. Despite the sergeant's threats to Niall, and his leer at Perna, neither of them had been taken from their cells for questioning. A young Guard brought them food twice a day and changed the stinking refuse buckets, and that was all. The lack of supervision might have aided their escape plan, if Niall had been able to devise one.

Actually, he'd thought of several, but they all involved being on the other side of the cell door first. And that was a problem. The Guard who brought the meals was practically a giant. He was armed with a short club, which seemed welded to his beefy hand, and he never took his eyes off his prisoner while the door was open. Niall was fast with his hidden dagger, but he didn't like his chances of going up against this one without incurring serious injuries. Still, after three mind-numbing days of tedium, he was almost desperate enough to try it.

He'd had plenty of leisure to wonder about the absence of other prisoners, too. There were ten cells in this corridor, all unoccupied except for his and Perna's. He couldn't believe the citizens of Welsea had suddenly become perfectly law-abiding. What were the Guards doing with their time, if not rounding up criminals or imprisoning innocent travellers? Something was going on. Perhaps this new prisoner might have some news that Niall could turn to his advantage.

He called out softly, but the only reply he received was a deep groan, followed by silence. Niall sighed and sank back onto his pallet. *Friend, I know exactly how you feel.*

SEVENTEEN

Cahira

Cahira couldn't seem to stop crying. A deep wound had opened at the heart of her, and it was bleeding tears.

Bram shouldn't have died like that. His death had been caused, not by his own actions, but by the twisted desires of greedy men far away. Cahira raged against the injustice of a decent and loving life cut short for no good reason. But even in the midst of her pain, she didn't dare indulge the anger too deeply. She was terrified of what she'd felt when she'd attacked the bear, and the way the song had taken her over. She couldn't let that happen again.

At Fortune Creek, her images had only caused fear, not harm. But she knew, beyond doubt, that anyone looking at that lightning for too long would have been blinded. If she'd increased the volume even a little more, eardrums would have burst. Skalsingers just didn't have that kind of power. At least, no one at the Academy had ever spoken about such a thing, and her tutors had included some of the most gifted and experienced Skalsingers in Algarth. She wished she had access to the Archives beneath the Academy, to find out for sure. But right now, she might as well wish for the moon.

When she finally slept, she dreamed not of Bram, but of Niall. He lay in a field of snow, pale and barely breathing. In the way of dreams, she knew exactly what was wrong with him. The deadly cold had stolen his vitality and his memories, his very self. If only she could bring him to somewhere warm, he would wake up and his memory would return. But there was no horse nearby, no wagon to carry him to shelter. He was too heavy for her to drag far on foot.

He needed fire, but the white expanse surrounding them was unbroken by so much as a bush or a fallen branch. She took off her cloak and wrapped it awkwardly around his body, bright blue on black, knowing, even as she did it, that it wouldn't be enough.

And then it came to her: the memory of singing lightning into the cave. If she could call light, could she call heat? As soon as she asked the question, she saw exactly how to do it. She knelt in the snow beside the still form of her friend and sang a song of the sun.

It was part of a children's ditty, one she'd known long before she'd even heard of the Academy. It was sung by mothers to their children, and later by the youngsters themselves in the skipping games they played with turning ropes. A rhythmic song, repeating the cycle of the seasons over and over: autumn, winter, spring, summer. But she only needed summer.

Sun is hot, day is long,
Time to sing a summer song.
Buzzing bees, flowers bright,
Fireflies light up the night.
Sun is hot, day is long,
Now I've sung my summer song.

Above her head, where before there had only been a blank expanse of grey, a ball of pale-yellow light appeared. It was fuzzy and weak at first, barely visible, but as she sang, it grew larger and glowed more intensely golden. She kept going, face upturned, willing the warmth to come. And it did. The new sun she'd created spilled its heat down upon her cold cheeks. She closed her eyes in thankfulness for a moment, then looked down.

The snow was melting, revealing fresh green grass beneath. Colour rushed into Niall's skin. His brown eyes flicked open, staring up at her in gratitude. She'd done it. She'd saved him. She broke off the song.

But something was happening to the grass. The tender shoots bleached to straw, as if spring had turned to late summer in an instant. They darkened as she watched, shrinking and curling in on themselves, until all that remained were skeletal brown wisps poking up from the dusty earth.

Niall's face had changed, too. His skin was fiery red. His eyes were black pools, reflecting the orange orb blazing in the sky above. He wasn't moving or even blinking. He was still unconscious.

She shook him by the shoulder. "Niall! Wake up!" He gave no sign that he had heard her. She shook him harder. "Niall!"

She peered into his face again and gasped in horror. His skin was as stiff and yellow as old parchment, stretched taut over his bones like the skin of a drum. It clung to the deep hollows of his cheeks, the jutting nose and chin, shrinking tighter and tighter until his head was little more than a grinning skull. Only his eyes were still alive, black and glistening in their bony sockets. He turned towards her, fixed his terrible gaze on her. A whisper hissed out between his parched and shrunken lips: "Why?"

Then the light went out from his eyes. He was dead. Cahira froze in place, her hand clenched on his shoulder, and felt brittle bones crumble beneath her fingers. She couldn't let go. Couldn't even scream. Her throat closed. She was choking.

"Cahira!"

She did scream then. And found herself alone in the dark, the sun snuffed out. She couldn't feel Niall, couldn't get a breath. Her heart was pounding at the cage of her chest, threatening to break free any second. When it did, she would die, too.

A small blurry light swam into view. Her eyes locked onto it like the hands of a drowning woman clutching a rope.

Something shook her until her teeth clacked together. "Cahira! Wake up!"

She drew in a deep, shuddering breath.

"Cahira!"

"I'm awake." Her voice came out as a croak.

By the dim light of the candle flame she recognised the familiar silhouettes of desk, chair and cupboard. She was in her room in the caves, sitting up in bed. Fadra was beside her, holding her by the arms. No sun, no snow, no Niall lying dead, killed by her skal. Another nightmare. She dropped her head and sobbed. She couldn't keep doing this. She didn't have the strength.

Fadra's arms came around her. "There, there. Hush now. It's over."

"It's not. It'll never be over."

Fadra rocked her like a child, and she allowed herself to be soothed. After a while, shame crept over her. She was so pathetic. She pulled away. "I'm all right."

"Another nightmare?"

"Yes."

"I was hoping there wouldn't be any more. Perhaps I can give you something to make you sleep better."

Cahira shuddered at the idea of going back to sleep. Tonight would be soon enough. Too soon. But maybe the Healer could help in a different way.

"Fadra?"

"Yes?"

"You said you were working to make skals stronger."

"Yes, that's my purpose here."

"Could you make mine weaker?"

Fadra drew back. "Why would you want that?"

"Because it's dangerous! Because it could kill someone!"

"On the contrary. You've already used it to save someone. Young Mia wouldn't be alive if you hadn't scared the bear away."

"I know, but—I had no control, Fadra. None. If it hadn't been for you—"

"Your skal is unique and powerful, Cahira. Never be ashamed of that."

"I don't want it!"

Fadra stood up. "It's about three hours to sunrise, but I don't think either of us is going back to sleep. I'll make some tea, and we'll talk."

The conversation was long and difficult. The image of Niall lying dead before her—because of her—wouldn't leave Cahira. She hated her skal, wanted nothing to do with it. But even as she insisted that, she knew it was only partly true. Fadra seemed to know it, too.

"Cahira, your talent is part of you. You can't get rid of it any more than you could wish away a leg or an arm. I don't know any way to weaken it, and I wouldn't do it even if I could. You need to learn to control it. I can help you."

"What if I stopped using it?"

"Could you do that? Really?"

Cahira considered the question honestly. She hadn't planned to use her skal against the bear. It had just happened, the same way it had at Fortune Creek when she'd seen Bram lying so still. She shook her head. "Maybe not."

"Then will you let me help you?"

In the end, Cahira agreed. If others were to be safe around her, she had no choice. Besides, a tiny hope had grown inside her. Even though she hadn't been able to save Bram, if she could truly learn to direct her wild skal, one day she might use it to protect Niall or Adric, or someone else she cared about. She'd give Fadra a chance to make good on her claim, and she'd work as hard as she could to harness her double-edged gift.

She was prepared to start right away, but Fadra declared that they both needed a good breakfast first. She went ahead to organise it while Cahira changed. The borrowed dress and jacket fitted well enough, but sat uncomfortably on her skin. They were a constant reminder that she owned nothing here. She was completely dependent on the goodwill of Fadra and the others. It was a new feeling in her life, and not one she relished.

Although it must still be well before sunrise, someone had been up before her: fresh candles lit the way to Fadra's quarters. Remembering what Ferdy had told her about the Metal Shaper, Cahira examined a holder. It was exquisitely made, in the form of a newly opened tulip, Shaped as perfectly as any metal-work she'd seen. If a man who'd only ever worked on horseshoes could learn to create something like this, perhaps Fadra really could help Cahira, too.

The study was as bright as before. In front of the crackling fire, plates of eggs and bacon lay on the table between the two armchairs, along with toasted bread and butter and cups already filled with tea. With Fadra's eyes upon her, Cahira forced herself to take a forkful of the creamy eggs and a tiny bite of bread. As soon as she began to chew, saliva rushed to her mouth. Her stomach suddenly felt as hollow as the surrounding cave. She swallowed quickly and reached for more.

At first, Fadra just talked. Her words sounded formal, like a prepared speech she'd delivered many times before.

"Your ability is a natural talent, one you are born with, but which doesn't manifest until years later. It has been generally believed that, while training may increase the mastery of a talent, the strength is fixed from the beginning and cannot be changed. I have proven that to be incorrect. Using infusions made from particular herbs, and practising mental and spiritual disciplines, I have strengthened my own abilities far beyond their previous limits. And I have taught others to do the same."

"I don't want to make my skal stronger."

Fadra dropped back into normal speech. "I know that. But you do want to control it. I believe we can achieve the one without the other."

"What do I have to do?"

"First, you need to accept your talent as it stands now. Its uniqueness, and especially its strength."

"I'm not sure I can."

"This will help." Fadra crossed to the work bench and lifted a squat glass bottle half full of pale green liquid. It looked identical to the contents of several other containers there, and Cahira wondered how the Healer could keep all the medicines straight in her mind when none of them bore labels. But Fadra didn't hesitate. She took down a cup from a shelf above the bench, uncorked the bottle and let fall a few precious drops. She sealed the bottle again, diluted the contents of the cup with water from a jug, and brought it to Cahira. "Sip it slowly."

Cahira took the cup and sniffed at the contents. She detected a faint smell of cut grass, and something else she didn't recognise: musty, earthy. "What is it?"

"A tonic Elise and I developed. It will relax your mind and open it at the same time." As Cahira still hesitated, she added, "It's completely harmless, I promise. I take it myself whenever I have a difficult Healing to perform."

Cahira lifted the cup to her lips and took a sip.

"Good. Just keep doing that until I return. I won't be long."

Fadra walked to a door that was set into the back wall between the workbenches. She passed through and closed the door behind her. Perhaps it led to her bedroom.

The liquid cooled Cahira's mouth, leaving a slightly bitter aftertaste that wasn't unpleasant, just strange. She'd expected the medicine to have some obvious effect on her, but she felt the same as before. She leaned back. The softness of the armchair cradled and held her. The fire warmed her. She continued to sip. Time passed.

Fadra returned and sat opposite her. "Now we can begin. Tell me when you first knew you were a Skalsinger."

"I was eighteen. I was in the field, by the river."

The sun had been shining in an unblemished sky as blue as sapphire. The grass sprang bright green all around. Birdsong, the buzz of insects, the music of the water, filled her ears. The sheer joy of being outside on a spring morning filled her heart.

"Sing what you were singing then."

Melody flowed from her throat, piercing and sweet. As the second voice layered its deeper theme beneath, tears welled. There was no feeling in the world like this. She saw the way to bring in a third voice, added it. And a fourth.

She opened her eyes. Sunlight filled the room. The aromas of grass, water, and flowers flooded into her nostrils. Without even a glance, she knew the image was there above her, bright and clear as a landscape fresh from the artist's brush.

Fadra was gently smiling and nodding. Cahira finished with a flourish and drew a deep breath. Sunlight and scents vanished. But an answering smile tugged at the corners of her mouth.

"I don't need to ask how that felt," Fadra said. "I can see for myself."

She was right. Cahira couldn't remember ever feeling this good. Whatever Fadra had given her had taken away her fear, but hadn't affected her singing. Or if it had, it had only made it more effortless. She felt as if she could do anything.

"Now, think back to your encounter with the bear," Fadra said. "What did you sing?"

"I don't know. It wasn't a song, really. There weren't any words. Just sounds."

"Can you remember them?"

Cahira thought about it. The bear had been growling. She'd been scared, but desperate to save the child. "A sort of growling, very low. Rumbling."

"Can you do it again now?" Fadra held up a hand, forestalling any protest. "There's no bear here, Cahira. No danger. Just try for a few seconds."

Fadra was right; there was nothing to fear. Cahira relaxed and brought back the memory. It was clear, but no longer frightening. She began softly, then stopped: she'd pitched it too high. She tried again. Yes, that was more like it. She increased the volume, with one eye on the space above them. Would the lightning appear? A small flash lit up the room, making her jump.

"It's all right. You're in control. Try again."

This time, the bolt was brighter and lasted longer.

"Good. Now, see if you can change the direction of the lightning. Imagine it shooting towards the corner over there."

Was that even possible? A tingle of excitement ran up Cahira's spine. Keeping the sound low, she visualised a small bolt of lightning streaking high across the room. And there it was. She stopped with a hiccough of surprise.

Fadra laughed softly. "See? It's your talent. Yours to direct."

Exhilaration thrilled through Cahira, abruptly followed by bone-weary exhaustion.

Fadra seemed to sense the change in her. "That's enough for now. You've made significant progress. I'm proud of you." She led Cahira to the door.

As Cahira was stepping into the passageway, she felt Fadra's light touch on her shoulder and turned.

"And please think about teaching Ferdy again. He needs your guidance."

"I will. I'll think about it."

"Good. Get some rest now. I'll send Elise for you after lunch and we'll have another session."

Heading for her room, Cahira's footsteps slowed, then stopped. As tired as she was, she didn't feel like going back yet. The first memory Fadra had drawn out of her had stimulated a longing for the sky, the real one. It must be close to sunrise by now. She made her way to the entrance cave.

The air was frigid in here. The guard fire, kept burning ever since the bear attack, smouldered untended just beyond the opening, lazy coils of grey smoke curling upwards in the predawn light.

Cahira huddled inside her jacket as the sky above the hills flushed tender pink and apricot, intensifying as she watched. The finest brush-stroke of gold limned the horizon, brightening and thickening moment by moment.

The call of a bird pierced the air, then another. Soon dozens were jostling for their places in the symphony. Cahira's ears filled with chirps and cackles, whistles and chuckles, from the joyous trills of blackbirds to the mournful complaints of crows. She drank in the crisp air, and it was like breathing happiness. She hadn't known how much she'd missed being outside, in the changing light under a broad sky, away from the fug of burning candles.

She had already accepted that she'd be living in the caves until she gained greater mastery over her skal. But that didn't mean she had to spend all day buried under tons of rock. Approaching winter or not, she'd come here as often as she could. And in fine weather she'd walk the hillside and venture down to the bank of the stream.

Another shiver ran over her. She'd need warmer clothing, but it shouldn't be a problem. The cave community was generous with both talents and possessions. In some ways they behaved more like a family than anything else, with Fadra as the mother to all of them.

But they weren't Cahira's family. Adric was her family. And in a way, Niall was too. She hadn't forgotten either of them, not for a moment. But going after them before she had control of these frightening new powers was unthinkable. She couldn't bear it if, trying to save them, she harmed them instead.

She spoke aloud, although she knew they couldn't hear her. Perhaps, wherever they were, they'd sense she was thinking of them.

"I'm coming. As soon as I can, I'm coming to find you both."

EIGHTEEN

Niall

Light was shining through the small, barred window. Another day. Niall rose to his feet and stretched, rubbing his back. His nose wrinkled at the stench emanating from his body. He could do with a bath. He could also do with a hot meal and a key to this cell. And a weapon. Might as well wish for the moon, if you were wishing at all.

He heard Perna moving around next door. She would be praying rather than wishing, but it came to the same thing. He called out softly to her.

"Good morning, Niall," she replied. "Aal be with you." She sounded as composed as she had every time they'd spoken recently. He was glad she'd found some calm, but he wondered what was going on in her mind.

"And how are you this fine morning?" he said. "Looking forward to our gourmet breakfast?"

From the cell on his other side came a man's voice, sounding incredulous. "Niall? Niall Crawley? Is that you?"

Niall blinked. "I'm Niall Crawley," he admitted. "Who are you?"

"Aal's teeth, it's good to hear your voice! It's me, Adric."

"Adric, what in blazes are you doing here? The last I heard, you'd gone to Eorna on some sort of errand for Berek."

"That's not exactly true, but I can't explain now. The thing is, we have to get out of here."

Adric, master of the obvious. "Do you have a plan, then?" Niall couldn't keep the sarcastic note out of his voice.

"Someone might be coming."

"Might be?"

"I'm not sure. But if he finds out I'm here, he'll come."

"Who?"

Silence. This secretiveness wasn't like Adric at all. Niall was about to press him further when heavy footsteps sounded from further along the corridor. An older Guard he hadn't seen before strode past him and stopped outside Perna's cell to unlock the door. He disappeared inside. A second later, there was a squawk, and he emerged, pulling a struggling Perna by one arm. She twisted in his grip. "Let me go!"

The Guard swung a meaty hand and slapped her across the face. Niall spat out a curse. Perna froze. The Guard yanked her back into motion, dragging her down the corridor to a door at the other end. They disappeared inside, and the door closed behind them.

Niall slammed his fist into the bars. He had to get out. He'd already judged the lock was too strong to smash. In desperation, he took the dagger from his boot and poked the tip around. He'd seen locks picked, but he'd never learned the skill. All he knew was you had to listen for a click. No click was forthcoming, and he was in danger of breaking the blade.

Out of the corner of his eye, he saw Adric's door swing outward. A moment later, Adric himself appeared and began fiddling with Niall's lock. It seemed to take forever, and Niall was becoming frantic at the thought of what might be happening to Perna.

After an eternity, Adric pulled the door open and grinned. "I've learned a few tricks since we last met." He tucked something away in his breast pocket and gripped Niall by the arm. "Do you have a weapon they didn't find?"

Speechless, Niall held up the little dagger.

"Better than nothing. Let's go get her."

As Niall joined him, a second figure appeared at the top end of the corridor: the weaselly sergeant. Seeing the prisoners out of their cells, he raised a short club and pointed it at them. "Back inside."

Niall thought fast. The sergeant wasn't a big man. If they could reach him before he called for help, they could overpower him. He was about to start sprinting when Adric grabbed his arm and pulled him back. Niall tried in vain to break free. "Curse you Adric, what are you doing?"

"He's got a crossbow." Adric sounded half grim and half impressed.

The sergeant was strolling down the corridor towards them now, holding the club out in front of him in one hand. Except Adric was right: it wasn't a club. It was flat and triangular, and the end facing them held a metal point.

"Dangerous?" he asked.

"You have no idea."

Whatever this weapon was, if it had Adric's respect, Niall wasn't about to argue.

The sergeant stopped about ten spans away. "That's right. Now get back in the cells before I put a nice big hole in one of you."

Niall was calculating if the distance was still too great for a thrown dagger to incapacitate the man. If only he'd come a little closer. As if the sergeant had decided to grant Niall's wish, he took two more steps and waved the strange weapon towards the cells. "Now."

Niall tightened his grip, ready to flick the knife underhand. He was about to let it fly when yet another figure appeared at the top of the corridor. The new Guard was big and dark-skinned, with close-cropped black hair. His biceps strained against his shirtsleeves as he raised a long staff in both hands and stepped up behind his superior. Niall's hand froze on the knife handle.

The sergeant spoke without turning his head. "Put them in the cells."

Even with Adric's skals of Swiftness and Strength and Niall's dagger, they couldn't take on two heavily armed men. Niall was momentarily tempted to throw the dagger anyway—at least he'd wipe the smile off the weasel's face—but he resisted and turned towards his cell. It was over.

There was an audible crack from somewhere behind him. Niall spun around in time to see the sergeant crumple to the ground. The crossbow clattered on the flagstones.

Niall stood, blinking stupidly as Adric pushed past him and strode up to the big dark-skinned man. "About time." He bent to pick up the fallen weapon.

"Sorry. Only just found out where they'd moved you."

Adric did something complicated-looking to the crossbow, and then slung it over his shoulder.

The new Guard nodded his close-cropped head towards Niall. "Who's this?"

"Niall Crawley, an old friend. Niall, meet Mundar." Adric grinned. "Just Mundar, you understand. Apparently he doesn't have two names like a normal person. At least, that's how he tells it. Okay? Let's get going."

Niall's brain started up again. He pointed at the closed door. "We can't leave Perna."

"We're not," Adric said. He turned to their new companion. "There's a young girl in there, with at least one Guard." Mundar didn't ask questions, just nodded and led the way down the corridor.

They halted outside the door, listening. Niall heard nothing. Adric unslung the crossbow. Mundar raised his staff again and nodded to Niall. Niall grasped the handle and pulled the door open in a single fast movement, then froze in shock. Perna stood facing him, less than an arm-span away. Streaks of crimson gore smeared her clothing and glistened on the blade of the little bone-handled knife she held out in front of her. Her eyes were wild.

Niall stepped carefully all the way around the door so she could see him clearly. "Perna? It's me. It's Niall." She stared at him blankly for a moment, then blinked and lowered the knife. "I want to go now." Her voice was without inflection.

Behind her, the Guard lay slumped in a chair, with his trousers around his ankles and his head tipped back as if he was gazing at the ceiling. But those eyes would never see anything again: his exposed neck and the front of his shirt were a mass of blood. Niall looked from the body to Perna, his mind refusing to accept what he was seeing.

She spoke again, her voice dreamy and detached. "He tried to…"

She shuddered, and her face twisted and crumpled. "I want to go *now!*"

"She's right," Adric said. "We have to get out of here before anyone else comes looking."

"Wait," Mundar said. He returned to the unconscious sergeant, grabbed him under the arms, and dragged him into the room with the dead man. He shut the door and gestured to Adric: "You and me first."

Mundar led the way up the corridor, followed by Adric. Niall brought up the rear, keeping an eye on Perna, who had reverted to her previous calm. He doubted she'd ever seen a dead body before, let alone killed anyone. She was in shock now, but reality was going to catch up with her, and there was no telling how she'd react when that happened.

When they reached the door of the Guard room, Adric turned and whispered, "Stay here." He and Mundar went forward, splitting to the right and left.

"Nobody move." Adric's voice was flat and hard. There was no sound for a few seconds, then came the crash of a chair hitting the floor and a babble of angry voices.

"I said, don't move." Silence again. Niall poked his head into the doorway. Three Guards were on their feet. Two held staffs, the other a sword. Adric was pointing the crossbow towards them. "Throw down your weapons."

The sword-wielding Guard was braver, or more stupid, than the others. "Why should we?" he growled. "There are three of us and you've only got one bolt."

"That's true," Adric answered. "One shot. And it's going into the throat of the last man to throw down his weapon."

The mouthy Guard's companions didn't share his defiant spirit. Two staffs hit the floor.

The swordsman's features twisted in fury. "You idiots!"

"Looks like you're the lucky one," Adric said cheerfully. He lifted the crossbow and squinted along the bolt. "Last chance."

The man swore viciously and laid down his blade.

"Not another sound," Adric warned. The Guard subsided, but his expression said if they ever met again things would go differently.

Mundar fetched ropes and strips of cloth from a cupboard in the wall. Niall admired the big man's competent movements as he tied their three captives to chairs and gagged them.

Niall's sword and knives were among other weapons stored in a wooden chest along with his purse, miraculously still full of coins. Adric joined him at the chest, taking a sword and half a dozen bolts for the crossbow. Mundar seemed happy with his long staff. The prisoners' packs lay against a wall, seemingly untouched.

Mundar's plan had been for him and Adric to escape dressed as Warrant Guards, but now they modified it to include Niall and Perna as prisoners being transported. Niall would have preferred to be a Guard too, thus keeping his weapons handy, but it would look too suspicious for three men to be escorting one small female. So he hid his newly retrieved knives in his pack, and gave the sword to Adric.

Perna was still clutching her own bloody knife. When Niall gently suggested she return it to her pocket, she stared at him for a moment as if she didn't know what he was talking about. Then she mechanically took out the scabbard, slid the weapon inside, and tucked it away again.

Mundar tied their hands behind their backs loosely enough for them to free themselves if they ran into any trouble, while Adric forced a Guard who was roughly his size to remove his blue shirt, which he put on over his own clothing. Then Mundar led them outside.

Niall had already sent his thoughts questing, and found Sienna, Dulcina, and Briar in a stable in the opposite corner of the marshalling yard. They passed a few real Guards on the way, but no one gave them more than a cursory glance. Adric went into fetch the horses while Mundar spoke to the stableman. The man disappeared inside and came back leading a big chestnut. All four horses were quickly saddled, and they mounted up.

When they reached the gate, Mundar addressed the Blueshirt stationed there. "Prisoners for the harbour."

The man waved them through. For a garrison, the security seemed very lax. Not that Niall was complaining.

About an hour later, they pulled up outside a nondescript house on a quiet street. After they'd removed Niall and Perna's bonds and settled the horses in the attached stable, Mundar unlocked the back door of the house and ushered them all inside.

"Are we safe here?" Niall asked.

"Safe as anywhere in Welsea," Mundar said. "Which is safe enough for now, but we shouldn't risk staying the night. We'll move as soon as it gets dark." He turned towards a door leading to another room. "I'll get us some food."

Adric bent to light the fire.

"Well, that gives us about seven hours to kill," Niall said. "So now maybe you can tell me what in the name of everything that's holy is going on. And who he is." He jerked his head in the direction of the door. "Is he one of Berek's Seekers? Did he come with you from the farm?"

"No, he's a real Guard, from Eorna garrison."

Niall's usual eloquence deserted him. "What?"

Adric took his time lighting the fire and then straightened up. "He's a Guard, working for Commander Oren." His mouth widened in a grin, as if he was about to deliver the punchline of a hugely funny joke. "Just like me."

At the look on Niall's face, Adric slapped his leg and gave a shouted laugh. "Ha! I knew I'd fooled you! I did it pretty well, didn't I?"

Niall's brains felt scrambled. "What do you mean, you're working for Oren?"

"I was never one of those stupid Seekers. Sit down and I'll tell you everything."

Niall sat. "Well?"

"I already told Cahira some of the truth. After I left, I started drinking too much and getting into fights. But it wasn't Berek who snapped me out of it, it was Oren. He found me in the drunk cells in Eorna and made me an offer. He said if I wanted to do something to pay back the people who caused Bram's death—instead of just drinking myself into my grave—he had a job for me."

"But they already caught Tarn."

"They never caught Commander Renn, did they? Oren's had people working in secret ever since, and they found out some things. After Tarn was arrested, Renn went to Bregia. Well, there were rumours about that at the time of the trial, but what we didn't know was that he came from there in the first place. He was a Bregian all along, part of some group called the Disciples of Kolos. Oren's agents heard whispers that they control the Bregian government behind the scenes, with the Imperator as their puppet. And they wanted to do the same in Algarth. Renn wasn't the only one they sent here, either."

"Berek?" Niall asked in surprise, putting two and two together.

Adric snorted. "He's not smart enough to be a spy. But Oren thinks someone might be pulling his strings. So he sent me to Mirston to be recruited and find out their plans. I was about to leave the farm to report to him when you and Cahira turned up."

Niall groaned. "Why didn't you just tell us?"

"I couldn't risk it. There are always people listening there—Berek's paranoid. I had to get my information to Oren, and I thought that once I'd gone, you'd leave, too. Aal's teeth, you could have knocked me down with a feather when I heard your voice in the cells." He suddenly looked alarmed. "Cahira's safe, isn't she?"

All Niall's elation at their escape drained away. He clenched his hands on the arms of the chair. "I don't know."

"What?"

"I was attacked, unconscious for two days. When I came to, she'd gone. Look, it's a long story, and it'll keep. But I'm going to find her."

Perna had been sitting all this time with her hands folded in her lap and her eyes closed. Now she opened them and looked up at Adric. "Thank you for rescuing us." Her voice was solemn. "It was very brave of you."

A faint redness coloured Adric's cheeks above the thatch of blond beard. He almost looked bashful, if such a thing was possible for him. "You did some of the rescuing yourself." He cleared his throat. "Where did you learn to use a knife like that?"

Perna's body stiffened and her eyes went deep and dark. Niall tried in vain to catch Adric's eye.

Oblivious to the effect his words were having, Adric blundered on, shaking his head in admiration. "I was never so surprised in my life when Niall opened that door and we saw you standing there holding out that little knife."

Perna blushed to the roots of her hair. Her chin trembled.

Niall scrambled to steer his clueless friend onto a different topic. "What are you doing in Welsea, anyway?"

Adric sat back and waved a hand. "That's easy. Oren sent me here. He'd already transferred Mundar to Welsea to work from the inside. They've been suspicious of the garrison for a while. Too much money in the town, too many people coming and going. Oren thought it was smuggling—luxury goods from Bregia—and that the garrison must be in on it because they'd never reported any trouble. We were down at the harbour when they caught me. Mundar got away without being spotted." He leaned forward again. "But we'd already found out what's going on. There are half a dozen Bregian ships down there, full of men. They're not in uniform, but they're acting like soldiers. It's not just spies and politics now. An attack is coming."

Niall went silent, trying to work out the implications. Algarth hadn't faced an armed enemy for generations. What would this mean for all of them?

While he was still thinking, Mundar came back, carrying plates of cold provisions. The men fell to—after days of prison slop, even salt beef tasted good to Niall—but Perna had reverted to her habit of hardly eating anything.

As they ate, they talked about their plans. Adric and Mundar were heading to Eorna as soon as it was dark to report to Oren. Niall fully intended to keep looking for Cahira. But the unspoken question was what to do with Perna. She couldn't stay in Welsea, but Niall didn't want to be saddled with her any longer, even if she'd shown she could take care of herself.

Before he'd worked out the best thing to do, Perna took the decision out of his hands. "I'm going with you to Eorna," she said to Adric. There was no doubt or hesitation in her voice.

Adric frowned and shot a questioning glance towards Mundar.

The big man calmly scanned Perna's face and then nodded pleasantly to her. "In that case, you had better change your clothes. A long dress isn't practical for fast riding." He tactfully didn't mention the rusty stain of dried blood blazoned across the bodice that might also cause them a few problems if it was spotted by the authorities. "We have spare clothing upstairs. I'll show you."

"You've got women's clothes here?" Niall asked Adric after the other two had left the room.

"No, only men's." Adric shrugged. "She'll have to make do."

Niall wondered what Perna would think of that.

NINETEEN

Perna

She hitched up the rough trousers and pulled the drawstring tighter around her waist. They were still too long. She rolled the legs up further and checked her reflection again, marvelling at the clarity. She'd never seen a glass mirror before she'd come to Welsea. At home there had only been a dented metal one that turned her into a strange, elongated creature, all big eyes and spidery limbs.

She'd never worn male clothing, either. Above the baggy fabric, her face was tiny, almost frail. She looked like a child. Was that how the others saw her? Even in these clothes, no one would believe she was a man, but perhaps she could pass for a young boy.

Except for her hair. It was too long. She searched the pocket of her discarded dress and found the little knife. The blade was rusty with his blood. She gripped the handle and steadied herself, pushing the memory away. She lifted a hank of hair and raised the knife, but her hand stopped partway there. Just the thought of the dried blood touching her hair was making her gag.

There was a jug and basin on a stand. She poured water and dipped the knife in. Reddish brown swirls flowed around it, turning the water in the basin a dirty pink. She swished the blade vigorously and examined it again. It was cleaner, but stubborn dark patches remained. Her hand trembled. He was dead. She had killed him, and Aal would never forgive her. She was like this knife: stained, disgusting.

But she had a job to do. She wouldn't be the one responsible for the others being caught again. The Guards would be looking for three men and a woman., not a boy. The hair had to come off.

Dropping the knife in the bloody water, she went back to the trunk and found a piece of rag. She fished out the knife and rubbed the blade until no trace of blood remained. The metal was bright and clean, as if it had never done any violence. She envied it.

She dried it carefully and lifted it again, clenching her jaw. The first cut was the worst. After that, it was just a matter of keeping going and trying not to think. Soon she stood amidst a litter of shed hair. Only a finger-length remained all over her head, sticking out in every direction. It changed her face, making the narrow planes of her cheekbones more prominent. She looked like a stranger. An ugly stranger. But what did that matter?

Her shorn head was cold, though. She found a knitted woollen cap and pulled it on, then added a thick felt jacket over the tunic instead of her new fur cloak. There. She was a boy.

She slipped the knife into a trouser pocket and went down to join the others. Adric was talking. "I overheard a couple of the Bregian crew. They'd sailed across Windras Strait from some place called Iantor, and then down the coast to here."

He glanced up at the sound of her feet on the stairs. His mouth fell open. The other two followed his gaze. Mundar's calm, serious expression didn't change, but Niall looked flabbergasted.

Of course, it was Niall who found his voice first. "Well, young Perna, I don't know if it's an improvement, but it's certainly a distinct look. You may start a whole new fashion among the ladies when you get to Eorna."

Idiot. She was glad she wouldn't be travelling with him tonight. Ignoring his foolish words, she leaned against the wall, listening to the conversation as it resumed, and wondering if there was anything she could ever do to make up for all the wrong choices she'd made. Perhaps in Eorna, she could join a different group of Aalden, dedicate the rest of her life to helping the poor and the sick. Aal had given her the gift of

Folk Healing. Maybe if she saved enough lives, it might balance the scale somehow.

Adric was speaking again. "They mentioned Eder Ford, too. They're meeting another force there, and they didn't think much of them—called them amateurs. The blasted Guards caught me before I heard anything else, but it's got to be Berek."

"If they march on the capital together, that's an army of four hundred or more," Mundar said. "There are a hundred Guards stationed in Eorna. After Adric's intelligence about the Seekers, Oren sent word to the other garrisons, but they're spread across the island. The message won't bring in more than another hundred in time to be any use." His broad brow furrowed. "Two to one at best. We could lose the city." His voice had remained low and steady as he spoke the chilling words. Perna admired his self-control. Her own heart was fluttering against the cage of her ribs.

"And we don't know anything about their tactics or weapons," Adric said, sounding angry. "What if they all have horses and crossbows?" He slapped the arm of the chair and burst out, "We can't leave yet! Not until we find out more."

Mundar nodded slowly. "We have to return to the harbour."

Perna thought it was a terrible idea. They'd be recognised and caught again, and there'd be no one to warn Eorna that the Bregians were coming. Adric and Mundar were very brave men, but this was suicide. She had to do something.

TWENTY

Niall

"You can't be serious," Niall protested. Adric and Mundar's plan to go back to the harbour in broad daylight was madness. "Someone must have discovered the men we tied up by now. Every Guard in Welsea is probably looking for us, with full descriptions to help them."

"I'll shave my beard," Adric said. "And Mundar can wear a hood." He leaned back and crossed his arms as if satisfied he had solved the problem.

Niall hardly knew where to start. "I don't think shaving's going to be enough," he said mildly, admiring his own restraint in the face of Adric's obtuseness. "And Mundar's size would give him away even if you put a bag over his head." He sighed. He'd known for the last few minutes it would come to this. He just hadn't wanted to admit it to himself. "It has to be me. I'm smaller and not so noticeable. And I can sense if they have horses on the ships."

Adric raised bushy eyebrows. "Wearing that?"

Niall glanced down at his expensive blacks. Excellent for melting into the shadows at night, but rather eye-catching in daylight. "Good point. I'll change, like Perna." He dipped his head to her, only to discover she wasn't there. She must have fled upstairs to escape his teasing.

Safely clad in shabby, nondescript brown, Niall went to check on Perna. There was no sign of her in the house. With a sinking feeling in his stomach, he tried the yard and the stable, hoping he was wrong. He wasn't.

As if they didn't have enough worries, Perna had run away, probably terrified by Adric's news about the Bregians. They had to find her before someone else did. At least Dulcina was still in the stable. Surely the girl wouldn't have gone far on foot.

Mundar stayed in the house while Niall and Adric searched the surrounding streets. They avoided contact with anyone, keeping their eyes peeled for any sign of a blue shirt. But they found no trace of their quarry. Niall wished now that she had taken the mare, after all. He'd be able to sense where she was. Finally, even Adric admitted defeat, and they returned to Mundar.

Niall was worried, but Adric seemed more angry than anything. He stomped around the room, muttering to himself behind his beard.

"Are you sure she hasn't gone up to the garrison to betray us?" Mundar asked.

Niall shook his head. "She killed a Guard, remember. She won't risk going back."

He wished he was as certain of that as he sounded. Perna had shown herself to be pretty unpredictable. If she thought Aal wanted her to tell the Blueshirts about them, she'd do it, no matter what. The mere possibility meant they had to forget about spying at the harbour. Their only choice was to stay on the alert and hope she came back—without an escort of Guards—before it was dark enough to leave.

TWENTY-ONE

Perna

She hadn't paid any attention to the location of the harbour when Niall had brought her to Welsea, but she reasoned it must be on the lowest level of the town, so she started off by following any street that sloped downwards.

She had pulled the cap low over her forehead to aid her disguise. Head bowed, she trotted along as fast as she could, silently praying that no one would accost her. She had no right to ask anything for herself, of course, but she was trying to help all the people in Eorna. So maybe the god would protect her until she discovered something useful and told the others.

After a particularly steep section, she turned a corner and found herself on the seafront. To either side of her, flat-fronted buildings stretched out in long lines, all the same. A broad wharf lay between her and the water, its timbers grey but solid-looking. Boats were tied up to it, bobbling up and down. And there were people everywhere: unloading carts, trotting in and out of the buildings, sitting or standing on the wharf, haggling at stalls, and striding along the waterfront. She tugged the cap lower and hunched her shoulders, trying to shrink into herself.

And it wasn't just the sights. Noise battered her ears. The wind moaned, the waves slapped against the decking, cartwheels creaked and rumbled, seagulls squabbled, and everyone seemed to be shouting at the same time. As if that wasn't enough, a gust of odour hit her full in the face. She recoiled, wrinkling her nose. She'd always hated the smell of fish.

Everything was telling her she didn't belong here. She wanted to turn and flee back to the house, but she couldn't. Not until she had done what she came to do. Anything else would be cowardly. Besides, she could just imagine the look on Niall Crawley's face. And Adric's.

Trying to ignore the sick feeling in her stomach, and the certainty that everyone was watching her, she crossed the wharf to the line of vessels, looking for the ships Adric had talked about. But none of these were big enough to carry hundreds of soldiers. And she could see men hunkered down on the decks, their heads bent over coarse black nets spread across their knees. Just fishermen. Had the Bregians left the harbour already?

She shaded her eyes against the bright sunlight and peered further out, where more boats were anchored. They might be large enough, but she needed to get a better look.

Trying to breathe only through her mouth, she made her way up the wharf, weaving around the smelly market stalls, until she was as close to the nearest vessel as she could get. There was no sail on the mast, no movement on the deck, and no markings on the side. She didn't know what else to look for. Her heart sank. Why had she thought she could do this? She was only an ignorant girl, with barely any schooling and no knowledge of the world. She should never have come here. Please Aal, she could find her way back to the house before they noticed she'd gone.

"Boy!" The shout sounded from behind her as she turned away.

"You! Boy!" The man was angry now.

She lengthened her stride, not wanting to be caught up in someone else's trouble. A hand grabbed her shoulder and spun her around, drawing a gasp of pain. A red face confronted her. "Are you deaf, boy?"

An icy shock ran through her. She'd forgotten how she was dressed. He'd been shouting at her. She pulled herself together and tried to deepen her voice. "No, sir."

"I've a message to be run. A quarter penny for you when you deliver it."

Maybe if she agreed, he'd let her go. "Yes, sir."

He released her throbbing shoulder and thrust out a folded piece of paper, sealed with a blob of red wax. "For the garrison. Give it to the sergeant on the gate. He'll pay you."

She nodded and tucked the stiff paper into the inside pocket of the felted jacket.

He glared at her. "Well, dolt, what are you waiting for? Get going!" He flapped an impatient hand.

She turned and ran like a rabbit. She took several wrong turns on the way back, and was forced to retrace her steps. Finally, she found the house. She pulled open the door and almost fell inside.

They were all on their feet. Niall had his sword half out, and Mundar's staff was raised. Worst of all, Adric was pointing the crossbow at her. She squeaked, not having breath for anything else. They lowered the weapons. Mundar walked over to the fireplace and sat down.

"Where have you been?" Anger had brought the blood into Adric's face. "We looked for you for an hour." His dark, hooded eyes glared at her. Her throat closed up.

"Well?" Niall said, and for once, there was no joke in his tone.

Fear and lack of air were making her light headed. She doubled over, bracing her hands on her knees. As soon as she felt able to speak, she straightened up and confessed what she'd done.

"Of all the stupid—" Niall exploded.

Adric let out a snort and turned his back on her. A hollow ache started inside her chest.

"Did you find out anything?" Mundar asked from his seat by the fire. He didn't sound annoyed, just curious.

"No," she admitted.

He nodded. "Come and sit down. You're shivering."

Feeling like a fool, but also very cold, she took the armchair next to him. But as she lowered herself, something crackled against her ribs. She drew the paper out with numb fingers.

"What's that?" Niall asked. He drifted over, followed by Adric, who was still scowling.

She refused to answer him, fixing her eyes on Mundar's placid face. "A man gave me this message, for the garrison." She handed it to him.

He examined it. "It's addressed to the sergeant in charge."

"That's what he said."

"Why would he give it to *her*?" Adric asked rudely.

Mundar broke the seal and unfolded the paper. "Because she's wearing that cap."

Perna pulled off the knitted hat and turned it over in her hands. Plain, dark green wool, just like she'd thought. What could Mundar mean?

"There's a messenger service, down at the harbour," Mundar said absently, his head still bowed over the paper. "Boys with green caps." He looked up again, and a rare grin split his face. "Listen to this." He read the words out slowly:

"Unloading cargo midnight tonight for transport to Eorna. One hundred and eighty packages. Arriving at Eder Ford in four days. Clear the way. Roldan."

Niall's face looked as blank as Perna's brain felt, but Adric's expression was jubilant. He slapped his leg. "Aal's teeth, she's done it. I don't know how, but she's done it."

"What do you mean?" Niall asked. "It's only a note from a smuggler. We already know they're operating out of Welsea and that the Guards are helping them."

Adric shook his head. "Not just any smuggler. Mundar and I know this Roldan. He's the one we overheard earlier, one of the Bregians from the ships. The one giving the orders. And now he's told us how many soldiers they brought, and when they're leaving."

Mundar nodded. "A hundred and eighty, at midnight tonight."

"Eder Ford in four days," Niall mused. "That means they're on foot. On horseback, we can be there in two. And in Eorna a few hours later."

"We need to get going before they do," Adric said. "We don't want to run into any Guards *clearing the way*."

Mundar folded the message and slipped it inside his jerkin. "It's two days to the full moon, probably why the Bregians chose this week for their attack. They can travel at night. Enough light to see by, but less chance of being seen. The same goes for us." He paused and looked up, as if gazing through the ceiling. "It will be a cold night, but clear and dry. We should go as soon as the moon rises."

They were talking as if Perna was invisible. As if all this had nothing to do with her, even though she was the one who'd brought them the message. They wouldn't know anything at all if it wasn't for her. "You're welcome," she said loudly and clearly.

Three surprised faces turned her way. They'd forgotten all about her! A hard lump of anger lodged in her throat, leaving no room for her voice to squeeze past. She was still trying to swallow it down when Niall inclined his head towards her, smiling.

"Why, thank you, Mistress Perna. I apologise for my bad manners on your arrival."

He gave a seated bow that she was sure was meant to be some kind of joke. She ignored him and turned her gaze on Adric, waiting for an apology from him, too. A real one.

His good-humoured smile had vanished. "You were lucky," he said flatly, "that's all."

How dare he? She opened her mouth to tell him exactly what she thought of him. But that lump was still there, strangling the words before they could come out. How could she ever have been attracted to this oaf, ever imagined them becoming more than friends? Remembering that she'd stayed on at Virtue Farm purely in the hope of seeing him again, her cheeks burned.

"You certainly were," Niall said. "What are the odds that this man should pick you out of all the boys at the harbour?" He shook his head. "When the luck's with you, it's with you."

At this last piece of stupidity, Perna found her voice. "It wasn't luck." She scorched the three of them with her gaze. "It was Aal."

She rose with dignity and turned to the stairs. She would travel to Eorna with them, because that was where she was going, anyway. But as soon as she reached the city, she'd find a group of Aalden, and never have to see any of them ever again. Especially Adric Gelt.

TWENTY-TWO

Niall

They departed Welsea without encountering any trouble, and reached Hem in the dead of night. Niall wondered how Perna felt about being back here, but she'd refused to speak to any of them since her outburst this afternoon, so he didn't ask. They passed through the sleeping village and continued eastwards.

By the time the sun lifted, they'd been in the saddle for eight hours. No one objected when Niall suggested a rest stop for the horses. They left the road and followed the sound of water to a fast-flowing, tree-lined stream. Niall let the animals drink their fill in a shallow side pool before picketing them. They wouldn't wander while he was awake, but he fully intended to grab some sleep while he could.

After a quick meal from the provisions in the packs, Mundar volunteered for the first watch. The others dug out blankets and settled down on the damp leaf litter. The pale fingers of sunlight shining through the bare canopy overhead did little to ward off the chill, but Niall dropped almost instantly into a deep slumber.

He woke with Adric looming over him, shaking his shoulder. "You said you wanted to take a watch."

He had said that. He regretted it now, but there was nothing for it. He stood, and Adric settled down in his place.

The sun was riding in a cloudless sky, but there was still a briskness in the air. Keeping a thread of attention on the dozing horses, Niall knelt at the pool and scooped icy water into his cupped hands. He drank enough to set his throat aching, then headed further along the bank in an effort to get his blood pumping, rubbing his hands dry on the coarse brown wool of his borrowed trousers.

It felt odd to be wearing anything but black. He'd taken to it originally as a sort of emblem against his father, a defiant mourning of all he'd lost. Not just his title and inheritance, but his family, his home, his place in the world. But the bitter choice had stood him in good stead in the years that followed.

Putting the skills he'd practised since childhood to profitable use, he'd travelled Algarth as a hired sword, defending baggage wagons and carriages, private residences and warehouses. People remembered the man in black, and passed on stories of his prowess, ensuring a steady stream of employment. He'd found he enjoyed the notoriety as much as the varied work. The unique, narrow lines of facial hair had been a later touch of showmanship, deliberately designed to make him even more recognisable. That his father would have abhorred the look—*a full beard is the mark of a true man, my son*—had been a bonus.

Now, of course, both hair and clothing had ceased being any kind of statement. They simply made him feel like himself. He'd be glad to resume his blacks tomorrow, and greet them as the old friends they were.

About twenty spans upstream, he came upon a wide, planked bridge. More trees rose on the far side of the crossing. But above them soared a steep, scrubby hill, bristling with boulders. A patch of shadow high up caught his attention. Probably the mouth of a cave, a big one. He was idly trying to work out just how large it might be when he noticed a veil of smoke rising in front of it. There was a ledge up there, and someone had lit a fire.

He'd heard of bandits making use of caves. He moved back under the cover of the trees and sank into a crouch. No sense in taking chances. At the first sign of anyone spotting him, he'd wake the others and get them moving.

He'd been watching for a long time, seeing nothing new, and was thinking of heading back, when two figures emerged from the cave. He couldn't make out many details at this distance. But one was shorter than the other, and the sunlight glinted off its red hair. A child, he thought, possibly a boy. The taller one was wearing a dress. Niall froze as she suddenly pointed her arm straight down at him.

He cursed himself for not leaving as soon as he'd spotted the smoke. He couldn't risk moving now. It seemed an eternity before the woman turned and vanished inside again, followed by the child. Niall sprinted back to the others with the news that they weren't alone. Minutes later, they were packed and on their way.

After that, they alternately walked and trotted the horses, stopping only for another quick bite around noon. They passed the occasional traveller, but no one spared them more than a casual glance. The hours dragged until they rounded the last bend and saw the rays of the setting sun gleaming on the whitewashed cottage at Eder Ford. It was owned by the garrison, kept clean and stocked for Warrant Guards needing to break their journey to Eorna. Adric and Mundar donned their blue shirts before approaching, but there was no need. Both house and stable were empty.

Niall settled the horses while Adric brought in wood for the fire. No one seemed inclined to talk, or to bother cooking anything. They ate bread and cold salted mutton from the pantry, then went to bed.

Staring up into the darkness, Niall considered his plans for tomorrow. This close to the city, he felt justified in leaving Perna with Adric and Mundar and setting out again in search of Cahira. If only he had a clue where to start. Maybe fresh inspiration would come in the morning.

He wished he had a way to tell her that he'd found Adric, or rather, that Adric had found him. But she was probably many reaches away, either with the woman Fadra or safely back home. It was maddening not to know for sure, but at least she was unlikely to be anywhere near Eorna, and that was a good thing. In a few short days, the city was about to become a very dangerous place.

TWENTY-THREE

Cahira

Ferdy was progressing quickly. In fact, Cahira felt a twinge of concern that he might outstrip her. Not that she was jealous, she assured herself. It was just that she wouldn't be able to help him anymore.

He'd already added another voice, making three altogether, and he seemed to be handling them with no trouble. His images had improved, too. They weren't as solid as hers, but getting closer all the time. Strangely, though, they were still static.

"Why don't you let the singing take care of itself for now," she suggested. "Just think about the images. And try not to look at them."

He dropped his eyes guiltily. His voice faltered to a stop. For some reason, he found the picture-making the hardest part, whereas for Cahira it flowed naturally from the singing. She tried again. "See if you can imagine the scene in your mind."

The blank stare told her she wasn't getting through to him. She fumbled to explain something she'd never had to think about before. "You know when you're remembering someone and their face pops into your head?"

Ferdy's own face showed only confusion, as if she was speaking a foreign language.

Cahira raked her fingers through her hair, trying to figure out what was wrong. It was such a simple thing, and yet she couldn't seem to make him understand. A change of scene might help, she thought in desperation. "Let's get out of here. Some fresh air will do us both good."

A few minutes later they stood near the smouldering fire on the ledge outside the entrance cave. The sky was the unbroken blue of a forget-me-not, the sun as pale and yellow as a primrose. *Spring colours on an autumn day*, Cahira thought. The clear light played on the patchwork of farmland and forest spread out below her. She gazed at the far hills and felt her hands unclench. Tipping her head back, she let herself enjoy the touch of the breeze on her face for a few moments. Right now, anything seemed possible, even teaching Ferdy to make moving images. But how?

Confidence, she thought suddenly. A good teacher had confidence in themselves. Fadra certainly did. Cahira had been too timid with her own pupil. She could fix that.

The student in question was kicking half-heartedly at a partly buried rock. Cahira pointed to the stream, flowing sedately between its banks again. "Look down there," she instructed firmly.

He stopped kicking and obeyed her.

"Now, pick a tree."

"Okay."

"Look closely at it. Memorise what you see. The colour and texture of the trunk, the angles of the branches, how tall it is, how wide. Everything."

She gave him a minute, idly watching the water as she waited. Something odd about the undergrowth on the far side of the bridge caught her eye. Was someone crouched down there? She peered harder, but couldn't tell if she was seeing brown clothing, the fur of an animal, or just a trick of light and shadow. It didn't matter; they had work to do. She turned back to Ferdy's absorbed face. "Got it?"

"I suppose."

She ignored the uncertainty. "Good. Shut your eyes and think about the tree."

His eyelids closed.

"Can you see it?"

"You said to shut my eyes."

"You don't need your eyes. Look at the memory of it in your head."

His eyelids snapped open. He frowned darkly at her. "You're not making sense." There was a touch of bad temper in his voice, the closest she had heard him come to anger. All her assurance fled.

"Never mind," she said quickly. "It's too cold to stay out here, anyway."

She almost ran inside the cave, not even checking that he was following. The sour taste of failure propelled her all the way to Fadra's study. One look at her face, and Fadra waved her in. "What's wrong?"

"I'm a terrible teacher. Ferdy needs someone better." She threw herself into an armchair.

Fadra seated herself opposite and cocked her head to the side. Her long grey hair was caught back with a thong today, meaning she'd been brewing medicines. Cahira had disturbed her at her work.

"I'm sorry. You're busy."

"It was time for a break, anyway. So, what's all this? I thought you and Ferdy were making progress."

Cahira raked her fingers across her scalp. "I thought so too. He has much better control over his voices now. But I can't seem to find a way to help him with the images."

"Perhaps you're trying to move too fast. You've only been working together for a few days."

"He has so much potential."

"Yes, but he's still very young. He probably needs a break. Spend a day apart and you'll both come back to the problem with clear minds."

It was a tempting thought. Ferdy was a nice boy, but the more time she spent with him, the less she had for working on her own skal. And she really wasn't ready to face him yet. "All right."

"Good. I'm glad you came, because there's something else I wanted to talk to you about." Fadra leaned forward. "You made great progress in our last session."

Cahira nodded. It was true. She'd sipped the same infusion, and it had freed her gift again. She'd varied the brightness of the lightning almost without thinking, sending it wherever she wished. And the hair-raising sound had proved as malleable to her will as any other melody. If she ever confronted another bear, she'd be the one in control, not the song. It was a good feeling. At least she wasn't failing at this.

"I think you're ready for the next step."

Intrigued, Cahira followed the Healer through the door in the back wall into a long, straight hallway with curtained openings along both sides. At the far end, another thick wooden portal blocked their way, black with age and seamed with cracks.

Time had worn the once-intricate carvings almost to illegibility, but in places Cahira could just make out the figures of people and animals, intertwined with a flowing ribbon of text. But even in the few sections where the angular shapes of the letters stood out clearly, she couldn't decipher the meaning. Perhaps it was Old Algarthian. She'd learned a little about the ancient language at the Academy, but hadn't been taught to read it.

Fadra took a heavy iron key from her pocket and fitted it into the keyhole. Given the age of the door, Cahira expected the lock to grate, but the key turned smoothly, with nothing but a soft click. Fadra pushed the door open and they entered a large cavern. Cahira stopped in surprise, taking a few moments to interpret what she was seeing.

The long, rectangular room was cool, almost cold. And it was dim, despite the lantern—many times larger than the ones in Fadra's study—suspended on chains from the high roof. The gigantic bronze bowl was pierced by hundreds, perhaps thousands, of tiny holes, arranged in swirling patterns. From each hole, a needle-fine ray of light laced through the darkened chamber, to splash a small pool of gold on wall or floor. Together, they revealed glimpses of something extraordinary.

Marching around three walls was an enormous tapestry, worked in rich, sombre colours: purple, deep green, inky blue, rust. The design was hard to make out in the confusing mosaic of light and shade created by the lantern. At one moment Cahira felt she was looking at a detail of a forest scene, with ferns below and many-branched trees above, but then her perception changed, and it seemed more like a bed of seaweed, its fronds waving beneath the ocean. Or were they green tentacles, belonging to a colossal sea creature? It was impossible to be sure. It might not be a picture at all, but merely an abstract pattern that her brain insisted on assigning meaning to.

One thing she was certain of: the lamp and the tapestry were the work of master craftspeople. Not even in the manor houses of her parents' wealthiest friends had Cahira seen objects of such quality. Each one must have taken years to complete, even by a highly skalled artisan. To find them here, hidden deep in the cave system, temporarily took her breath away. And why had Fadra shrouded them in the dark like this? They deserved to be appreciated in the full light of day.

"Welcome to my sanctuary."

Cahira found her voice. "How did they get here?"

"I brought them with me, on a ship."

Cahira's admiration for the Healer increased. Fadra must be incredibly rich. She could have had a mansion in the city, servants, carriages, fine clothes, anything she wanted. She could have moved in the highest level of society. And yet she chose to live simply, doing her chosen work, with this chamber of treasures her only personal indulgence.

"Come and sit with me."

Cahira hadn't even noticed the long table of polished timber near the centre of the cavern, surrounded by eight high-backed chairs. The surface was bare except for a glass flask, half-filled with clear liquid, and a plain wooden cup.

When they were seated, Fadra leaned across the table and took Cahira's hands in hers. "This is a place of clarity and power. Close your eyes. Do you feel it?"

Perhaps it was only the influence of Fadra's words, but Cahira did feel something. A kind of excitement, and yet a calmness at the same time. Keeping her eyes shut, she nodded.

Fadra let go of her hands. "You have been using the green infusion. You know the effect it has, how it relaxes you and helps your talent to flow freely." Cahira heard liquid pouring. "This elixir is different. It brings mental clarity and insight." She wrapped Cahira's fingers around the cup. "You might find it a little bitter. It's best if you drink it straight down."

Cahira lifted the cup to her nose and sniffed, but detected nothing. Fadra misunderstood her hesitation. "It's safe, I promise you."

She sounded hurt, and remorse filled Cahira. She put the cup to her lips and drank. There were only a few spoonfuls of liquid and she finished it in a couple of swallows. It was indeed bitter, and yet not exactly unpleasant. It had a sort of pleasing astringency.

"Keep your eyes closed and clear your mind of any thought or expectation."

Cahira tried, but found herself constantly checking to see if she felt any different. Perhaps the elixir wasn't going to work on her. She still hadn't noticed any change when Fadra broke the silence.

"Now imagine yourself looking up into a clear blue sky. No clouds, just pure blue."

Cahira pictured the bluest sky she could think of. Deep, cornflower blue, rather than forget-me-not.

"Push your gaze higher. Past the blue and into the blackness."

Feeling a little like Ferdy, Cahira confessed, "I don't see any black."

"The sky as it appears at night is always there, Cahira, even in the day time. It is simply hidden from us by the glaring light of the sun. The stars and the dark spaces between, they lie beyond. Look for them. Reach for them."

Cahira didn't really understand, but she would take Fadra's word for it and try. And there it was, a hint of darkness hovering on the edge of the blue. Exhilarated, she willed herself to push into it. Soon, a field of ebony surrounded her, pierced by a thousand twinkling points of light. It was beautiful.

"Come further. Beyond the stars."

The sparkling motes lengthened to streaks of white. They streamed past, faster and faster, thinning out as they went. Finally, the last remnant was left behind. Only the blackness remained, perfect in its own way. Unblemished. Pristine.

"You see it now."

"Yes."

She felt completely calm and yet alert. She wanted nothing, strove for nothing, was content just to be.

After an age, she sensed they weren't alone. Another mind was here: cool, curious. A question drifted towards her:

Who are you?

Cahira, she thought.

I have been waiting for you.

She couldn't have said whether the words had been spoken aloud, or written inside her head for her to read, or sent some other way. She felt no pressure to reply. She merely drifted in the darkness, hoping for more.

Your talent is strong. Few can reach out so easily.

A sweet feeling of approval flooded her. It was the way she felt when Fadra praised her, but magnified a hundred times.

What is your desire?

That was easy. *To know that Adric and Niall are safe.*

They will be.

A thrill ran through her.

But you must do your part.

Anything.

Do not fear your power. Embrace it.

She blinked, and was abruptly back in the lamplit room, staring across the table at Fadra. The Healer patted her hand. "You did well. I knew you would."

"Who was that?"

"For now, you can call it the Unity. The mind of all."

"All the people?"

"Not just people. Everything. The stars, the animals, even these rocks that surround us. We are all parts of a greater whole. It has another name, which you will learn in time."

Cahira had a hundred questions, but a wave of exhaustion abruptly washed through her.

As usual, Fadra sensed her mood. "You should eat now. And get some rest. You made exceptional progress today."

"Can I come back here?"

"Anytime you like. But eventually, you won't need this room. You will be able to contact the Unity wherever you are."

The noon bell rang as Cahira stepped into the passageway. She must have been in there for almost two hours. It had seemed only minutes. Despite what Fadra had said, she wasn't hungry, just tired. She made her way to her room and lay down.

She woke with a raging hunger and no idea how long she'd slept. Although the dining cavern was empty, platters of roasted meat and vegetables remained on the sideboard. They were cold, but Cahira was too starving to be picky.

She'd only been eating for a few minutes when three more late-comers arrived: two men and a woman. They piled their plates high and came over to where she was sitting.

"Mind if we join you?" the dark-haired man asked. "These two are Jon and Nattie, and I'm Aidan."

So this was the Metal Shaper Ferdy had told her about. "Not at all," she said truthfully. "I could do with the company. My name's Cahira."

"Oh, we know." The woman plumped herself onto a chair. "I'm Nattie, in case you didn't guess."

She spoke as though she couldn't get the words out fast enough. She was small, with skin the colour of bronze, eyes a shade darker, and short black hair attractively shaped to her head.

The man introduced as Jon merely nodded to her as he sat down. He had very fair skin and close-cropped snowy hair.

"I've been admiring your work out in the passage," Cahira said to Aidan.

"The candle holders? Mere trifles," he said, waving a hand in the air. "You should see—"

"Stop boasting, Aidan," Nattie said. "We all know how talented you are."

Aidan grinned and began eating with gusto.

Cahira cast around for something else to say. She was going to be part of this community for a while, and it was time she got to know some of them. Finally, she fell back on that tired old standby, the weather. "It's nice and warm in here. When I went outside it was freezing."

"It's the caves," Aidan said. "The further in you go, the more stable the temperature is. Winter or summer, it doesn't make much difference."

"It's why Fadra settled here when she came to Algarth," put in Nattie. "She's from Mallorna, you know. Nothing up there but snow and ice. She says she can't stand the heat here in summer."

When Fadra had said she'd come on a ship, Cahira had assumed the Healer was from somewhere in Bregia, just across the Windras Strait. Mallorna was much further north, on the far side of the Bregian Mountains. Cahira had never met anyone from there.

"Why did she come all this way?"

Nattie shrugged. "She doesn't like to talk about it. But I think something bad happened to her and she had to get away. All she'll say is she felt like a change of scenery, so she went to the nearest port and got on the first ship that agreed to take her on board. It was an Algarthan trader, sailing home to Eorna."

Now that the ice had been broken, the conversation flowed easily. Nattie seemed especially friendly, asking about Cahira's own background and what had brought her to the caves. Cahira kept her explanation simple, saying only that Fadra had been looking after her injured friend, and that they'd been separated when bandits attacked them on the road. Nattie and Aidan made sympathetic noises.

"It's a pity you couldn't manage to bring your friend here," Nattie said. "Fadra's one of the best Healers I've ever seen."

"I know," Cahira said. "She showed me her papers and the medicines she's working on."

"And that's not all," Nattie said. "She's helping us with our skals. And that's a big job. There are nearly twenty of us now."

"More like thirteen," Aidan said. "You always exaggerate, Nat."

Nattie tossed her dark head. "I'm sure it's closer to twenty." She started counting rapidly on her fingers. "The three of us, and Elise, and

Ferdy, and that new one, the Wood Shaper, what's his name, and now you, Cahira, and Darin—oh no that's right, he left, didn't he, I never did find out why—"

"It doesn't matter," Aidan interrupted. "No, pipe down, Nat. Darin was an idiot, afraid of his own shadow, even if he was good with stone. We're better off without a coward like him." He turned to Cahira. "Fadra says the only limits to what we can achieve are the ones we invent for ourselves."

John raised his head from his plate for the first time. Serious grey eyes met hers. "Fadra is a fine and visionary leader. You should trust her." He went right back to eating before Cahira could think of a reply. There was a slightly awkward pause.

Nattie had been looking sulky ever since Aidan had interrupted her. Hoping to restore the good mood of the conversation, Cahira turned to her. "What's your skal, Nattie?"

She brightened up immediately and rushed into speech. "Oh, I'm a Charm Shaper. When I came here, I could only do minor charms, but I'm sure I'm up to at least Level Three now and Fadra says I'll go even further. But Jon's the rare one. He's a Mind Wender."

Jon shot her a disapproving look from under his pale brows. Cahira wasn't surprised he was uncomfortable with his skal being discussed. Mind Wenders could only persuade, not control, but people were naturally wary of anyone who could influence their thoughts to any degree. And sometimes the persuasion was very effective: look at all the damage Chairman Tarn had done before he'd been found out and stopped. But Cahira resolved to give Jon the benefit of the doubt. After all, no one chose what skals they received. It was what they did with them that counted.

And these three all had impressive skals. Metal Shaping was common enough, but the skill Aidan displayed was not. As for Nattie and Jon, few Charm Shapers reached Level Three, and Mind Wending of any kind was rare. And then there was Ferdy. If the rest of the community were anything like the ones Cahira had met so far, Fadra was leading an amazingly talented group. Perhaps Aidan was right, and there really were no limits. It was an exciting thought.

Jon finished his meal, excused himself quietly, and left, followed not long after by the other two. Cahira sat on alone, disinclined to move. Her body felt heavy but also somehow empty, despite the large meal. The experience in Fadra's sanctuary had taken a lot out of her, it seemed. But it had also given her food for thought, as had the conversation over lunch.

The voice—the Unity—had said she should stop being afraid of her skal. Until now, even under Fadra's instruction, she'd kept a tight rein on it. She'd been scared that if she let it loose, like she had against the bear, she wouldn't be able to control it. But her new friends seemed to have complete confidence in Fadra's training, and they should know. Besides, the Unity had also told her she had to become stronger if she wanted to help Adric and Niall.

So, no more fear. From now on, she'd trust Fadra and stop putting limits on herself. And when she found her family again, she'd be powerful enough to keep them safe.

Returning to her room, she pulled aside the door curtain and stopped dead, her brain refusing to register for a moment what she was seeing. She'd tidied up before she'd left this morning. She'd even swept the floor. But while she'd been away, someone had tipped rubbish all over it. Torn paper, broken candles, shards of pottery. And food scraps—crusts of mouldy bread, curled brown vegetable peelings, rotten fruit.

Cahira retreated a step, her heart hammering, her eyes darting into every shadowed corner. But whoever had done this was gone. Her gaze went to the small desk, where she'd been trying without success to write a new song. The pen and parchment were there, just as she'd left them.

The bed looked undisturbed too. She picked her way through the garbage and sank down. Who would do something like this to her, and why? She hadn't argued with anyone, had made no enemies as far as she knew. But this spoke of hatred, contempt. Abruptly, nausea rolled in her stomach. Pressing a hand to her mouth, she ran.

She was halfway along the passage when Elise rounded the corner, her expression quickly shifting to concern. "Cahira! Are you all right?"

Cahira shook her head and pushed past, not caring if she was being rude.

She pelted through the entrance cave, out into the low afternoon light. She drew in gulps of air, expelled them in white clouds. Her stomach settled, but her eyes filled and overflowed. As she stood there sobbing, shame seeped through her. *Look at me*, she thought, *crying like a schoolgirl because someone doesn't like me*. She had to be stronger than this.

Then, from somewhere deep inside, reassurance came: *You are stronger than this*. She clung to the declaration like a lifeline. She gulped and sniffed, wiped the tears on her sleeve, and went back.

She had another moment of weakness when she saw her room again, but she pushed it down and got to work. As she cleared out the mess, she wracked her brain for a clue to the culprit. The only person she could think of was Ferdy. She had pushed him hard this morning, and he'd failed. He hadn't been happy with her about that. Dirtying her room was exactly the sort of thing a child might do in a fit of spite, and the boy was barely out of childhood.

She heaved a sigh of relief. Ferdy wasn't an enemy or a threat. He probably regretted his action already. She wouldn't mention it to him, or to anyone else. She didn't want them to think she couldn't take care of herself.

TWENTY-FOUR

Niall

When Niall entered the main room of the cottage next morning, dressed comfortably in his blacks, he found all three of his companions silent and busy. Adric was laying fresh wood in the fireplace. Perna stood at the table with her head down, slicing bread and cold bacon. Mundar sat opposite her. He was writing in a book. Curious, Niall stepped closer.

The big man was scribing word after word onto the smooth, cream paper, stopping only to dip the pen into the ink bottle.

"What are you writing?"

Mundar's hand didn't even pause. "A journal. I write so that when I die, my words will live on. This page is an account of everything we discovered at Welsea."

"Huh." Niall couldn't think of what else to say.

Mundar completed another steady line, blotted his work carefully, and closed the book. Its thick leather cover was the colour of mahogany, tooled with a design that reminded Niall of ocean waves. The quality of the workmanship, together with the paper, told him that the journal had been expensive. It seemed a strange possession for a Warrant Guard.

Mundar tied a leather thong around the book, wiped his pen on a piece of rag, and capped the ink bottle. He returned pen, bottle, rag, and book to his pack. Every movement was as deliberate and precise as his handwriting. Size and strength had led Niall to expect a certain clumsiness, even a lack of intelligence, in the big Guard. That had been stupid, and Niall wasn't used to feeling stupid. Mundar's dark eyes met his, and a faint smile played around his mouth, as if he could read Niall's thoughts, and was amused by them.

No one seemed inclined to talk as they packed and saddled the horses. They splashed across the Ford and headed north. Sometime in the night, Niall had decided to go to Eorna with the others. Searching for Cahira was pointless when he had no clue where to start. He'd ridden the entire length of road between the farm and Welsea, without finding Fadra's house. Doing it again would serve no purpose. The only other place he could think of was her parents' estate south of Edervale, and if she was there, she was already safe and didn't need him.

Eorna, on the other hand, might need him badly in the next few days. A strong Beast Speaker could be very useful to the defence of the city. Besides, Logen Rush was Chairman of the Council now, and Logen was his friend, had been for years. His closest friend, except for Cahira. It would be good to see him again.

They rode along the edge of the Greenwood Forest, stretching many reaches south and east from here. Deep in those trees was the spot where Sara, the foreign Greenhaelan, had tackled the Blight. Tarn had been defeated in there, too, and his corruption exposed. Now, less than half a year later, Algarth was in danger again, not from disease or political machinations, but actual armies intent on conquest. The island hadn't faced conflict on this scale since the days of Tana Lossil, the last King.

According to legend, King Tana had won his war by Shaping a Gateway to another world. There, he'd obtained a powerful stone that made his castle invulnerable to attack. The invaders had been forced to lift their siege and retreat.

Sara, a descendant of the King, was a Gate Shaper, too. That might be very useful in the battle preparations. She could transport people and supplies much faster than a horse-drawn cart. She might even be able to bring more Warrant Guards to the city before it was attacked. If Logen or Oren hadn't already thought of sending her a message, Niall would suggest it when he reached the garrison.

Thoughts of Sara had reminded him of the others of their company back then, and he wondered how they were faring. Fin, Tulley's gentle wife, had passed away peacefully a few weeks after they'd all returned to Eorna, but Tulley, Mena, and young Kelan were still living in the city. Mena had her Healing practice, and Kelan must have started Charm Shaping classes at the Academy by now.

He should send word to the three of them to leave as soon as possible. Tulley would refuse, of course—the stocky Metal Shaper had never run away from a fight in his life—but Mena and Kelan at least should go. Although, given Kelan's stubborn refusal to stay out of danger, that was probably a lost cause, too.

As the horses ate up the reaches to the city, Niall's mood turned melancholy. Things were about to change, perhaps forever. For the first time, he wondered if he'd ever see these former companions again.

TWENTY-FIVE

Cahira

Ferdy seemed the same as always when they met at breakfast the next morning. Cahira couldn't detect any sign of guilt in that open face. She doubted now that he'd been the one who'd dirtied her room. She gave him the news that they were taking a break from their lessons, the way Fadra had advised. He looked disappointed, but she wasn't tempted to relent. She needed some time for herself.

She ate quickly and hurried to the study. Fadra ushered her into the sanctuary and left her, saying she had work that needed attention. That was fine by Cahira. The elixir waited on the table, and she knew what to do.

She glided without effort into the blackness and the presence of the Unity. With its encouragement, she sang with even greater freedom. Jagged light played around her, thunder crashed, and none of it touched her. She wondered why she had ever been afraid of this. It was her talent, to be used as she pleased.

Delighted with her success, she began to experiment. In place of the lightning, bright birds soared across the sanctuary. They dipped and wove around the hanging lights, their jewel colours rivalling the tapestries. She laughed in delight.

Concentrate. It is the songs of power you need.

It had the flavour of a rebuke. Cahira flushed. She was wasting time. She dismissed the frivolous birds and called the lightning once more.

On the walk back to her quarters, she felt energised and full of purpose. Even so, she couldn't suppress a slight thrill of apprehension as she approached the door curtain. But her fear was baseless: the room was just as she'd left it.

As she undressed for bed that night, she lifted the stone from her pocket and cradled it briefly in her palm. It felt cold, and somehow heavier than usual. She'd been sleeping with it under her pillow, but she turned to the desk and tucked it away in the little drawer. Memories of Bram, and the grief they brought with them, only made her vulnerable. That was the last thing she needed.

She woke in darkness, some instinct warning her she wasn't alone. Being careful not to move or make a sound, she strained her eyes in an attempt to pierce the blackness. It was no good. The night was a solid wall, repelling her vision.

She held her breath and listened. Nothing for a few beats. Then her ears picked up a tiny scrape from the corner nearest the doorway. She stiffened, blind eyes swivelling in that direction. She hadn't imagined it; someone was in here with her. Her heart knocked against her ribs, but she made herself breathe normally, as if still asleep. Another scrape, a little louder, from the same spot. What if they had a weapon?

You have one, too. Of course, she did. She could light this room up in a few seconds, expose the intruder, even blind them if necessary. But as soon as she began to sing, they would hear, and they might reach her before her skal affected them too badly to act. She wished she knew if they were armed.

Was that the scuff of a footstep? Someone could be moving towards her right now. She couldn't afford to hesitate any longer. Willing the power to come quickly, she let out a single low note. The room filled with white light. The blackness returned an instant later, but the lone flash had been enough to show Cahira that she was alone. The interloper had fled.

She felt her way to the little desk and lit a candle. The surface looked undisturbed, papers and pen just as she'd left them. What had the trespasser been up to over here? She slid the drawer open, immediately recognising the scrape she'd heard. She looked inside, then brought the light closer and stirred the contents to be sure she hadn't missed it. But there was no mistake. The sky stone was gone.

She set the candle down with a shaking hand and balled her fists. The token was useless to anyone but her. The only reason to take it was spite, the same motive for throwing rubbish all over her floor. This wasn't Ferdy's work. He was impulsive, but not a sneak. He wouldn't creep around in the night and steal from her. Someone else had done this. Someone who wanted to cause her pain. They had no right. She hadn't harmed a single person here.

She sat at the desk and tried to think past the anger. Despite the darkness, the thief had gone straight to what they wanted. If they'd just opened the drawer at random, there would have been nothing in the feel of the small piece of rock to make them think it was of any value to her. Stealing the rolled song parchments would have made more sense. The fact she was a singer was well known by now, but she'd spoken to hardly anyone about the sky stone.

Fadra knew, but Cahira couldn't believe the community leader would stoop to burglary. If Fadra wanted to hurt her—and why should she—there were easier ways to do it. She held enough authority to make Cahira's life very unpleasant, without stealing from her.

The most likely explanation was that someone had overheard her telling Fadra about the stone. The conversation had taken place in the dining hall, and Cahira hadn't been whispering. She couldn't remember who else had been there that day. It could be anyone.

Tears threatened, but this time she refused to let them come. Crying wouldn't help. She needed a plan. She briefly considered telling Fadra, but rejected the idea. She didn't need anyone's help. She'd find out who was doing this to her and deal with them on her own.

She went back to bed, but sleep wouldn't come. She tossed and turned, nursing her rage. Half out of her mind and ready to tear her hair, she finally heard what she'd been waiting for: the clanging of the breakfast bell. She leapt up and ran along the empty passages to the dining hall.

The first to arrive, she filled a plate with steaming food she had no interest in eating. As she picked at it, she eyed each new diner, assessing if they could be the one. No one stood out. Joining briefly in a few conversations, she used the talk as an excuse to scan faces for a hint of malice, but found none. Afterwards, she lingered in the main hallway, greeting everyone she saw, looking for signs of guilt. She caught some surprised looks at her sudden sociability, but that was all.

"Cahira! I haven't seen you for a few days. How are you?"

Elise had come up behind her while she'd been distracted by yet another fruitless conversation. Cahira assured the younger woman that she was well. Elise took her by the arm in the quick, impulsive way she had, the movement setting her high ponytail swinging. "Come to my room for a cup of tea? Fadra gave me some of her special blend."

After a moment's thought, Cahira accepted the invitation. She didn't care about the tea, but as Fadra's assistant Elise went everywhere and knew everyone. She might be able to help.

Over steaming cups, Cahira explained. Elise's blue eyes widened. "But that's serious. Someone in your room at night? Stealing from you? You have to tell Fadra."

Cahira shook her head. "I just want to find out who it was and get my stone back." Not quite true—she also intended to teach the thief a lesson they wouldn't forget—but Elise didn't need to know that.

"It's not going to be easy, with the stone being so small," Elise mused. "It could be hidden anywhere. How will we find it?"

Cahira blinked. Why hadn't she thought of this approach before? She'd been wasting time trying to identify the thief. She could pinpoint the stone instead, and then she'd know who'd done this to her.

"It doesn't matter if it's hidden. It's Charmed to respond to my singing."

Elise frowned. "What do you mean? Charmed how?"

"If it's nearby, it glows when I sing."

Elise's birdlike features smoothed out. "That's amazing. I've never owned anything Charmed." She took a sip of tea. "So, you're just going to start singing all over the place and hope it's somewhere out in the open so you can see it?"

Cahira shook her head again. "When it's glowing, and I'm close to it, I can picture it in my mind, whether it's visible to others or not. That's part of the Charm on it."

The look of concern had returned to Elise's face. "I don't know, Cahira. It sounds dangerous to me. I mean, what if you find it in someone's room, and they catch you? They might hurt you to keep you quiet."

"I can defend myself against a petty thief." She bent her head and sipped her own tea, her thoughts on exactly how she would do that.

"I guess you can. I heard about the bear." Elise gave an odd little laugh. "And Fadra's been teaching you, hasn't she? In the sanctuary."

The sudden hard note in the younger woman's voice alerted Cahira. She looked up sharply. Elise was on her feet, clutching the heavy teapot in both hands. In a fluid movement, she drew it back and swung. Cahira ducked. The vessel flew over her head, close enough that the breeze from its passing brushed her hair.

The momentum of the failed attack sent Elise sprawling across the table, still grasping the teapot. Before she could recover, Cahira shoved her own seat back and stood, shaking with rage. First, the weapon. She called the thunder, just the right pitch. The pot shattered in Elise's grip. Crying out in pain, the girl dropped the fragments and leapt up.

Her eyes blazed at Cahira, all pretence of friendliness gone. "You think you're so *special.*" The word dripped with venom. "So talented, with your wonderful skal. I've been here two years, serving her. Learning from her. But since you came, she barely looks at me. Messing up your room and taking your stupid stone was nothing. You've stolen the most important person in the world from me. *You're* the thief."

Elise's pretty face had changed out of all recognition. Eyes wild, teeth bared, she advanced around the table with her fingers curled like claws, as if she intended to rip out Cahira's throat. Lines of blood crisscrossed her hands where the sharp edges of pottery had cut into them, and thin scarlet trails ran down her wrists. She looked insane. "I'm the one who helped her with all her research," she spat. "*Me!* And I've never been allowed in the sanctuary, not *once.*"

Cahira backed up a few steps. Then she stopped, remembering herself. Crazy or not, Elise was no threat to her. Barely drawing breath, she expelled a short, high note. The compact bolt of lightning flashed into existence in front of the angry, congested face, exactly where Cahira had planned. Elise staggered back with a shriek. Elation at her success filled Cahira. She fired a second shot, just as clean and precise. The girl wailed again, lifting bloodied hands to cover her eyes. There was no need for Cahira to do any more. Blinded and defeated, her enemy sank to the floor, moaning softly.

Ignoring her, Cahira sent out the three notes that would find the stone. It had been tossed into a corner among a heap of dirty clothes. She strode over and dug it out. Straightening up, she addressed the pathetic bundle whimpering on the floor. "Be thankful I stopped with your eyes. If you try anything else against me, I'll use my *wonderful skal*, as you called it, to finish the job."

Satisfied, she tucked the stone into her pocket and left.

Fadra wasn't in her study, but the sanctuary door stood open in invitation. Cahira sat down in the dimly lit cavern and poured herself a generous measure of elixir. She got up again and paced while she waited for it to take effect, examining the tapestries and fingering the stone through the fabric of her dress.

I am here.

She'd made contact even faster this time, almost without effort. Perhaps she no longer needed the sanctuary or the liquid. Fadra had said she wouldn't always. But the familiar surroundings were reassuring. And for now, she wanted that. *No*, she thought sharply, *I don't need reassurance. I'm not so weak.* Guidance, that was more like it.

She spoke aloud, finding it easier to organise her thoughts that way. "Someone has been acting against me."

You have dealt with them.

"Yes, but—"

You cannot afford to be distracted by such things.

"But is there anyone else I should be wary of?" The thought had been bothering her ever since Elise revealed herself. What if she was surrounded by enemies, trying to bring her down, delay her, weaken her?

None can harm you.

"But what if—"

You are stronger than this.

Cahira opened her mouth to reply, then stopped. She'd experienced those words before, flavoured with exactly that tone. But not in here. She'd been crying on the ledge outside the entrance cave, and then the assurance had come. She had believed it was her own thought, but now— "Was that you, too?"

It was.

"You've already been speaking to me outside this room?"

Your talent is exceptional. It has made our connection strong from the first. You will carry me with you when you go.

Her doubts fled. Everything would be all right. She'd leave the caves and find Niall and Adric, and she'd be strong enough to help them, no matter what trouble they were in. With this new ally, she couldn't fail. A stray thought skittered annoyingly, like a mouse scrabbling in the corner. Only a small thing, but it sowed a seed of doubt.

"Why couldn't I teach Ferdy? His images—"

He is weak. Take control.

Of course! She'd been wasting time trying to teach the boy something he wasn't capable of. She knew what to do.

Cahira pulled back the curtain, setting the rings rattling. Ferdy lifted his head from the pillow and sat up with a grin. "Are we having a lesson today?"

He sounded like a child who'd been offered an unexpected treat. Why hadn't he been practising on his own, if he was so keen about strengthening his skal? Instead, he was just lazing around in bed. The Unity was right: the boy was weak. But she could fix that.

In the singing cave, she fidgeted while he lit the candles, then spoke firmly. "No scales today. Let's hear you sing something more challenging. The River Song. Three voices, verses and chorus."

"Should I try the images?" He sounded uncertain.

"No, just the voices. And whatever happens, keep singing."

She let him complete the first verse before doing anything herself. He sang it competently enough. A faint, blurred image of a waterfall formed above him. She concentrated on it, not making a sound herself, but holding the words and notes in her mind. The image sharpened. Even though he wasn't looking at it, Ferdy's voice faltered slightly.

"Keep going," she snapped, irritated that she had to tell him again.

He flushed and pulled himself together. Better. He was singing strongly now; she could work with this. She brought the image into greater focus, added detail. But it was still static.

What should I do? she silently asked the Unity.

The answer came immediately. **Draw on his power. Like this.**

An indescribable sensation—the closest she could come was that it felt like drinking from a stream of sparkling light—and then new energy flowed through her. She concentrated on the image once more, willing it to move.

Above Ferdy's head, white spray flew as the waterfall cascaded into its pool, sending foam-topped waves rippling outwards. No image of her creation had ever looked more vibrant, more real. It was like one of her dreams. She could hardly wait to see the rest of the song. But then her ears detected a change. Ferdy's voice was trailing away again.

"Keep singing!"

Instead, he stopped completely. The waterfall vanished. Cahira flicked her gaze to the boy, ready to rebuke him. Something was wrong with his face. It was frozen in a grimace, as fixed as a mask. His eyes had rolled up, leaving only the whites visible.

She took a step towards him, but he was already falling backward. Before she could reach him, he hit the cave floor hard, limbs splaying out. He lay like a puppet whose strings had been cut, not uttering a sound. Was he dead?

She bent over him. His eyelids were clenched shut now. A bright scarlet thread trailed from one nostril across his downy cheek, glinting in the candlelight. Cahira reached out a fingertip to touch the warm, wet blood. A shiver passed through her. She laid a hand on his chest and felt a faint rise and fall. Her own breast heaved as something brittle broke inside her, its shards slicing into her heart. She choked out a sob and ran, screaming for Fadra.

Ferdy was going to live. Cahira kept telling herself that as she stalked the hallway outside Fadra's study. The Healer was in there, doing everything she could for him. He would be all right. If he wasn't—

Calm yourself.

She stopped pacing. "Why did you let me go so far?"

You are strong.

"I used him."

He is not important.

Was that what she'd been thinking when she took over Ferdy's skal, drew on his power? The truth was, she hadn't been thinking of him at all. Like she hadn't been thinking of Elise. The girl had been jealous and tried to harm her, but she didn't deserve what Cahira had done in response.

Calm yourself.

The tone was sharper than before, almost impatient.

"*Calm* myself? What about Elise? I blinded her!"

She will recover. Concern for such a one is a waste of your time. She has no talent.

Cahira's pulse hammered in her temples as if she was holding her breath underwater. She felt as if she might be going to faint.

You are stronger than this.

The same words that had brought her comfort now chilled her to the bone. "Get out of my head! I'm not listening to you anymore."

Silence. The thundering of her blood receded. She took a deep breath, another, then lifted a hand to knock on the door. Fadra needed to know she was mistaken about the Unity. It wasn't benign.

Do you think you can be rid of me so easily?

Her fist froze a hairs-breadth from the wood.

You invited me in, Cahira Gelt. Accepted my help. We are connected now.

She squeezed her eyes shut, as if that could keep its voice out of her skull. "Go away!"

A dry chuckle slid between her ears, sending icy shudders down her spine.

She'd seen danger coming from so many places. Berek and his cult at the farm. Dostig and the ambushers on the road. The bear in the entrance cave. Even her own skal, trying to wrest control from her. She'd been wrong about all of it. The real threat—to her and everyone around her—was this monster inside her head.

"Who are you, really?" It came out as a whisper.

Silence.

Cahira's hand went to her pocket, where the stone lay. She gripped it and thought about Bram. He hadn't just loved her. He'd believed in her, and in the goodness and beauty of her gift. But both she and it had changed so much since then. She had the power to hurt, maybe to kill, and she'd used it without mercy. What would he think of that?

Suddenly, she knew exactly what he would say. She could almost hear his slow, warm voice—a brown voice, she'd always thought—serious but kind. He would tell her she couldn't undo the past, no matter how much she wanted to. But she could learn from it. She could fight hard to resist the urgings of the Unity from now on. And never forget that the same ability that had harmed Elise and Ferdy could also protect, as she'd protected the little girl from the bear.

As you protected Kelan, she thought sadly, *when you stood in front of him in that horrible room in Fortune Creek, and died for it.* But at least she knew now, as perhaps Bram had known already, that there were far worse fates than that.

She opened her eyes and drew a breath. The vile, deceitful voice in her head had uttered one truth: she was strong. Stronger than it knew. Not because of the power of her skal, but because she had memories of love and courage to draw on, and always would. She raised her hand and knocked on the door.

Fadra answered almost immediately, with the good news that she believed both Elise and Ferdy would recover completely. She invited Cahira to visit them. But Cahira wasn't ready to face either of them, or anyone else in the community. They probably hated her, and that was all right. She was just so thankful she hadn't caused any lasting damage.

No, she'd slip away quietly, speaking to no one but Fadra. It was past time. The lessons in controlling her skal were the only reason she hadn't left before now. She'd learned them well, and she was grateful to Fadra for teaching her. But the presence of the Unity was strong here, and Cahira had no intention of letting it manipulate her into hurting anybody else. Gaining some distance from the caves might be the first step in silencing it completely.

Fadra listened to her halting attempts to explain all of this, with puzzlement growing on her intelligent face. "I haven't experienced anything like that, Cahira. The Unity always speaks to me about positive things. It encourages me to be stronger, better." She laid a hand on Cahira's arm. "Are you sure they weren't your own thoughts? You seem confused. Perhaps you need more time in the sanctuary to clear your mind. We can try a different elixir."

Fadra meant well, but Cahira knew in the depths of her being that the Healer was wrong about this. "Thank you for all your help, but I really have to go."

Fadra reluctantly accepted that. She did insist on supplying extra clothing and plenty of supplies for the trip, including bottles of the two infusions Cahira had been taking. Cahira accepted the last gift only to spare Fadra's feelings. She had no intention of touching either of the liquids again.

When everything was packed, Fadra took her to a cave lower down the hill where horses were stabled, and presented her with a mount, a quiet little mare with none of Blackbird's temperament. Even as Cahira thanked the Healer sincerely for her kindness, she wondered sadly if she'd ever see her own horse again.

She was heading back to Virtue Farm, following Fadra's directions. A moment of doubt assailed her as she mounted up. Perhaps she should go to the city instead, and report Berek's activities to the Council. Scant seconds later, she rejected the notion.

Anything could have happened while she'd been in the caves. The authorities might already know about Berek. Even more likely, she and Niall had simply let their imaginations run away with them, and there was no danger of an attack at all. Besides, Adric should have returned from Eorna by now, and she needed to see him.

Crossing the bridge, she realised she'd forgotten to ask the mare's name. Names were important, even for horses. This one was gentle and grey, and a little plump.

"I'll call you Dove," she said aloud.

Dove made no response, which Cahira took as approval.

TWENTY-SIX

No one gave Cahira a second glance as she hurried between the buildings with her head lowered. Giving silent thanks that Fadra's parting gift had included this drab grey dress and jacket, she passed through the deserted dining hall and into the kitchen. A few women were still cleaning up after lunch, and Cahira felt the beginnings of a small smile tug at her lips. She'd found Bett on her first try. Perhaps it was a good omen that she'd be seeing Adric soon, too.

The teenager glanced up, then grinned and threw down her rag. She bounced over and flung her sound arm around Cahira's shoulders in a tight hug. "You're back!"

"Can we go somewhere to talk?" Cahira whispered in her ear.

Bett angled her head towards the door of the storeroom. As soon as they were alone, the questions tumbled out, and Bett was happy to answer them. Yes, she was fine, and Mara too. No, Adric wasn't here, but Niall had been back, looking for Cahira.

"We was all worried about you," Bett said, "but he were near frantic. Almost knocked Berek down, or so I heard. I woulda liked to see that. But he went off again come mornin', must be a week or so ago."

This was better news than Cahira had dared to hope. Niall had not only regained consciousness, but was in his right mind. She would have liked to let him know she was safe, but he could be anywhere by now.

As far as Bett knew, Adric was still in Eorna. That was a relief, too, in a way. He was probably better off there than with Berek. But she still had to find him.

"Do you have any idea what part of the city he's in?"

"Well, I knows the house they took me an' Mara to before they brung us here. He might be there."

Cahira memorised the address and thanked Bett profusely.

They returned to an empty kitchen. Cahira took leave of her friend, and had just clasped the handle of the dining hall door when a deep voice sounded from beyond it. She froze. She hadn't understood the short rumble of words, but the identity of the speaker was unmistakable. It was definitely time to go, but not the way she'd come.

She was halfway to the rear door when the sound of her own name, uttered by a second male voice, stopped her in her tracks. Did they know she was here? Were others waiting in the yard to take her as she emerged? She edged back, and risked easing the dining hall door open a tiny crack. A glance over her shoulder showed Bett tiptoeing across the floor to join her.

The blood pulsed against Cahira's skull, making it hard to hear anything else. She pressed her ear to the narrow opening, and the words came through clearly. The second man was speaking, his voice higher than Berek's and vaguely familiar.

"There can be no doubt. The Skalsinger is here."

A tiny gasp escaped Cahira. She held her breath, fearing the worst. But there was no sound of approaching footsteps.

Berek's voice came again: "How do you know?"

"Not your business. But she's on the farm."

Cahira's insides went weak with relief. They hadn't heard her.

"Very well." Berek sounded defensive. "I'll order a search, tell the men to bring her here. Will that satisfy you?"

"No. Leave her alone. She must believe she is a free agent."

Cahira's lungs were bursting. She released her breath carefully and allowed a trickle of air to enter her nose. She desperately needed to swallow, but her throat was so dry she was sure she'd choke and give her presence away.

"As to other matters," said the unknown man, "are you ready to move?"

"Of course." Berek was offended again. "We march tomorrow, and reach Eder Ford the day after. As agreed."

"Make sure you arrive before noon."

The same familiarity nagged at Cahira. Where had she heard that assured voice before? And why was it giving Berek orders?

"We'll be there. You worry about your own people. And the others, off the ships."

"They are on the way. Have beds and provisions ready."

"Don't know why we need 'em at all," growled a new voice. "The Warrant Guards are weak. My men can take 'em, sir, with no help from no cursed foreign scum."

Beside Cahira, Bett's eyes widened, but she didn't utter a sound.

"Now, Commander," Berek began. "We agreed—"

"Do not question your betters, Ruston." Chill steel rang in the rebuke. "Fadra's stratagems are beyond your meagre understanding."

Angry protests arose, but Cahira had stopped listening. Blindly, she reached out to the wall to steady herself. She knew the identity of the third man. The name he'd spoken had given her the clue she needed.

As crazy as it seemed, Fadra had sent the Mind Wender, Jon, to coordinate a treasonous attack on Eorna. And if the men in that room discovered they'd been overheard, they wouldn't hesitate to kill her and Bett to keep their secret.

Bett must have been thinking the same thing. She jerked her head towards the back door. Cahira nodded. Moving on the balls of her feet, she reached the door a few steps ahead of her companion. She grasped the handle and pulled, hearing the alarmed squeak from behind her a split second too late. The long, tortured shriek of the rusted hinges paralysed her in horror.

The scrape of a chair broke the sudden silence from the dining hall. They were coming, and Cahira couldn't move. A hand thrust past her and pushed the door shut, eliciting another hair-raising screech. Bett grabbed Cahira's arm, dragged her to the storeroom with surprising strength, then shoved her in. Cahira stared blankly as the door closed, with Bett on the wrong side.

Footsteps entered the kitchen.

"Oh sir, you scared me," Bett exclaimed, finishing with a little gasp.

"Why are you still in here, girl?" Berek demanded.

"I'm not. I mean I am, but I wasn't, if you see, sir." She sounded flustered, not like herself at all. "I come back for me apron. It's dirty, see, an' I forgot to take it to the laundry. I'm always forgettin' things, forget my own head next, Mara says—"

"What did you hear?" Jon fired the words through Bett's ramblings, like stones from a catapult.

"Hear?"

"Did you hear us?"

A pause, and then Berek said, "It's all right, girl. Just answer the question."

"Well, I hears you comin' into the kitchen, sir. An' then I hears you askin' why I'm still here, an' I hears me own voice, tellin' you I forgot me apron. An' then the gentleman says *what did you hear*, an' *did you hear us*, an' you says *answer the question*, so that's what I'm doin'…" She trailed off.

Even to Cahira's discerning ears, the confusion sounded absolutely genuine. She could almost see the blank, gaping expression. Bett was displaying an unexpected gift for acting. And the strong-mindedness to resist Jon's skal. She hadn't exactly lied, but she'd certainly left a lot out.

"All right, you can go," Berek said.

"Thank you, sir."

The back door cried out again as Bett made her escape.

"Are you sure she heard nothing?" Jon asked.

Berek scoffed. "You saw her. She's practically half-witted, like all the kitchen women. Forget about her. If you're worried about eavesdroppers, we'll finish this conversation in my office."

Cahira waited until their footsteps had completely faded away before poking her head out. No one was in sight, either in the kitchen or dining hall. And bless Bett, the back door was open. No fear of the hinges betraying her again. But she had to take a deep breath and set her jaw before she could force herself to move.

Bett was waiting in the yard. She grabbed Cahira in a hug, and Cahira clung to her just as tightly.

After a few moments, Bett stepped back, giving her a gentle push. "Time for you to go. Get to Eorna, tell 'em what you heard."

Cahira couldn't help it. A snort of laughter burst from her. She slapped her hand over her mouth, fighting the urge to giggle hysterically.

Bett grinned, sharing the joke. "Well, maybe not *everythin'* you heard."

Cahira got herself under control with difficulty and gripped Bett's good arm. "Come with me."

Bett shook her head. "If I goes missin' after this, they'll know somethin's wrong. Anyway, you got two horses with you?"

"Just one."

"That's what I thought. You need to travel fast, give the city as much warnin' as you can. Two of us on one horse, that'd just slow you down."

She was right, but leaving her here still felt like abandonment. Bett seemed to understand. "I'll be safe enough. They think I'm an idiot, remember?" She smiled impishly.

"You were brilliant," Cahira said. "And when this is over, I'll come back for you, I promise."

"I might be gone myself by then. Not much reason to stay, now."

"But where will you go, and how will I find you?"

"Get along with you." Emotion roughened Bett's voice, too. "We'll see each other again, never fear. Friends forever, that's you an' me." She gave Cahira a second push. "Now go."

Cahira went. She sped past the outbuildings and picked her way across the stubbled fields, shooting nervous glances over her shoulder to make sure she wasn't being followed. She untied the little mare from the fence with shaking fingers. She was free, thanks to Bett's quick thinking and a healthy dose of luck.

When she'd put a comfortable distance between herself and the farm, she slowed Dove to a walk. The mare was moving well, but Cahira doubted she was used to hard riding. No sense in exhausting her. At this pace, it would take about four hours to reach Eder Ford, and the same

time from there to Eorna. She'd arrive very late tonight, but someone in
the garrison would be on duty.

She'd tell them about Berek and the planned attack, but she was in
two minds about accusing Fadra. Could the woman who'd Healed Niall
and cradled Cahira as she wept be involved in a plot to take over the
government? Or was Jon a double traitor, using Fadra as a scapegoat to
protect himself if things went wrong? She gnawed at her lip, undecided.

A thought occurred to her a few minutes later: the voice in her head
had been silent the whole time she'd been on the farm. As she'd hoped,
its influence seemed limited to the caves. It was a huge relief to have one
less thing to worry about.

The sun had almost set when Dove lurched to the right and pulled
up, trembling. Half asleep, Cahira grabbed at the front of the saddle
to stop herself sliding off. She dismounted and ran her hands over the
mare. When she came to the off foreleg, Dove flinched away. There was
a definite swelling above the hock, hot to the touch.

Cahira wanted to scream in frustration. They must be close to the
Ford by now. But her mount was lame, and the daylight was almost
gone. There was no chance she'd reach the city tonight. She only hoped
they could make it to the river. There was a cottage there, built in the
days when Eorna had levied a toll for crossing the water. There was no
toll-keeper now, but someone might have taken over the house. Maybe
she could beg a bed for the night, and hope Dove was better by the
morning.

The wind was blowing freezing blasts at her. She untied the bulging
pack and dug out a fur lined jacket and matching gloves. Another sign
of Fadra's thoughtfulness. Trying to sort out her feelings towards the
Healer was too confusing. She gave it up.

She hefted the pack over one shoulder, and considered removing
the saddle, too. But it was well made and heavy, and she quailed at the
thought of carrying it. Perhaps if they went slowly, Dove could manage.

The mare ignored the first gentle pull on the reins. Cahira set her feet and tugged a little harder. "Come on, girl, we can't stay here all night. Just a bit further."

Dove took one step and stopped again.

Tears threatened as Cahira briefly leaned her forehead against the mare's warm neck. "Please, Dove, I need you to walk. Just try."

Leaning forward, she put a steady drag on the reins, not letting up when the horse began to move. But progress was agonisingly slow. The mare halted every dozen steps, and had to be bullied and coaxed to go on.

Darkness fell, and the stars came out. Cahira's arms ached. Her burning eyes strained to make out the way ahead. The surface under her feet was only a shade lighter than the black masses of the trees on either side. She was wondering how long she could keep this up, when the moon lifted over the horizon. The road transformed into a ribbon of silver, flowing between dark banks.

But even with the increased light, Dove was becoming more and more reluctant to move. She'd just balked for what seemed the thousandth time when hoof-beats sounded from behind them. A rider was catching up, moving fast. Had Berek or Jon seen through Bett's deception and sent someone after Cahira?

Desperation gave her the strength to tug Dove into the shadow of the trees. Seconds later, a horse thundered past, with a dark figure crouched over the withers. The hoofbeats died away. A false alarm. But it was even harder to move Dove after that.

It took longer than Cahira would have believed possible, but she finally caught sight of the cottage, shining white in the moonlight. It looked in good repair, but the windows were dark. Perhaps no one was home. That might be even better.

She left Dove at the gate and crept all round the building, listening for any sound. At last, she took her courage in her hands and knocked on the door. No response. She tried the handle. The door creaked open. She went in, moving as quietly as she could.

The moonlight from the single window revealed several chairs pulled up to a table and three well-upholstered seats in front of the fireplace. Cahira cautiously checked the rest of the cottage, finding a kitchen and two bedrooms, all equipped for occupation but empty of people. So far, so good. She dropped the pack in the front room and went back for Dove.

The mare moved more willingly when she caught sight of the stable. Safely tied up inside, she sucked water from the stone trough, snorting and blowing. There were remnants of hay in the rack, but she didn't seem interested. Trying to ignore the ache in her arms, Cahira removed the saddle and rubbed Dove down with the blanket, avoiding the injured leg.

Shivering despite the exercise and her thick clothing, she returned to the cottage. A fire was laid in the hearth, and a basket of logs stood waiting. Whoever had done that wouldn't be happy she was making herself at home in their absence. But a thin crust of frost was already forming on the window pane. She'd freeze in here without the fire.

She lit the twigs and watched the greedy flames lick upwards. When she was sure it had caught, and that the chimney was drawing properly, she sat down and opened the pack. She drank first, long swallows of icy water that made her shudder, but relieved her parched throat. The small loaf was still fresh, and she tore chunks off, leaning back as she chewed. Her last meal had been breakfast, back at the caves. It seemed a lifetime ago.

When the bread was finished, she started on the package of preserved meat and cheese. The salty food made her thirsty again. She drank some more. Fadra had even included nuts and dried berries for dessert. Why would she do all that, if she was the villain Jon had claimed?

She laid a second log on the fire and watched the flames dance, relishing the heat playing on her face and the feeling of being well fed and comfortable. She'd sit here a while longer in the wonderful warmth, then claim the bedroom with the east facing window. The morning light would wake her early. Hopefully, Dove would have recovered enough by then to carry her the rest of the way to Eorna.

TWENTY-SEVEN

Perna

Perna woke in the bedroom of yet another tavern. This one was called Bella's and it was in Eorna. She and Niall had arrived here late last night, after spending weary hours at the garrison. Adric and Mundar had stayed up there, but Niall had brought her to this place, where the owner had greeted him enthusiastically, her dark eyes shining in the lamplight. No doubt he was a frequent customer.

Bella looked young for a tavern keeper, and was the exact opposite of Nathan in every way. The black mass of her hair was long and wavy, her brown skin clear of blemishes. She'd laughed a lot, too, stretching her reddened lips wide. When she'd led them up to the bedrooms, she'd taken the stairs two at a time, her skirts flying out shamelessly at every turn.

Perna sat up and looked around the luxurious room. All this waste discomforted her, but she'd agreed to stay for one night, and it was almost over. It would be light soon, and she'd be able to leave. She'd seek out a poorer area of the city, find a group of Aalden who worked with the people there—surely, they'd be glad of a Healer—and she'd never enter another tavern. If she worked hard and sacrificed enough, maybe Aal would forgive her one day.

She lit a candle—pink and smelling of flowers, another ridiculous extravagance—and dressed. As she smoothed down the modest brown skirt, relief washed over her. She was herself again. Nothing remained of her disguise except her short, choppy hair, and that would grow back. She was tempted to leave the murderous little knife behind, but a sharp blade was a useful tool in the hands of a Healer, so she dropped it into her pocket instead. She would put it to better use in the future.

Downstairs, the big lamps were glowing and breakfast was laid out. She was still feeling tired, and she might have to walk a long way to find what she was looking for. She should eat something. Scorning the steaming meats and elaborate, glazed pastries, she chose bread and cheese and sat down at a small table.

At the first taste of the bread, saliva sprang to her mouth. The loaf was fresh and soft, fragrant with yeast and herbs, and she had to force herself to chew her portion thoroughly before swallowing it and reaching for a second bite.

She'd just lifted a piece of cheese to her lips when a shadow blocked the light. It was Niall, carrying a plate piled high with food. He sat opposite her without being invited. She opened her mouth to rebuke him, but there was no point. She'd be gone soon, leaving him behind forever. Knowing that, she could tolerate him for now.

He scanned her plate and narrowed his eyes. "Why aren't you eating?"

"I am eating," she pointed out, waving the piece of cheese in front of his face as if he was near-sighted.

He raised one black eyebrow. "Barely."

He cut himself a generous chunk of meat, ate it with gusto, then smiled his crooked grin. "Very passable, and not even a little bit poisoned, as far as I can tell. Why don't you give it a try?" He held his plate out in invitation.

Perna bent her head and kept eating. Just a few more mouthfuls, and she'd go.

"Perna, I'm worried about you." The quiet, serious tone had her raising her eyes in surprise.

"You hardly eat anything," Niall went on. "You'll make yourself sick, and what use will you be to your god then?"

"You're not my father or my Elder," she snapped, furious at his blasphemy and presumption. "It's none of your business."

Someone like him would never understand. She was controlling the desires of her body in dedication to Aal, just as her mother had taught her. The god would honour that and protect her. If she needed proof, she only had to remember how she'd already been rescued from her foolish infatuation with Adric Gelt.

The first time she'd seen Cahira's brother-in-law, as he came striding across the training grounds at the farm, an actual shock had gone through her body. With his golden hair shining in the sunlight, his handsome face and broad shoulders, he'd seemed like one of the heroes out of the old songs, higher and nobler than other men.

And she'd dreamed—it didn't matter what foolish things she'd dreamed. She'd been caught in the snare of physical beauty, when all her devotion should have belonged to Aal alone. And her weakness had led to nothing but disillusion and hurt. Adric had turned out to be just an ordinary man after all, and a stupid one at that, who barely noticed Perna and valued her not at all. Aal had shown her the truth for her own good.

And now another idiotic man was upsetting her all over again. Her throat closed, and she knew she couldn't manage another bite.

"Perna, I only want to help."

Why couldn't he mind his own business? She scraped her chair back and stood. "I don't need your help and I don't need you to tell me what to do."

Without giving him another glance, she hurried upstairs to get her things.

Of course, he didn't leave it at that. Emerging from the bedroom with her pack on her shoulders, she found him planted in front of her, his eyes hard. "Where are you going?"

"To find some Aalden."

"Good idea. We'll warn them about the attack, and you can go with them when they quit the city."

Perna regarded him with disgust. Did he truly think she was such a coward? She had no intention of leaving Eorna to save her own skin, and neither would any Aalden who took their duty seriously. She didn't waste time explaining this, but simply skirted around him and started down the stairs.

"Look, just wait a minute, will you?" He sounded annoyed now. "I'll come, too. Make sure you get there safely."

"No."

He overtook her at the bottom of the stairs and barred her way to the front door. "Don't be a little fool. You don't even know the city."

"Aal will guide me to the right place, just like in Welsea."

There, let him remember that she had found the information they needed, not him.

"That was just luck."

She glared at him. Not only stupid and blasphemous, but ungrateful.

He flung up his hands, as if she was the unreasonable one. "Perna, I'm not letting you go alone. I'll use my skal if I have to. Dulcina won't move a step unless I tell her to."

She tossed her head. "I'm not taking Dulcina. I'm walking. Don't follow me."

She edged around him, her body stiff with tension, half expecting him to grab her the way he had in Mirston. If he dared to do it again, she'd scream this whole place down. Perhaps he sensed that, because he dropped his arms and let her go.

Her heart beat hard and fast as she crossed the street. She halted on the other side and spun around, expecting the worst. But the tavern door was closed, and there was no sign of him. Good. Hitching the pack higher on her shoulders, she looked around. The paved road was lined with upright stone buildings, some with intricately wrought iron balconies. Smartly-dressed pedestrians strolled past her. A closed carriage came around the corner, pulled by two high-stepping, glossy black horses. As she'd suspected, this was a prosperous area, not what she was looking for at all. Muttering a quick prayer, she picked a direction at random and began walking.

TWENTY-EIGHT

Niall

Niall ground his teeth as he watched Perna stalk out of the tavern. She was infuriating. He took a step to follow her—despite what she'd said, she could hardly stop him—and heard Bella calling his name.

She strode up to him with skirts swirling and anxiety marking her mobile face. "We've got trouble. We need to talk."

Niall shot a glance towards the door. Anything could happen to a naïve young girl in this city. But in the end, he trusted Bella's judgement. If she was worried, he'd better listen. He'd told her everything he knew last night, and she'd started sending messages right away. She must have got a reply.

He followed her into her private parlour and shut the heavy, felt-lined door. "What have your people heard?"

Bella's *people* ranged from scruffy street dwellers and servants offering information for a few copper coins, through a middle tier of artisans and merchants, some honest and others slightly shady, who welcomed a little lucrative work on the side, to full employees. These last ran the various businesses Bella had inherited from her father, and the ones she'd established herself since his death. Finally, there were those exalted beings who were not in anyone's employ, but with whom Bella had mutually beneficial *arrangements*, as she called them.

There was no telling how many people answered to Bella in one way or another, but between them they had access to every part of the city

206

and every level of society. If there was something worth knowing, they found out about it, and passed the message on.

Bella seated herself behind her desk and leaned forward. "Have you ever heard of a woman called Fadra?"

Niall tried to maintain a neutral expression, but his stomach was churning. "Yes, I know who you mean. What about her?"

"She claims to be Mallornan, but my sources say she's from Bregia."

"A spy?"

"More than that. She's been gathering a force together, somewhere south of here and off to the west. They've been living in a system of caves."

"An army?" Could she mean Berek's Seekers? But he'd seen no caves on the farm.

"Not in the way you're thinking. Two of my people met one of her group who fled to the city about a month ago, with quite a story to tell. It's only the word of one man and I can't vouch for its truthfulness, especially as he was as scared as a rabbit and drinking heavily at the time, but he said this Fadra has found a way to increase the strength of skals, way beyond anything we've seen before. He claimed she's training a group of followers, steering them towards using their abilities as weapons."

"*Weapons?* How?"

"Well, for instance, this man—Darin—is a Stone Shaper. He used his skal to make the caves more comfortable for living in. He said he was happy to do it, especially after Fadra showed him how to increase his power. He claimed that in the end he could enlarge and smooth an entire cavern just by passing his hands over the walls. I'm not sure I believe that."

Niall wasn't sure he believed it either, but it seemed harmless enough. He said so.

"If he only used it to Shape rooms for people to live in, yes," Bella said. "But then this Fadra had him practising outside, boring holes in the rock cliffs, seeing how big he could make them, and how quickly. The faster and more destructive he was, the more she praised him.

"He got suspicious, so he started listening. And he heard her saying to someone that Eorna Garrison was built of much softer rock than the caves and wouldn't be any problem. That's when he got scared and ran away."

"You mean, in an attack on the city, he could—"

"Blast a hole straight through the garrison wall, or undermine the foundations."

Niall sat back, stunned. "But you said he's not working with her anymore?"

"No, but he claims there are at least a dozen others, with all kinds of skals, just as strong as his. Niall, think what damage an immensely powerful Metal Shaper could do, or a Mind Wender, or a Beast Speaker, if they attacked the city."

Niall felt as if he'd been punched again. "Or a Skalsinger," he said reluctantly.

Cahira had used her skal to force those Guards at Fortune Creek to surrender, and she hadn't even known what she was doing back then. If this Fadra had got her hands on her, who knew what she might be capable of now? But he was being stupid. Cahira would never help anyone attack Eorna. Which meant she could be in danger for refusing.

"Why are they all following the blasted woman?" he burst out.

"Who knows? But Darin believed he was the only one with any qualms. He said the others are fanatically devoted to her and to something they call *the Unity*. Even as drunk as he was, he wouldn't say any more. My people said he seemed terrified that he'd mentioned it at all."

"Where are these caves?" Niall heard the iron in his own voice. Eorna could take care of itself. He was going after Cahira right now.

"I don't know." Her eyes widened at the expression on Niall's face. "They tried, Niall, but Darin wouldn't say."

Of course not, Niall thought sourly. Why should anything be that easy? Cahira might be a prisoner, forced to use her skal to save her life. Or she could already be dead. No, he wouldn't believe that, not unless he had absolute proof. She was alive. He just had no way to find her.

If only he hadn't been ambushed in that stable, they could have faced this threat together. But he'd stupidly allowed himself to be distracted by a horse, and then knocked out by those oafs. He should have been on his guard. It was all his fault.

Bella broke into this self-excoriation. "They've probably left the caves already, anyway. The attacks must be planned to happen at the same time, don't you think? The important thing is that there aren't two armies coming to Eorna like we thought—the Seekers from the farm and the Bregians from the ships—"

"There are three," Niall finished.

He sighed and bowed to the inevitable, but not with a good grace. "I'll go tell Logen and Oren. We can't let Fadra's followers get anywhere near the city. Somehow, we have to stop them at the Ford."

At least he could make sure he was included in the force at the river. And then he'd find out for certain if Cahira was with the enemy or not.

TWENTY-NINE

Perna

Beneath the felted jacket, shivers rippled over Perna's skin. She sped up, hoping to warm herself, giving a wistful thought to the green woollen cap she'd left behind. Then she shook her head at her own weakness. Bodily comfort wasn't important. Besides, she was seeking a group of holy women, and she couldn't afford to give a negative impression. It was bad enough that she'd cut her hair off, without turning up in a boy's cap too.

She had to remind herself of that more than once as she pushed on. Her feet were hurting, and she felt tired and weak, despite the bread and cheese at breakfast. But each time she slowed down to rest, the freezing wind drove her forward again. The sunlit morning had been swallowed up by clouds. She wrapped her arms around her body and forced herself to keep going.

The tall stone houses gave way to more modest dwellings. The people hurrying past were dressed in plain, workaday clothes. She was getting closer to where she needed to be. A few more turns, always choosing the least attractive way, and she found herself on a wide road lined with cracked and faded timber buildings. A few bulged and leaned alarmingly, as if their upper storeys might topple into the street at any moment. Perna gazed, with great satisfaction, on sagging balconies, rows of flapping laundry, and piles of broken furniture.

Carts and wagons clogged the road, more than she'd ever seen in one place. They were moving slowly—loaded ones one way, empty ones the other—all forced to walking pace by the sheer press of numbers. Perna's heart gave a tremendous thump as a gang of children exploded from between the houses, yelling and laughing as they raced around the carts and dodged the cudgels of the drivers. The vehicles were stirring up a cloud of dust. The breeze caught some of it and whirled it across the street. The people in its path bent over, coughing and pressing cloths to their faces. Perna felt glad she was on this side.

As if it had read her thought, the spiteful wind swung round. Grit flew into her eyes. She squeezed them shut and gasped, drawing dust into her nose and lungs. Sneezing and coughing, she groped for the nearest wall, feeling her way along the splintery wood until she came to a corner. She rounded it and bent over double, heaving and snorting, desperate to clear her airways. She hacked and spat until her throat was raw, then sucked in breath after breath in the lee of the building.

The coughing gradually subsided, but her legs were trembling. She slid down with her back against the wall and opened her eyes, just a slit. The lids felt as if they were grating over sand, and everything was blurry. She needed water to rinse out the dirt, but how was she going to find some if she couldn't see? She wasn't even sure she had the strength to rise to her feet again. She leaned back against the building and prayed for help. She was on her way to become an Aaldan. Surely the god would send someone to her aid.

"Who are you, then?"

Perna started as the hoarse voice sounded from right in front of her. Had Aal answered her prayer already? She held out her hands. "Please, can you help me? I can't see."

"Sure, I'll help you. What'll you pay?"

"Pay?"

"Pay?" mimicked the girl.

"I don't have…"

"Let's see what you do have, then."

Hard hands gripped Perna's upper arms and yanked her forward, then wrenched the pack from her shoulders. She blinked desperately, but the world was still blurred. She couldn't make out anything except vague patches of light and shadow.

She heard a rustling as the girl went through the pack.

"Just clothes? Where's your money?" The thief sounded angry.

"I don't have any."

A hard slap across her cheek rocked Perna's head on her neck, drawing a cry of pain.

"Don't lie to me again. You've got expensive clothes, good boots. This pack is new. So where's the money?"

"At the tavern," Perna whispered.

It was the truth. Niall had bought all these things, and he was still at Bella's, as far as she knew. But true or not, the answer earned her an even more vicious slap. Perna's head slammed into the wall. She bit her tongue, tasted blood. She raised her hands in front of her face in an effort to defend herself. Why was this happening to her? Where was Aal?

"One last chance. Give me the money or I'll call my friend to come and search you. You won't enjoy it. He's big and mean, and he won't be as gentle as me."

Perna sobbed, terrified at the thought of what the man might do to her when he didn't find anything. She'd brought nothing but the pack. Even her pockets were empty. No, that wasn't true. She had the little knife. For the first time, her heart thumped with more than fear. Maybe she could frighten the thief off.

She eased one hand into the pocket and closed her fingers around the hilt, then turned her blind eyes in the direction of the voice. For this to work, the girl had to believe Perna could see her. Gathering her courage, she drew out the knife and waved it rapidly back and forth. "Leave me alone."

A hand clamped down on her wrist and twisted it until she dropped the weapon with a little scream.

"That was stupid."

Perna braced herself for another slap in the face. Instead, there came a cold, stinging pain at her throat. The thief was pressing the knife against the soft skin. Not even daring to breathe, she clenched her teeth to stop the trembling in her jaw and pulled her head back as far as she could, until it was stopped by the wall. Sharper pain, accompanied by a trickle of warmth. It was her own blood, flowing from where the thief had cut her. She tried not to swallow, terrified any movement of her throat would cause the blade to bite deeper.

"Where. Is. The. Money." The low, grating voice was hard as stone.

Perna had no more answers to give and nothing more to try. The thief would slit her throat, and she would die alone in this nameless alley. Aal had abandoned her.

A voice called out nearby, and was answered. The words were unclear, but the pressure on Perna's throat vanished. She heard running footsteps, quickly fading away. She blinked furiously. Still nothing but light and moving shadows.

Something else claimed her attention: a throbbing pain where the knife had been. Her life's blood was draining away. She pressed a hand to the gash, hoping to stem the flow. The blood was hot and slippery under her fingers.

Boots scraped on the cobbles. A shadow loomed over her. "Are you all right, miss?" It was a man.

Perna tried to answer, but her voice refused to respond.

"She's bleeding." That was a woman.

Perna's hand was lifted away and something soft pressed against her skin.

"Can you walk?"

Perna didn't know. Her head was swimming.

There was a conversation that sounded like the speakers were under water, followed by a gentle touch on Perna's arm that made her jump.

The woman spoke again. "We're going to help you to your feet and take you to a Healer. All right?"

All right, Perna thought, but couldn't tell if she'd managed to say it out loud. She felt very strange. Someone grasped her under the armpits and hauled her up.

"She's passing out," someone else said, very slowly and from a long way away.

"Wake up, child. You've slept enough for now."

Perna opened her eyes. They seemed to be working again, but all she could see was a dirty white wall about an arm's length away. Her eyeballs felt raw and gritty. She rubbed them.

"Leave them alone, girl. You'll make them worse."

Perna rolled over to face a plump woman standing with her legs apart and her hands on her broad hips. She had more hair than anyone Perna had ever seen. It was a streaky mixture of yellow and grey, and it looked as if its owner had tried to tame it and then given it up as too much effort. Half of the tangled mass was piled haphazardly on top of her head like a gigantic bird's nest, stuck here and there with long pins, while the rest fell in unruly curls and waves over her shoulders and down her back. Resisting the urge to run a hand over her own cropped head, Perna sat up.

The woman smiled, revealing a gap where one of her front teeth should have been. "Good girl. Now, let's see you stand."

Perna gathered her legs under her. Her head felt like it might float off her shoulders, and she swayed a bit, but she pushed herself to her feet without help. It seemed like a victory.

The woman held out a man's grey woollen coat. "You'll need this. No firewood this week."

Already shivering, Perna shrugged the garment on and wrapped the belt twice around her waist.

The woman regarded her with her head on one side. A pin slid partway out, and Perna's fingers itched to push it back in. "Skinny little thing, aren't you?"

That was rude, but Perna chose not to take offence. She was in the poor quarter now, and the gap-toothed woman probably didn't know any better.

"Where am I?"

"In Aal's House, Dyers Lane. I'm Tabia. One of the Sisters here."

"You're an *Aaldan*?"

Tabia huffed. "No need to sound so surprised, girl. We come in all shapes and sizes, you know."

"I—I'm sorry, I just—how did I get here?"

"Jake and Minna brought you. Said you'd been robbed."

Memory flooded back. Perna lifted a hesitant hand to her throat, afraid of what she'd find. But her fingers felt only the tiniest ridge of raised skin. Pressing on it caused no pain at all.

"Oh, you're Healed now. I saw to that. Not as bad as it looked. Just a shallow cut."

So she wasn't about to die after all. "How long?"

"Only a few hours. But lunch is ready, and you need feeding up. Can't have you collapsing again. The food's not fancy, mind. But it's hot, and it's filling." Tabia turned and limped slowly to the door, favouring her right leg.

Perna followed her down a hallway to a room that seemed too small to hold all the people and noise inside. Men, women, and children stood in crowded groups. Others sat shoulder to shoulder around the walls. Standing in the doorway, Perna caught a glimpse of a table in the middle of the space, before the clustering backs hid it again. Even the stairs leading to the upper storey were occupied, and everyone was talking at the same time.

If some of the women were Aalden, Perna couldn't tell which. She didn't see a single cream robe. Come to think of it, even Tabia wasn't wearing one. Her dress was of yellowish, wrinkled linen, its wide hem decorated with blue daisies. But the thread was faded, and there were gaps in the stitching.

An odour floated out, wrinkling Perna's nose. Part of it was the savoury smell of hot food, but something sour lay beneath. She recognised it from the tavern back home: unwashed, beer-soaked bodies in close proximity.

She couldn't see any way through the crowd, short of pushing and shoving. But as she trailed in Tabia's wake, people bunched up tighter to let them pass. They stopped at the table, where a heavily muscled man was filling bowls from a steaming pot. The pleasant part of the smell was stronger here. Perna's mouth watered.

Tabia gave the man an unladylike thump on his meaty arm. "What's on the menu today, Jake?"

"Turnip and a nice bit of mutton, Elder, compliments of a butcher down at the market."

Perna started in surprise. How could this woman, with her common manners and her ridiculous, undisciplined hair, be the spiritual leader here? The man must be making some kind of joke. But then she remembered the way everyone had stepped aside to let them through, and she wondered.

The Aaldan planted her hands on her hips and shook her head vigorously, shedding a couple of pins. "How many times, Jake? My name is Tabia. Just Tabia."

"Sorry." His grin wasn't repentant at all. "A bowl for you and our new friend?"

"Small one for me, large one for her. Make sure there's meat in it. I don't think this one's been eating too well lately."

Perna wanted to say she wasn't hungry, but that would have been a lie. She felt hollowed out. She carried the bowl carefully to a slightly less crowded corner. Sitting on the cold floor, she took a spoonful. Rich flavour filled her mouth. The stew was good—really good. She swallowed, and it warmed her all the way down. But she forced herself to stop when she'd eaten half the portion. Greed was an offence to Aal. She set the bowl aside so she wouldn't be tempted, then folded her arms and leaned back against the wall, closing her sore eyes.

Multiple conversations ebbed and flowed, and Perna let them wash over her. She felt surprisingly content. She was in a House of Aal. It wasn't what she'd been picturing, and Tabia certainly didn't match her idea of an Elder, but she'd come to Eorna to help the poor and needy, and a lot of them were gathered in this room. Aal had answered her prayer. She wouldn't think beyond that for now.

THIRTY

Bett

The frost-stiffened grass crunched under Bett's thin shoes. She blew on her frozen fingers and shoved them into her pockets, hurrying as fast as she dared on the treacherous ground. She was fed up with these early mornings, tired of the darkness and the deep cold that made her crippled arm ache even more.

She crossed the yard and pulled open the kitchen door, wincing as it squealed its shrill greeting. Someone should fix the thing. It was bad enough to be up and working at this hour. No one needed to be screamed at by a stupid set of rusty hinges.

Mara was already at work, carefully preparing a breakfast tray for Petir, Berek's bed-ridden uncle. She always liked to do it herself, and take it up to him in the main house.

The only time Bett had gone with her, she'd seen how fond Mara seemed to be of the old man, how gentle she was with him. Mara had a good heart. Uncle Petir obviously liked her, too, and was delighted to meet Bett. He chatted away to them both, his mind sharp even though age had weakened his body. As he smiled and winked at them, Mara had forgotten to pull her hair over her scars. She'd looked happy.

It was hard to believe that the bullying, puffed-up Berek could be related to such a sweet old man. But he'd given his uncle a home here, so maybe there was a touch of kindness in him after all. Bett's mother had always said that no one was all bad, although some folk came mighty close.

Mara glanced up at Bett's noisy entrance into the kitchen, nodded to her, and went back to work. Dismissing the memory of Uncle Petir's cosy room with a sigh, Bett clumped across the floor to fetch the jar of leaven, kept alive and bubbling on its shelf above the stove. She lingered there, rubbing her stiff hands and taking her time checking the fire inside the black iron box. Then she carried the leaven to the workbench and began mixing her first batch of bread for the day. Over the next few minutes, the other women trickled in, until the room filled up with chatter and busyness.

While the dough was proving, Bett and Mara made a pot of tea sweetened with honey for the workers. Bett took her cup to the back door. She opened it just a crack, gently enough to avoid a repeat of the squealing. The action reminded her of Cahira's visit yesterday, and she hid a secret smile. Fooling Berek and the other men had been fun, and really important too. If the warning got through to Eorna, it would be partly because of her. That felt good. She hoped Cahira was okay. They hadn't brought her back anyway, or the news would be all over the community by now.

Cradling the warm cup in her hands, Bett craned her head to the side, her eyes seeking the sunrise. Despite the hated cold, she liked to do this when she could. The beginning of a new day always seemed hopeful somehow, full of promise. It was a good one this morning. A line of red fire kindled across the horizon, throwing a sheet of gold over the frosted fields. Bett sipped the sweet, fragrant tea, content for the moment.

A noise caught her attention, coming from somewhere out of sight. She frowned, trying to place the sound. Footsteps? If so, there were a lot of them, and they were getting closer. She jumped as a gruff voice called out, his words nonsense to her ears. Another answered the same way. Had they been drinking? Berek wouldn't be happy.

A moment later, two men came into view. They were strangers to her, both wearing dark grey cloaks and trousers. They weren't moving like drunks, but she still couldn't understand them.

"What are you looking at?" Bett jumped again, but it was only Mara, who had come up behind her.

Bett moved aside. "I'm not sure."

Mara only gazed through the narrow opening for a few seconds before backing away.

"Bregians," she whispered tightly. "Bregian soldiers."

"Bregians?" Bett said blankly.

And then she remembered Ruston's words from yesterday: *cursed foreign scum*. Her hands clenched so hard on the cup it was in danger of shattering. She forced her fingers to loosen, but her heart was tight in her chest. Berek and Ruston had betrayed Algarth to the Bregians. They were the scum. She'd been stupid to think for one moment that there could be any good in Berek at all.

Almost as if Bett's fury had conjured him, the Seeker leader appeared in the doorway to the dining hall. The kitchen sounds died away as the women noticed him.

His dark eyes found Mara. "A word with you."

Mara carefully put her cup down, pulled her hair forward, and followed him stiffly back into the dining hall. Bett watched the two of them cross to the far side of the room. Berek was speaking, but the rumble of his voice was so low that she couldn't make out any words. Finally, Mara gave a brief nod, and Berek turned on his heel and strode away. Mara returned to the kitchen, her face set.

"What did *he* want?" Bett snapped.

Mara sat down. All the women gathered around to listen.

Mara's lips were pressed together. She looked scared or angry, maybe both. "It seems we're to have *guests*." She almost spat the final word. "And we must look after them well. Twice the normal food preparation for today's meals, and another portion for them to take with them when they leave."

"Twice?" Bett grated. "How many of them are there?"

Mara's eyes glittered. "A hundred and eighty. A hundred and eighty Bregians."

A stunned silence filled the kitchen for several seconds before some of the women began to exclaim angrily.

Mara held up a hand. "I know. We'll need more help, but it's only for one day. They'll be moving on tonight."

"But why are they here?" someone asked.

Mara's expression grew grimmer as the mobile side of her mouth pulled down to match the other. The red puckering of her scars stood out against her bloodless skin. "He told me they're going to help him *destroy the corruption in our nation.*" She mimicked Berek's pompous tones perfectly, then lifted her chin. "I know what that means. They're marching on Eorna. And our men are joining them."

The women gasped and protested, some in outrage, others in denial.

Bett's heart was fluttering like a bird trapped in a cage. Even though she'd known the truth before Mara spoke, hearing it put into words was still shocking. "How can we stop 'em?"

Other voices echoed the question, but Mara stared them all into silence. "We can't. We'll do what we're told, prepare the food and stay out of it. Back to work now." Her voice allowed no argument, but many faces were flushed with anger as they bent to their tasks.

No matter what Mara said, Bett had no intention of *staying out of it*, and her mind was turning like the wheels of a runaway cart as she lifted the jar of leaven. She didn't know what she could do to stop the Bregians, but she was going to do something.

As she was kneading her second batch of dough, the solution came to her. The best thing about it was that it didn't involve killing anyone. Oh yes, she'd considered that. Hemlock grew wild near the bottom stream, and it wouldn't be too hard to chop some of the huge leaves extra fine and add them to the food intended for the soldiers. But after a moment's reflection Bett had realised she couldn't do it. She wasn't a murderer, not even of Bregians. This idea was better.

After setting the basin of dough near the stove to prove, she caught Mara's eye and jerked her head towards the storeroom. Mara followed her in, and Bett closed the door. She put her hands on her hips. "You don't really want us to help 'em, do you?"

"I'm not sure what else we can do. Even if we refuse to cook the extra food, it won't stop them. A few days' march on empty stomachs won't kill them."

"Funny you should mention stomachs," Bett began, a smile twitching her lips.

Mara narrowed her eyes. "What are you thinking?"

"I'm thinkin' about bread. An' I'm rememberin' that brown medicine you gave me last month. You know, when I was havin' trouble…"

Mara nodded, understanding dawning on her face. "You mean the goatbean powder," she said slowly.

"Do you have much left?"

"Oh, I always keep a supply on hand." Mara's sloping smile answered Bett's own grin. "Wait here a minute." With her fingers on the door latch, she turned back. "Don't tell the others. I'm not sure we can trust them all to stay quiet. At least a few of them genuinely believe in Berek's nonsense."

Bett only had to wait a few minutes before Mara returned to the storeroom carrying a cloth-wrapped bundle. She unfolded the linen to reveal dozens of crisp brown pods, broad and wrinkled and as long as Bett's hand.

"Now, normally I only grind up the shells," Mara said. "But today I think we need the seeds. They're stronger." She fetched down a bowl and began breaking the pods over it. As the brittle skins shattered, smooth cream-coloured beans tinkled into the bowl.

Bett frowned. "They won't kill no one, will they?"

"No, but for a few hours, our Bregian friends might just *wish* they were dead. It should slow them down a bit, anyway, give the Warrant Guards a chance against them."

Back in the kitchen, kneading the finely ground beans into the dough, Bett pictured the effect her special bread would have on the Bregian soldiers, and had to bite her lips to keep from smiling. For once, cooking felt like a truly satisfying occupation.

THIRTY-ONE

Cahira

Cahira dragged her eyelids apart, then immediately squeezed them shut against the dazzle. After a few more tries, she blinked away the obscuring tears and looked around. She was still in the armchair, and sunshine was flooding in through the window. The fire had burned down to fluffy grey ash.

She pushed herself to her feet, wincing as her cramped muscles protested. Her mouth felt sticky, and there was a bitter taste on her tongue. She opened the pack to get some water, then hesitated. It was a long time to sleep huddled in a chair, even after such an exhausting day. Could Fadra have drugged her? She uncorked the water bag and sniffed at the contents, but her nose couldn't detect anything strange. She might be imagining things, but she took the bag outside to the pump and rinsed it out several times before filling it with clean water.

The sun was even higher than she'd guessed, a sickening confirmation of how much time she'd lost. After splashing her face and taking hasty swallows from the pump, she hurried back inside and started going through the pack. To be on the safe side, she dumped out all the food that was left, and emptied and rinsed the two potion bottles before discarding them. Rapidly searching through the rest of the contents, she found nothing more sinister than clothing. She changed out of the dress into a tunic and trousers, then tipped the empty pack upside down and shook it to make sure she hadn't missed anything. An object fell out, catching the sunlight as it tumbled to the floor.

She reached out and picked it up. A small oval disc made of dull grey metal, smooth and unmarked. She turned it over. The opposite side was engraved with an eight-pointed star, like the ones drawn on maps to represent the compass directions.

Cahira felt as if she'd been punched in the stomach. Jon's words at the farm came back to her: *she's here, somewhere*. He'd been very certain, and now Cahira knew why. This disc was a locator, a Charmed object linked to a map. She hadn't escaped from Jon at all. He could find her whenever he wanted.

She stuffed the clothing into the pack as fast as she could, but hesitated about the disc. Her first impulse had been to leave it here. But if Jon didn't know she'd found it, she might be able to mislead him about where she was going next. She dropped it into her pocket, where it clinked against the sky stone.

Outside, watching closely for any sign of movement, she almost stopped in her tracks as a thought hit her. Jon hadn't been near this pack. Fadra had assembled it, with Cahira looking on. There was no doubt now. Fadra was involved in the conspiracy.

Inside the stable, Dove nickered a welcome. She really was a very sweet horse. Cahira ran a hand down the lame leg. It was warm but not hot, and Dove didn't flinch at her touch. If leading her for a while didn't cause any problems, Cahira would try mounting up. It was about twenty-four reaches from here to Eorna, and even riding at a walk would be better than travelling there on her own feet.

She heaved the saddle onto Dove's back and considered again what to do with the disc. Some locators needed to be fairly close to their paired map to work, but the more expensive ones could function from many reaches away. Cahira wondered if Nattie had Shaped the charm. If so, the disc could be powerful.

At least Jon didn't seem to be here yet. Perhaps he'd stopped for the night too, seeing no reason to hurry when he could find her anytime. And thanks to Bett's subterfuge, he didn't know Cahira was on her way to warn the city. She wanted to keep that advantage. If the conspirators thought Eorna was unprepared, they might get careless. She should send the disc off in a completely different direction.

She'd take it to the river. If she saw a cart or wagon heading south across the Ford, she'd toss the disc into the back. Her parents lived to the south, which made it more plausible she'd go there. If there was no vehicle, she'd throw the disc in the water and let the current carry it away.

She'd only led Dove a few steps from the stable when a flicker near the corner of the house snagged her eye. A blown leaf? Or the edge of a cloak whisking out of sight? It might not even be Jon, but a stranger wanting to prey on a woman travelling alone. For all she knew, there could be a dozen of them. If Dove had been completely sound, Cahira would have mounted up and galloped off. As things were, she didn't want to be looking over her shoulder the whole way to Eorna. She needed to be sure.

She dropped the reins and sidled back behind the stable door, hoping the thick timber would provide some protection if anyone decided to shoot at her. Ducking down, she put her eye to a wide crack in the planking. Time passed, and nothing moved. Had she imagined the whole thing? She had to know what she was dealing with, force anyone watching to reveal themselves while she stayed safely hidden. But she wasn't prepared to harm them, not unless there was no other way. What could she do?

Wracking her brain, she remembered the story of how Logen and his companions had once been saved by the appearance of a swarm of wasps. She didn't know any musical pieces about wasps, but something close came to mind. Beneath her breath, she began to murmur a song of bees. When a score of furry golden bodies were flying above her head, she sent them zooming to the place she'd seen the flutter of movement.

A shout split the air. A man came pelting out from behind the cottage, thrashing his arms to fend off the imaginary insects. The sun lit up his white hair. He was heading for the river, but then he stopped. Ignoring the darting bees, he turned slowly in a circle, his eyes scanning all around. The sound died on Cahira's lips. The bees vanished.

"Cahira," he called. "It's all right, it's just me, Jon. From the caves. You can come out."

What should she do? Was she willing to hurt him, the way she'd hurt Elise? The sick feeling in her stomach told her she wasn't. She never wanted to do that to anyone again.

"The bees were a clever idea." Jon went on circling, searching for her. "They fooled me at first, until I noticed they weren't making any sound."

Cahira felt like kicking herself. She hadn't thought of that. He stopped, facing her. She shrank back behind her wooden barrier. He cocked his head, as if listening to something. "Are you in the stable?"

Cahira's mind raced as he took a step forward. She drew a deep breath and moved out of the shelter of the door.

"There you are. Didn't you recognise me? I'm sorry if I scared you."

This was a very different Jon. The icy tone and formal speech were gone. He sounded harmless and friendly. Cahira wasn't fooled, but she did her best to smile at him, still thinking fast. She mustn't let him see she knew the truth. She spread out her hands. "Sorry, Jon. I just saw someone and panicked. I didn't know it was you."

He smiled at her. "No harm done. I'm glad you chose bees instead of lightning this time."

He was being so forgiving, so reasonable. Could she have got everything wrong? *No*, she thought, giving herself a mental shake. *It's all an act. I know what I heard.*

He nodded towards Dove. "Are you leaving?"

"Yes, I'm heading south to visit my parents." The lie came easily, fitting with her earlier plan to throw him off her trail.

"Oh? Where do they live?"

"South of Edervale, almost to the mountains."

Somehow, he'd come nearer without her noticing. They were face to face now, less than an arm's length apart. She wanted to step back, but that might reveal her true feelings.

He frowned, holding her in a steady gaze. "A long way to travel on your own." Did he suspect something?

"I have a friend at Edervale," she blurted, the half-truth giving her a twinge of discomfort. Sara did live at Edervale, but she was more an acquaintance than a friend. They'd known each other for two days before Bram's death had driven Cahira back home, and they'd only met once since then. Nevertheless, she ploughed on. "I thought I'd stay a night with her on the way."

As she looked into Jon's clear grey eyes and spoke the lie, her uneasiness grew. It was wrong to deceive him when he was just concerned for her. But she wasn't supposed to tell him she was going to Eorna. At least, she didn't think so, but she was having trouble remembering why.

He nodded, accepting her words at face value and making her feel even worse. "We were all surprised when you left the caves so suddenly. We'd hoped to have time to get to know you better."

He sounded so wistful that Cahira wished she'd been able to stay and get to know him better, too. She'd enjoyed talking with the three of them over lunch that day. They'd been so welcoming, telling her all about themselves and their community.

"You can return with me, if you like," Jon went on. "Elise and Ferdy are fine, and no one blames you for what happened. We know you didn't mean any harm. You're not the first one to have made a mistake. It's all part of learning to control our abilities."

Could she really go back? She'd made a lot of progress in just a few days of Fadra's mentoring, and she knew she could do even better, given time. She'd left because she'd been ashamed, that was all. She hadn't meant to hurt anyone. It had just been a mistake, like Jon said.

"There's no rush to visit your parents, is there?"

No, of course there wasn't. They didn't even know she was coming. She could do anything she wanted. She'd go back to her new friends and learn more about her power. With Fadra's help, who knew what she could achieve in the future?

Greater things than you can imagine.

Cahira actually felt the blood drain from her face as the familiar whisper brushed against her mind. For a few moments, listening to Jon, she'd forgotten all about the Unity, Fadra's treachery, everything. Jon was a Mind Wender. He'd been influencing her, and she'd fallen into the trap. This time, she couldn't hide her shock and dismay.

His smile disappeared. His eyes bored into her. "Listen to my words." His voice echoed oddly, entwined with the hissing of the Unity. *Listen.*

Panic swept away Cahira's reluctance to harm anyone. She strove to bring the lightning, the thunder, but the whispering kept dissolving her thoughts before she could utter a sound.

Jon held out a hand. "Come with me." *Come.*

Cahira tried to run, but her feet were glued to the ground. A moan of frustration burst from her. Immediately, a dark cloud formed above Jon's head. Relief leapt up. She could do this. She increased the volume of the groan until it drowned out the voices. Free of restraint, she backed away.

Jon was eying the growing cloud warily. Jags of lightning flickered. He threw her a sudden look of alarm. Triumphant, Cahira bared her teeth at him. Then he drew a long dagger from somewhere in his clothing and started forward. Her voice faltered. The cloud faded. He came at her with the blade held low, poised to strike upward. Her throat closed in terror. The last wisp of cloud vanished. She turned and fled.

Driven by pure instinct, she raced for the water. She had no plan, just the hope that there might be other people at the crossing. She tried to suck in a breath, but her throat still refused to open. The blood pounded in her ears. Every second, she expected to feel the sharp blade plunge into her back.

Help me! she thought in despair.

A horse neighed from somewhere up ahead. Cahira's chest heaved violently, and she could breathe again.

"Stop!" Jon's shout drilled into her skull, and the echoes twisted greasily through her thoughts. *Stop… stop… stop…*

Cahira's legs slowed. She gritted her teeth and pushed harder. Her body responded sluggishly. It was taking an enormous effort just to keep moving. Her leg muscles were burning, and her head was splitting. He was going to catch her, and then she would die. The relentless voices filled her brain to bursting.

"Get out of my head!" she screamed.

Cruel laughter cascaded through her mind.

But she'd reached the river now. She lifted her head to see a pony splashing towards her, pulling a vehicle.

"Help!" she cried out to whoever was driving, and had no breath left for anything else.

She lurched into the shallow water, her thigh muscles on fire. At the first touch of the river, the maddening laughter stopped. Jon was still shouting, but the compulsion was gone. Cahira's legs, suddenly freed, carried her forward in a lurch. She fell to the stony river bed, landing on her hands and knees.

The pony reached her and bent its shaggy head to nose at her shoulder. Heart hammering, Cahira twisted around, expecting to see Jon right behind her. He was nowhere in sight. Not in the water, not on the bank. He hadn't even bothered to chase her, relying on the power of his mind. But he'd soon realise his mistake. Cahira hauled herself up, fighting the pain and fatigue, and splashed past the rough-coated pony towards the vehicle.

To her surprise, the driver was a pink-cheeked, elderly lady. She smiled down as if she was used to finding desperate, bedraggled women in the river. "Are you heading to Eorna?" Her fluting voice was like the chirping of a bird.

Cahira nodded, still too winded to speak.

"It has been some time since I visited the city, oh my, yes." The lady's hands fluttered in excitement. "A little trip will do me no harm, no harm at all. Would you like to join me? There is room to hide in the back, yes there is." She indicated a red-curtained opening behind her seat.

Cahira nodded again. The tall, boxy vehicle was made of wood that had cracked and weathered to silver grey. Here and there, scraps of paint clung on forlornly. It looked ancient, ready to fall apart. But the important thing was that it was completely enclosed. Even the windows were shuttered. It would hide her from Jon's sight.

She used the last of her strength to climb up to the seat and crawl through the opening. She pulled the thick curtain across and sat down in the darkness, panting hard. Too late, she wondered if she'd brought danger to the woman by taking refuge here. But the die was cast. All she could do now was wait in the softly creaking vehicle, dripping water and hoping Jon wouldn't catch up with them.

The large wheels grated and stalled on the bottom of the river as the vehicle slowly turned beneath her. Then, with a lurch that threw her sprawling onto her back, it swung all the way around. Another crunch and a second jerk, and it rumbled forward, swaying gently.

Pushing herself painfully to her hands and knees, Cahira pressed her ear to one shuttered window, listening for a hint that Jon was following them through the water. But the grumbling of the wheels, the splashing of the pony, and the constant creaking of the old vehicle drowned out every other sound.

Her bruised knees were protesting badly. As she eased herself into a crouch to relieve the pressure, something shifted under her and slid away, almost sending her sprawling again. It was too dark to see clearly, but she felt around, hoping she hadn't been kneeling on anything alive. She encountered an object twice as long as her hand, with a smooth, flat surface and four straight edges. It was a book, bound in leather. She wriggled her fingers under it and lifted it free. Another lay beneath.

In fact, as her eyes adjusted to the dimness, she saw the whole floor was covered in them, several layers deep. This dilapidated vehicle held a staggering collection. Even if the pages were blank, the sheer number of volumes represented a small fortune. If they were all printed inside, she couldn't even imagine what they might be worth.

Suddenly afraid that her wet clothing was going to ruin them, Cahira stacked a dozen to one side to give herself a clear space to sit. What were all these books doing here? It made no sense.

The splashing stopped, replaced by the sharp clopping of hooves on shingle. They'd reached the opposite shore. As the vehicle slowed and tilted, Cahira grabbed onto the lower edge of the window to stop herself from sliding backwards. They must be climbing the bank. By the time the floor had levelled out again, the air inside the closed box had grown unpleasantly warm. It tasted stale, too.

If Jon hadn't caught up to them by now, he wasn't going to. Cahira carefully shuffled forward and eased the curtain open, blinking in the light and relishing the cool breeze on her sweating skin.

"You can come out now, dear, yes you can."

Cahira clambered onto the seat. "Thank you."

"Oh, it is my pleasure, yes, it is. Oh my, yes," the old woman twittered.

Clear blue eyes met Cahira's, shining out from a face as wrinkled as a winter-stored apple. Wisps of white hair poked out from underneath a shapeless black cap. Something nagged at Cahira, some memory of having seen this woman before, but she couldn't quite place her.

"I'm Cahira."

"My name is Enge, yes, it is."

The name sounded familiar too, but again the memory eluded her. Confident it would come if she didn't force it, she looked around to see where they were. A wide empty road stretched ahead, bordered on both sides by trees.

"The man who was following me?" Cahira asked.

"Wouldn't cross the Ford, oh dear me, no. Couldn't."

Couldn't? What did that mean? But the thought of Jon had reminded Cahira of the locator. She still had it. He could follow it and find her again. She had to get rid of it, fast. She scrabbled in her pocket, her fingers recognising and rejecting the smooth, familiar shape of the sky stone, questing further. The disc wasn't there. It must have fallen out when she'd been tossed to the floor of the vehicle. Her heart sank at the prospect of blindly feeling around for it among that mass of books.

"Can we open the shutters?" she asked. "I've lost something, and I need to find it."

"Yes, yes, time for a stop anyway, so it is." Enge held up a finger. "Just a moment, just a moment."

She didn't seem to do anything with the reins, but the pony turned off the road onto a track leading through the trees. It trotted along, its hooves making barely any sound on the soft surface. The back of

Cahira's neck prickled. She knew this trail. The last time she'd been on it, she'd been hiding in fear of her life with Bram, Adric, Niall, and the others. She gripped the seat, feeling she might fall off at any moment.

"Courage."

Cahira shot a glance at her companion, but the old woman's eyes were on the pony. Cahira could almost believe she'd imagined that single, soft word. *Courage*, she thought. Bram had been courageous, and she wouldn't disgrace his memory by falling apart now. She unclenched her hands, took a few deep breaths, and lifted her head.

They emerged from the trees into the clearing. Stumps stood around it, the same ones she and Fin and Logen had been sitting on when the others had introduced Kelan to them. The boy's news, about a foreign Greenhaelan imprisoned in Eorna, had started the entire train of events that had led to Tarn's defeat, but also to Bram's death. Cahira gently touched the sky stone in her pocket, wondering at the cruel coincidence that had brought her here again.

The pony stopped. The old lady climbed down, and Cahira followed. When Enge swung aside the first pair of shutters, a surprise met Cahira's eyes. Without thinking about it, she'd expected the window space to be filled with more weathered wood, in the form of bars or a lattice. Instead, a panel of intricate ironwork depicting flowering vines decorated the opening. Her curiosity piqued, she examined the vehicle more closely as Enge moved around to the opposite side, wondering what else she might have missed.

The scraps of peeling paint weren't random as she'd first thought, but were concentrated into two large sections flanking the windows. Blue predominated, and seemed to have been the original base colour, but there were traces of red and yellow and green, as well as hints of fine black outlines. There had been some kind of complex, colourful pattern here. Cahira put out a finger and traced a fragment of black line, curled and as delicate as filigree. Too little of the design remained for her to make any sense of it.

Enge came back to join her. "You are interested in my caravan, yes you are. I have had it for many years now, so I have."

The odd word seemed to suit the vehicle somehow. "It must have been beautiful once," Cahira said.

"Yes, yes, very beautiful. Still beautiful." The little woman patted the caravan as if it was a favourite pet. "Come, look inside now."

Dropping her pack on the ground, Cahira climbed up and through the curtain again. With the shutters pulled back, the interior was transformed. Sunlight laced through the ironwork of the window openings, illuminating the volumes stacked on the floor. There were even more of them than she'd imagined, and they weren't the only books in this space. Shelves covered the walls, each one crammed tightly with leather or cloth spines. Some looked as old and faded as the caravan, cracked and threadbare. Others might have been bound yesterday. Cahira stared in awe. Then, remembering why she was in here, she began to search.

She was hot and frustrated by the time she gave up, and sure she had moved every book on the floor at least twice. The locator wasn't here. It must have fallen out when she'd dropped to her knees in the water, back at the Ford. She'd wasted time looking for it, time that the city didn't have.

Glaring at the books as if it was all their fault, she fumbled for the stone in her pocket, seeking its comforting touch. As she folded her fingers around it, an image flashed into her mind: a street market, a book stall, and an old woman in black. Enge had been the stall holder who had sold them the sky stone.

Ice trickled down Cahira's spine, immediately followed by a hot flush of anger. She scrambled outside and dropped to the ground. The old woman was sitting on a nearby stump, eating a piece of bread.

"Who are you?" Cahira demanded.

Enge merely glanced up and continued chewing.

Cahira advanced a step. "I mean it. Tell me who and what you are, right now."

Enge took her time swallowing the mouthful before replying. "That is the wrong question, yes, it is."

Cahira was so tired of being manipulated and kept in the dark—by Fadra, the Unity, Jon, and now this mysterious old woman. Thunder rolled below the surface of her mind, yearning to be set free, but she held back the storm. She was in control, not the song. And she wouldn't attack an old woman, however sinister, who had made no move to harm her.

She faced Enge squarely and planted her feet. "What's the right question?"

"Something you need to discover for yourself, Cahira Gelt." She wiped the crumbs from her fingers onto her shabby black robe, and shuffled over to the caravan. Without haste, she climbed up and settled herself. "Your friend will be here soon, yes, very soon."

The pony pulled the vehicle around in a half circle until it was facing the way it had come.

"What friend? What are you talking about?"

"Remember," Enge said, swivelling her blue-eyed gaze towards Cahira again. "Courage."

She clicked her tongue, and the pony headed down the track towards the road.

Cahira was forced to let it go. It was infuriating, but she couldn't think of what else to do. Enge picking her up and then abandoning her here was certainly starting to look like some kind of trap, but despite everything she couldn't be absolutely sure. Not enough to harm the old lady, anyway.

At least she didn't have to sit around waiting trustingly for the *friend* who might be coming along. The pack was on the ground where she'd left it. She shouldered it and set off.

She'd only been back on the main road for a few minutes when the wind rose. Icy gusts battered against her face. Ducking her head, she made for the shelter of the treeline again. But it was worse there. Leaves and twigs whirled through the air until she could barely see. She battled her way back to the road and pushed on against the gale, staying low and concentrating on planting one foot in front of the other. Even the weather was conspiring against her.

A warning shout rang out from behind. She spun around and came face to flank with a horse. Had Jon found her again? Fearful of what she might see, she raised her eyes to the cloaked and hooded rider.

"Cahira?"

She just caught her own name before it was whipped away by the wind. A woman's voice, though, not Jon's. The speaker's face was half-covered by green wool, only the eyes exposed. She laughed as if in disbelief, lifted a gloved hand and tugged the scarf down to her chin. "Cahira! It's me, Sara."

It was a long moment before Cahira found her own voice. "What are you doing here?" she yelled.

"Let's get out of this wind, and I'll tell you!"

Sara tugged a glove off with her teeth and reached down. Cahira grasped the lowered hand, guessing what Sara was about to do, and wondering what it would feel like. Dizziness assailed her. She almost fell, but Sara's firm grip kept her upright.

"It's a bit startling the first time, isn't it?"

Startling wasn't the word. In an instant, Cahira's surroundings had changed. She was standing on a thick layer of straw inside a stable. Sara released her hand and dismounted. Unlike Cahira, the horse didn't seem at all disturbed by its sudden change of location. Perhaps it was used to it.

Cahira watched in mute astonishment as Sara unsaddled her mount and rubbed it down. She'd heard about this skal of Sara's, the ability to open Gateways between locations, but having just experienced it herself, she had no words.

Sara turned to her, a look of concern on her face. "Are you okay? It's all right, we're at Bella's. We'll go inside and talk."

Cahira suddenly remembered her mission. "There's no time," she said, gripping Sara's arm. "We have to go and warn the garrison. There's an army on the way to attack the city. They'll be at the Ford tomorrow."

But Sara only nodded. "They already know. Niall and Adric came two days ago, and Commander Oren's been preparing since then. They sent a message to me at Edervale. That's why I'm here."

Cahira's mouth fell open. Her thoughts whirled and shifted as she struggled to adjust to this new information.

Sara placed a hand over hers. "Come on, we'll warm up and get some food, and catch up with each other's news. Bella too. She knows more than I do about what's been happening."

Inside the tavern, Bella greeted them with her usual energy, and quickly organised a substantial lunch for three, to be served in her cosy private parlour with its blazing fire. Now that she knew the city had been warned, Cahira was more than content to rest for a while. She ate Bella's delicious food, sipped some luscious wine, and listened as the others talked.

She didn't know either of them well, but she trusted them. They'd both played their parts to defeat Tarn's plans and clear the names of the Greenhaelen. Her thoughts turned to the last time she'd been at the tavern, just after the trial. Something about that meeting nagged at her, a piece of information that felt important, but she couldn't catch hold of it. It was probably nothing, just her tired mind playing tricks. She pushed the feeling aside and focused again on the conversation going back and forth across the table.

The two women were very different narrators. Sara, her voice soft and her blue eyes serious, kept everything in chronological order and stuck to the facts, but she wasn't allowed to continue this way for long. Time and again, Sara's words would remind Bella of something else the other two needed to know, and she'd jump in to tell them, tangling the careful thread of Sara's narrative and sometimes breaking it altogether. But Cahira had to admit that Bella was entertaining. Her mobile face and expressive voice mimicked each character and conversation as she added to the story, and her dark eyes shone with pleasure. She was a born performer.

However, as the jumbled tale unfolded, Cahira's enjoyment slowly seeped away, to be replaced by something close to anger. The whole time she'd been so anxious about Niall and Adric, so desperate to find them, they'd been safe and having adventures of their own. Well, not completely safe—they'd spent some time in a gaol cell—but nothing truly terrible had happened to them. And Adric hadn't even been a Seeker of Virtue. He was a Warrant Guard, of all things!

She'd wasted so much energy worrying about the two of them, she didn't know whether she wanted to hug them or shout at them. Probably both. They hadn't needed her help at all. They'd even found Perna and brought her here.

"She left yesterday, after a fight with Niall," Bella added. She lifted her chin in a passable imitation of Perna at the height of her dignity and pitched her voice low and tight: "I'm joining the Aalden. Don't follow me." Then she smiled and reverted to her own lively tone. "Niall would have gone after her anyway, of course, but I had to tell him about Darin."

"Darin?" Cahira asked, startled. Where had she heard that name recently?

"A Stone Shaper, a very dangerous one. He had some strange things to say, about a woman named Fadra."

Cahira must have made an involuntary sound, because Bella stopped and stared at her. "You know this name?"

Cahira took a deep breath. It was her turn. She told her tale rapidly and mostly honestly, but held back any mention of the Unity. She didn't want the others to know that some sort of evil being had been living in her head. What if they thought she was dangerous and wanted to lock her up? What if they thought she was mad? Anyway, there were more important things to think about right now than her own personal problems. If Algarth fought off this invasion, that would be soon enough to tell the full story.

She finished up by saying she'd escaped from Jon across the Ford, without bothering to explain how. It didn't matter. She was tired and deflated. She'd come all this way for nothing. She slumped down in her seat and smothered a yawn.

Bella's sharp eyes noticed. "You've been through a lot. It's time you rested. Come on, I'll get you both settled in."

Cahira didn't argue. To be honest, now the burden of anxiety had been lifted, she felt like she could sleep for days. Saving Algarth wasn't up to her any more. Other people were taking care of it, people who were equipped to deal with this kind of thing. She could leave it to them.

THIRTY-TWO

Niall

Niall stood beneath the trees on the river bank and aimed a sour glance upwards. The weather was changing, and not for the better. A cold wind was blowing from the north, and heavy grey clouds were scudding in. Rain was the last thing they needed. Poor visibility and damp bowstrings would seriously hamper the archers tomorrow.

The thirty skilled longbowmen were key to the defence of the Ford. Eorna's Warrant Guards were spread thin in the effort to protect the city. First, Oren had sent a large contingent to the northern waterfront. The Bregians had been prepared to land soldiers on the west coast and march them overland. They'd hardly baulk at sailing the shorter distance across the Strait to Eorna's harbour. Mundar, who had experience with ships, had been promoted to captain and assigned to the docks. A second force had been left behind to hold the garrison—the most defensible structure in the city—if the worst came to the worst. The rest of the fighters were here: the archers under Adric's command, three troops of Guards, and Niall's Beast Speakers.

Niall eyed the sky again. He wasn't happy about the plan, for several reasons. It was true that if the weather cleared by sunrise tomorrow, the archers would have a chance to do some damage. The enemy would be exposed on a stretch of bare, featureless ground on the other side of the Ford, with the sun in their eyes. But gambling on the weather was a loser's game, and he wasn't hopeful.

The second problem was Oren's order for the bowmen to prioritise anyone on horseback, in an effort to take out Fadra's group before they could use their enhanced skals. The Beast Speakers would also target the riders, telling their horses to throw them and cross the Ford on their own, after which Niall and the others would lead the animals to the city. If any of Fadra's people survived this encounter, they'd be forced to walk to Eorna, slowing them down and perhaps removing some of them from the fight altogether. Twenty-four reaches was a long way if you weren't used to travelling on foot.

And all that would have been fine by Niall, and Adric too, if every rider was guaranteed to be an enemy. But Cahira might be among them. And so, last night, the two of them had made a plan of their own.

They'd stand together, and if either of them spotted her, Niall would force her horse to bolt and carry her straight to them. He was by far the strongest Beast Speaker here. He could overrule any command urging her mount to unseat her. The danger would come during the crossing, when an arrow might find her before she reached them. But they couldn't think of any way of preventing that. All they could do was trust in their ability to identify her before the shooting started, and the speed of the horse. *Plus a huge slice of luck*, Niall thought gloomily, not at all confident of his chances of being handed something so useful.

He tried again to convince himself he was worrying about nothing. Cahira would never have joined Fadra. Oh, she was impulsive and strong-willed, even stubborn, ruled by emotion rather than sober logic. Not that Niall was so fond of sobriety himself, but he usually stopped to think before rushing headlong into trouble. Not so Cahira. She was the most alive person he had ever met, and at times the most exasperating. Her moods could change as swiftly as the weather.

But he was certain of one thing. She would never willingly help anyone who harboured ill will towards her home and her friends. And so there was no reason for her to come here, was there? But no amount of arguing with himself could take away this restlessness, this feeling of unease.

He watched the sun dip below the horizon, wishing the night was over instead of just beginning. When nothing remained of the light except a narrow band of dull orange beneath lowering clouds, he stirred himself and set out for his tent. Dumping his pack and bedroll inside, he settled himself in a spot sheltered by the trees, but with a glimpse of the dark water flowing over the Ford. A young Guard came around, giving out food. Niall took his share, but he chewed mechanically, barely tasting it. His mind churned with bleak imaginings of what tomorrow would bring.

A fat drop splashed onto the leaf litter beside his boot, then another. By the time he'd crawled back into the tent, rain was drumming on the waxed canvas. One by one, the others arrived and crowded in. No one spoke. There was no need. They all knew what this could mean. Niall stretched out on his bedroll and wrapped himself in the blanket. Nothing to do now but try to get some sleep.

He woke with a start, every sense alert. It was completely dark, and the rain was still beating. He sat up. By the soft sounds around him, the others were doing the same. What had woken them all? Then he sensed the horses, about a dozen of them. He probed for direction and distance. They were on the other side of the Ford, maybe a few hundred paces from the water. Near the cottage, then. This could be Fadra's group. The officers needed to be told.

"I'll go," he said, knowing he'd get no more sleep tonight until he knew for sure.

No one protested. He heard them settling back down, resting while they could. He pulled his cloak tightly around him, drew up the hood, and crawled outside into the rain.

He could just make out the solid masses of the evergreen canopies against the charcoal sky, but the terrain at ground level was all undifferentiated shadow. He'd have to rely on senses other than sight.

Even through the hiss of the downpour he could hear water rushing over the stones of the Ford. He used the sound to keep himself oriented towards the centre of the camp. He took as direct a line as he could, but kept having to dodge the tree trunks that loomed up without warning in his path. The wet, slippery mulch beneath his boots slowed his progress further, and there were low shrubs and fallen branches everywhere.

Remembering that the horses were picketed behind the command tent, he touched minds with Sienna so he'd know when he was close.

It felt as though he must have covered the distance three or four times when a hoarse voice came out of the darkness in front of him, setting his heart thumping.

"Halt! Who goes there?"

"Niall Crawley. I have news for Commander Oren."

Metal scraped as a lamp was unshielded. The thin beam of light played over his face, dazzling him.

"Pass." The Guard stepped aside.

Spots and streaks danced in Niall's vision. He took one tentative step forward and then another, hands held out in front of him, until he came to a wall of wet canvas. Another Guard, a second brief glare, and he was ushered in.

"Wait," said a voice.

Niall stood blinking until the bright spots in front of his eyes had faded into the darkness. And then, without warning, a glow bloomed above his head. A metal and glass lamp hung from the roof, and as he watched in growing alarm, the flame inside it brightened and grew until the whole interior of the tent was flooded with light. This was madness. The command group was supposed to be hiding their position from enemy eyes.

The burly form of Commander Oren was bent over a table covered in papers. He looked up wearily. "It can't be seen from outside when the tent is laced shut." He rubbed a hand vigorously over the dark brown stubble on his head, as if to stimulate his brain into greater wakefulness. "Something new from the Charmers at the Academy. The lamp itself and a coating painted on the inside of the canvas."

Niall squinted up doubtfully. "Are you sure it works?" He'd never heard of a charm that could do anything like this.

"See any light as you approached?"

Niall admitted he hadn't.

"Been burning all night. Only shrouded it to let you in."

That was intriguing, but Niall reluctantly set his curiosity aside. They had more urgent things to talk about. "There are people across the Ford. Twelve to fifteen horses."

The tiredness vanished from Oren's broad face, and there was a stir from the others inside the tent. Niall recognised the three sergeants he'd already met at the garrison, but the fourth man was unfamiliar. He was unremarkable in height or build, but the dark blue of his Warrant Guard shirt threw his pale skin into sharp relief. Despite his snowy hair, he only looked about Niall's age. Oren introduced him as Jak, a recruit from a town further south, who'd been on his way to join the muster at Eorna when he'd come across their camp.

"There was no one on the other side when I crossed, sir, honest." Jak's face was twisted in anxiety, his grey eyes round and pleading. "I would have told the officers if I'd seen anyone."

"It's all right, Jak," Oren said. "No blame to you. They must have come afterwards."

Jak nodded vigorously. "Yes, sir. Thank you, sir."

Niall briefly hoped this scared rabbit of a man wasn't a typical example of the calibre of Warrant Guards that would be arriving in Eorna to bolster the defence. He seemed afraid of his own shadow, and not overly bright.

Oren addressed his sergeants. "So, some of them are here early. How does that change our plans?"

They discussed the possibility of the enemy attempting the river before daylight. The rain would cause the water to rise, making the crossing more difficult as time went on, but on the other hand, this might just be a small advance group. In that case, they'd wait for the rest of their forces before moving. Each of the sergeants had his own view and put it forward strongly.

Oren listened patiently to all the speculation and argument. Then he held up a hand. "We don't know their intentions, so we have to be ready for anything. Post more sentries along the bank to listen for anyone trying to cross."

He nodded to Niall. "You and your men join them. If they're mounted, deal with the horses."

His steady gaze returned to his sergeants. "If they wait for daylight, and if this cursed rain stops, we stick with the original plan. Otherwise, the archers will be useless and it'll have to be pikes and swords as they climb the slope." His voice hardened. "But make them pay for crossing the river. Until you hear the retreat, your orders are to stand and hold. At any cost."

Niall made his slow, wet way back to rouse his companions, his thoughts as dark as the surrounding night. Just as he reached the tent, the rain seemed to slacken. He looked up. High above, the tiny spark of a single star shone out from the gloom. Another kindled to white fire beside it.

The clouds were breaking up. Perhaps the luck was with him after all.

THIRTY-THREE

Roldan

Overseer Roldan covered the distance from one side of his command tent to the other in three long strides, then turned and set out again. It was always like this before an engagement. He was consumed by a restlessness composed of equal parts nervous energy and anticipation.

An hour to go until the assault, and the rain had slowed from a furious pelting to a mere drizzle. He'd be glad to finish the campaign and leave this soggy little country. But rain or not, his job was to secure the Ford before noon: a nice warmup for his troops before the major event, when they'd be taking the city itself.

He only hoped all these amateurs he'd been ordered to work with wouldn't get in the way of what he had to do. He'd already judged the Algarthans from the farm as soft, ill-trained, and practically useless. As for the others, at least the Disciple and Jon were Bregian, but they both made his skin crawl with their talk of *enhanced talents* and *spiritual power*. He had to admit that the white-haired Mind Wender had gathered good information in the enemy camp, but the deception involved didn't sit well. Truth be told, this whole situation didn't sit well.

Roldan scowled and lifted a hand to his head, rubbing it vigorously across the stiff grey bristles. He was a soldier, born and bred, and he didn't need help or advice from anyone in order to take one insignificant, unwalled city. But the orders had come from very high up, and there was no use griping about it. That was part of being a soldier, too.

He lifted the last piece of bread from the tray on the table and chewed it as he resumed his pacing. He'd ordered food and rest for his men after their march from the farm, so they'd be fresh for the day's fighting.

At least this first encounter would be conducted in proper military style, with no amateurs butting in. After they'd heard Jon's intelligence, even the Disciple had seen the sense of holding her mounted group back until Roldan's forces had dealt with the Beast Speakers on the other side.

And he'd deal with them swiftly. He had the advantage here, and not only numerically. These *Warrant Guards* weren't real soldiers, and Jon had said they'd be using traditional longbows. The arrows would never penetrate toughened Bregian oak shields. Armed with the new crossbows, they might be more of a threat, but Roldan doubted anyone in this backward little country had ever heard of a crossbow. Even in Bregia, the superior weapons were still rare, and his force had been issued only a dozen of them.

If there were any decent shots among the Algarthan bowmen, he could lose a handful of soldiers to the crossing, but once they closed in on the enemy line, his troops wouldn't have any trouble. He knew each of them—their training and their years of experience. Most had already fought in several campaigns under his command. They were battle-hardened professionals, facing glorified thief-takers.

He'd hold his own archers in reserve for now. They'd be of limited use against an enemy hiding in the trees. Much better to save them for the assault on the city. As soon as he'd secured the first section of streets, he'd station them on the rooftops to provide cover as the infantry pushed towards the garrison and the harbour. It was a tried-and-true strategy, and he wouldn't need any help from the local yokels or Disciple Hellin's pupils to make it work.

He chewed and swallowed the last mouthful of bread. The Algarthans could cook, he'd say that for them. He ran his thumb along the ridge of scar tissue bisecting his throat—a souvenir from the campaign against the Mallornans five years ago. Now, they were a people who knew how to fight, as tough as the harsh land that had spawned them. Not like these soft islanders. A nation of farmers and bakers. That was who he was facing. They didn't stand a chance.

245

THIRTY-FOUR

Cahira

Cahira tucked the shirt into the soft woollen trousers with great satis-faction and reached for the belt. She wondered if Sara or Bella had left the fresh clothing on the chair beside the bed. Probably Sara, who knew her preference for practical garments. Bless her, she'd even found a blue cloak, not exactly the same shade as the lost favourite, but an intense sapphire that Cahira liked very much. She put it on and twirled around, admiring herself in the long glass. Then, laughing at her own vanity, she removed it again. No need for a cloak inside the warm tavern. Still, she folded it carefully before laying it down.

Feeling more like herself, she tied back her hair and retrieved the stone from under the pillow. She rubbed its smooth surface gently with her thumb for a moment, then slipped it into a pocket.

Judging by the shadows outside, she'd slept well into the morning. Sara was probably already at the garrison, meeting with Commander Oren. At least it had been a natural sleep this time, not Fadra's drugs. She felt clear-headed and rested. And hungry. Starving, now that she thought about it. Downstairs, breakfast would be long over.

She crouched and untied the flap of her pack, looking for something to eat. Then she remembered. She'd thrown all the food out, afraid Fadra had contaminated it. Sitting back on her heels with a disappointed huff, she noticed the corner of a book sticking up. She clearly recalled going through the pack at the cottage and finding only clothing.

Frowning, she lifted the book out and turned it over in her hands. It was a small leather-bound volume with no title on the cover. Could it have got in by accident while she was sliding around in Enge's caravan? She didn't see how. The pack had been fastened. Later, though, she'd left it on the ground when she'd gone into the vehicle to search for the disc. The book must have been slipped in then. And the only other person there had been Enge.

Cahira's heart beat faster. She carefully laid the volume down on the floor and wiped her fingers on her shirt. Books could be Charmed, for good or ill, and she didn't trust the old woman. Too many coincidences surrounded her. But the memory of the word that Enge had spoken twice came back to her: *courage*. It had been an odd thing to say, especially if she meant Cahira harm.

What would courage look like right now? Well, not lounging around in her room thinking about breakfast and leaving the defence of the city up to others. Why hadn't she thought of that yesterday? Fadra had given her a gift, even if she hadn't intended to. Cahira's new control over her skal might save lives. She'd go up to the garrison and offer her services to Commander Oren. Hopefully, she'd see Niall and Adric there, too.

The book caught her eye again, and an elusive memory tugged at her mind, the same thing that had been nagging at her while she waited for lunch yesterday. Something Sara said at their previous meeting. Cahira wracked her brain. And then it came to her. Sara had spoken about her encounter with the archivist at Edervale Castle. A woman, surrounded by books and papers, who'd later disappeared. A woman named Enge.

Cahira caught her breath. Why did the old lady keep turning up, and what were her intentions? According to Sara, the archivist had helped her escape from the castle and given her a book containing information she needed to know. Was it possible that Enge had placed this book in Cahira's pack for the same reason? Cahira bit her lip. She'd just been thinking about courage. Was she really afraid of such a small, inert thing? It was only leather and paper and ink, after all.

Her fingertips didn't tingle when they met the smooth cover. No strange thoughts came into her head as she opened it. The first page was blank. She snorted at her foolish fears and turned it over. And there was the title:

THE BOOK OF KOLOS

by a Disciple

Who, or what, or where, was Kolos? Cahira sat cross-legged on the floor and hauled the book onto her lap. She soon discovered that Kolos was a spiritual being that the writer believed in and worshipped. Several pages were filled with grandiose statements about how awesome and terrifying Kolos was, how it destroyed its enemies and offered power to its Disciples. Was Enge a Disciple? Had she hoped the book would convince Cahira to become one, too? If so, the woman knew nothing about her.

She turned another page. Instead of the rows of text she'd been reading, a dense tangle of lines met her eyes. She yawned and rubbed her temples. Her brain felt fuzzy, as if she hadn't had enough sleep. Well, it had been a busy couple of days. She peered at the mass of lines coiling over and under each other. Strangely, she didn't see any ends. Slowly the truth dawned on her. The drawing wasn't composed of multiple lines but a single, continuous one, looping and crossing itself many times before joining up at the point it had begun. It was smoothly drawn and the same thickness all the way, with no breaks or blots. The writer hadn't lifted the pen from the page until the whole thing was done. It was skilful scribing, but she couldn't find a pattern in it, or figure out why it was here.

Idly, she traced a small section, then jerked her hand away. For an instant, she could have sworn something had moved under her finger, something cold and alive. And was that a drop of ink on the tip? It couldn't be. All the ink on the page had been dry for a long time, maybe years. It was gone now, anyway. She rubbed the unmarked finger, which was slightly numb, and eyed the drawing again. It was unchanged, nothing but a clever scribble. Her imagination had been playing tricks on her.

She closed the book, suddenly feeling the need to be somewhere else. Pausing only to stow the new cloak in her pack, she left.

Bella was downstairs. She confirmed that Sara had gone up to the garrison. "You seemed exhausted last night. We thought we'd let you sleep."

Bella nodded when Cahira told her she was leaving, too, but insisted she eat something first. Cahira made no objection. Her hunger had multiplied tenfold.

"I'm sorry I can't lend you a mount," Bella went on.

Cahira's conscience smote her. She'd completely forgotten about Dove, left behind at the Ford. She hoped the gentle little mare was safe. But she belonged to Fadra, after all, so perhaps Jon would make sure she was taken care of.

"We're closing the tavern today," Bella continued. "Boarding it up in case the fighting comes through here. I'd already sent the spare horses away before you came."

Cahira assured her it was all right, but her heart sank at the thought of more walking. If only Sara had waited. As she finished eating, she briefly considered telling Bella about the book, but there wasn't really any point. Nothing had happened to her when she'd opened it, and she'd left it locked in her room, anyway. She quickly thanked the tavern keeper and took her leave.

The sun was lower than she'd expected, and in the wrong quadrant of the sky. She must have slept all the way into the afternoon. Sunset couldn't be more than two hours away, and the garrison was several reaches to the north, perched on a headland overlooking the harbour. Should she wait until tomorrow, when she could start out earlier? But who knew what the city would be like by then, if the defenders failed to hold at the river? Today might be her only chance to get through. She'd just have to hurry. She could rest when she got there.

She surged into motion, running until lack of breath forced her to slow down. As soon as she was recovered, she sped up again, dodging carts and wagons, riders and pedestrians. Most were heading east, abandoning the city. And getting in her way. It was maddening.

She was stumbling through the choking maze of alleys north of the marketplace when she came upon the barricade. A long wagon had been dragged across the road, leaving only a narrow gap guarded by two men in blue shirts. One of them held up a hand. "Halt! What's your business here?"

"I need to get to the garrison."

He shook his head. "No civilians allowed through without authorisation. You'll have to go back."

How could she convince him? Lifting her chin, she rapped out, "Urgent message for the commander."

The Guard thrust out a grimy palm. "Let's see it, then."

"It's a verbal message. For his ears only."

He shook his head again, but this time with a smug smile on his face. "I don't think so."

Cahira gritted her teeth, fighting to control the anger that suddenly threatened to burst out of her. She couldn't seem to catch her breath, and her heart was pounding strangely. Blue-black spots, like blotches of ink, hovered around the edges of her vision.

The Guard was leaning forward in concern. "Are you all right, Miss?"

He wasn't going to let her through. What could she do now?

Your talent.

Cahira's head cleared as the answer came to her. She didn't want to hurt these men, but she had to get past them, and she could only think of one way. Her heart steadied. She could breathe again. And she could sing.

She emerged from the tangle of alleys onto the broad road that led up to the garrison. In the streets behind her, several pairs of Guards lay peacefully in front of their barricades. She'd been very careful, very controlled. They'd probably wake with headaches, but certainly nothing worse. She felt a little guilty about it—they were all on the same side after all—but later, after she'd helped protect the city, they'd realise that she'd done the right thing.

THIRTY-FIVE

Niall

It was four long hours past dawn, and Niall's nerves were stretched to breaking point. The rain had stopped, but the enemy hadn't come. A cold wind was blowing across the river into his face, making his eyes water. He caught his hand creeping towards the hilt of his sword yet again, snatched it away. A bird called from above, high and piping. He flinched. How much longer?

He sent a steadying thought to Sienna and the other mounts picketed deeper in the forest. They were grazing peacefully, in no need of his reassurance. For a moment he wondered who was supposed to be calming whom.

A soft hiss passed up the line, "They're coming."

Niall couldn't make out any movement on the low bank across the water. Someone had sharper eyes than him, or a more vivid imagination. He directed a probing thought towards the other horses he'd sensed last night. They were stationary and still a long way back from the shore. If the enemy was advancing, they were doing it on foot, which meant no mounts for him to influence, and no priority targets for the archers. *Of course not. That would be too easy, wouldn't it?*

He sent the intelligence tersely down the line: "No horses."

He had almost concluded that the sighting had been the product of overactive nerves, when a faint, smoky smudge appeared along the top of the bank, accompanied by a hint of sound, like the susurration of waves against a seashore. The greyness thickened until it revealed itself as a tightly packed line of Bregian soldiers. The murmuring grew to a roar as they spilled over the edge and began racing down the bank.

Niall's pulse was beating as fast as if he was running with them. Beside him, Adric was preparing the crossbow, grunting at the effort as he hauled back the cord and locked it in place. He'd been practising in the garrison forecourt, often accompanied by a group of curious and admiring Guards. The weapon took longer to load than a normal bow, but Adric had declared it was worth it because of the extra power and distance. Niall was dubious, but the big man, enamoured of his new toy, had insisted on lugging the cumbersome thing along. At least he'd brought his longbow and arrows, too.

"Archers stand ready!"

The Bregians reached the shore and splashed into the shallow water in disciplined lines. The first row held large rounds of thick wood in front of their bodies. Oren's plan was already showing cracks—no horses, and the soldiers tightly packed together, protected by shields. The archers would have their work cut out for them. And why weren't they shooting yet?

"Come on," Niall muttered.

"Wind's against us," Adric said. "We'd be wasting arrows. We need them closer."

"Wonderful."

Adric turned his head and actually grinned. "You worry too much. Like Oren said, we'll make them pay a hefty toll for this crossing."

The soldiers had reached the middle of the Ford.

"On string," came the order.

Adric slid the bolt smoothly into its slot and raised the bow to his shoulder. His broad hands were steady, unaffected by nerves or doubts. For perhaps the first time in his life, Niall wished his own mind wasn't so agile. He could use some of Adric's confidence and lack of imagination right now.

Despite the heavy shields and the current, the Bregians were making good progress. The roar had resolved into individual voices.

The command finally came. *"Let fly!"*

Bowstrings twanged and arrows hissed. Niall held his breath as the long, slim shapes arched out over the water, hanging in the air for longer than he would have believed possible.

They've overshot, he thought, sure that the arrows would fly past the soldiers and fall uselessly into the river. But he'd forgotten the wind. Abruptly, the missiles faltered in their flight, tilted, and dropped with deadly accuracy onto the Bregians. Shrill cries rose in response—some of the arrows had found targets—but the advance continued.

Despite the order, Adric hadn't shot yet. He was swinging the bow slowly from side to side, squinting along it. Halfway through an arc, he stopped and uttered a small grunt of satisfaction. He went completely still for a second, and then Niall heard a dull *thwack* as the bolt sped away, too fast for his eyes to follow. He couldn't tell if it had hit anything. Adric was already bent over the crossbow, reloading.

"Shoot at will!"

Another rain of arrows flew up, followed by more cries. Gaps appeared in the ranks as the injured crumpled to the riverbed and were left behind.

Niall reached out one last time to the unfamiliar horses. They hadn't moved. It looked as though no one intended to ride them into this fight. It was time to bring them across, leaving Fadra's group unmounted. The animals were too far away to be influenced by the other Beast Speakers. It was up to him.

But as he filled their minds with thoughts of running, they became agitated and panicky. They were tied or hobbled, he realised, unable to get free. Grinding his teeth in annoyance, he lifted the pressure off them, just as the first Bregians stepped onto the shore below him.

From the corner of his eye, he saw Adric raise the crossbow again. This time, he heard the dull thud as the bolt hit. Chips of wood exploded from a spot near the centre of the front line. A soldier dropped like a rock.

"Got him!" Adric exulted. "That should make a difference." He sounded vastly pleased with himself.

It annoyed Niall, whose own failure still rankled. "Why?" he asked sourly. "There are plenty more of them."

Adric grinned. "Not with painted shields, there aren't. He's the only one I saw. Must've been someone important. Maybe the commander himself."

If he was right that the Bregians had lost their leader, it didn't slow them down. As they crowded onto the shore at the foot of the slope, they closed ranks again. Despite the archers' efforts, only a small minority had been left behind in the river. Their fellow soldiers pushed on, ignoring their cries.

Niall wished he could do the same. The hideous shrieks and moans lifted the hairs on his neck. He imagined himself wounded, struggling to keep his head above water, knowing that no one was coming back for him. He shuddered.

The front row raised their shields over their heads and began the climb towards Niall and the others. A last flurry of arrows dove on them. Many stuck in the shields, making them look as if they'd sprouted feathers.

Adric shot one more attacker before abandoning the crossbow and drawing his sword. Niall's was already out. His heart hammered as he and the archers pulled back to the main line of defence in the trees. He was a good swordsman—expertly trained and with years of experience behind him—but he'd never been in a battle like this. No one in Algarth had.

His greatest fight before now had been at Fortune Creek—their group of ten against a troop of twenty Guards. They'd prevailed back then, but not because of their swordsmanship. It had been Cahira's skal that had saved them. Her absence might be the only bright spot in this whole situation, but they could certainly use a similar surprise right now. *Might as well wish for a flying horse*, he thought. *Or a never-ending ale barrel.*

Then the first grey-clad man reached the top of the slope, and there was no more time for wishing. The Bregian lowered his shield, drew a long, flat-bladed sword, and ran straight for the Algarthan line. A tide of his fellows came after him, spreading out to both sides. They yelled—fierce, wordless cries that finally drowned out the sounds of their companions in the river.

"*Hold the line!*"

Niall raised his own sword. The closest enemy was only ten strides away and coming on fast. At least this one carried no shield. With the ease of long practice, he overrode his body's automatic desire to turn and run. He planted one booted foot forward of the other, bent his knees slightly, and tightened his grip.

The dictums of his weapons tutor, drilled into him from the age of seven, unrolled in his mind: *"Every fight is a dance. Find the rhythm. Feel it in your bones."* Familiar words, from the days when Niall had been the favoured eldest son, before his skal had appeared and his father had disowned him. He thrust aside the anger, as he'd done so many times before. It was a distraction he couldn't afford. But the advice still held. *Feel the rhythm. Flow with it. Then lead the dance.*

The soldier came at him, his own sword raised in a double grip. Niall's vision narrowed. His nerves disappeared. Time slowed. Silence enveloped him. He danced.

He felled the first attacker without breaking a sweat, and the second almost as easily, but the third was more experienced. A grizzled veteran with shoulders like a bull, he pressed hard, keeping his centre of gravity low and his strokes economical. Niall's chest was heaving by the time he finally saw the tiny break in the man's defence. His quick thrust missed its target at the last second, but it had forced the soldier to twist awkwardly, sending him off balance.

Fast as a snake, Niall turned his own blade and slashed the exposed side. The man gasped and staggered back, giving Niall the chance to snatch a knife from his belt. With a weapon in each hand, it was his turn to press the attack.

It was over in seconds after that, but Niall only had time to draw a single breath before the next man was on him. The pattern repeated over and over: engage with one Bregian, find his weakness, put him down, face the next. There seemed no end to them. He couldn't even look away to see how Adric and the others were doing. Was the line holding, or had they been forced back, leaving him out here on his own?

No time to speculate, either. No time for anything except the next block, the next parry, the next thrust. His knife dealt with one, his sword with another. But he was slowing with every encounter, losing the rhythm, making mistakes. He took a stinging cut on the forearm, ducked, and felt the blade stir the hair on his head. *Too close.*

When two enemy soldiers ran straight past him, Niall guessed he was in deep trouble. Others followed. The line had collapsed. Death was more than a possibility now, perhaps a certainty. No time to think about that, either. He blocked again, clenching his jaw as the shock travelled down to the soles of his boots.

"Disengage! Retreat!" Several voices took up the command. But they were all a chilling distance behind him.

His sword bit deep into the meat of an upper arm. The man yelled and turned away, clutching at the bloody wound and exposing the side of his neck. A quick thrust from the knife finished him off. He staggered aside and crumpled to the ground. But a replacement had already stepped up, swinging back his weapon in a long arc.

Disengage? If Niall had any wind left, he would have laughed out loud. He was being pressed too hard to catch a breath, let alone open enough space to turn and run.

At least this red-faced youth was no natural swordsman. He slashed wildly, using his whole body and signalling every stroke. There should have been plenty of time to parry the blows, but the muscles of Niall's injured arm were reacting more and more sluggishly. Another swing, another clang as the blades clashed together. Suddenly, the hilt of Niall's sword twisted in a hand made slippery by blood. He might have died then, but the youth reacted too slowly, giving him the chance to drop the knife and take a two-handed grip on the sword.

With the uninjured arm doing most of the work, he swung the weapon like a broadsword, which it definitely wasn't. Not enough reach, too narrow, and too light. It was keeping him alive for now, but it was a doomed strategy and he knew it. A swordsman of even average skill would make short work of him.

"Retreat! Retreat!"

Shut up, Niall thought. The certainty that he was going to die made him angry, but what truly incensed him was the fact that it would be for nothing. Oh, he'd killed a few Bregians, but that hadn't been his real job here. He'd meant to be handicapping Fadra's group, and he'd failed. They could gallop straight to the city and create whatever havoc they chose. Worst of all, he still didn't know for sure that Cahira wasn't with them.

So this is it, he thought grimly, blocking another swing. *My luck's finally run out. It was bound to happen sometime. But that's no reason to make things easy for this cursed Bregian, is it?*

He disengaged, noticing that the soldier's flushed, dirt-streaked face was contorted in pain. Was he injured from a previous encounter? The blades met again, then Niall's slid down the edge of the other with a rending screech. As the hilts locked, the discomfort in the Bregian's eyes turned to panic. Niall wasn't the only one expecting to die today. That cheered him a little. The dance hadn't finished yet.

Taking a ragged breath and firming up his grip, he strove to push the other weapon away. He and the youth swayed together for a few seconds, neither able to prevail. Then the Bregian cried out, and the pressure on Niall's sword disappeared. The Greyshirt staggered backwards a couple of steps. Panting, Niall raised his blade and prepared to defend himself one last time.

There was no need. The weapon fell from the Bregian's hand. He bent forward, wrapping his arms around his midriff and uttering low, guttural sounds. He must have a stomach wound. It was amazing he'd fought so long with such a serious injury. But he was done now. Still groaning, he dropped to his knees and fell over, his body curled tightly as he rolled on the ground.

Niall raised his head in search of the next attacker. But there was no one to fight. In every direction, grey-clad figures were collapsing, to join those already writhing in the mud. Niall stared, his exhausted brain trying to make sense of it.

"Retreat! Retreat!"

The shout brought him to his senses. Stopping only to retrieve the discarded knife, he made for the trees as fast as his weary legs could carry him.

THIRTY-SIX

Cahira

"Commander's orders," the big Guard repeated, his face as stupid and placid as a cow's. His partner was more like a sheep, with his curly white hair and mild, worried expression. Neither of them posed any threat to her, but they were armed and standing in her way.

Holding onto the shreds of her fraying temper, Cahira tried again. "I need to talk to Commander Oren. He'll know who I am. Just send the message."

The sheep smiled condescendingly at her. "Look, Miss, we're all a bit busy right now. Trust me, the commander won't want to be disturbed by a social call. Best you go home."

"Of course he's busy, you dolt," she practically growled. "This city is about to be attacked. That's why I need to see him."

The bovine Guard's heavy eyebrows lowered. "Commander Oren has it all in hand. And he doesn't have time to deal with hysterical women. Neither do we." He levelled his spear at her, the tip almost touching her breast. "Now, turn around and go home."

The last fine threads of Cahira's patience snapped. She'd trudged all the way up here, the pack growing heavier with every step. The straps dug viciously into her shoulders, her feet hurt, and now she was being obstructed by these two idiots. Enough. They'd forgive her later, like the others. Or not. At this point, she didn't really care, as long as she got inside.

The discordant notes travelled in a sibilant whisper across her tongue and between her slightly parted lips. For an instant, she fancied she could taste them—bitter, metallic—but that was impossible.

A startled expression came over the big Guard's face. The spear clattered on the ground as he lifted trembling hands to cover his eyes. He bent over, his broad shoulders quaking. The other Guard's mouth fell open, and then the sound reached him, too. He gave a low moan and scrabbled at his ears before dropping into a crouch. His head was tipped back and his eyes darted around in panic. No longer a sheep but a rodent, paralysed by fear of the winged death that it sensed high above.

For a moment, Cahira was dismayed. She hadn't meant to terrify the poor men, just incapacitate them like the others. But after all, she told herself, it served the same purpose in the end. They weren't permanently harmed, and she was free to go on. She swept through the gates into the courtyard. Something was bothering her, some sense of disquiet, of warning, but she pushed it away irritably. She didn't have time to stand here dithering.

She'd never set foot inside the garrison, but it had originally been a castle, and she'd visited her share of them with her aristocratic parents. They all tended to follow a similar plan. She'd head for the central tower. High above the city, with views in all directions, it would make a perfect command post. Oren would probably be there.

Crossing the outer yard, she entered the tunnel that would take her into the castle proper. She went through the inner courtyard and the first hall with quick, authoritative steps. No one challenged her. Three corridors branched off from here, and she chose the broader, central way. Guards and officials were hurrying in both directions, but they seemed intent on their own business. Only a few even spared her a glance. In each case, she sped up slightly and fixed her gaze straight ahead. It did the trick. Which was more fortunate for them than for her, when she came to think of it.

She came to the base of the tower and ascended the winding staircase, her earlier weariness gone now she was so near her goal. Reaching the top landing in no time, she banged her fist on the door and entered without waiting for a response.

Four men were bent over the table in the middle of the circular space. They straightened up and turned to her, their faces contorted in surprise. Oren wasn't among them. Two wore good quality clothing and held themselves as if they thought they were important. The others had blue shirts with plain yellow badges. *Not even sergeants*, Cahira thought in disgust. She'd been wasting her time. She spun on her heel, then reconsidered. They might still be of use. "Where is Commander Oren?"

One of the wealthy-looking men stepped forward. "Who are you? How did you get in here?"

Cahira bristled. "That is none of your concern."

His eyes travelled down her body, and a sneer lifted the corner of his mouth. "A woman, dressed like a man, asking to see the commander. Seems very much my concern. I'll ask you one last time. Who are you?"

She dropped the pack and straightened to her full height. "Cahira Gelt."

"Never heard of you." He addressed the nearest Guard. "Take her away for questioning." Dismissing Cahira from his thoughts, he returned to the large parchment laid across the table.

Both Guards came for her, swaggering. They didn't even bother drawing weapons—their mistake. She opened her lips. The whisper slid through the air.

Something clamped around her waist and jerked her backwards, squeezing until her ribs creaked. The whisper ended with an undignified squeak as her feet left the floor. She kicked and struggled, but whoever had hold of her was too strong. She couldn't even draw in enough breath to sing.

"Gag her," barked a voice from over her shoulder.

Surprise crossed the Guards' faces, but they hurried to obey. One of them pulled a crumpled handkerchief from the pocket of his trousers. She tried to bite him as he brought the revolting thing to her face, but he evaded the attack and stretched the rag across her mouth. He leaned forward and passed the ends behind her head, pulling them tight enough to mash her lips painfully against her teeth, before knotting them at the back.

Her captor lowered her to the floor and released his grip. Sucking in air, she whirled to face him, fingers clawing for his eyes. He grabbed her wrists in mid-air and grunted, "Tie her hands, too."

She glared up at him, panting. Blue shirt, yellow badge edged in red. A sergeant, with a wide, squashed nose and ears that stuck out from his head like jug handles. There was no fear on his broad face, and no anger either. He looked slow and stupid, but his movements hadn't been slow at all.

She stared him in the eye as they pulled her arms behind her and wrapped the rope around her wrists, her mind racing while she caught her breath. Could she sing with this gag obstructing her mouth? Why not? She didn't need words. She could hum. But the uneasiness that had nagged at her at the gates suddenly rose up again. She'd already used her skal against innocent men who were only doing their duty. How many more? Perhaps she should reconsider, try harder to get them to see reason. If she went quietly—

They dare to touch you, bind you.

Rage boiled up. She tasted gall and iron. How dare they lay hands on her? Bind her like this? She'd come to offer her services to defend their city, and this was how they treated her. She could bring all these men to their knees right now, and they thought they had power over her? She would show them power, and fear, too.

"I know who you are, Skalsinger," the sergeant said evenly, "and if I hear a single sound from you, I'll knock you out."

She stiffened, the hum dying in her throat.

He lifted her again and spun her to face the doorway. As her feet touched the floor, a shove in the small of her back sent her stumbling forward.

"Walk, and remember what I said."

The hateful voice ordered her down the stairway and along a different corridor. Another set of steps, followed by a maze of hallways. After several turns, he stopped her in front of a closed door. His hand reached past her and lifted the latch. "Inside."

She obeyed. The humiliating walk through the garrison had transformed hot temper to cold fury, but also given her time to think. If this man knew who she was, why was he treating her like a criminal, or a traitor? There was only one explanation: he was a traitor himself. A Bregian spy, or one of Fadra's group, sent here to undermine the defence of the city.

The small room contained a desk and two chairs. The sergeant dropped her pack onto the floor and moved behind the desk. "Sit."

She lowered herself carefully to the chair in front of him. He remained on his feet.

"Why are you here?" His voice was low and flat.

She stared at him in contempt. How was she supposed to answer, gagged like this?

But it seemed he was only thinking aloud. "And what do I do with you?" He rubbed his eyes. "I can't let you go. Not with that—*ability*—of yours." For the first time, his face showed some expression. His upper lip curled in what looked like disgust.

Cahira's eyes narrowed. What did he know about her *ability*? She twisted her hands, trying to loosen the bonds, but only scraped her skin raw on the coarse rope. She had to get away from him and warn Oren that the garrison had been infiltrated.

He was going on, still in that deep, slow voice, as if he was working it out as he went along. Not exactly a sparkling intellect. And yet he had her under his control. It was infuriating.

"I know who you are. You fooled the Council, but you don't fool me. I was there, at Fortune Creek. Where did you get that sort of power? And those images…" He shook his head. "Only an evil mind would conjure up things like that. You're a witch, aren't you?" He nodded, agreeing with his own ridiculous conclusion. "And you'll stay in a cell until the commander comes back and decides what to do with you."

Oren wasn't even in the garrison? Cahira slumped, her chafed wrists stinging as they contacted the chair. Tears sprang to her eyes, born of frustration more than pain. She turned her head away. She wouldn't let him see her weakness.

Not weak. Strong.

Because she wasn't weak, was she? She was strong. Who did this little man think he was, to call her a witch and try to contain her power? The vibration rose from deep in her chest, buzzing up through her throat and into her nose. A low note, almost below the threshold of hearing, something she'd never tried before. But she knew she could do it.

Wait.

On second thoughts, it might be wiser to wait for a better opportunity. No matter what she did to this man, her hands would still be tied, her mouth would still be gagged. That would hamper her. The vibrations subsided.

Oblivious to his close escape, the sergeant bent over and unfastened the straps of the pack, keeping his eyes on her. "What devilry do you have in here?"

He lifted the things out, squinting at each one as if it hid some secret peril. He sniffed the contents of the water bag, held out every piece of clothing at arm's length and shook it hard. It was a good thing she'd left Fadra's bottles at the cottage. Gods knew what he would have made of them. Everything she'd brought with her was blatantly harmless; even this oaf would have to admit that eventually. But then he drew out the last item, and disquiet uncoiled in Cahira's stomach.

He turned the book over in his clumsy hands. "What's this?" His eyes drilled into her, trying to gauge her response. "Important to you, is it?"

Cahira held herself very still, barely breathing. After a moment, he returned his attention to the book. Laying it on the desk, he opened it and stared at the first page. His head shot up. "Kolos? Are you Bregian, witch?"

What was he talking about? He said something else, but she wasn't listening. Her own thoughts were too loud. She was sure she'd left the book in the bedroom at Bella's. How could it be here? She must have put it into the pack—there was no other explanation—but she had no memory of doing it, none at all. Nausea gripped her. What was this book?

A tool. To strengthen those with the talent to use it.

A tool? It was a strange thought. But she had been feeling stronger and more in control these past hours, even after she'd been tied up.

If that was the book's doing, she had to get it back. She'd need all the strength she could get when the city was attacked. Without thinking, she stood and took a step forward.

The sergeant snatched up the Book of Kolos and dropped it into the pack. His sword rang faintly as he slid it from the scabbard. "Get back. Or I swear to Aal I'll skewer you, woman or not."

She lifted hot eyes to his, and saw fear there, but also determination. He meant it. She stepped back. He came around the desk, keeping the point of the weapon angled towards her.

A knock sounded from behind her.

The sergeant rapped out, "Come in."

Cahira twisted her head to see two Guards entering.

"Take her to a cell," the sergeant ordered. "Keep her tied. And the gag stays on."

"Aye, Sergeant Donard."

They stepped up and grabbed her arms, one on each side. Bound and outnumbered, she didn't resist. She was confident she wouldn't be in their power for long. She'd think of something, and then she'd return for the book.

Yours to use.

It was meant for her to use, she knew it.

"If she gives you any trouble, or makes a sound, knock her out," Donard growled. "She's more dangerous than she looks."

The threat sent an unexpected thrill of pleasure through Cahira. *Oh, Sergeant, you have no idea how dangerous I can be.*

THIRTY-SEVEN

Perna

It was Perna's third day in the House on Dyers Lane, but already she'd seen and learned enough for a month or more.

This was nothing like being trained by Elder Meril at Mirhome. There was no reliable means of heating water, no cupboards stocked with clean, neatly rolled bandages and rows of salves and tinctures. It was dirty and smelly, crowded and chaotic, and the Healers depended almost completely on the power of their skals. Many of the people who sought help had serious diseases or horrific injuries, too.

The first time Perna had glimpsed white shards of bone sticking up from a bloody, gaping wound, she'd only just made it to the yard outside before heaving up her breakfast. Jake told her later that the man had been knifed in a street fight between the rival gangs that strove for control over this part of Eorna.

After Perna's stomach had emptied, she'd forced herself to go back and watch the two Healers work on their silent, scowling patient. They stemmed the blood, stitched the wound closed, and willed away any infection, all the time speaking gentle, soothing words to the ungrateful thug. His only response was a grunt of relief when they were done.

That hadn't even been the worst of it. She'd seen death, too. Some injuries and illnesses were too severe to be Healed, or the sufferers arrived too late. Most weren't gang members or criminals like the first man, either. And far too many of them were children, or young adults no older than Perna. They should have been looking forward to decades more of life, perhaps to marriage and offspring of their own. Instead, they lay on the floor, soaked in blood and filth, as death slowly claimed them. Perna could do nothing but ease their pain as they slipped away.

Anger at the sheer waste, the unutterable cruelty, replaced her shock and disgust. Bursts of fury assaulted her without warning, like flames blazing inside. But as the hours grew into days and the dying kept coming, the fire banked down to hard, red coals of rage. They warmed and filled her like that first bowl of stew, and gave her the strength to go on.

She stopped only when she could do no more. Then she claimed a bed or chair—or sometimes just a vacant space on the floor—for a few hours, until she could force her body to rise again. It was beyond exhausting. But even as she grew physically weaker, she felt her skal strengthen.

She still ate little, but from necessity rather than choice. Food was scarce. The merchants who normally thronged the market place had fled at the first word that danger was coming to the city. The street people, who'd stayed because they had nowhere else to go, raided the vacant houses and brought portions of their spoils to Tabia, but it was never enough to fill the bellies of everyone in the House. There must be plenty of stores in the warehouses behind the docks, only a short distance away, but the Warrant Guards had built barricades across every road and lane, and they weren't letting anyone through.

Perna was trying to find space for another emaciated youngster who'd probably die before the day was out, when she noticed a new patient being carried in. It was a frequent occurrence, and she wouldn't have paid any further attention, but the Aaldan bending over the arrival caught her eye and waved to her.

Quickly settling her own charge as comfortably as she could, Perna trudged over to examine the slightly built girl. Her scruffy blond hair was thickly matted with blood on one side of her head, and her eyes were closed. Her face was almost as grey as the blanket she was wrapped in.

So that was why the Aaldan had called on Perna. Head injuries were very difficult to treat, but she seemed to have a knack for them. She'd pulled a few patients through who had been considered hopeless cases by the other Healers. Even so, with a wound as severe as this one, the girl might never be fully restored to her previous self.

Gazing down at the still, pinched face, Perna felt the familiar mix of rage and pity. Such a young life, possibly destroyed forever. A memory assailed her, of another grey-faced patient with blood on his head: Niall Crawley, lying in the stable at Virtue Farm. It seemed a lifetime ago. She hadn't been able to do anything for him back then, but she'd come a long way in a short time.

She was almost dead on her feet, but she judged she had enough energy left for one more Healing before she'd need to sleep. She knelt beside the girl and placed gentle hands on the site of the injury. She closed her own eyes and concentrated, feeling out the extent of the hurt.

Thank Aal, it wasn't as bad as she'd feared: there was only the surface wound, no bleeding in the brain. Messy, but the girl should recover fully. Relieved, Perna prayed briefly, willed the damage to Heal, and lifted her hands away, gasping even at that small physical effort. Yes, she was done for now. Time to find a bed and get her head down for a few hours.

The patient stirred and opened her eyes. "What happened? Where am I?"

The hoarse tones rocked Perna back on her heels. She knew that voice. It belonged to the thief who had cut her, and would have done worse if Jake and Minna hadn't frightened her off. She raised a trembling hand to the narrow, ridged scar under her chin. She'd been blind and helpless, and this girl had taken advantage of her weakness.

If she'd known who she was helping, Perna would never have wasted her time and her skal. There were so many others more deserving. She heaved herself to her feet, grimacing at the effort, and turned away.

"Wait," the thief called out, a tremble in that husky voice.

A part of Perna rejoiced at how frightened she sounded. It was only right that this criminal experience what she herself had felt with that knife at her throat. She lifted her chin and kept going.

"Come back! *Please!*" The last word was almost a sob.

Perna halted with her foot on the first step. Why was this merciless, violent girl so scared of being left alone? Did she think she was dying? Was it the thought of meeting Aal face to face that terrified her? Well, that was her own fault. If she'd chosen a different path, sought to earn an honest living instead of attacking innocent people, she'd have no reason to fear the god's anger after death.

Of course, the thief wasn't about to die from her injury, but it wouldn't be a bad thing to let the girl believe it for a while. It might make her repent of her wickedness, and that would be pleasing to Aal. Ignoring the cries, Perna dragged her tired body up the stairs.

THIRTY-EIGHT

Cahira

The beefy Guards marched her along more corridors and down two flights of stairs. They were below ground level now, traversing passages carved into the soft stone of the headland. Cahira ignored the rough prods and coarse jokes of her irksome companions and concentrated on memorising the twists and turns. She'd last glimpsed Sergeant Donard—and she'd remember that name—taking a seat at the desk, with the pack resting on the floor nearby. After she freed herself, she planned to find her way back.

She didn't know how she'd get rid of the rope and gag, just that she would. The thought of these brutish men holding someone like her against her will for long was almost laughable. They had no idea of her potential, no clue of what she could do. And they would never save Eorna without her help.

The Guards dumped her into an empty cell and left her there. As soon as she was sure they'd gone, she began the search. If she could find something to free her hands, she could untie the gag. Most of the stone-walled room lay in darkness, but a candle fixed to the wall outside shed flickering light a short distance through the bars. Cahira examined everything in the span of that wan glow, looking for a weakness or a possible tool. But the bars were thick and well-forged, and the lock and hinges showed no trace of rust. The uneven floor was bare, except for a thin layer of gritty dust.

She'd have to search further back, in the shadows. She turned and waited for her eyes to adjust, closing them to speed the process. With nothing to see, the odours of this place pressed in on her: sour, nauseating. She swallowed hard and tried to breathe through her mouth, but the gag was too tight, and she gave it up. She waited, doing her best to ignore the imaginings conjured by the stench.

When she opened her eyes again, her gaze was immediately drawn to something low and humped, lying in a corner. It resembled the huddled form of an animal, and her heart beat faster as she pictured it springing at her, teeth bared. But there was no sign of movement. She edged a little closer, peering into the darkness. Another step, and her breath huffed out in relief. It was only a blanket, rucked and crumpled against the wall, the rough fabric blotched with ominous stains. Cahira screwed up her nose. Here was the source of at least some of the smell. Despite the dank chill creeping through her, she backed away. She wasn't that desperate for warmth.

It didn't take long to check the rest of the tiny cell. Cahira's shoulders slumped. She'd been so hopeful of finding something useful.

Sleep.

She yawned around the gag. It must be dark outside by now. It had been an exhausting day, and she couldn't do anything more tonight. Easing herself down as far from the fetid blanket as she could, she stretched out on her side, then winced as a stone dug into her hip. She wriggled sideways, but the irritation persisted. An image flashed briefly into her mind: clouds in a stormy sky. A snatch of melody played softly and was gone, leaving her aching for more. She sat up.

Sleep.

Another yawn. She had to get some rest. She settled down, but the mysterious pain was back. So was the image. Layers of smoky cloud, ragged-edged and streaked with black, in a slate-blue sky. It reminded her of something.

Recognition hit her like a dash of cold water. She struggled upright, her heart thudding. It was the sky stone she'd been seeing in her mind— and feeling against her hip. How could she have forgotten that it was in her pocket? And that melody, sweet and yet sharp as a knife cleaving her to the core, was their song. Hers and Bram's. The one she'd written for their wedding day. The one she'd sung in the cave after the bear attack, to bring her back to herself. Back to her grief.

She couldn't get her hand into the pocket, but she clutched the stone through the fabric. Hot tears coursed over her stiff, cold cheeks. A hollow opened inside her, deep and wide enough to swallow her whole. If she looked even once into that black, bottomless chasm, she'd tip over the edge and go down into endless heartbreak and loss. Part of her wanted to let herself fall, to surrender to the despair. To be finished with the absurd, exhausting business of life—eating and drinking, thinking and striving, day after day—without him. But she mustn't give in, not yet.

She unclenched her fingers from the pocket. She hadn't saved Bram, and that was an agony and a guilt that would never heal. But she was more powerful now, unless she allowed her feelings to weaken her. She had to stay focused and protect the others. Adric and Niall, Bella and Sara—all the people in Eorna—needed her to be strong. And she would be.

Not strong enough.

She bit her lip as sudden doubt assailed her. She was only one person, however talented. What if she simply didn't have the power? She'd rejected Fadra's training and the Unity's help. What more could she do? A new picture formed in her mind.

A tool, she remembered. The book might contain what she sought. She had to retrieve it.

You will. Sleep now.

Cahira lay down on her other side, fresh confidence running through her. There was nothing to worry about. She'd rest tonight, and morning would bring her the opportunity she needed. And then the enemy would pay for wanting to hurt her friends.

THIRTY-NINE

Perna

Resentment filled Perna's thoughts as she dragged herself down the stairs. She felt as though she'd only had a few minutes' sleep before she'd been woken by the tap on the door and the message that she was wanted in the kitchen. Surely there must be someone else to chop the scant vegetables left in their store and set them boiling for dinner? Someone who hadn't already been working since before dawn.

Bitterness turned to puzzlement when she found the big black pot simmering on the grate, puffing out onion-scented steam. The only other occupant of the kitchen was Tabia. The Elder straightened up from bending over the fire, pushed the bird's nest back from her moist forehead, and limped over to the scrubbed table. Stiffly lowering herself, she gestured for Perna to take the seat opposite. Perna sat, wondering what this was all about.

"Perna, you're a hard worker and you've saved lives. I'd be happy for you to stay, if that's Aal's plan for you. But we need to talk."

Perna frantically searched her memory for anything she'd done wrong since she'd been here, but there was nothing. She'd tried her best to please Aal and gain Tabia's approval.

The Elder's grey eyes were fixed on her. "This afternoon, a young girl was brought in. A head wound. You treated her."

Panic gripped Perna. Had she made a mistake? "Is she—"

"She'll be fine. Physically, anyway."

"I don't understand."

"You used your skal and left her?"

"I'd finished the Healing. I was tired. There was no reason to…"

"Did she beg you to stay?"

Perna clasped her hands together to stop them from trembling. She nodded.

The Elder leaned forward. "Why didn't you?"

"She's a thief, Elder," Perna blurted. *A thief who cut me, and might have killed me if the others hadn't come along.*

"How do you know?"

There was no choice but to explain it all. Perna's heart pounded as she re-lived the awful encounter. The Elder listened in silence until the words ran out.

"That must have been frightening," Tabia said gruffly. "I'm sorry."

Perna sighed in relief. The Elder understood now. She would agree that Perna had done the right thing by leaving the thief to contemplate her wickedness and repent.

"Perna, we don't judge if someone deserves our help. We give it because it's needed. The rest we leave in Aal's hands."

"I did help," Perna said, stung. "I Healed her, didn't I?" *Even though I was already exhausted.*

"You used your skal. But she needed more than that. She needed kindness."

"She didn't show any kindness to me!"

"She is a child." The Elder's tone was reproving, but Perna didn't care anymore.

"Even children know right from wrong!"

"Sometimes. And sometimes it's hard for even an Aaldan to tell them apart." Tabia levered herself up from the table, grimacing slightly. "Just think on what I said, Perna. And pray about it. Aal will show you the truth."

Alone in the kitchen, Perna fumed. Tabia was an Aaldan, dedicated to the god. She should support Perna, instead of siding with a vicious criminal. Right from the moment Perna had met the woman, with her coarse, abrupt way of speaking and her messy, uncontrolled hair, she'd felt reservations. She'd pushed her doubts aside when she'd seen how much good she could do here. And she had worked hard, she had. Even Tabia admitted that. But now the Elder had shown her true colours. She cared nothing for virtue or goodness, just bleated on about being kind.

Aal demanded obedience and self-discipline, not sloppy emotion. Being nice to people who ignored the god's laws only encouraged them in their wicked ways. Perna's mother had taught her that long ago.

It had been a hard lesson at first, for an only child who hungered for friendship and acceptance, but eventually Perna had learned it well. While the other village brats ran around the schoolyard in the lunch break, playing and shouting and doing whatever they felt like, she sat primly, her clothing neat and clean, her hands folded, and her mind going over the morning to make sure sure she hadn't done anything to offend Aal.

Soon they stopped inviting her to join in and began taunting her instead, calling her names. On the worst day, one hateful boy grabbed the ribbon on the end of her plait and pulled it right off, waving it in the air like a flag as he ran off, whooping. Face flaming, hair shamefully unravelling around her shoulders, Perna made her miserable way home.

After scolding her for losing the ribbon, her mother declared that she should spend more time at home improving her sewing so she could bring in extra income for the family. Mother was a Fibre Shaper and a natural needlewoman, sending her creations to be sold in the market at Welsea, but in Perna's clumsy hands the malicious threads knotted together, and the spiteful needle pricked her fingers until they bled.

Day after day, Perna prayed to Aal to make Mother let her go back to school. Not just to avoid the hated sewing, but because of Mistress Bent, the teacher. She was an Aaldan, a holy woman, who had once lived in a faraway house called Mirhome, where everyone spent all their time serving Aal.

There were no horrible boys at Mirhome, no spiteful teasing girls, no Father staggering home from the tavern every night to shout at Mother and stumble around the house before falling into a drunken stupor by the fire.

Perna wondered why the Mistress had ever wanted to leave somewhere like that and come to a sorry village like Hem. She even began to dream of going there some day to become an Aaldan herself. But Mother wouldn't relent. Perna was to be a seamstress. She just had to try harder.

She was washing away the scarlet drops of blood after an especially painful session, when the stinging vanished. She dried her hands, then stared down at them with her mouth open. For the first time in months, her fingers were pink and smooth, with no trace of scratches or scabs. She knew at once what had happened. Her skal had come in. She was a Folk Healer, not a Fibre Shaper.

Wild with excitement, she rushed to tell her mother. In response to the words tumbling from Perna's lips, Mother merely bowed her head and said: "As Aal wills." And the needlework lessons continued as if nothing had happened.

Perna was disappointed to discover that, after the first time, she couldn't Heal her own pinpricks and scratches, no matter how hard she tried. Mother said it was because skals were for the benefit of others, and not to be used selfishly to please herself.

She eventually became a competent needlewoman, although never an enthusiastic one. Her work brought in a small but steady income. But what she loved best was using her skal. When anyone in the village was sick or injured, Perna visited them. She couldn't always make them well, but it was the most amazing feeling when she succeeded, even though all she ever got in return was some gratitude and perhaps a few turnips or an egg or two.

But she hadn't given up on her dream. One day, she was sure, a prosperous citizen travelling through Hem would fall sick and call for the village Healer. They'd pay her in coins instead of vegetables, and she'd be able to afford to travel to Mirhome.

For now, though, it was the sewing that brought in the money they needed, and there was none to spare. And then Mother herself fell ill. She was afflicted with some kind of wasting sickness. Perna could do nothing except ease her pain and give her rest. Father finally agreed to pay a Healer, but Mother slipped away before she arrived. Perna was trapped, keeping house for Father and trying to stretch her tiny income to feed them both, while all his earnings went to the tavern.

And then he proclaimed her betrothal to Nathan. The dream of Mirhome, grown thin and brittle with time, shattered into pieces. Perna even considered throwing herself in the river and ending her sorry life, but she knew that would be the wickedest thing of all. Aal would never forgive her. There was no way out, until the miracle happened.

A stranger came to the village to visit Mistress Bent. She had white hair and black clothes and drove an odd-looking vehicle, a big grey box flecked with bits of coloured paint, pulled by a pony. The Mistress invited Perna to her house for the first time and introduced her to the old woman. She had a strange name—Inge? Enyi?—Perna couldn't remember. But the important thing, the truly wonderful thing, was that the woman was on her way to Mirhome. And she offered to take Perna with her.

Faced with this undeniable proof that Aal wanted her to be a holy woman after all, Perna didn't hesitate. She ran home, packed her few belongings and left while her father was still in the tavern. She didn't even prepare his supper for him to find when he came home. She spent the night in Mistress Bent's house and set out with the old woman next morning.

They travelled further than Perna had ever been before, way up north. The trip took four whole days, and she loved every minute—the countryside passing by, the silent companionship of the old woman, the slow clop of the pony's hooves that were carrying her further and further away from Father and Nathan. But the best thing of all had been imagining her new future among the Aalden.

Now, sitting alone in the kitchen of the House in Dyers Lane, Perna thought that those four days had probably been the happiest of her whole life. Because she hadn't found what she'd been looking for at Mirhome, and she hadn't found it here either.

She needed a place of discipline and purity, where she could atone properly for all the wicked things she'd done, especially after Welsea

Garrison. Tears dripped onto the table. She wiped them away with a sleeve. She wouldn't give up. Somewhere on Algarth there must be a community of Aalden who took their sacred trust seriously.

She couldn't leave yet, with the streets barricaded and the fighting about to start any day, but she'd go as soon as it was possible. She was so tired, though. Her head bowed forward. The tears flowed again.

She jerked upright when heavy footsteps entered the kitchen. It was Jake, come to fetch the pot of soup. He spoke to her, asked her what was wrong, but she couldn't bear the idea of trying to explain it all. She blundered past him and fled upstairs, where she locked the door and threw herself on the bed.

She woke in darkness, a new notion stirring. Tabia wasn't the kind of Elder she'd hoped to find, but the woman had been right about one thing. She'd told Perna to pray. Unable to bear the thought of getting up to tidy herself, or even compose her mind and body for addressing the god with proper respect the way Mother had taught her, Perna nevertheless took the advice.

Lying on her stomach with the pillow wet with tears and her clothes crumpled under her, she pleaded with Aal to lead her to somewhere she could start again, and earn forgiveness for all the things she'd done wrong.

FORTY

Roldan

Roldan's empty stomach and bowels were still fighting him as the first fingers of sunlight crept between the tree trunks. He stroked the scar on his throat and resisted the powerful urge to double over.

By now he should have been marching his troops through the city, carving a way to the docks. Instead, they'd spent the night puking up their guts, soiling their trousers, and rolling on the ground in agony. Roldan had refused to do the latter, but the rest had been completely out of even his control.

Only one conclusion could be drawn: they'd been poisoned. Not a large enough dose to kill, but that was scant comfort. The Algarthans, instead of being annihilated, had retreated from the Ford in good order and were no doubt shoring up Eorna's defences right now.

And against all reports, they had crossbows. Two of his men had died with bolts sticking out of them. One was a fool who had won some money gambling and spent it on having his shield embellished. Painted a target on himself, that was what he'd done. And he'd paid even more dearly for that piece of vanity than he had for the useless decoration.

Roldan gritted his teeth and thumped a fist hard against his thigh as his stomach reminded him again how unhappy it was.

"Overseer, when will your men be ready to leave?" The voice was clipped, the tone impatient and lacking in respect. If anyone else had spoken so to him at this moment, they would have received a swift and possibly fatal response. But that satisfaction was denied him.

Holding his back ramrod straight, he turned to face her. She wasn't alone; that toad Berek was with her. Roldan was pleased to see that the man was slightly hunched, and had his hands on his stomach. The facial skin not covered by his unkempt beard was grey and pinched, and deep blue hollows lay beneath his red-rimmed eyes. A weakling, like Roldan had suspected, unable to control even his own body.

The Disciple, on the other hand, was standing every bit as straight as Roldan himself, and apparently managing it without effort. Her complexion was its usual tan, and not a hair of her grey tresses was out of place. When he didn't answer immediately, she raised a slim, dark eyebrow.

"Within the hour," Roldan replied. Curiosity at her composure vied with his natural reluctance to engage with her more than he had to. Curiosity won. "Were any of your people affected, Disciple?"

"No. We brought our own supplies. It seems the bread from the farm was contaminated."

The black-bearded man stirred. "If you are insinuating this is somehow the fault of my Seekers..." He glared at her. Roldan almost admired his courage, before he realised it wasn't bravery at all, merely blind stupidity.

The Disciple's eyes hardened, but she gave the fool a soft answer. "We have no way to know how it happened, and it hardly matters now. The question is, when can we move?"

Berek bristled as if she had insulted him again. "My men are ready to march as soon as I give the order."

Having seen some of Berek's men only a few minutes ago, Roldan doubted that, but it was typical of the man's empty boasting. How he hated working with amateurs. They were always fanatics. Religious ones, like the Disciples of Kolos, or political ones, like this idiot's *Seekers of Virtue*. Fanatics were unpredictable and dangerous, not only to the enemy, but often to their supposed allies. Give him professional soldiers any day, fighting for nothing except reliable paydays and regular meals.

Something in Roldan's face must have conveyed his distaste. Berek abruptly stepped up to him, straightened his back, and actually poked him in the stomach with an insolent finger. "Don't look down your long Bregian nose at me. This is my country. As soon as my men have dealt with the Council, I will be the ruler of Algarth, and you'll still be nothing but a soldier, taking orders from your betters. And your orders now are to go ahead and subdue any opposition in the streets, clearing the route for my forces to reach the Council building."

Only Roldan's iron self-control kept his hands off the twin daggers in his belt.

"Of course, Master Berek," the Disciple said. "I am sure Overseer Roldan meant no offence." Her cold eyes slid to meet Roldan's gaze. "No doubt he is still feeling a little unwell." The tone was as silky as oil sliding across the edge of a blade. But it was a command, from the woman who, rightly or wrongly, had been put in charge of this expedition.

Still ignoring the roiling in his guts, Roldan snapped to attention and stepped back smartly. "No offence meant at all, Master Berek."

Berek huffed, but said nothing more.

"So, we are agreed," the Disciple continued. "Roldan, you will move your soldiers out first, in one hour's time. Master Berek and his Seekers will follow, and my people will bring up the rear, staying in reserve until we are needed."

Berek stumped off to get his stricken men into some sort of order. Roldan was about to do the same when the Disciple held up a hand. "Wait a moment, Overseer."

She stepped closer and spoke under her breath, beckoning to a young woman who had been standing a short distance away, holding a large pack. "Two things. First, Elise will accompany you as you gather your soldiers. She has brought something to increase the efficacy of their weapons. There should be enough for at least a quarter of your force. Your troops only, mind. The Algarthans are not to know anything about this. A few drops on the tip of arrow, sword, and spear. They should not allow the affected metal to touch their skin. The solution will make no distinction between our fighters and theirs."

Roldan lowered his own voice. "Poison?"

Her smile was condescending. "Nothing so crude, I assure you. But it will serve our purposes."

He refused to give her the satisfaction of begging for more information. "And the second thing?"

"I need to inform my contact in the fleet that we have been delayed. They must remain offshore until we are close to the city, so we can co ordinate our attacks. I will be in my tent for the next hour. Make sure no one disturbs me. Questions?" She gave him a meaning look.

"No, Disciple Hellin."

Roldan already understood the fleet was another thing the Algarthans did not need to know about. He briefly wondered how she would send the news to the ship, but felt no desire to ask her. Nothing as clean and straightforward as a messenger hawk, that was certain. He had heard the rumours like everyone else. They said the higher-level Disciples communed with Kolos itself, and that bloodletting was involved.

"Good. Prepare your men."

Roldan went, but he had an ominous feeling, quite separate from the pain in his gut. This was what happened when civilians were put in charge of a military operation: religious fanaticism, mysterious potions, and dark rituals.

He should be in command. He knew how to fight a war efficiently while retaining his honour and the honour of his nation. Only his unshakable loyalty to Bregia—and the oaths he had taken—stopped him from pulling his people out of this mess right now.

FORTY-ONE

Cahira

Escaping from the cell was easier than she'd expected. The young Guard who brought gruel in the morning must not have received the order about keeping the gag on her. Or maybe he simply didn't see how temporarily removing it could cause any harm. Either way, as Cahira glanced up at his entrance, his gaze went from her blocked mouth to the bowl and spoon in his hands, and back again. He frowned, then set the food down on the floor and moved behind her to untie the piece of rag. He hadn't even closed the door.

Cahira worked her tongue around her stiff mouth, wincing at the stinging of cracked lips and bruised gums, and waited to see if he would free her wrists as well. But he left them alone and sat in front of her, picking up the bowl and spoon. She was hungry enough to consider letting him feed her, but one glimpse of the sickly grey paste, with its yellow globules of floating grease, and her appetite fled.

He lowered his eyes and dipped the spoon. Cahira let loose the melody that had been playing in her mind since she'd woken. The rising series of discordant notes filled the space between them. Shock froze his face. His hand tightened on the bowl, which shattered with a resounding crack. He dropped the shards and the utensil, staring down at the blood on his fingers as if he couldn't understand what had just happened.

Cahira drew out the final note, but only until his eyes rolled back in his head and he toppled sideways. Then she cut off the sound. He hadn't tried to harm her, and she had no desire to maim him permanently.

Shuffling on her knees until she was alongside him, she bent forward and twisted her shoulders to bring her hands around as far as the bindings would allow, then reached her fingertips to the hilt of the dagger in his belt. After some patient work, she lifted it free and carefully rotated it until the edge met the rope. Then it was just a matter of sawing. It took longer than she'd expected, but finally the tough strands parted.

An involuntary cry escaped her lips as she brought her stiff arms from behind her back. Tightening her jaw, she worked her shoulders and wrists to get the blood flowing. As soon as the worst of the sensations had passed, she pushed herself to her feet, tucked the dagger into her own belt, and walked out.

Excitement prickled along her spine, confirming what she already knew: the book lay waiting for her behind this closed door. She'd left the cell with every intention of retracing her steps to the room where she'd last seen Donard, but each stride in that direction had felt more and more wrong. Finally, she'd followed the intuition, and it had led her to this seemingly unfrequented part of the garrison, just one level up from the prison.

She scanned once more for movement in the hallway, then eased up the latch and pushed the door slightly ajar. A low mumbling reached her ears. The narrow strip of wall she could see through the gap told her nothing. She took a breath and readied her talent. Then she slammed the door back with a crash.

Half a dozen figures lurched to their feet, some from pallets laid on the floor, others from chairs. Cahira opened her mouth, and then realised there was no need. These men were in a sorry state: bloodied heads and dirty bandages, and no weapons she could see. All of them wore blue shirts, mostly torn and filthy. As they took in her identity, they sank back, grumbling and cursing. A few kept murmuring, as if they had no means of stopping the stream of sound once it had begun.

The attack on the Ford had been planned for yesterday, she remembered. These Guards must have been wounded there. Had they stopped the armies at the river? Or had the Bregians and Seekers overwhelmed them and marched on the city? Even now, Niall and Adric might be fighting for their lives somewhere. She had to get the book.

An old man, wearing the robes of an Aaldan, stepped forward to meet her. "Can I help you?"

Cahira thought fast. She bobbed a curtsy and smoothed her voice to honey. "I'm sorry to disturb you, sir. Sergeant Donard's regards, and he's asked me to bring him the belongings of a spy he caught yesterday. A pack, he said, with clothes and a book in it." She gazed up shyly through her eyelashes.

A ruddy tide swamped the man's withered cheeks. "Ah, hmm, yes, yes," he stammered, "I am familiar with the book you mean."

Cahira rewarded him with a brilliant smile. The Aaldan puffed out his scrawny chest. "The good sergeant asked me to examine the work," he quavered. "I'm considered— not to be immodest, you understand— rather an expert on such matters. I believe he suspected it might contain some type of Charm." He shook his grey head at such ignorance. "But, as I expected, it's completely harmless, merely a Bregian religious text, and a common one at that. Of little value even to a collector. You can tell him I said so. Now, where did I put it?"

While she waited, doubt gnawed at Cahira. Had she been wrong about the book, after all? Was she just wasting her time here?

The Aaldan shuffled back, holding the book in one hand and dragging the pack with the other. After a brief expression of thanks, she was outside the door, looking for somewhere she wouldn't be disturbed.

Not far away, she discovered a deep, shadowed alcove set back from the hallway. The thick layer of unmarked dust on the floor was reassuring. It seemed no one ever came here. Crouching down with her back to the wall, she opened the book with trembling fingers. She leafed through until she found the tangled skein of ink that had almost felt alive. Her eyes bored down, and she willed something to happen.

At first, she was afraid it was wishful thinking, that the sheer strength of her desire was causing her to imagine things. But no. Right across the page, the matte lines were darkening and taking on a sheen. Tiny glints of light—reflections from the candles in the hallway, she realised— winked out at her. Within seconds, the entire drawing was gleaming as wetly if it had just been laid down.

But it didn't stop there. The lines swelled and thickened. Dark liquid was welling up from the paper, adding to what was already there. Cahira had never heard of anything like this. It was amazing, and a little unsettling. But she'd wanted power, and some sort was at work here. The old man had been wrong. This book was special.

As more fluid rose to the surface, the outer areas lost definition. The carefully inked lines overflowed and bled into each other, all flowing in the same direction. Inward, towards the heart of the drawing. Finally, Cahira found herself staring at a puddle of ink, shimmering darkly in the centre of the page.

Holding her breath in wonder, she reached out a forefinger and dipped it in. A jolt of cold shot up as far as her knuckle. She reared back, rubbing the affected digit with her thumb. It seemed unharmed, just a little numb. She bit her lip. For a split second, she had felt the energy, the power. It had repelled her and drawn her at the same time. But it was what she needed.

She lowered the finger again, holding it as still as she could. A slight vibration ran through the inky pool. Then the chill, viscous liquid slowly drew itself up around her skin, coating it to the second joint. She shivered. The sensation wasn't pleasant, but it was bearable. The jolt came, but this time she was ready for it.

Coldness travelled up her finger, spread through her hand and into her arm. It made its way past her elbow and shoulder. It hesitated when it reached her fluttering heart, and she thought it might stop there, but it was merely gathering itself. As the stream from the book filled it, the rapidly beating organ quietened. A new rhythm of slow, steady beats sent pulses of strength throughout her body. Fear and uncertainty, weariness and pain, were things that no longer existed.

Her eyes still on the page, Cahira watched the pool shrink. Finally, the last dark, shiny drop slipped its way into her. The paper was clean and unmarked. Cahira lifted her finger and examined it. Not a spot or stain marred the skin. It looked exactly the same as it always had. But it wasn't the same. She wasn't the same.

A voice broke her out of her reverie. "Send three more troops to the docks, tell 'em to report to Captain Mundar."

Cahira pushed herself further into the shadows.

"How many ships are we expecting to cross the Strait, sir?" a second voice asked, sounding closer. "And how many soldiers?"

The footsteps halted just short of her hiding place.

"Aal knows. Probably more than we can stop, to be honest. That's for your ears only, mind. But we'll thin their numbers a bit, eh? Force 'em to pay in blood for their landing."

"Yes, sir."

"And get the troop leaders to inspect the barricades on the way. Make sure they're closed up tight."

The two Guards started off again, still talking. They moved past without a glance in Cahira's direction. But their words had sparked a response inside her. *The docks.* There was going to be fighting there, against ships coming from Bregia. And the defenders were too few. They needed her help. She was filled with new power, but she was in the wrong place.

At least the waterfront wasn't far, and she could use her talent on anyone who tried to stop her. But any commotion in the crowded garrison would bring more Guards running and waste precious time. It would be best to slip out without being challenged. A disguise? She rifled through the pack. Plenty of blue, including the intensely coloured cloak, but no shirt that could pass as a Warrant Guard uniform. And nothing to hide her long hair. She bit her lip. What now?

New footsteps. A single Guard, this time. She assessed him as he passed. His height and weight were close enough, and he was wearing a cap. Perfect. She just had to get him out of the corridor into an empty room.

She pitched her voice high, added a touch of uncertainty. "Oh, sir, can you help me?"

He spun around with an oath, impatience stamped on his coarse features. "What is it, Mistress?"

She lowered her eyes modestly, then raised them to his. "Miss."

Taking her in, his expression went from bored to interested.

"I came to find my brother," Cahira continued. "He volunteered for the Guards, but I don't know where he is. Our mother is so worried about him."

"You're all alone here?"

"Yes." Cahira sank slightly at the knees. "Oh dear, I'm not feeling very…" She collapsed artistically, slowly enough for him to step forward and catch her.

Close up, his breath smelt of cheap ale, and his body like week-old fish. She turned her choke of revulsion into a little gasp. "Oh, thank you, sir."

He gripped her tighter. "Do you need a Healer?"

"Oh, no, I'm just a bit faint, that's all. Perhaps a chair?"

"Of course. We can go in here."

He kept his arm around her as he steered her into the room. It held only a table, covered in rolled-up bandages, and a chair. Her gallant rescuer helped her sit and went to close the door.

Cahira readied her song, the same one she'd used on the Guard who'd brought her breakfast. An upwelling responded from deep within. This was going to be easy. He turned towards her, said something else. Ignoring him, Cahira set both song and power free.

He stiffened and went silent. Then he began to shake. As he lost control of his body, he fell to the floor and flopped over onto his back. Cahira felt as if she was looking down on him from a great height. He was twitching now, his mouth opening and closing like a stranded fish. It was almost funny. But it would be easier to take off his uniform if he wasn't moving so much. She sang the next note in the sequence.

A violent convulsion seized the Guard's body. His back arched upwards and his heels drummed against the stone before he collapsed again. This time he lay still, with his mouth gaping and his eyes staring at the ceiling. That was better. Crouching down beside him, she grabbed the front of his shirt and began dragging it over his head.

Without warning, her mind flashed back to another prone body: Niall, on the floor of the stable. Where was he now? Had he been at the Ford? Had Adric? Were they lying injured somewhere, or already dead, like Bram? Her hands stopped moving. Dread sat heavy in her chest.

Weakness.

She drew a breath, pushing the emotion down. It only weakened her. Bram was gone. But Adric and Niall might still need her. They could even be at the docks. She had to be stronger than this. She *was* stronger than this. She bent again to her task.

Despite the rank smell of the man, his uniform was relatively clean. It was loose on her, but passable after she tucked it in. She crammed her hair up into the cap, made sure the dagger was secure at her waist, then tied the Guard's hands with his own belt. She gagged him with a wide strip of bandage from the table, pulling it as tight as she could. Then she left him, closing the door behind her.

In the stolen uniform and with the cap pulled down over her eyes, none of the Guards in the upper hallways gave her a second glance. Neither did the dozens marshalling in the courtyard outside. Even the new pair posted on the gates ignored her. They were turning away anyone trying to enter, but didn't seem to care who was leaving.

She rounded the first curve of the road at a fast trot, and then the full force of the wind hit her, almost sending her tumbling. She staggered and found her balance, jammed the cap firmly on her head, and continued the descent more slowly. The sun was high—it must be nearly noon—but it shed no warmth. By the time she reached street level, her teeth were chattering.

She ducked into an empty alley and unlaced the pack with stiff fingers. It should be safe enough now to ditch the uniform. And the cap was already making her scalp itch. The previous owner hadn't just been a disgusting, smelly pig, he'd been infested with parasites. She shuddered and scratched vigorously beneath her hair. The first chance she got, she was having a bath.

Armoured against the chill in the thickly woven blue cloak, she passed through two barricades without breaking her stride—leaving four more Guards unconscious behind her—before reaching the line of warehouses on the docks. The area was swarming with both Blueshirts and armed civilians. Probably more than even she, with all her skill and power, could tackle in one go.

She slowed to a stop and shook her head, confused. For a moment, she'd been thinking of these people as enemies to be stopped. But they weren't. They were here to defend Eorna, just like she was. She'd been willing to incapacitate a few Guards to make sure she got here in time, but now she needed to talk to them and offer her help.

She approached the nearest group. "Excuse me."

They stared at her. One stepped forward, grinning around a mouthful of half-rotten teeth. "What can we do for you, sweetheart?"

It was time for Aunt Alys again. "You may escort me to Captain Mundar." Head high, spine as rigid as a pole, she added, "Tell him Lady Cahira Gelt wishes to speak with him."

The brown-stained smile faded as the Guard saw his fellows edging away from him. They might be willing to fight shoulder to shoulder against the Bregians, but in a skirmish with a noblewoman, they were making it clear he was on his own.

Cahira stared into his eyes, gently tapping one foot.

Shooting a glare at his faithless companions, he bowed to the inevitable. "This way," he growled, stumping off.

Allowing herself a small smile of triumph, Cahira followed him.

FORTY-TWO

Niall

"Stay alert!" Adric's bass voice reverberated off the high, stone walls.

From his doorway, Niall eyed the makeshift barricade at the end of the street. Last night, he'd been hopeful that whatever had struck the Bregians at the Ford might have thinned their numbers, but scouts had reported the whole force marching north this morning.

The jumble of barrels and furniture wouldn't stop them for long, but it wasn't meant to. Its purpose was to slow the first few ranks, encouraging those following to cram up behind them. Crowded into the road, with their own troops preventing a retreat, they'd be prime targets for Adric's archers on the rooftops.

Commander Oren and the Council had been forced to guess the enemies' route through the city, but Logen had argued strongly in favour of Market Street. It was the broadest and straightest path to the garrison and harbour, and passed Eorna's civic buildings, including the Council Chamber, on the way. Oren had agreed: Market Street was the key. He'd posted most of the barricades and archers along it, with support forces nearby to contain any overspill when the shooting started. Weaver's Way, where Niall waited, was one of these secondary positions. The main force of Eorna's Guards were concentrated further north. Their turn would come later, after the archers were done.

The order had gone out for civilians to either volunteer their help or stay out of the way. Streams of them had been crowding the eastern road towards Gadara for days. Others had gone south to hide themselves in the Greenwood Forest until the crisis was over. But many had offered to stay and fight alongside the Guards, or use their skals in other ways. These last included Healers to treat the injured, Shapers to keep up the supply of weapons, and five Beast Speakers, of which Niall was the only one left in the city. Three had died in the debacle at the Ford and the other, a widow with young children, had changed her mind and fled last night. Knowing what she'd seen at the river, Niall didn't blame her.

He absently rubbed the fresh scar above his wrist. The Aaldan in the garrison infirmary had done a good job closing the wound. Only a thin white line showed that he'd been in a fight at all. Later today he might find himself in another one, but for now his only task was to deal with Fadra and her students, as he'd failed to do at the Ford. He had no intention of letting that happen again.

"Enemy sighted!"

It was time for him to pull back. Retreating inside the building, he closed the heavy door. He'd created a spyhole by patiently digging out a large knot with his dagger. Applying his eye to it, he sent his skal questing. The horses had drawn closer, but not near enough to be in the city yet. Fadra's group must be bringing up the rear.

"Market Street and Weaver's Way!"

Niall tensed, then forced himself to relax. Adric and the others knew what they were doing, and conditions were perfect for shooting. The freezing wind, blowing hard from the west all morning, had chased away the clouds and then dropped to a whisper. Even without the new coating from the Charm Shapers at the Academy, the arrows would fly true.

He'd been surprised to recognise Kelan among the students distributing the vials to the archers last night. The nineteen-year-old had sprouted a beard, and seemed at least a hand taller. He'd addressed the bowmen with confidence and authority. "Only one drop per arrow. We don't have enough to waste. Dab it on the tip, don't rub it in. Let it dry naturally."

But afterwards, when Niall caught up with him in a quiet corner, this new maturity dropped away. Kelan's green eyes glowed with boyish enthusiasm.

"It's amazing stuff, Niall. Brecca's been working on it for ages; she meant it for coating keys, so you could put them into locks in the dark. But she never thought of using it on arrow heads to make them go where you wanted. That was my idea."

"Brecca?" Did Kelan have a crush on another girl, so soon after being abandoned by the treacherous Rassil?

"Instructor Brecca," Kelan said. "She's about a hundred and she talks funny, but she's okay."

"Talks funny?"

"She uses all these old words, really long ones. But she's better than the others. At least she listens, sometimes." A brooding expression settled on his face. The headstrong teenager wasn't enjoying his time at the Academy.

No surprise there, Niall thought. He remembered Kelan's look of horror when he'd first discovered he was a Charm Shaper and would be spending the next few years in a classroom. A sardonic response sprang to his lips, but he suppressed it. The boy needed cheering up.

"So, you suggested using the liquid on the arrow heads. That was smart."

Kelan brightened again. "Brecca wasn't sure it would work, but she gave me some and let me go into the forest to test it. I got a rabbit, but I didn't know if it was the Charm or just me. So, when the next one came along, I closed my eyes." He grinned at Niall's raised brows and nodded. "Yep. One shot, straight through the heart. They don't give us much meat at the Academy, so I was pretty popular that night, I can tell you."

The tramp of footsteps brought Niall back to the present. Kelan's innovation was about to be tested on something more dangerous than rabbits.

The horses were getting closer, too. Near enough that he could disperse them if he liked. He considered the idea, then rejected it. Better to wait until Fadra's group was in range of the archers before unhorsing them. Then they could be taken care of for good. He ignored the voice in his head that suggested strategy wasn't the only reason he wanted the riders in sight before he acted. *She's probably not even with them*, he told himself.

"Arrows on strings!"

Through his peephole, Niall watched a line of men approach, marching shoulder to shoulder, followed by another close behind. But they wore no uniforms, carried no shields. His eye was drawn to a figure in the centre of the front row. His blocky body took up the space of two normal-sized humans, and his ruddy face glowered beneath a fuzz of red hair. It was 'Commander' Ruston, leading Berek's army. The forces must have split up, with the Bregians taking the broader route. Niall silently wished the archers over there good hunting.

Meanwhile, scores of Seekers had already followed Ruston into Weaver's Way, and the barricade was working. As the advance stalled, Ruston sent men to dismantle the obstacle. But he gave no order for the others to halt. They kept coming, pressing up tighter as they waited for the way to be cleared. There must be a hundred of them now. A few started eying the surrounding buildings, sensing something wasn't right. Their caution came too late.

"Let fly!"

Hissing filled the air, followed by cries and groans. Ruston's voice boomed out, but his words were lost in the confusion. Panicked Seekers milled around, some trying to force their way through the massed ranks behind them, others clambering over their fallen comrades in a desperate but doomed attempt to rush the barricade. A second flight of arrows drove the survivors to the sides of the road to seek the protection of the buildings. But there was no escape. One by one, they were picked off as the Charmed arrowheads found their marks.

Despite his contempt for Berek and everything he stood for, Niall felt sick. This wasn't a battle. It was a massacre. Apparently, the archers didn't share his distaste. Death continued to rain down until the few Seekers who were still on their feet fled raggedly back the way they'd come. Niall scanned the dead and injured, trying to ignore their hair-raising cries, but failed to spot Ruston's fiery head among them.

Oren's strategy had worked spectacularly, but it would be foolish to think that one small victory meant Eorna was safe. The Seekers' inexperience and arrogance had been their downfall. They'd marched in with no caution, no plan. But surely even Ruston and Berek wouldn't make that mistake again with the remainder of their force. And the Bregians a few streets over wouldn't have made it at all. Not to mention Fadra's group.

Niall sent his senses out. The horses were closer. They were inside the city, and moving fast. If he wanted to catch sight of them before they passed, he'd need Sienna, who was waiting in a stable in the next alley. He dashed through the building, heading for the back door.

But halfway there, a flash of blue on the internal staircase stopped him in his tracks. A Warrant Guard cartwheeled down the iron spiral, his arms and legs flailing. He came to rest, with a sickening crunch, in a huddled heap at the bottom. One look at the angle of his head and neck told Niall the man was dead.

A voice called out from above, "Bregians on the roof! Take cov—" The warning cut off with a cry.

Another movement to Niall's right. He spun in that direction, reaching for his sword, but something arrested his wrist before his hand touched the hilt. He looked up to see a human wall confronting him. His mouth went dry.

Above his massive chest, Ruston's scarred face wore a feral grin. He waved a long-bladed knife slowly back and forth in front of Niall's eyes. Niall's sword was still in its scabbard, and his right hand was immobilised. His left snaked towards one of the blades tucked into his belt.

"None of that," Ruston grated. "Move another finger and I'll bleed you like a pig."

Ridden by fear, Niall's brain was galloping at top speed. He couldn't reach for his weapons, but his mind had always been as sharp as any blade. He doubted Ruston's was the same. In a battle of wits, Niall was better armed. And every battle was a battle of wits, when you came right down to it.

"I have no intention of moving, friend," he said pleasantly. "Being skewered sounds most uncomfortable, not to mention messy. Blood all over the floor and so on. And this isn't my house, you know. It would be rude to bleed all over it."

A frown creased the coarse skin between Ruston's sandy brows. "Keep joking. See what happens."

Despite the low, vicious tone, the knife didn't move closer. Why hadn't Ruston killed him already? Why stand here making threats? Only one answer: the man wanted something. And Niall was an excellent negotiator.

"No joke, I assure you," Niall said. "I have no wish to die today. Tell me how to avoid it."

Contempt showed on Ruston's face. "I want a horse, a fast one. Use your pathetic skal to call one to the back door."

Niall froze at the sound of his father's words, echoed by this thug. *No son of mine could inherit such a pathetic skal.*

"What are you waiting for? Move!" The knife gestured.

Niall turned and headed for the door, all thoughts of cleverness swept away by the flood of memory.

"Take your things and get out! I'll have no bastard heir with a peasant's skal!"

"Father, please. Wait."

He should never have stooped to begging—it had only increased the disgust on his father's face—but he'd been a very different person then. Twenty-five years old, and so delighted that his skal had come in. So eager to tell his father. So desperate to make the Lord Crawley proud. Such a fool.

"You're no son of mine. If your whore of a mother was still alive, I'd send her packing, too."

That was when shock had turned to rage, and Niall had hit him. No chance of repairing the situation after that, even if he'd wanted to.

"Where's the beast?" Ruston's grating voice snapped him back. They were outside the door, standing in the street. "Any tricks and you'll be making that mess you're so afraid of."

Niall's brain started working again. He needed a horse. He'd throw himself onto the end of Ruston's knife before he called Sienna here. But there were other mounts in the same stable. *Not you, old fellow*, he thought. *And you're too timid, sweetheart.* He went on to the next and found what he'd been looking for.

He turned to Ruston. "It's coming."

"It had better be fast. And no tricks."

"I remember."

The big gelding, having kicked down its flimsy stall door in response to Niall's urging, trotted around the corner and headed towards them, ears pricked and stirrups flapping gently against its sides. Ruston grunted, presumably in approval.

Niall was under no illusion that Ruston intended to let him go unharmed—the man enjoyed violence, it was written all over him—but he judged he had a fifty-fifty chance of coming out of this alive. Less favourable odds than he liked, but you played the cards you were dealt. He held one ace, and he'd make the most of it.

Ruston turned to face him again. His scarred cheeks rippled in a feral grin. Holding the knife low, he took a step forward. Shooting a brief apology to the gelding, Niall flooded its mind with fury.

As the animal's scream rent the air, Ruston spun around, blindingly fast. But instead of backing away from the rearing horse, he closed in, dodging the flailing hooves and jabbing the knife upwards with what looked like impossible speed. Before Niall had time to do more than register the blurred movement, it was over.

Ruston darted aside, giving Niall an unobstructed view of the long arc of blood that spurted up from the gelding to splatter against the wall near his head. Hot droplets sprayed his face. He flinched. As the horse's forelegs came down, its knees buckled. It screamed again and crashed to the ground. Pain and panic filled Niall's brain, the sensations threatening to sweep him away.

He tore his mind free and pressed his shaking body to the wall. He'd never imagined the heavy man's major skal might be Swiftness. And now he was face-to-face with Ruston again, right back where he'd started. He'd gambled and lost.

Still grinning, the Seeker of Virtue licked his lips and raised the gore-covered blade.

A sound like an axe hitting wood, and Ruston's head snapped back on his thick neck. The knife fell from his hand. Without thinking, Niall slid along the wall and into the doorway. Someone shoved him roughly aside. Pulling his knives, he turned to face the new threat.

"Get down!" Adric's legs were planted wide, and the crossbow was in his hands.

Niall dropped to the ground. A red-headed fury leapt over him, barrelling straight at Adric. The crossbow went *thwack*. Ruston roared. The two men staggered together in a grotesque parody of a dancing couple before Ruston sat down abruptly on the floor.

He coughed twice, then his head nodded forward, and he fell slowly sideways. When he came to rest, Niall could see the end of an iron bolt in his stomach and another in his chest. Blood trickled from the wounds.

Niall looked up with heartfelt thanks on his lips. But Adric's eyes had gone wide, and his mouth hung open. He gave a little grunt. The crossbow tumbled to the floor, revealing a wet, red stain on his shirt. Something was sticking out of it. *The hilt of Ruston's knife*, Niall realised in shock.

Adric swayed. Niall scrambled to his feet, barely getting a shoulder under the bigger man as he headed for the floor. But Adric was a dead weight, and all Niall could do was break his fall. They landed in a heap, with Niall pinned painfully underneath.

He was trying to free himself when three blue-shirted men, with bows slung over their shoulders, came down the iron stairs. They rushed to help, lifting Adric and gently laying him on the floor. His breathing was shallow and rapid, and his eyes were slitted in pain. The hilt of Ruston's knife jutted out obscenely from under his ribs. One of the archers reached for it, his intention clear.

Niall's hand clamped down. "Don't pull it out. You'll make the bleeding worse." He flicked a glance to the stairwell. "The Bregians on the roof?"

"We got two." The man who'd answered was older than the others. "His friends moved on, except for one taking pot shots at us from behind the chimney next door. We had no cover, so we came down for orders." His gaze went to Adric, and he shook his head. "Poor lad."

"Where's the nearest Healer?" Niall demanded.

The archers looked blank. Then a youngster spoke. "Everyone's gone. We evacuated them."

"Some Healers were staying," Niall said with brittle patience. "Find one." The youth rose to his feet uncertainly.

"There's a House of Aal in our street." The voice was slow and hesitant. Niall's head swivelled towards the third Guard, whose round, beardless face flushed at the attention. "Ma said the Aalden were going to look after the hurt ones. Ma said—"

"How far?" Niall snapped.

The broad forehead creased.

"You live in Dyers Lane, north of the marketplace, don't you, Matty?" the standing Guard put in.

The frown smoothed out. The beardless youth nodded vigorously.

Not close, Niall thought, but nearer than the garrison. "Go and see."

Matty stared blankly at him.

"I'll come with you, Matty," the same Guard said. "Show me the way to the House of Aal, eh?"

Matty nodded several more times and stood up.

"Wait." Niall concentrated for a moment, found what he wanted. "Turn left outside the back door. Around the next corner you'll find two horses, in a stable. Take them, it'll be faster." At the doubt on both their faces, he added harshly, "Do you want to save the life of your troop leader, or not?"

Matty screwed up his eyes and began a low keening.

"Come on Matty," said his companion, throwing a reproachful look in Niall's direction. Finally, they left.

"Matty's a bit slow," the older man said. "But he's a good Guard for all that, and one of the best archers I've ever seen."

"Sorry," Niall said shortly.

"You're worried, lad, I can see that. And with reason." He squinted down at Adric. "But he's still breathing, and where there's breath, there's hope."

Niall didn't answer. Overlaid on Adric's prone form was the image of another man who'd been stabbed under the ribs: Bram, stretched out on the floor of the tavern in Fortune Creek. The blood seeping into Adric's shirt—a blue Warrant Guard shirt, how ironic was that—was in almost exactly the same place. Twin brothers with twin wounds. And Bram's had killed him.

Worse, this time Niall couldn't blame it on the Guards or their corrupt leaders. If Adric died here, it would be Niall's fault, no one else's. He'd stupidly allowed Ruston to surprise him, and then failed to put an end to him.

A sound from outside had Niall on his feet, sword drawn. But it was only the gelding. To his shame, he'd forgotten it. The poor beast was lying on its side, its flank heaving with each panting breath. It moaned again as Niall approached. Blood pooled around it, bright crimson on the dusty cobbles. A single glance told Niall all he needed to know. Ruston's vicious slash had cut through the artery in its groin.

"I'm sorry," he whispered as he reached gently into its mind, spreading calm. The horse's breathing slowed. Its eyes closed. Niall laid a hand on its neck and bowed his head. The pulse faded away. Another needless death. He went inside.

He was crouched beside Adric, lost in dark thoughts, when something else intruded on his mind. The horses he'd been tracking were very close. No more than two blocks from here, he guessed.

He scrambled to his feet and strode to the doorway, cursing. He could incite the animals to toss their riders right now. Oren would order him to do it in a heartbeat. But the same problem remained. Without physical eyes on them, he couldn't be sure of not hurting Cahira. He'd already killed an innocent animal, and probably Adric, too. He had to know if she was there before he made another fatal mistake.

He called Sienna, telling her to be calm and ignore the smell of blood and death. She came at a trot, then stepped delicately around the fallen gelding and pushed her soft nose into Niall's hand. With one foot in the stirrup, he hesitated, sending a troubled gaze through the doorway.

The older Guard nodded, as if he understood the conflict in Niall's mind. "He's still breathing, lad. Go if you need to. I'll stay with him until the Healer comes."

Niall stared for another stretched-out moment, mired in guilt and misery. But not uncertainty, he realised. Not if he was being honest.

Because no matter how long he drew out this decision, the outcome would be the same.

He'd made his choice back in their childhood, and never yet wavered from it. He wasn't about to start now.

FORTY-THREE

Cahira

The Guard with the bad teeth led her to a small warehouse. He mumbled her name, and after a short delay she was ushered inside.

A tall, heavily muscled man with the complexion of the southern islands came forward. "Adric has told me about you, Mistress Gelt." His voice was slow and deep. "I am sorry for your loss, and his."

"Thank you, Captain. Please, call me Cahira."

"And I am Mundar. Just Mundar. There is no need for titles between friends."

For a moment, Cahira wondered if this was a sly dig at her 'Lady Cahira' impression, but his calm, serious expression hadn't changed.

"Will you walk with me?" he continued. "I want some fresh air."

Cahira had already had plenty of that today, but she was willing to be buffeted a little more if it would convince this man to use her in the defence of the docks.

They headed in the direction of the water, passing small groups of Guards and civilians hunkering down behind barriers built from barrels and crates. Some had bows with them.

"Is Adric here?"

"No. Most of the archers are further south, protecting the streets."

They reached the edge of the dock and stood side by side with the wind pressing hard against their backs. Cahira looked out, straining to see anything moving on the choppy, grey surface. "Are there really ships out there? Has it been confirmed?"

Mundar nodded. "A fleet was sighted from the garrison early this morning. They dropped anchor near the middle of the strait. They haven't moved since then." He peered up at the clear sky. "But the wind is going to switch north soon. A hard, gusty blow. Two hours from now, maybe less." He shook his head. "Good for the Bregians, and very bad for us."

"Is that why they're waiting out there? They need the breeze behind them?"

"It would be best for them. Bregian vessels are wide and heavy, with a single, square-rigged sail. They're designed for slow travel along the broad lakes and rivers of their country, not open water. That is why they use Algarthan traders to move their goods across the strait. Our ships are more manoeuvrable in unfavourable wind."

This discussion had begun to feel oddly significant, as if something was coming that Cahira needed to hear. "So, they can't reach us until the wind changes?"

"They could tack against it, but they won't. They would be too vulnerable."

"Tack?"

"It means making long sweeps across the bay, back and forth, coming nearer with each pass. It is slow, and it needs concentration." He directed a meaning look towards her. "And steady, experienced hands on sheets and tiller."

With her mind on high alert, Cahira instantly understood, despite the unfamiliar words. "You'd order your archers to shoot at the sailors."

"Yes. And with the wind in our favour and the fleet travelling broadside to us, every flight of arrows would find many targets. As the ships lost crewmen, they would sail slower, giving us more opportunities."

"That's why you said they won't risk it."

He nodded. "The Bregians are not stupid. They'll wait for better conditions. And they are about to get them. As I said, bad for us."

"But even if the wind doesn't change for days, we'll still have to face them, sooner or later."

"Yes, but reinforcements from the eastern garrisons are on their way. If they reach the city before the ships come in, we won't be so badly outnumbered. But that isn't going to happen, now."

"Oh, I see."

"Indeed."

As they set out walking again, she chewed on her lip, thinking. "Wait a minute. How do you know what the wind's about to do?"

"My parents are traders. I grew up on board, barely touching land. You learn to read the water, the feel and taste of the air, the look of the clouds. And—" He stopped, as if was reluctant to say any more.

She still hadn't got what she needed from this discussion, so she pressed him. "And?"

"It's my skal. Weather Seeing." He sounded almost apologetic about it. Or perhaps he was afraid she wouldn't believe him. Weather Seers were rare, and Cahira had never met one, but she saw no reason for him to lie.

"It's a shame you can only predict the weather, not change it. You could call up a hurricane and blow the ships all the way back to Bregia."

It had been a flippant remark, but Mundar seemed to take it seriously. "No one is strong enough to control the wind, not even the smallest breeze."

"Why not? It's only air. It's flimsy." She waved her hand around to prove her point.

He smiled slightly. "You wouldn't think so if you'd been under sail in a storm."

His calm certainty nettled her. "But that's a gale. You said a small breeze."

"All weather is connected. Everything affects everything else."

They'd reached a group of defenders, and Mundar stopped for a word with their leader. Cahira bit her lip again while she waited. She was getting closer; she could feel it.

She tackled him as soon as they moved on. "But we control air whenever we breathe in and out." She pursed her lips and demonstrated. "It's easy."

"Weather is the breath of the entire world. It would take immense power to influence it even a little. Trust me."

And there it was, at last. The clue she'd been waiting for. *Immense power*, she thought.

"And you've never heard of anyone with such a skal?"

He stopped walking and stared at her. "Have you?"

"No," she said slowly, trying to disguise her excitement. "But that doesn't mean there's no such thing."

She'd already controlled thunder and lightning, hadn't she? And that was a kind of weather. And what was singing, except manipulating air, making it vibrate? She flexed her fingers, feeling an echo of strength ripple through them. Whatever had flowed from the book into her, it was at her disposal.

Mundar turned to look out over the water again. "We're as ready as we can be. But when the wind rises against us and drives those ships in, we'll be hard pressed to hold here."

It was her moment. "I may be able to help with that."

He fixed a solemn gaze on her. "Adric told me what you did at Fortune Creek, Cahira. Distracting some of the Bregians could be useful, I won't deny it. But I cannot guarantee your safety. I think you should leave."

A distraction? Was that all he thought she was good for? And she didn't need anyone to 'guarantee her safety'. Fury boiled up, but he was in charge here, and there was no sense in antagonising him. He'd soon see exactly how 'useful' she could be.

She forced her voice to calm reasonableness. "I understand the risk, Captain. And I'm not going anywhere."

She shaded her eyes and counted the grey squares suspended above the sunlit water. Seven Bregian ships. The wind had dropped to nothing, and the sails hung flat.

She was alone on the small lookout platform. A long line of docks stretched away to her left, and the headland rose on her right. Mundar had been at pains to explain that the shallowness of this part of the harbour meant the Bregians couldn't land here. They'd have to make for the deep-water docks further along. Also, the platform should give her a good vantage point from which to use her skal in the first clash, while allowing her to escape to the garrison before the fighting came near her.

She hadn't needed his assurances, and she'd been glad when a message had taken him back to the warehouse, giving her the chance to try her experiment. She cleared her thoughts of everything except the approaching ships, then blew gently out. She didn't add any sound, simply imagined her breath pushing the sails away. At the same time, she rehearsed suitable melodies in her mind.

A song emerged from her memory. It was one she'd learned at the Academy and almost forgotten until now. It described a cold, moonless night and an unseasonable storm at sea. The violent wind and waves slammed into a fleet of fishing boats, overturning them and drowning every man on board. In their hovels on the shore, families waited fearfully for husbands and brothers and fathers who would never return, except as grey corpses strung out along the stony beach.

It was a dark, melancholy song, and she'd never performed it since, but it was still there in her memory, every note and word. If she could use it to whip up a similar storm—a small one, only around the ships— she could sink the Bregians, rather than just hold them off temporarily. That would be a far better solution. Her storms until now had consisted of thunder and lightning, never wind, but it couldn't hurt to try.

Choosing a vessel that lay some distance from the others, she took a deep breath and held her arms out, flexing her fingers. She'd never used gestures in her singing, but it felt right for this. Fixing her mind and her gaze on the ship, she began softly.

Tingling cold suffused her chest, then raced with terrifying speed to her fingertips. Power crackled through her lungs like lightning and surged up into her throat, eager for release. She choked off the song and felt the pressure recede. Shaking, she grabbed onto the railing and closed her eyes.

Whatever she'd expected, this was so much more. The flood of strength had almost overwhelmed her. But even as she'd flinched away from it, she'd known without a doubt that she could sink every ship out there, drown every soldier on board.

She licked her lips and looked at her hands, clenched on the rail in front of her. They seemed exactly the same as always, with no sign of the power that had rippled into them. She glanced towards the men behind the nearest barricade. They were talking and joking, bolstering each other's spirits. They hadn't noticed anything.

Her heart settled into its normal rhythm as she shifted her attention back to the sea. Was it her imagination, or had the sails grown larger? A breath of wind caressed her face and lifted a few strands of hair from her forehead. The breeze was picking up again, and it was blowing onshore, just as Mundar had predicted. It would carry the enemy ships straight into the harbour.

The men waiting below were no match for Bregian soldiers. They'd be slaughtered, and it would be Cahira's fault. She could save them—she knew that now—but she was too scared to try again. The mere memory of that power, leaping like a wild animal in response to her song, had set her heart hammering in fear once more.

Not fear.

Or was it truly only terror that she felt? Wasn't there some excitement mixed in, too? Like riding a galloping horse at breakneck speed. Dangerous, but exhilarating. Such energy, and it had been in her hands, literally at her fingertips.

Yours to control.

Greater forces than she'd ever imagined had come at her call, then drained away when she'd dismissed them. She'd been in control.

Yours to use.

It was her talent, to use as she chose. There was no need to be afraid, and nothing to worry about. Except those Bregians ships, sailing closer every minute. She couldn't let them land.

A gust whipped the hood of the cloak from her head and blew her hair out behind her. On the water, the sails bellied forward, as if the vessels were eager to spring to the attack. She lifted her arms.

This time she was ready for it: the tingling, the lightning, and the pressure. And this time, she let it go. The storm song poured from her throat, soft and low. There was no need for volume. Her voice was only the instrument of the power, not the source. And it wasn't terrifying. It was glorious.

Pale streaks of cloud appeared in the sky above the ship. They swelled and solidified, darkening to match the sail. Slowly, but inexorably, they spread over the fleet, brooding and sullen.

She heard shouting from somewhere far behind her, but it wasn't important. She leaned into the wind. The massed clouds were swirling, and their colour had changed to deepest ink.

Bring them in.

Power thrummed through Cahira until her whole being was alive with it. She called the storm to her—the magnificent tempest of her creation—and it came, blotting out the sunlight. The little ships raced before it on white wings of foam.

This was her destiny. She could hardly bear to think of the years she'd wasted her talent on peasants in backwater taverns. Her life had been so small, her ambition so weak, her understanding so limited.

She glanced down at the tiny men cowering behind their paltry barricades and laughed aloud. How stupid to think they could stand against her strength, her fleet, her perfect storm.

The gale roared past. The indigo clouds boiled overhead. The ships flew on.

FORTY-FOUR

Niall

Niall hauled himself onto the tiled roof, nodding tightly to the pair of archers already stationed there. The barricade that stretched across Market Street behind him was one of the larger and sturdier ones—four massive wagons, roped together and then piled high with all kinds of junk. He checked again on Sienna, who was waiting in yet another back alley, hopefully out of the way of the fighting to come. He'd pushed her hard, and overtaken the riders he was tracking. They were still several blocks away. The news from the Guards was that an enormous force of Bregians marched with them.

His nerves hummed like bowstrings as he fixed his eyes down the length of the street, anxious to see who would arrive first. If it was the Bregians, all bets were off, and he'd soon be battling for his life, along with everyone here. But if Fadra's people were in the lead, he should be able to do something more useful than going down fighting.

He drew one tense breath, let it out. Two riders burst into view from a side street with a clatter of hooves, pulling up abruptly as they spotted the barricade. They were both men, and the horses belonged to Fadra's group. So far, so good.

He raised his eyebrows at the nearest archer, who shook his head regretfully. "Not close enough. No point wasting arrows on 'em."

Too far for the bowmen, perhaps, but not for Niall. He'd make the animals bolt into range, carrying their riders with them. The horses' heads turned his way as he made contact. At the same time, one of the men stood in the stirrups and pointed up the street.

An almighty *crack* split the air somewhere over Niall's shoulder. He spun, almost losing his footing on the slick tiles. His eyes darted around, searching for the source of the noise, but he couldn't identify it. Another *crack* smote his ears, followed by a drawn-out, agonised creaking that set his teeth on edge. But both at roof and street level, everything appeared normal.

And then he spotted it. A long, wooden plank, part of one wagon supporting the barricade, was twisting as if it was being wrung between two enormous hands. The groaning intensified. Neighbouring planks began to warp. A rivet popped under the strain. Then another. They shot out like stones from a catapult.

Niall stared down in disbelief, his task forgotten, until instinct kicked in and threw his body flat on the tiles. A final, deafening *bang* set his skull ringing, and the entire barricade burst apart, hurling chunks of debris in every direction. A wickedly pointed shard, half as long as Niall's arm, whirled past his face and smashed into the chimney.

Beside him, one archer was swaying on his feet. Niall snaked out a hand and hauled the man down to his knees. Blood was running from a gash on the Guard's temple, but he ignored it, staring over Niall's head and fumbling behind his back for an arrow. He put it to the string with practised hands, sent it on its way, and reached for another.

Staying low, Niall twisted around to follow the archer's gaze. The two riders had disappeared, but a grey tide was pouring up the street towards the shattered barricade. The soldiers' legs were pumping, and their mouths were open as if they were yelling, but all Niall could hear was a gentle hissing. The explosion had temporarily deafened him. At least, he hoped it was temporary. He shook his head and swallowed hard, but it made no difference.

His companion wasn't the only Guard busy at his work. Arrows arched over the Bregians and plummeted down. Dozens of soldiers fell in eerie silence, but the rest kept coming. And some were already climbing the buildings. At any moment, there'd be hand-to-hand fighting on the roofs.

Niall couldn't afford to get caught up in this battle, not yet. The rider who had stood in the stirrups was a Wood Shaper, with his skal turned into a weapon to destroy the barricade. Niall had to find him and the others before they did any more damage.

He slipped around the chimney stack and skidded down the opposite slope of the roof. Swinging himself over the lip of the eave, he hung by his hands for a moment, then dropped into the back lane where Sienna was waiting. He vaulted into the saddle and peered around, alert for any threat.

A figure strolled around the corner of a building, and Niall's hand went automatically to his sword before he recognised the man. It was Jak, the recruit he'd met in Oren's command tent at the Ford. He was out of uniform today, but that white hair and pale skin were unmistakable.

Jak approached with his hand held out. "Master Crawley, it's good to see you alive and well."

Niall's ears still felt odd, but his hearing must have come back, because Jak's soft voice was crystal clear. He leaned down from the saddle and shook the young Guard's hand. He tried to locate the horses, but couldn't seem to get a fix on them.

"She's a fine mare," Jak said, stroking a hand down Sienna's neck.

It was true. Niall had only taken one of his father's possessions when he'd been exiled, but he'd chosen well. Sienna was the best mare to have been bred in the district for generations. His father must have been furious to discover her missing. Niall had expected to find Warrant Guards on his track, but apparently the senior Master Crawley didn't want word of the family conflict to get out for the gossips to chew over.

Even if he had been pursued, Niall would never have regretted his choice. In those early weeks and months of his banishment, the beautiful, spirited mare had been his only companion. His newly discovered skal might have been anathema to his father, but to Niall, who had always been drawn to horses, it was pure, unalloyed joy. On many days, it was the only brightness in his life.

He could tell what Sienna was thinking, what she was feeling. He knew if she was hot or cold, hungry or thirsty, content or irritated. And she was aware of him, too. She liked him! She was willing to go where he wished, as fast as he pleased. Most of the time, at least. On some days he chose their route; on others he bowed to her wishes.

This bond with a different kind of being was magical, immeasurably precious. And as he explored it further, he discovered that he could sink even deeper, until he almost believed he was a horse himself. On those bleak nights when the memories wouldn't leave him alone, she would nudge him gently, and he would take refuge in her mind. He would see through her eyes, hear with her sharp ears, smell all the rich odours of the world that were denied to a mere human nose. And find respite from his pain in the simple patterns of her thoughts.

She turned her head now and pushed at his leg, as if she knew he was thinking of her. Niall came back to the present with a start. His mind had been wandering. There was something he needed to do, something about horses.

"Look, they're coming now," Jak said.

Niall nudged Sienna forward, following Jak's pointed finger to a shadowed gap between two buildings that provided a clear view of the destroyed barricade in Market Street. Bregian soldiers were marching through without opposition. The archers must be dead or in retreat. Niall couldn't believe it had all happened so quickly. He'd hardly been with Jak any time at all. Then a group of riders appeared, and he forgot his confusion as relief swept over him. He'd found them.

"Oren's instructions have changed," Jak said. "He was wrong about them being dangerous. Your orders are to let them pass, unharmed."

Let them go? Niall stared, trying to understand, as the horses pulled up directly ahead of him. A woman with long, grey hair was in the lead, and at least half of the others were women, too. They all sat relaxed in their saddles, and they carried no weapons. Oren was right; this group posed no threat. It was a good thing Jak had found him in time, or Niall might have hurt them.

Beneath him, Sienna fidgeted. He reached out to calm her, but her agitation only grew. Now she was dancing in place, tossing her head. He spoke aloud, and his own voice sounded strange—faint and muffled—as if it was coming from underground or far away. "What's wrong with you, girl?"

"Perhaps you should get down," Jak said, his words still as clear as a bell.

Niall dismounted the skittering mare and laid a comforting hand on her neck. She flinched from him. It was as if she didn't know who he was.

"Steady girl, it's me. It's Niall."

Her skin shivered under his touch, but he sensed her mind calming. But something else was nagging at him now. It was about his companion. He turned to Jak. "Why aren't you in uniform?"

"Special assignment. I'm a messenger, remember?"

Of course, Niall thought. *He brought me orders from Oren.* But how had Jak known where to find him? Niall had told no one about his plans after leaving Adric with the old Warrant Guard. His heart gave a great leap as he remembered: Adric was hurt, maybe dying, stabbed by Ruston. Niall had left his friend bleeding on the floor, because he had to make sure Cahira was safe.

Sienna had calmed completely now, and was standing steady beside him. Niall peered out at the riders, trying to see if she was with them.

"She's fine," Jak said. "Everything is fine."

The young Guard meant well, but things didn't feel right to Niall. There was something he needed to do; he was sure of it. Not just finding Cahira. A different task, just as important. But his thoughts had grown as slippery as eels. He'd take hold of one, and another would slide away into the murk. Had the explosion addled his wits as well as his ears? He leaned against Sienna's warm flank, trying to think it through. First, he had to find Cahira—he stiffened as something cold touched the back of his neck.

"Stay very still. The edge of the blade is against your skin, but there is poison on the tip. It would be a shame to kill you by accident." Jak's voice sounded different. More mature, surer of himself. And a lot nastier.

Niall's mind cleared as if a fog had been lifted. Fadra's group was the enemy, and Jak was working with them. He must be a Mind Wender, and he'd been messing with Niall's thoughts. Icy rage settled like a stone. He'd make this white-haired villain pay for his betrayal.

"I almost had you," Jak mused, "but your obsession with the Skalsinger is persistent. Walk forward. Instruct the mare to follow. Do not even think of trying anything. There is enough poison for you and the horse." He raised his voice. "Fadra, we are coming out."

FORTY-FIVE

Cahira

A low drone issued through her lips. She watched from her high platform as the lead vessel reached the central dock and swung broadside. Small waves destroyed themselves against the unforgiving hull, sending spray flying upwards. Cahira's eyes tracked the movement mechanically. Her mind was dull, incurious.

She saw the flapping sail being hauled down, the snakes of rope uncoiling through the air and slapping the timber. Grey figures followed, leaping onto the boards and wrapping the lines around the bollards. They looked as small as ants to her. Perhaps she was dreaming again, and she'd wake to find herself back in the caves, or in the bedroom at Bella's.

Long, narrow missiles streaked towards the ants. Some of them fell. *Wounded*, she thought, *maybe dead*. But they were unimportant, after all, nothing more than tools. And there were plenty more. Laughter rolled through her mind. She wondered where she'd heard it before, then forgot about it. Another ship docked. The ants scurried. The missiles flew.

"Cahira!"

A different voice, but also familiar.

"Cahira! Get down!"

Mildly curious now, she twisted around. Her eyes were drawn to two men on horseback at the far end of her dock, near the warehouses. One was dressed in black, and the other's pale hair shone in the sudden shaft of yellow light slanting beneath the livid clouds.

Cahira's body jolted. Memory rushed through her like the icy water of the Ford, where she'd fallen to her knees trying to escape a Mind Wender who wanted to control her. And here he was, threatening her again.

She broke off the droning and screeched, high and wordless. The white-haired rider stiffened, then arched backwards. His hands clawed the air before clutching at his temples. Cahira drew a breath and let out another scream. Her pursuer pitched forward, still holding his head, and slumped onto the horse's neck. The animal whinnied and stamped. The man—his name was Jon, she remembered suddenly—slid off sideways, landing face-down on the dock. Cahira panted hard as she examined the distant figure for any sign of movement. She saw none.

The other rider leapt from his mount. Ignoring his companion, he swung himself up into the other saddle and turned towards her. His mouth opened. "Cahira!"

It had been his voice she'd been hearing. The horse sprang into motion, pounding along the dock.

He is nothing. Ignore him.

But somehow, she couldn't. Her eyes were glued to the black-clad rider. A name sounded in her mind: *Niall.*

Roars and screams reached her ears, but still she stood and stared. What was Niall doing here? Why had he shouted at her? Another shock of memory, rocking her on her feet. The fleet! The Bregians! What had she done?

Calm yourself. Everything is unfolding as it should.

She turned to face the water. Ships. Ants. Meaningless noise. Nothing to do with her.

Then a high, haunting call drew her eyes to the sky. Far out over the grey waves, a seabird soared, its long tilting wings flashing white against the bruised clouds. The colours reminded Cahira of something. Her hand dipped into her pocket, closed around a smooth, hard object. Warmth flowed up her arm, across her chest. Her lungs opened. Fine tendrils of heat crept through her frozen body. But the cold rose up like a swirling, murky fog, filling her inner vision and smothering the golden threads one by one.

Hands caught her shoulders from behind, dragging her attention outward once more.

"Cahira! Are you all right?"

She was far from all right. But it wasn't his problem. She turned to face him and shouted over the wind, "You need to go. It's not safe."

"That's why we have to get out of here!"

She couldn't meet his eyes. "Leave me."

"No." His tone had hardened. He was going to be stubborn about it.

She tried to push him away, but her fingers clamped onto his arm instead, refusing to let go. She released the stone so she could use her other hand.

All sensation cut off. She couldn't feel the wind, or hear the screams, or see Niall standing in front of her. All that existed was the lake of grey fog within. A new and horrible conviction crept into her mind, sliding into every corner and cranny. Hidden below the swirling surface, some monstrous thing waited to emerge. And when she saw it, she would die.

Time stretched out, and her terror grew beyond anything she had ever experienced, even in a nightmare. An age later, when she thought she could feel no more, a dark whirlpool formed in the murk. It was coming.

A thick, fleshy snout, covered with green, crusted growths, broke the surface. It rose higher, swaying and twisting. It was a tentacle, like that of an octopus, but shaded deepest indigo between the green. The same colour as the storm clouds. And the ink that had flowed into her at the garrison. The Book of Kolos had done this, put some hideous thing inside her.

No, she thought. *I did it to myself.* She'd sought the power, welcomed it, hungered to use it. But it had used her instead.

And yet, despite her fear, she was alive. Perhaps there was still a chance for her.

"I don't want it anymore!" The tentacle shrank back a little, curling in on itself. Could it be that easy? Cahira held her breath, willing it to vanish completely.

"What don't you want?" Niall's voice echoed in her head. He sounded confused.

The outside world sprang to life. He was holding her, and she was gripping his arm. The stone was warm in her other hand. She'd picked it up again without noticing. The wind howled around them.

She forced herself to meet his eyes, to see the worry and the unbearable tenderness she'd known she'd find there. He deserved the truth—what she truly was, what she'd done.

"The power," she said, and her voice came out thin and hoarse. "I wanted it, thought I needed it."

She looked away, to where Bregians were still streaming onto the docks. Hugely outnumbered, the defenders were failing to slow the tide. Not ants, but people. Living, breathing human beings, that she'd killed as certainly as if she'd wielded a sword herself.

"It's my fault, Niall," she whispered. "I brought the ships in."

Even above the tempest, somehow he heard her. He shook her shoulders gently. "This cursed wind blew them in."

"No, it was me." The tears chilled her cheeks.

She could still see him, but inside her the inky tentacle was unfolding once more. Another emerged from the murk, and then a third. Soon, the head would follow. The monster would snatch her up and drag her into the depths. She imagined she could feel it pulling already.

But it was only Niall, tugging at her. "Come on! We can argue about it later."

She let him lead her off the platform and down the ramp to the dock. What did it matter where her body was? The gale grabbed at her hair, lifting it off her neck and flinging it forward. Strands wrapped around her face. Like tentacles. She raked them away violently, careless of the scratches. A large drop of rain hit her scalp. By the time they reached Sienna, they were being pelted by stinging sleet. Niall boosted her, unresisting, into the saddle, and swung himself up behind her.

Cahira's vision was split. Inside, the monster was writhing. Outside, the fighting had moved closer, as the fierceness of the Bregian attack pushed the Algarthans out to the flanks. Niall turned the mare and galloped her towards the warehouses.

They had almost reached the first of these when a figure appeared in front of it, its green cloak flapping in the wind. Sienna tossed her head and snorted, pulling up at the sudden apparition. The woman gave a quick glance all around. Seeing them, she held up a hand, then vanished. A split second later, she reappeared, but not alone. An entire cart had popped into existence beside her. It was Sara. It must be. Only she could go from place to place in an instant like that. But what was she doing here?

A stooped, bandy-legged man in a ragged tunic climbed down from the driving seat and joined the Gate Shaper, jamming a shapeless felt hat down over his ears as the wind threatened to snatch it. Two Guards trotted towards him, with a third slung between them. The driver helped them hoist their companion into the vehicle. A second pair approached, but this time the carter gestured to the green-cloaked woman. She laid a hand on the injured Guard. Then both of them disappeared. Sara was using her abilities to transport the most seriously wounded off the docks. Probably up to the garrison, where Healers could tend to them.

Shame flooded through Cahira. This was how a skal should be used: to protect, to save. But what had she done with her own power? She'd brought the Bregians to Algarth's shore. All the dead and injured were her fault. She twisted her head away, unable to watch any longer.

The world flashed white. Thunder cracked, as if the sky had been split with an axe. The roaring wind flung needles of ice from every direction. She could barely feel Niall's arms around her.

Inside, the tentacles twined sinuously. There were more of them now.

Take hold of the storm. Bend it to your will.

Cahira's whole body shuddered, but amid her misery, a spark of defiance was born. She was a terrible, worthless excuse for a human being, and she would be overwhelmed soon, but while she was still able to resist that voice, she would.

She turned her gaze back to Sara, who had reappeared, and drew inspiration from her. "No."

Your people are dying.

She didn't reply.

Turn the storm against your enemies. Destroy them.

"No. Never again. Leave me alone."

A dry, spiteful chuckle writhed through her mind, mocking her. *Never again.*

"Who are you?" She had asked that before, and received only silence. But this time, it answered.

You know.

And she did. "Kolos," she said. "You're Kolos."

Very good. But my name is only the beginning.

She had heard enough. Using all her will, she tore her attention back to her surroundings. More time had elapsed than she'd thought. Sienna had carried her past Sara and the warehouses and onto the road leading up to the garrison. The skin over the mare's withers shivered as the lightning flared again, and her ears twitched at the deafening peal of thunder that followed, but she kept going.

Cahira was exhausted, wet, and freezing, but what she felt most was relief. Her mind was clear, her vision undivided. She could see the road ahead and feel Niall's warm arms around her. The hateful voice had fallen silent.

She didn't delude herself that it had vanished forever. She'd invited it inside her, and it had no intention of leaving. She would need more than a burst of defiance to dislodge it. But for now, she leaned back against her friend and gratefully accepted the respite she'd been given.

FORTY-SIX

Niall

The insane wind had eased a little, and the sleet was letting up. Taking advantage of the better conditions, Niall pressed Sienna to greater speed around the tight bends of the garrison road. He had to get Cahira to a Healer.

When he'd seen her standing above the dock, with her arms outstretched and the blue cloak streaming behind her, he'd thought of an ancient warrior queen, defying the elements and the oncoming fleet. He'd been immensely relieved that he'd found her, and yet deathly afraid for her. He was still afraid.

She was alive, yes, but there was something deeply wrong with her. When she'd turned at his shout, her face had been barely recognisable, even to him. She'd looked wild, desolate, and at the same time almost terrifying.

What had she said? "I did it. I brought the ships in."

Impossible, of course. She'd been lost in some kind of delusion. Probably Jak playing his tricks again. And that was a strange thing, the way the traitor had fallen, senseless, from Sienna's back. Perhaps a stray arrow had struck him, although Niall had seen no sign of a wound on the unconscious body.

But only Cahira mattered now. She was slumped like a sack of grain in the saddle, her head bowed as if under a heavy weight. Niall held her tightly, afraid she'd fall if he let her go. Her unresponsiveness reminded him of the first days following Bram's death, when the vivacious, passionate young woman he'd known had disappeared completely, replaced by a pale waif who didn't speak or smile. But on the road searching for Adric, traces of her old self had shown through. Niall had been glad of it, even though it resulted in frequent arguments. He'd give almost anything for a good, robust quarrel now. Urging Sienna on, he bestowed a vicious, silent curse on the woman Fadra, who must be at the bottom of all this.

At the next bend he twisted his head to observe the melee seething over the docks. It was impossible to tell who had the upper hand down there. But his countrymen were outnumbered, and more Bregians were marching north through the city. Not to mention Fadra's people, who'd stayed behind while Jak brought Niall here. As leverage against Cahira? He'd never know. Then there was Berek's ludicrous cult, if any of them remained alive. Most likely, any survivors had scuttled back to the farm after their first taste of a real fight.

Even without them, Oren wouldn't be able to hold the streets, or Mundar the docks. The odds were too heavily against them. They'd have to pull back to the garrison, where they'd be besieged by both Bregian forces. *Assisted by traitorous vermin who can blow things apart just by pointing at them*, Niall remembered.

Whether the end came in hours or days or weeks, Eorna was doomed. As soon as Cahira had been seen by a Healer, he'd spirit her out of the city. Bella would help. No, better yet, Sara. She'd been transporting wounded from the docks to the garrison. He'd find her, and ask her to whisk Cahira to safety.

Sienna rounded the final turn and approached the gate. One of the Guards on duty recognised Niall and waved them past. Something about her new surroundings roused Cahira. She raised her head and turned a pale face towards him. He stifled an involuntary cry, as eyes like dark holes stared through him without recognition.

He dismounted and lifted a hand to her. "Come down, you're safe now."

She was gazing into space, but she started at the sound of his voice. The empty eyes found him, then widened. "Niall?"

He'd scorned to shed a single tear since the day he'd left home, but at that lost, wondering tone, moisture gathered and threatened to spill over. He swallowed and murmured as he would to a spooked horse. "Yes, it's me. Still me. Come down, now."

She hesitated, then swung her leg over the saddle and slid to the ground. Her hand was icy. He put an arm around her shoulders. "You're chilled. Come inside."

The infirmary floor was covered in pallets, most of them occupied. Servants and Healers bustled between them, carrying bandages and basins of water. The only sounds were the crackle of the fire, the soft groans of the injured, and the low mumbling of the Aalden as they prayed.

Niall found a place near the hearth for them. He helped her sit and began chafing her hands to get some warmth into them, while she stared blankly ahead. Not wanting to leave her, he tried unsuccessfully to catch the eye of one of the Healers.

He was about to call out for attention when someone struck up a tune on a stringed instrument and began crooning. Cahira stiffened. A look of horror came over her face. "No," she whispered, shrinking into herself. "No, please."

He laid a hand on her shoulder. "What's the matter? Is it the music?"

She shuddered. "Stop it, please. Oh, make it stop." She began to rock and moan.

A blind fury took hold of Niall, against whoever had turned Cahira's greatest joy into her worst nightmare. If Fadra had done this, she was a dead woman. Unable to exact revenge on her, he sprang up and made for the singer instead.

When he drew close enough to the shadowed corner to see that his target was only a young boy, he forced some of the anger down. His voice still came out harsh and blunt. "The lady near the fire needs rest and quiet. Take a break."

The song died, and the red-headed lad's fingers jangled on the strings before he stilled them. He clutched the instrument to him as his eyes followed Niall's curt gesture towards Cahira. "No problem," he said hoarsely. He cleared his throat. "It's time for my dinner, anyway."

The boy had just reached the doorway when someone pushed through from the other side, almost sending him flying. The newcomer was a young Guard, and his chest was heaving. He stopped and burst out, "They're coming up the hill! They've overrun the docks. We couldn't stop them. They're coming!"

A burly man with a yellow badge on his shirt sat up from his pallet. "Don't tell us, fool of a boy!" he roared. "What d' ye think we can do about it? Get up to the command room."

The young Guard gaped. The other waved an arm. "In the tower, boy! The tower!"

The messenger fled.

"Lie still," the robed Healer kneeling beside the sergeant scolded. "You'll start that leg bleeding again."

The wounded man growled, but lay down.

Niall had been wending his way between the pallets towards the nearest Aaldan. At the sound of that voice, he changed direction and headed for the speaker instead. He stared down at the bent head with its cropped, steel-grey hair, and knew he'd been right.

"Elder Meril," he said.

She looked up from the bowl where she'd been washing her hands. "Master Crawley, isn't it?"

"And Mistress Gelt. She needs your help."

"Is she injured?"

"No, but something's wrong. And she's freezing."

Meril dried her hands and followed him. Cahira was still staring into the flames, showing no awareness of their arrival. The Aaldan gave her a piercing look, then crouched down. "Hm, let's see."

She clasped Cahira's unresisting fingers between her own and bowed her head. Niall lowered himself to the floor on the other side. Long seconds crawled past. Neither of the women moved. And then a series of shudders ran through the Elder. She dropped Cahira's hands and turned a burning gaze on Niall. "What has she been doing? What is she involved in?"

"I—I don't know," he stammered, shaken by the expression of near-loathing on the Aaldan's face. A fresh burst of anger chased away his shock. "Can you help her or not?"

Meril was wiping her hands on her robe again, but this time as if she was trying to scrub something dirty off them. "Perhaps, but this is more than a physical sickness. Stay here."

FORTY-SEVEN

Perna

As the fighting reached the area around Dyers Lane, the House filled up with wounded until there was no room for any more. Then the Aalden went into the streets. Taking her courage in her hands, Perna joined them.

She'd thought she'd grown used to death—the sights and sounds and smells of it—but she'd been wrong. Out here, horrors lurked around every corner. Corpses stared at her from bloody holes where ravens or crows had pecked out their eyes. Gaping wounds writhing with bloated maggots grinned evilly. Groans and cries chilled her to her bones. And an obscene stench invaded her whole being until she was sure she'd never feel clean again.

She vomited until her aching stomach was empty, then wiped her mouth and forced herself back to work. Searching out the living souls among the dead, she did what she could for them. It was little enough. The fighting had been fierce. Most of the fallen had gone beyond help before she reached them.

For the first time, she saw enemy soldiers, in dark grey uniforms, lying alongside the Warrant Guards in their blue shirts. There were many men in ordinary clothes, too, and even some women. They might be volunteers who had stayed to defend their homes, or they might be Berek's Seekers of Virtue, in league with the Bregians. Without uniforms, there was no way to tell.

And Perna found she didn't care. Attacker or defender, all the dead were dead alike, and all the wounded were suffering. Face to face with the aftermath of such violence, such evil, she couldn't ignore any of them.

She knelt beside a beardless youth in Bregian grey, with blood soaking through his tunic and moisture leaking from his terrified eyes, and put all the energy she could muster into Healing him. Immediately, she knew it wasn't enough, and she could have screamed in rage and frustration. But that wouldn't help him. She changed her focus, aiming only to relieve his pain and allow him to slip away in peace. He turned those drowned eyes towards her, croaked out something that might have been *thank you*, and gave a little cough. His head fell to the side. Bright red oozed from the corner of his mouth and dripped down into the dust. Perna bowed her own head and sobbed.

A warm hand squeezed her shoulder. The touch seemed to give her strength, but when she turned, no one was there. She closed the boy's eyelids and pushed herself to her feet, ready to continue.

"Hey, you!"

A ginger-haired man was scowling at her from the other side of the street. "Get away from that Bregian dog! There are good Algarthan men here who need your help. Save your tears for them." He gestured to a figure with the same carroty hair lying in the gutter at his feet.

"Your son?" she asked gently as she crouched down to examine him. The wound was on his neck, but the exact nature of it was obscured by a sheet of blood.

"My nephew," the man replied hoarsely, "but as good as any son to me."

Perna called for water and a cloth, and a volunteer came running with a basin.

The young man's eyes were closed, and his face was pale and still. He didn't react as she sponged away the gore to see what lay beneath. It was as she'd feared. His throat had been slit. A deep, clean cut, and a fatal one. At the sight of it, Perna's mind flashed back to a small room in Welsea garrison. To a man slumped in a chair, with hot blood spurting from his neck. She thrust out a hand to stop herself from falling.

She was a murderer. Somehow, in the last few days, she'd forgotten that. She'd been so quick to judge everyone else for their failings. She'd criticised Niall's flippant attitude, Tabia's messy appearance and tolerance of bad behaviour, and the thief's attempt to rob her. But she had done worse than any of them.

She stared miserably down at the thick blood oozing from the wound. Soon, another young man would lie dead in the dirt, beyond her ability to save. As if he had read her thought, he made a small sound of fear. His eyes flicked open, and he turned them towards her, just as the Bregian had.

"I'm so sorry," she whispered.

"What do you mean, you're sorry?" The older one shook her roughly by the arm. "You're a Healer, aren't you? Fix him!"

"I can't."

"Look! He's still breathing!"

Perna's shoulders slumped. "There's nothing I can do."

"You wasted your skal on that Bregian cur, and now you don't have any left for my boy?"

"No, that's not…"

"Traitor! Bregian-loving filth!"

A fist slammed into the side of her head, jarring her neck. She bit her tongue and let out a yelp, which only seemed to incense him more. Blows and curses rained down. She fell beneath them, making no attempt to defend herself. Aal was punishing her. She would bear it as best she could.

"Hey, stop that! What do you think you're doing?"

There were sounds of a struggle. Perna twisted around painfully and peered up through blurry eyes. Her attacker was being restrained by two other men. When he couldn't break free, he screwed up his mouth and spat at her. Curses floated backwards as he was dragged away.

Perna slowly raised herself on one elbow, her tear-filled eyes going to her patient. Life had fled from him, as she'd known it would. She laid a hand briefly on his forehead, then rose shakily. Her head pounded, and her tongue throbbed where she'd bitten it. Pain was blooming in almost every part of her body, but it all seemed to work. She was a murderer, and probably damned by Aal forever, but her skal could still save lives, still comfort the dying. She wiped the spittle off her cheek and moved on.

She stayed out until after dark, saving a precious few and easing more on their journey into the next life. How many were Bregian and how many Algarthan, she couldn't have said. All she saw was their desperate need and her ability to help them.

At one point, someone brought food and water, and she ate and drank everything she was given. Then she went back to work. She was vaguely aware of others doing the same. Several times more, she felt that comforting touch on her shoulder, that flow of renewed strength. There was never anyone there. Once, she thought she heard a whispered, "Take heart, beloved daughter."

Just my mind playing tricks, she told herself, *probably because of that blow on the head.* Nonetheless, the gentle words filled her with joy. Neither of her parents had ever spoken to her so tenderly.

She was stumbling with exhaustion by the time she returned to the House. Making her way through the packed room, she had to concentrate hard to stop herself from falling on anyone. She was watching her feet so closely that she almost missed him.

She'd reached the stairs when some flicker of recognition paused her steps and turned her around. And there he was, sitting with his broad back to the wall and his shaggy blond head bowed over his drawn-up knees. His face was hidden, but she didn't feel a moment's doubt of his identity. A strange warmth surged through her. Her body acted on its own, retracing her path until she stood in front of him.

She crouched down. "Adric?"

He raised his head and stared at her. "Perna? Is that you?"

She nodded. Her gaze flicked over him, noting with relief the unstained bandage around his chest, his good colour, his clear breathing.

He was gazing at her as if he couldn't believe his eyes, and she suddenly imagined how she must look to him: dirty face streaked with tears, hair greasy and tangled, and clothes stained with blood and filth. Her cheeks burned. No wonder he was staring. She should stop embarrassing herself and go upstairs, but she couldn't make her body rise.

She sat down instead. It was so good to see him! All the feelings she'd rejected swept over her again. She felt her mouth curve into a smile. "Hello, Adric."

For a moment, he looked puzzled at this sudden friendliness. Then he cleared his throat. "Um, how have you been?"

A ridiculous question, and she gave an equally foolish answer. "I am well, thank you."

A long, awkward silence followed. This was pathetic. She should go. She stayed.

"You look different," he said at last.

Somehow, she knew he wasn't just talking about the dirt and the messy hair. "I am different. I've seen some things…" She bit her lip. "Adric? I'm sorry for the way I—"

He shook his head. "Doesn't matter. We've got more important stuff to worry about." His gaze turned inward, and his generous lips thinned and tightened.

Perna's fingers itched to stroke the deep lines from his brow. She sat on her hands. "How is the fighting going? In the rest of the city, I mean."

"It's not good news." His tone was grim. "I've been listening to the ones who came in after me. They're saying the enemy punched through our barricades as if they were nothing. Our men couldn't hold them back. And they landed ships. We might have lost the docks by now."

Even with all the dead she'd seen, she hadn't imagined things could be so bad. "The garrison?"

"Still holding, as far as I know." His face twisted. "Aal's teeth, I should be out there! Not sitting here, safe and useless."

"I'm glad you're here." The words had burst from her on their own, but she couldn't regret them. They were nothing but the truth. She was very glad indeed.

He seemed uncomfortable now, and no wonder. But at least his anger had vanished. "I'm happy you're all right, too," he said, and cleared his throat. "So, you've been Healing people?"

Suddenly she wanted to tell him everything, make him understand. "Oh Adric, I had no idea what it means to be a Healer. How terrible it is, how heartbreaking and exhausting and filthy, and how wonderful, too. To bring comfort and even save lives. It's…"

Words failed her. Miraculously, he seemed to know what she was struggling to say. "It's what you were born to do."

"Yes." She stared at him in wonder.

He nodded. "It's how I feel when I'm running, or climbing, or about to let an arrow fly."

Perna smiled as irrational happiness bubbled up. If the battle was going as badly as Adric said, they could easily die tomorrow, together with everyone in this room, but she couldn't seem to make herself care, or feel afraid.

She'd found him again. And in this one precious moment, they understood each other. It was enough. It was so much more than enough.

FORTY-EIGHT

Cahira

Wind.
Waves.
Ships.
Screaming.
Death.
Fog.
Tentacles.
Kolos.
Niall.
Blackness.
Silence.

Slowly, the disjointed sounds and images reassembled themselves. Memories unfolded, harsh and painful. But the darkness and quiet persisted.

I'm dying, she thought, and felt only relief. It was for the best. Her parents would grieve for her. Niall, too. But they were all safer without her. And surely, the monster couldn't follow her into death. She only needed to stay here, hushed and still, until she faded away to nothing.

A nudge at the edge of her mind—a thread of sound where no other sound existed. She tried to block it out and sink into the void, but it refused to be ignored. A voice, speaking her name. "…Cahira… back."

A woman's tone, one she'd heard before. Despite herself, she caught more. "Listen… Cahira… wake… back to…"

A slow stirring in the darkness, sensed rather than felt. Cahira flinched away from it. The words resolved. "Listen to me, Cahira. Wake and come back to yourself." A pause, and then the voice started again. "Listen…"

It wasn't going to stop until she responded, and the thing inside her was rousing. She couldn't bear to be trapped in here with it. She willed her eyes to open.

Nothing happened. The blackness was absolute. It was like struggling to wake from a nightmare. Well, she had plenty of practice at that. She pushed harder.

"She's coming out of it," the voice said. "Speak to her. Gently now."

"Cahira? Can you hear me?" That was Niall.

She tried to say yes, but nothing came out. She swallowed. This time, she managed a croak.

Inside her, the agitation increased.

"Cahira, open your eyes."

She was doing everything she could, but her lids were too heavy. She couldn't lift them.

Kolos was thrashing now. She pictured the tentacles flailing in all directions, blindly seeking her. There was no escape. The monster would wind her in its cold embrace and drag her down, never to rise again.

"Be still, demon." A new voice, as hard as steel. "Aal, we invoke your protection over this precious soul."

Sensations rushed in—orange flaring against black, a blast of heat on her face, a crackling noise, and the bitter tang of smoke. She was lying on her side, gazing into a fire. Human sounds intruded on her awareness: shuffling, whispers, a low groan. She rolled over onto her back to see three faces staring down at her, lit by flickering light. First, Niall, then a woman she didn't recognise, and finally the owner of the voice.

"Elder Meril?" Cahira's voice scraped its way through a throat that might have been coated with sand.

"How do you feel?"

Cahira coughed and licked her dry lips. "I'm not sure."

Meril leaned forward and stared hard into her eyes. "It's subsided for now, but we couldn't expel it completely." Her gaze pinned Cahira like a rapier. "You understand what I'm talking about?"

Cahira nodded, her heart in her mouth. How could Meril know? And how much had she told Niall?

"We need to talk," Meril said. "But not now. Now, you should rest."

Cahira struggled to sit up. "No. I want…" She couldn't finish the thought.

"Right now, I don't much care what you want." The tone was gentler than the words. "This garrison is under siege, and we've other patients to deal with." She turned to Niall. "Try to get her to eat, then sleep. Send for me if she grows cold again."

"I will."

Cahira bristled. She could make her own decisions. "I'm not hungry, and I'm not tired. Tell me what's happening."

"Well, that sounds more like the woman who came to Mirhome demanding answers," Meril said dryly. "I suppose it's a good sign." She left, followed by her unnamed companion.

Despite her denials, Cahira's eyes were threatening to close again. She fought to keep them open. She wasn't returning to that darkness, knowing what awaited her there. "What time is it?"

"Three hours past sunset."

She looked around the crowded room. "You brought me to the garrison?"

"Yes. You were—"

"And we're under siege," she said quickly. She didn't want to think about how she'd been.

He nodded. "They took the docks at last light, then made camp at the lower end of the road. They haven't come up any further, but we're cut off from the city."

She was almost afraid to ask. "Adric?"

He looked away. He was trying to protect her again.

"Tell me!"

"I don't know. Honestly, Cah. He was injured, south of the market, but a Healer was coming. Odds on, they brought him in this morning." This time, he held her gaze, but she could hear in his voice that he was still keeping something back.

"Niall—"

He made an exasperated sound. "Look, I'll answer all your questions, but first I'm going to get us both some food, like the Elder said."

She would have kept arguing, but a sudden flare from the fire shed more light on his face, revealing things she hadn't noticed before. She stared at the bruised shadows under his eyes, the sunken grey hollows of his cheeks. He looked like an old man. No, he looked like the figure lying in the snow in her dream, the one who'd shrivelled into a corpse as she'd watched.

He's been sitting here for hours, she realised, *waiting for me to wake up*. And before that, he'd been fighting in the streets. He needed food and rest more than she did.

She swallowed her protest and nodded.

Stepping into the corridor, she closed the door softly behind her. She took a deep breath and blew it out, feeling some of the tension drain away. She'd made it this far without waking him.

Despite her fear of falling asleep again, she'd succumbed to exhaustion almost as soon as she'd eaten, but this time she'd woken to full alertness with her course clear. While Niall snored, she would search the garrison for Adric. If he was here, she'd find him, and be back before Niall knew she was gone. She crept along the candle-lit hallway, the dank chill setting her shivering.

Unlike the infirmary, the other chambers on this level were small and cold. Most lay in a darkness broken only by the dim light of thin wax tapers. But the floors were crowded with the injured, lying on pallets, blankets, or just pieces of sacking. As she made her way between them, her ears rang with an awful symphony of guttural moans, mumbled prayers, shouted curses, babbled strings of nonsense, and an occasional hair-raising scream. The infirmary hadn't smelled like this, either. The stench of bodily fluids, mixed with the sweet, stomach-churning odour of putrefaction, forced its way into her nostrils, her lungs, her very being. She swallowed convulsively, feeling as if she'd never be rid of it again. She pinched her nose, gritted her teeth, and tried to think only of Adric.

Room after room, and all the same; it was a horrifying testament to the way the Bregians had stamped their dominance on the city. And how many other poor souls lay dead on the streets, or huddled in whatever bolt-holes they'd been able to find? Was Adric one of those?

She'd searched this whole level now and found no sign of him. She returned to a stairwell she'd passed earlier and started down. But she'd only reached the first bend when the view below stopped her in her tracks. The next landing was jammed with men, women, and children, packed in like beasts penned for slaughter. Except the butchering had already begun. Many lay unmoving, the light of the stair candles gleaming on patches of still-wet blood. Others sat, or stood leaning against the freezing walls. The all-too-familiar smells and cries emanated from them, but the narrow well concentrated both and made them even more hideous.

Faces tilted up towards her. She saw anger in some of them, and hope in a few, but most of the expressions were simply blank. There were no soft pallets here, no blankets, no Healers. Nothing but desperate people needing help she couldn't give. Suddenly, she couldn't bear the thought of pushing her way between those tightly packed bodies, feeling their clutching hands as she passed. If she'd known for certain that Adric was among them—but she didn't know. She wasn't even sure he was in the garrison. She would search all the higher levels first, and only then venture down into this nightmare. She turned and fled.

One floor up from the infirmary, the air was fresher and the illumination stronger. The cries of the wounded had been left behind. But Cahira couldn't get the memory of what she'd seen out of her head.

Red hatred welled up in her—at the Bregians, the Seekers, Fadra and her acolytes, anyone who'd played a part in this. She wished them all dead and buried. No, more than that. She wanted them blotted out, leaving nothing to mark the fact they'd ever existed. She imagined herself doing it. She'd send the lightning over and over until they burned to ash, then raise a hurricane to blow every last speck away. Her fury carried her onwards, all caution forgotten. She sped along hallways, in and out of rooms, up another level. The rage gave her energy, buoyed her up. And then it betrayed her.

Flying around a corner, she ran into the last person she ever wanted to see again: the loathsome man who'd put a knife to her throat, tied and gagged her, and ordered her imprisoned. Sergeant Donard's eyes widened in shock, and then he reached for her. She twisted away from his grasping hands and pelted back the way she'd come. He let out a curse and followed, his boots thumping unevenly. He must have been injured since they last met.

She took random turns, skidding through corners with no care for her safety, and was rewarded when the limping footfalls faded behind her. She slowed to a walk, waiting for her breathing to return to normal. As soon as the blood stopped thundering in her ears, she noticed the buzzing. It was soft—only just within hearing—but it tickled the inside of her skull unpleasantly. It was coming from an open doorway ahead. She drew level, and a jolt of shock pulled her up. He was sitting in a corner with his head bowed. The candlelight shone on his red curls. Cahira grabbed at the door frame to steady herself.

Ferdy showed no sign that he'd noticed her. He was strumming on a lute and singing—a wordless, vibrating melody that curdled Cahira's insides. Heaviness filled her limbs. Her leaden head dropped forward until her chin rested on her chest. The flagstones beneath her shifted and dissolved into thick, sucking mud, trapping her feet and engulfing them up to the ankles. She couldn't move, not even a finger. She was exhausting herself trying.

Why am I still struggling? she thought. *What's the point?* All her efforts had been doomed to failure from the start. The Bregians were too many, too strong. Fadra's people were too skilled and powerful. And Kolos would never release her. Better to give up now and wait peacefully for the end.

Far back in a corner of her mind, something was scratching, trying to get her attention, but Ferdy's song held her like a bird in a snare.

"You!"

The shout broke through her frozen state. Her head swivelled slowly. Donard stood at the end of the hallway. Without meaning to, he had saved her. She could move again, think again. The flagstones were firm beneath her feet. He lurched towards her, his face a mask of hatred. She clapped her hands over her ears and ran.

She was gaining on him again, but as she passed a dark recess under some stairs, a hand grabbed her elbow with steely strength and jerked her to a stop. She spun to face her assailant—an old man in a crumpled brown hat that only came up to her chin.

"This way, daughter." He released her arm and retreated into the shadows.

She went with him, although afterwards she couldn't have said why. Perhaps she was just too surprised to react quickly, or perhaps it was the way he'd called her 'daughter', as if he knew her and was on her side. Foolishness, and yet there was something familiar about him. He put a finger to his grey-bearded lips, and they watched Donard clump past.

When her pursuer was out of sight, Cahira spoke. "Do I know you?"

"Well now, it's true we met before, or close to, anyhow." White teeth flashed in a broad smile. "You was lyin' low in the back of a wagon, as I recall, and I'd just gotten reacquainted with my old friend Dobbo."

This was the drunk who'd distracted Dostig and his men, giving her—and Fadra—the chance to escape. So, was he on her side or Fadra's? He pulled open a door set into the wall under the stairs. "Me and you need to part ways again now. Your path goes through here, all the way out to the east. You'll know what to do when you gets there."

She stared blankly at him, rubbing the elbow. Why would she want to leave the castle?

Blue eyes gazed up at her solemnly from under the brim of his battered hat. "Think on it, daughter. The dark ones—curse 'em—they'll be searching for you, looking high and low now they knows you're here. Already found you once, and trapped you like a fly in a web, ain't that so?"

Ferdy, she thought. He meant Ferdy and his song. How could he know about that?

The old man gestured to the darkness beyond the open door. "Besides, come morning, you'll be needed out there." He lifted his nose and gave two short sniffs, like a dog trying to scent something in the air. "Not long to first light. Time you was on your way."

He produced a lantern—from where, she couldn't tell—and thrust it into her hands. The candle was lit. Turning her, he pushed her gently through the doorway. She took a few more steps, then twisted around and shook her head, discovering her voice again. "I can't. I have to find Adric."

Already backing towards the hallway, he stopped and gave a brief snort like a cat sneezing. "Don't fret yourself. Safe as a bird in a nest he be, and far from here. Aal's own truth, my word on it."

She stared into eyes the colour of a rain-washed sky and saw no sign of deceit. But she had to be sure. "How do you know? Who are you?"

"Name's Garst." He turned away and trotted off with a jaunty wave.

As soon as she made to follow, the door swung shut in her face. Heart thumping, she shoved at it. To her surprise, it gave way without resistance. He hadn't locked her in. She poked her head out, but he was nowhere in sight. For an old man, he moved fast. She was about to emerge when limping footfalls broke the silence. She pulled the door shut, whirling and pressing her back against it in case Donard tried the handle. She was facing the darkness now. The wavering light from the lantern revealed a narrow, straight-sided tunnel lined with close-fitting blocks of stone. A low roof of the same material arched overhead.

She couldn't hear Donard anymore, but that didn't mean he'd gone. He might be waiting right outside. After a short debate with herself, she crept forward on the balls of her feet, holding the light high. She'd see if Garst had told the truth about where the passage led.

She knew the name, of course. Logen and Niall had talked about him. Sara, too. He was the old man who'd met them when they were hiding in the hills. He'd guided them safely to where they needed to go. He'd also had something to do with the swarm of wasps that had allowed them to escape, or at least Sara thought so. And he'd warned the Guards in the house near Fortune Creek that a group of mercenaries were coming. Apparently, that had been important, but Cahira couldn't remember why.

She hadn't really been listening that day. She'd been sunk in grief, wondering what kind of future she could have, now that Bram was gone. But it seemed as though the old man had been true to his word back then. And he'd helped her escape—twice now—from men who intended her harm. That counted in his favour.

After going straight and level for some time, the route suddenly plunged down a set of stairs, descending into obscurity. Cahira lay on her stomach and dangled the lantern over the abyss, but the light still didn't reach the bottom. The darkness was unsettling, but it also drew her. Garst had said the passage led out of the castle, and that she'd be needed there. She badly wanted to know if he was right.

She stood and considered her next move. Niall was probably looking for her by now, anxious to bring her back to the infirmary for more rest. Between his determination to protect her, Ferdy's disturbing performance, and the sergeant's dogged pursuit, the search for Adric had become fraught with obstacles. If she returned to the hallways, one of them would find her. And if Garst was to be believed, her brother-in-law wasn't even here.

She smiled wryly, fully aware that this careful reasoning was only leading her to the path she really wanted to take. It had never been in her nature to ignore a mystery. Or to willingly retrace her steps, which was the only other option she had. Going forward—following her curiosity—was what she did, for better or worse. Holding the lantern out, she started down.

FORTY-NINE

Niall

She was gone. Niall scrambled to his feet, wincing as his stiff muscles protested the sudden movement. Curse it, why couldn't she ever just stay put?

Nearby, an Aaldan was nodding beside her patient. He bent and asked if she'd noticed Cahira leaving. The woman started up from her doze and shook her head, giving him a resentful look. He didn't care.

Outside the room, he considered which direction she might have taken. She'd been in such a strange mood after they'd fled the docks, almost as if she'd been emptied out and replaced by someone else. He rejected that thought angrily. She'd just had a shock, that was all. Meril and the other Aaldan had brought her back. She'd recognised him, spoken normally, asked sensible questions. The haunted look that had turned him inside out had left her eyes.

He peered along the hallway, more anxious than he wanted to admit. More than he'd been at the Ford, or in the fight for the streets, or when he'd faced Ruston. If Cahira was back to her normal self, that probably meant she was being impetuous and fearless. Right now, that could be a very bad thing. Perhaps someone had seen her go past. He'd ask in every room until he tracked her down.

He'd searched most of the infirmary level, leaving countless tired, disgruntled people in his wake, when he came across the red-haired singer again, strumming and murmuring. Niall supposed the music was meant to soothe and ease the wounded, but to his ears it sounded more like a dirge than anything else.

This room was the most crowded one yet, with bodies lying wall-to-wall. They appeared more seriously hurt, too. Many cried out in their sleep, tossing from side to side. The air itself seemed to hold a miasma of despair and death. Niall drew his cloak tighter around himself as he pushed through, as if to avoid contamination. There weren't any Healers here, but no doubt their numbers were thinly stretched in the garrison. The singer broke off as Niall reached him, lifting a freckled face.

"Do you remember the lady I was with earlier?"

The boy gaped at him for a moment, then bobbed his head.

"Have you seen her again? Did she come in here?"

"No, sir."

"Are you sure?"

The annoyed look that had become familiar in the last half hour was stamped on the singer's face. "I'm sure." He picked up the instrument. The dirge droned on.

Niall's shoulders slumped. The castle was enormous, and Cahira could be anywhere. He was never going to find her. Even though his body felt like it had been trampled by a herd of horses, the agitation in his mind told him sleep was out of the question. Maybe Logen or Oren could give him something useful to do.

Growling under his breath at the thought of all reckless, headstrong women—and a certain dark-haired, green-eyed one in particular—he turned his steps towards the command room in the tower.

He crouched in the thick cover that lined the road, his presence cloaked in shadow. Above the horizon, the grey sky was streaked with pink and gold. In the dim light before dawn, he watched the horses pass in front of him.

The woman called Fadra occupied the centre of the group, on a fine black stallion. There was no sign of the traitor Jak, and that was some satisfaction, but the dark-haired man who'd blown the barricade apart was sitting beside his leader, stiffly upright and on the alert for any threat. Eight others rode with them.

They were heading towards the garrison, surrounded by a tightly packed mass of Bregians. It was a smart move. The greyshirts would protect them from direct assault, while the Wood Shaper could snap arrows into kindling before they reached the soldiers.

Niall considered stirring up the animals, unseating the riders. It would give him some satisfaction and might inconvenience Fadra's group, even cause some injuries. But it would also result in the beasts' quick deaths. The Bregians would have no compunction about killing maddened horses to protect themselves. In fact, the only reason to do it would be to salve his own ego after his failure to stop them yesterday. It wasn't worth it. He knew that, but he didn't like it. He shook his head, cursing under his breath at his impotence.

He'd come out with the scouting party to distract himself from worrying about Cahira. But the strength of numbers—and military discipline—of the enemy were only depressing him, and there was nothing for him to do here.

Not for the first time, he wished for Adric and his crossbow. One nicely-aimed metal bolt would solve the problem of the Wood Shaper permanently. If only he'd retrieved the weapon after Adric had fallen, he might have figured out how to use it himself, but his mind had been on other things. Still, he should have thought of it. Come to think of it, his brain hadn't been working too well last night, either. Why in Aal's name had he given up looking for Cahira so soon? His decision made no sense to him.

The scout leader raised his hand in a prearranged signal. Niall nodded. Time to leave and report what they'd seen. Commander Oren had a bird's-eye view of the road from the windows of the tower, but had sent the small party for a closer look at the assault force. Niall fervently hoped the other scouts had spotted some weakness that he'd missed. Otherwise, the near future was looking grim for all of them.

FIFTY

Cahira

She descended the last few steps to find nothing but another stone-lined passage stretching out beyond the reach of the lantern. But rather than being straight like the first tunnel, this one curved and twisted as she followed it. At times she even suspected it of doubling back on itself, although it was hard to judge directions with no landmarks to guide her. The constant ache in her legs told her that she was steadily climbing.

More than once, she stopped and chided herself for continuing this journey in near-darkness to who knew where. She should turn around and go back to Niall. But each time she halted, something urged her on. It could have been the memory of the look in Garst's eyes, or the way he'd said, *Come morning, you'll be needed out there.* Most likely, it was just her own stubbornness. She refused to give up without finding anything, to waste the effort she'd already spent. And of course, the further she went, the stronger that argument became.

She pushed on until a dead end brought her up short. She hadn't passed any other passages, and now a thick wooden door blocked the way ahead. The candle was a slumped mass of half-melted wax. As she watched, the last fraction of wick sank below the molten surface, taking the final gleam of flame with it. Chill blackness pressed in. Whatever lay beyond the obstacle, it must be better than this freezing, lightless tunnel.

She ran a careful hand over the splintery timber and discovered a flaky, rusted handle. She curled her fingers around the cold metal and pulled. The hinges creaked in protest. The old wood grated against the stone floor and stalled. She took a firmer grip and tugged with determination. Moving in fits and starts, the grumbling door surrendered to her will. Light sliced through the narrow opening, bright enough to make her eyes water.

Blinking away the tears, she hauled the door fully open. In front of her, the sun was breaking free of the horizon. She'd reached the eastern wall of the castle as Garst had promised, and it was just past dawn. Lowering her eyes, she saw only a stretch of tawny grass that told her nothing. She stepped into the daylight.

Before her lay more grass, topped by blue sky. To her right, the ground sloped down past the castle before abruptly dropping away to reveal a patchwork of farms and forests below. The city, which must be in that direction, was hidden from sight. To her left, a long stretch of frost-yellowed turf led upwards, lapping at the base of the stony rise that marked the end of the headland.

There was no one nearby, but the light breeze carried faint cries and the distant clash of metal. *They're fighting on the road in front of the gates,* she thought, and wondered what she was doing up here, when the battle was elsewhere. And then, beneath the other noises, on the very threshold of hearing, a familiar hum vibrated, accompanied by a dry scratching in Cahira's ears and a stirring in the pit of her stomach.

She swivelled towards the grey stone. The sound was coming from up there, where the rock levelled out into a broad platform at its summit. Two tiny figures were silhouetted against the sky, the distance too great for her to see any details. But she knew at least one of them, and this time, she wouldn't allow herself to be stalled or distracted. She'd confront him face to face.

As she made her way closer, the figures resolved themselves. Fadra stood there, tall and straight, gazing upwards with her long grey hair blowing behind her like a flag. And beside her, his copper mop blazing in the sunlight, was Ferdy. His arms were raised, his head also tilted back. He was using his skal to do something she couldn't quite define yet, but it wasn't anything good. Of course, she'd known that before she'd seen him. Known the instant she'd heard the same tone he'd been singing last night, and felt that thing inside her wake in response.

As if sensing her thought, Fadra tipped her head downwards, the sharp movement reminding Cahira of a raptor fixing its gaze on its prey. She straightened her own spine and stared back in defiance. She wouldn't be cowed by Fadra. And certainly not by Ferdy. She'd taught him; she knew his limits.

Your power is greater. Your will is stronger.

"Shut up," she muttered. Surprisingly, it did.

A little out of breath now, she strode on. Down below, men were fighting for control of the garrison and the city, but Garst had been right: her battle was here. And after a night of frustration and uselessness, she was more than ready for it. She had no plan beyond reaching Ferdy and stopping whatever he was doing—without harming him in the process.

Once more, it was as if the older woman had read her mind. Fadra turned towards the boy and laid a hand on his shoulder. The volume of his song increased. So did the complexity. The loud, ugly harmonics boomed through Cahira's head and churned in her stomach. Darkness crowded in on her thoughts, making it hard to concentrate. He wasn't forming any images, but the power in the music alone was appalling, beyond anything she'd believed him capable of.

It slowed her, but she fought it. She swallowed to ease the weight pressing against her ear drums, then forced her heavy legs to carry her on. Just ahead of her now, a shoulder-high cluster of sharply angled boulders rose from the grass. Behind them lay a long slope of dark grey stone, and above that the platform that was her destination. She was so intent on moving forward that she failed to notice she wasn't alone.

They must have been there all along, crouched down among the boulders, but her attention had been fixed higher up. They appeared in front of her like spirits risen from the ground: the Metal Shaper, Aidan, and another man, a stranger. She pulled up with a jerk and tried to back away, but Ferdy's destructive melody had compromised her control over her body. Her feet slipped from under her. She fell awkwardly, limbs sprawling.

Aidan had a sword blade at her throat before she could move. "Stay down. Don't open your mouth. I know exactly what you're capable of, traitor, and I won't hesitate. Trust me."

He was the second person to call her a traitor since she'd returned to Eorna, and she'd had enough of it, especially from one of Fadra's followers. The melody was there before she even stopped to think. She didn't need to open her lips. The sound travelled along her sinuses and out through her nostrils, whining and burring.

Aidan's eyes rolled back in his head. Cahira scrambled out of the way just in time to avoid being skewered by the falling sword as he dropped to the ground. The other man opened his mouth in shock, and she felled him, too. Ignoring them both, she lifted her gaze to Fadra and Ferdy. Both their heads were angled to the sky again. It didn't look as though they'd noticed anything. And perhaps her use of her own skal had provided her with some protection, because Ferdy's song was far easier to resist now. She made her way between the boulders and started climbing.

The rocky slope wasn't as smooth and uncluttered as it had seemed from down below. Thin plates of stone with sharp, broken edges were strewn several layers deep all across the surface. In places they were stacked up knee high or more. No matter how carefully she stepped on them, they teetered and cracked, threatening to slide away and take her with them. How had Fadra and Ferdy managed this? Then, after several close calls, she spied a clearer section winding around some taller stacks. She stopped and followed it with her eyes. A narrow track looped back and forth across the slope, leading to the summit. She'd missed the start of it below, but she carefully made her way to the nearest stretch and discovered that the stone surface was solid underfoot.

Now that she didn't have to concentrate so hard on where to tread, the memory of what she'd done below nagged at her like a sore tooth. She'd resolved never to use her skal again—at least not to harm anyone—yet at the first sign of danger, she'd lashed out without thinking. Had Kolos taken control of her?

Stopping to catch her breath, she cast her mind back to the moment she'd attacked Aidan. She'd been scared, yes. Indignant, angry, even desperate. But the writhing tentacles, the dry laughter, the murky coldness—and especially the surge of power she'd felt on the docks—were absent. This time she couldn't blame her actions on anyone else; she'd made her own decision. And what did that say about her?

She bowed her head. Impetuous. Thoughtless. Reckless. She'd been called those things in childhood by her tutors and older relatives like Aunt Alys, and they were still true. That was why she'd opened that cursed book in the first place, let this thing invade her and bring in the ships. She'd doomed Eorna because she had no self-control.

Ferdy's wordless song filled her ears, scratched and buzzed against her brain, roiled in her stomach. Her gaze dropped to the hilt of the dagger she'd taken from the Guard in the garrison, still tucked into her belt. What use was a single weapon when everything was already lost? She lifted it out with two fingers and let it fall with a clang. But even as she stood listening, frozen in place, a tiny seed of curiosity sprouted. She felt a sudden, perverse desire to understand what Ferdy was doing, and how, before the end came. It wouldn't change anything, but she was a Skalsinger, and she wanted to know. Fighting against the dulling effect of the song on her brain, she scraped together every morsel of knowledge and experience she could recall and aimed it at the problem. If she had chosen that melody, that rhythm, that tone, what would her intentions have been?

Understanding slowly unfolded. That low, buzzing hum, penetrating through flesh and bone to the heart and brain, carried a message. *Despair*, it said. *Surrender.* When it reached the defenders down below, it would steal the resolve from every one of them. It would crush their hopes, overwhelm their minds with fear and doubt. Some would freeze as she had. Others would flee like wounded animals, their purpose forgotten, seeking nothing more than a dark place to curl up and hide.

The revelation was like cold water thrown over her. She gasped and raised her head. Niall was down there, and maybe Adric too, along with every able-bodied soul that remained of Eorna's Warrant Guards and volunteers. If they surrendered, the city would fall. Algarth itself would be next.

But analysing the song had broken its power over her once more. She could think and move freely again. She might be the only one in hearing range who could. It was up to her. She bent and retrieved the dagger.

Even now, it wasn't easy. Every step forward was an act of will. She had to stay outside the music, continuing to dissect it second by second, lest it overwhelm her. It was exhausting, but she wouldn't give in. However long it took, she would reach the unscrupulous woman who'd pretended to be her friend and the young singer who'd betrayed his own people. And she'd stop them.

FIFTY-ONE

Niall

From his vantage point in the tower, he took in the scene below. The narrow, unglazed opening was one of many, placed at intervals around the wall that encircled the command room. When he'd left for the scouting trip, they'd all been veiled in darkness. But on his return, the early morning light had revealed long vistas in every direction. After reporting, he'd walked the perimeter, gazing out of each window.

In the east, the rising sun had transformed the coastal way to Gadara into a shining ribbon. People and vehicles crawled along it, all heading away from the city. Southward lay the garrison gates. The broad road winding down the hill was clogged with a grey mass of Bregian soldiers. There was no sign of the horses, although he could still sense them somewhere below. Not wanting to be reminded of his failures, he'd passed on quickly. To the west, the land sloped gently for a short distance before ending in a sheer drop above the harbour. Nothing moved there, except birds diving with white splashes into the water.

The northern view had held his attention the longest, although he couldn't have said why it drew him so strongly. The garrison lay halfway up the tilted finger of the headland, surrounded by a sea of grass. As the ground continued to rise, the turf gave way to stone. Above a tumbled hem of boulders, a bare expanse of charcoal-grey slate thrust upwards before levelling out into a broad platform. It looked as though an enormous sword had descended from the sky and sliced horizontally through the rock. But right on the very end, a tiered stack rose, spared by the wielder of the blade.

It was the highest point on the coast and a perfect spot for a permanent lookout post, but everyone in Eorna knew the stories. The stone up there was unstable, liable to sheer off without warning. It had happened many times before. One day that last pile, too, would tumble into the sea. When Adric and Mundar had brought news of the invasion to the garrison, Commander Oren had sent Guards up there to keep watch on the strait. They'd been withdrawn after the docks fell, leaving the high perch to the wind and the seabirds again.

After gazing at the bare, rocky shelf for several minutes, Niall had abandoned it too, crossing to the south-facing window where he stood now. In the mustering yard below, the Algarthan forces were lined up behind the gates. They shifted restlessly as they waited for the order to move out.

Logen and Oren murmured quietly together at the next opening. The two men could hardly have been more different in temperament and appearance. Warrant Guard Commander Harl Oren—his round, coarse-featured face stamped with its usual humourless expression— looked exactly what he was: a plodding man who'd been thrust into high command by an unforeseen chain of events. Oh, he had integrity, Niall thought, and even brains of a kind, but he was so dull and serious, so wedded to duty, so lacking in any kind of charisma.

Logen Rush, on the other hand, had always been a natural leader, with his tall stature, thick golden-red hair and beard, and a mouth more suited to smiling than frowning. They'd met on the road six months after Niall had left home. Taking to each other immediately, they had remained friends ever since. It was only because of Logen's influence that Niall had been allowed to stay up here. Oren neither liked nor trusted him—an attitude that owed more to his flippant manner than anything he'd actually done—but as acting Chairman of the Council, Logen had overruled the dour commander.

But as different as they were, the one thing the two leaders had in common was their determination to act in the best interests of the city and the nation. They'd both do whatever they could to end this invasion and drive the Bregians back from their shores.

Their tones had been too low for Niall to understand what they were saying, but now they seemed to reach a decision. Logen nodded and moved aside. Oren beckoned to one of the uniformed runners standing at attention behind him. When the young Guard came forward, Oren bent his head and spoke quietly. The messenger stepped back, saluted, and sped from the room. Niall turned his eyes to the yard again. Things were about to start.

The minutes crawled as he waited, white-knuckled and tense. Then a horn sounded, and the massive gates were flung open. The vanguard—armed with steel pikes and swords impervious to the power of the Wood Shaper—rushed out with a roar and broke over the front ranks of the Bregians. Availing themselves of the high ground, they pushed the greyshirts back without effort, leaving dozens lying on the road in their wake. Raising his voice this time, Oren gave the order for the next wave to make ready.

Niall was familiar with the plan, having heard it from Logen last night. This second force would split into two groups and attack from the flanks. When Oren judged the Bregians had been pushed downhill far enough, he'd sound the retreat and all the Algarthans would pull back behind the gates again. In this way, with repeated sorties and retreats, he hoped to harry the enemy and prevent them storming the castle, while keeping their own casualties to a minimum.

Niall's grip on the sill loosened, and he breathed a little easier. It was early in the battle, but if his countrymen kept fighting like this, they might defend the garrison until help arrived from the other cities. The odds of completely defeating the invaders were still very long, especially if they couldn't wrest back the docks, but at least they were holding out for now.

And then, for no reason that Niall could discern, the tide turned. The first Algarthan sortie wavered in its tracks, slowed almost to a stop. The Bregians firmed their line and forged uphill once more. Niall's jaw was clenched as hard as stone. Oren let out a low curse and ordered out the next wave. For long agonising minutes, the battle-front surged repeatedly a few spans up the road and down again. But with each cycle, the greyshirts seemed to press forward a little more, fall back a little less.

"Come on," Logen muttered.

Then the desertions began. Only a few at first, then more and more. They fled in every direction, through any gap they could find. Some even tried to force their way downhill through the bulk of the enemy. It was as though they'd lost their minds. Others simply dropped their weapons and stood stock still, as if asking for death. The Bregians obliged them.

Niall's heart pounded in shock. He shifted his weight from foot to foot, torn between an insane desire to be down there swinging his own sword, and an intense, shameful relief that he was safe up here. Not that anywhere would be safe if the enemy breached the castle, an outcome that was looking more and more likely every minute.

The sortie had failed. Worse, they were being annihilated. And why hadn't the second wave gone out yet? Despite Oren's command, they were still in the mustering yard, milling around aimlessly.

"Pull them back," Logen burst out.

Oren didn't respond.

Logen rounded on him. "Pull them back, man, or we lose them all."

For long seconds, they stared one another down. Oren's eyes fell first. His deep voice was steeped in bitterness as he snapped out the order.

FIFTY-TWO

Roldan

Something vibrated against his eardrum, as if a tiny insect were trapped in there. Observing the battle from his secured position beside the road, Overseer Roldan tilted his head and shook it again.

Scratch. Buzz. Scratch.

No use. Trying to ignore the discomfort, he straightened up. At least the first encounter of the day was proceeding according to plan. His soldiers, disciplined and well-equipped, were having no trouble pushing back the rabble that had spilled through the gates at dawn. Victory was inevitable.

Yes, it was going smoothly, he told himself, absently twisting a fingertip in his ear. But the usual sense of satisfaction at his troops' success continued to elude him. His gaze shot upwards to the pile of rock crowning the headland. It was all her fault. She was too far away to see clearly, but he knew she was there—knew it in his marrow. She would be poised on the highest point, like a noblewoman gazing over her estates. Or a queen looking down on her subjects.

She was doing something up there, worse than poisoning his people's weapons or using arcane means to contact the ships. It was the cause of this infernal buzzing in his ears, this restlessness and dissatisfaction. This wrongness, deep inside his being. And it had affected the enemy even more strongly, snatching away any joy Roldan might have had in this battle and stealing the honour that should have belonged to him and his soldiers.

The Algarthans had poured from the garrison just after dawn, undisciplined but hot and ready for a fight. They'd fallen on the grey ranks filling the road, and the fierceness of their attack had pushed the line backwards. Roldan's force had rallied quickly, and for a while neither side had been able to gain a decisive advantage. He'd had no doubts his soldiers would prevail in the end, but the enemy were making more of a battle of it than he'd expected. But then, everything had changed.

In a single moment, all along the line, the Algarthans checked and slowed, and the Bregians waded into them like reapers slashing a wheat-field. Many of the enemy broke then, fleeing towards the side of the road or back to the garrison. A handful were so panicked they tried to escape downhill. It was as if they had lost their minds. But strangest of all had been the ones who'd stopped moving altogether and just stood there, waiting for the blow to fall.

Those who hadn't been cut down already were still frozen in place, even now. It was unnatural, and it made Roldan's flesh crawl. He was beset by a strong impulse to call a withdrawal and allow their fellows to fetch them in. They were all finished, anyway. They had no choice now but surrender. What harm could it do to allow the survivors to retreat?

In four decades of fighting for his country, he'd never felt this way. It would be a defiance of orders, and an abandonment of sound military policy. In any conflict, the enemy must be utterly crushed, lest they dare to rise later in revolt. That he wished to do otherwise shocked and bewildered him. But he couldn't let the idea go. The consequences of acting on it played through his mind.

At the very least, his distinguished career would end in disgrace. He'd be stripped of his honours, scorned and reviled by everyone he knew, disowned even by his own family. At worst, he'd be executed for treason. And how would Bidi manage then?

The last time he'd seen her, she'd been talking about them leaving the city and buying a farm. He wished now that he'd given in and resigned his commission before this campaign, but he'd hungered for just one more victory. A last shiny bauble of fame to add to his collection. His mouth twisted. He'd been a fool.

But regrets were useless. He had to decide what to do, before his soldiers overran the garrison and took matters out of his hands. Pulling his forces from certain victory would be a betrayal of his nation, the troops under his command, and his innocent wife. But how could he live with himself if he let this travesty of a battle continue? There was no way out, and the buzzing inside his brain was driving him mad. He threw his head back and roared his frustration at the uncaring sky.

His new adjutant spun around. "Sir?"

The blank incomprehension on the young woman's face brought Roldan to himself. Staring into those startled eyes, he recalled their conversation after the briefing last night. With eagerness and pride suffusing her voice, the aide had expressed her gratitude at being considered worthy to take part in this engagement on foreign soil. She'd vowed to live up to the confidence that Roldan, and Bregia, had placed in her. Her manner and phrasing had been almost comically pompous, but sincerity had shone from her. She'd meant every word.

Roldan's indecision vanished. He couldn't order his soldiers to withdraw. For better or worse, he was a loyal Bregian, too. Even more than that, he was the scion of a noble family, whose military fame stretched back centuries. That history, that inheritance, had shaped his entire life. He wouldn't set it aside now.

"Never mind," he said.

The adjutant looked confused at his gentle tone, but nodded and turned her attention to the road.

The moment of weakness over, Roldan tugged his tunic straight, checked his sword hilt was exactly where it should be, and stiffened his spine. Behind him stood more than a thousand years of Bregian culture and progress. What was Algarth, to think it could hold out against that? A nation of farmers and bakers he'd called them, and he'd been right. Bregia was the superior civilisation, destined to increase its territory and rule over lesser peoples.

It embarrassed him that he'd forgotten that, even for an instant. He must be getting soft in his old age. Perhaps it was time to retire, as Bidi had urged. But that was a decision for another day, after he'd returned home in victory. Right now, he had his duty to do. And he wouldn't allow doubt to creep in again.

FIFTY-THREE

Cahira

The dagger was slippery in her hand as she halted to catch her breath and gather her thoughts.

She'd panted all the way up the looping path and then trudged across the long, flat platform, all the time assuming that Fadra and Ferdy would be waiting for her, as aware of her presence as she was of theirs. She'd expected them to confront her as soon as her head crested the stack at the end.

But she'd negotiated the last shallow tiers of slate with her heart in her mouth and the dagger at the ready, only to reach the top and find herself gazing on two backs, still a dozen paces away. Even now, they seemed oblivious to her presence, staring at the sky in front of them, or perhaps the waters of the strait below. The situation left her temporarily at a loss.

She wiped her hands on her cloak and took a fresh hold of the dagger. She told herself sternly that nothing had changed. Ferdy was still singing, encouraged by Fadra. If they didn't know she was here yet, so much the better. She'd creep up close behind them and threaten to use the weapon unless they stopped what they were doing.

At least there was no danger of them hearing her coming. Up here, the song filled her skull almost to bursting. But she'd kept up her analysis, noting exactly how Ferdy was stringing the notes together, and even this close, her mind remained shielded from the full effect.

She dared a quick glance below. A grey tide was moving uphill towards the gates of the garrison, and hardly anyone seemed to be resisting them. The Algarthans were in disarray, many of them standing stock still. She had to act now.

But she'd only taken one step forward when Fadra turned in a leisurely way to face her. "Cahira, I knew you'd find us." She didn't appear to be speaking louder than normal, but her words cut cleanly through the din.

Ferdy gave no sign he'd heard anything. Keeping a hand on his shoulder, Fadra motioned with the other. "Join me."

Cahira wondered if the invitation held a double meaning. If so, the woman would be disappointed. Taking an even firmer grip on the dagger, she approached, stopping just out of arm's reach.

Fadra smiled. "It's good to see you again. I'm glad you made it to Eorna safely."

Cahira raised the weapon higher. "Tell him to stop."

"Why should I do that? He's singing magnificently."

"If you don't silence him, I will."

"Oh, I doubt that."

"You have no idea what I'm capable of."

Fadra lifted an eyebrow. "Go ahead, then."

A vivid image of the sharp blade arcing down and biting deep into Ferdy's unguarded back invaded Cahira's mind. She flinched, and a shiver ran up her spine. Fadra was right: she couldn't do it. Not like this, with Ferdy helpless and unaware.

"You see? I understand you, Cahira Gelt. I've been inside your head. Mostly empty, of course, except for some weak sentimentality, easy to manipulate."

Cahira's mouth dropped open. *Inside her head?*

"Oh, I'm not a Mind Wender, like Jon," Fadra went on. "He's dead now, poor man. You killed him."

Cahira's heart was pounding, and she was incapable of speech.

"Of course, you didn't do it on purpose, did you?" False sympathy rang in Fadra's voice. "Murder isn't in you. Oh yes, I know you, Cahira, through and through."

"How?" Cahira choked out.

"Are you truly this slow? It was the potions, my *herbal infusions*. They opened your mind and gave me access. The Unity, too."

"You mean Kolos." Cahira grated it out in defiance, half-expecting that speaking its name would draw it up from the depths. But she detected nothing.

"Found your wits again? Yes, the great Kolos, may it be praised. Now I wonder how you discovered that?" Fadra paused, then nodded. "Of course, the book. Planted in your pack at the tavern. Kolos has servants everywhere, even in the heart of Eorna. And naturally you opened it, as we knew you would. That foolish curiosity. I'm only surprised you worked it out so quickly. Perhaps you're not quite as stupid as I thought." She eyed Cahira and then gave a short laugh. "Bear got your tongue?"

Cahira pulled herself together. She had to show this hateful woman she wasn't afraid of her. She paused for a few seconds to gather the threads of Ferdy's song again, having almost lost hold of it in her shock at Fadra's words. When she spoke, she was pleased to find her voice didn't shake.

"No, I got the bear. Remember? And that's the least of what I can do. I could sing up a gale to blow you right off this rock. Give up while you still have the chance."

"Are you talking about what happened down on the docks? Idiot girl, you didn't bring the wind. Oh, you have some talent. Enough to interest me when I heard you at the farm, and to keep your friend unconscious so you'd agree to come to the caves. But no human can control the weather. Kolos did it, not you. But your pathetic shame about it was very useful. Guilt is a good way in, although there are others. Fear, for instance."

Could it be true? For the first time since she'd left the docks, Cahira recalled Mundar's prediction: *the wind is going to switch north soon*. A hard, gusty blow. The weather had done exactly what he'd said it would. Which meant she hadn't been responsible for bringing in the ships. And neither had Kolos, despite what Fadra wanted her to believe. Fresh strength flooded her as the enormous burden she'd been carrying lifted. She still felt foolish for ever trusting the woman to care for Niall. But at least she wouldn't be tricked again.

Fadra was still talking. "Kolos will have you yet, you know. Or destroy you. Because a storm of a different kind is about to descend on your precious island. One none of you will be able to weather."

About to reply hotly, Cahira stopped herself. Why was Fadra wasting all this time on explanations and insults? The woman was stalling, trying to keep Cahira's attention on her. But why bother if she truly believed nothing could stop Kolos? She must know their plans could still be upset. All Cahira had to do was figure out how.

Forget about Fadra. She was just a distraction here. Ferdy was the key, Cahira knew it. And if she couldn't bring herself to harm him, she only had one other choice, didn't she? Skalsinger against Skalsinger, that was the way. She had to neutralise the effect he was creating with a melody of her own. Only not entirely her own, she realised, as the solution bubbled up inside her. Instead of fighting against Ferdy, she would turn his solo into a duet, by resolving every discord into harmony.

To a Singer with her experience, the musical problem was absurdly simple, especially as she knew Ferdy's part as well as he did by now. Holding the counterpoint steady while fighting the debilitating effect of his dirge would be the hard thing, probably the most difficult performance she'd ever given. But she was ready, even eager. She could do this.

Keeping her eyes on Fadra in case she tried anything more than talk, Cahira waited two beats, expanded her lungs and sent out the first note. She did not try to form an image. Matching Ferdy's melody, without succumbing to the despair woven through it, would be enough to deal with.

As the third tone flowed from Cahira's lips, the mask of calm superiority slipped from Fadra's face. Her features twisted in rage. Cahira recoiled from the inky darkness that filled the older woman's eyes, but she steadied herself and kept singing.

Fadra's fingers clamped down on Ferdy's shoulder like talons and hauled him around to face Cahira. A wince of pain crossed his face, and then the volume of his song increased again, setting Cahira's skull pounding. Her thoughts flew to the moment she'd taken control of his skal in the caves. The same thing was happening now, except it was Fadra controlling him. A faint, dark smudge appeared above their heads, the beginning of an image. How was the woman doing this? She was no Skalsinger.

The darkness grew until it resembled a storm cloud. Something shifted and swirled within, as if struggling to come into focus. A brief suggestion of greenish tentacles flickered in the murk, nauseating Cahira, but giving her the clue she needed. Kolos was acting through Fadra, using her as a channel to send power to Ferdy. Too much power for a young boy with an untrained skal to contain. Back at the caves, Cahira had loosened her control just in time to prevent Ferdy's death, but neither Fadra nor Kolos would have any such compunction.

None of this was Ferdy's fault. He was being used, and he'd die here if Cahira didn't do something fast. She stared into his hazel eyes, seeing no darkness there. Kolos hadn't taken possession of him directly. If she could break Fadra's grip on his shoulder, she could save him. Still singing, she lifted the dagger. With an innocent boy's life at stake, this time she wouldn't hesitate.

At the sight of the rising blade, Fadra's free hand dipped into her pocket, as fast as a snake striking, and drew out a knife of her own. She set it to Ferdy's bare throat. "Touch me and he dies right here."

Ferdy sang on, unaware of danger. A drop of blood emerged from one nostril and slowly trickled over his parted lips. His time was running out. Cahira had to reach him.

She broke off her own song and shouted at the top of her voice, "Ferdy, stop! It's too dangerous."

An expression of shock crossed his face, as if he was a sleepwalker abruptly wakened. The maddening dirge fell silent. His bewildered eyes fixed themselves on Cahira. As recognition dawned, rage replaced confusion. He lunged forward, almost slitting his own throat on Fadra's blade. She flicked it away just in time, but lost her grip. The knife skittered across the rock and disappeared over the edge. Alarmed by the blind fury on Ferdy's face, Cahira took a hasty step backwards.

"Dangerous?" he yelled. "What do you care? I *trusted* you and you nearly killed me!"

Cahira gulped. "Ferdy, you're right, and I'm so sorry. But I do care about you. It's Fadra who doesn't."

"Liar! She saved me after you left me to die!"

"No, I tried to—"

"You tried to make me into something I'm not," he flung at her, his voice cracking. "To make me like you. I did everything you told me to. I worked so hard, but it wasn't enough for you!"

This was so close to the truth that it silenced Cahira completely.

"Go away and leave me alone." His tone was soft and bitter. "I'll use my skal however I want."

"Ferdy, please, this isn't the way," she began, but he'd already turned from her and started singing again. She had no choice but to resume her own part in response.

I am too strong for you, Cahira Gelt. The words issued from Fadra's lips, but it was the same voice Cahira had been hearing in her head ever since that first time in the sanctuary.

You will sing my song now.

A new refrain pressed in on her thoughts, one that would heighten the discords rather than resolve them. She struggled to block it out, partition it off, keep her own melody line true, but a single jarring note slipped past her lips, then another. She gasped for breath, felt her arm fall to her side, the dagger dangling from a limp hand. Her head thrummed and sweat poured down her forehead, stinging her eyes.

But she couldn't give up. The lives of Ferdy and the people down below depended on her. She clenched her jaw and fought back, one beat, one note at a time. She was prevailing, but for how long?

FIFTY-FOUR

Niall

"Wait," Logen called out. "Don't sound the retreat yet. Something's happening."

Oren held up a hand to halt the messenger.

Niall followed Logen's pointing finger, wondering what his friend was talking about. Nothing below seemed to have changed. The Bregians were pushing towards the gates. The Algarthans were falling back in disarray. Perhaps sheer desperation was deluding the Chairman into seeing things that weren't there.

But then Niall's attention was caught by a huge man in a blue shirt, rising to his feet at the edge of the road. He must be one of the deserters who'd fled to the cover of the bushes. He'd stopped fleeing now. Swinging a massive broadsword, he waded straight through two Bregians, then another. He was cleaving his way back to the centre of the fighting. And he wasn't alone. Small knots of men were re-engaging the Bregians all across the battle site.

And here came the second wave at last, pouring through the gates. At the sight of them, something halfway between a cheer and a sob rose to Niall's throat. Embarrassed, he turned it into a cough. When he could trust his voice not to betray him, he spoke. "Any idea what just happened?"

Logen grinned at him. "I don't know, and I don't care. We're not done yet, that's all that matters."

With the injection of fresh Algarthan troops, the fighting became fiercer and uglier. After several minutes, Niall raised his eyes from the bloody slaughter. Clouds were gathering. It looked like another storm was coming.

A flash of white flickered against the grey. A long-winged bird, dipping and soaring. It captured and held his gaze. When it flew out of sight, he sought it through the other windows. It skimmed low over the rock platform at the north end of the headland, where the clouds were darkest. A narrow pillar of sunlight shot down, illuminating not only the bird, but also a group of tiny figures standing below. Niall's mouth dropped open.

A second later, he was racing for the stairs.

FIFTY-FIVE

Roldan

Roldan rubbed his thumb absently along the scar on his throat and grunted in satisfaction. He'd been afraid the Algarthans were about to sound the retreat, but they had begun to push back again, and now his troops were earning every piece of ground they took. This was the way battle should be: clean and honourable, with no quarter asked, and none given.

But despite his pleasure at the turn of events, it had created a dilemma for him. Expecting a quick victory when the defence collapsed, he'd followed his forces almost to the gates of the garrison, and now the renewed fighting swirled around him. He had no doubt of his ability to carve his way back to safety, only of his desire to do so.

A decade had passed since he'd personally participated in a battle, but he'd never slackened off his daily training. It had been a matter of self-discipline, and of setting an example for his subordinates. His blood sang at the prospect of putting those skills to use against a real adversary. He longed to lead from the front one more time. To feel that familiar surge of adrenaline, laced with fear, as he measured himself against an opponent who truly wanted to kill him.

But Bregian Overseers didn't engage in personal combat. Their value lay in devising strategy, instilling discipline and motivation. An old man's role. *And I am an old man*, he told himself. No matter that in this moment, he felt younger than he had in years.

A blue-shirted foe fell beneath his blade before he knew he'd made the decision. Blood pumping, he roared in triumph. His people echoed him and redoubled their own efforts. The battle heat was upon him now, not to be denied. He raised the sword again and again. His arm was tireless, his skill undimmed.

Then a man stepped up who refused to die so easily. He was agile and quick, dressed all in black. A worthy opponent, with expertise enough to challenge his own. Their blades clashed, then clashed again. Joy sang through Roldan. His mouth widened in a feral grin. No answering smile on that set face, though.

And something in the eyes as they flicked momentarily towards the top of the headland—desperation? Another sideways glance, and Roldan was sure of it: the man was fighting with all his skill, but not to defend the garrison. His only desire was to free himself long enough to race up there, to the stack of rocks lying beneath the purple mass of storm clouds. The place where the Disciple stood, practising her foul magic.

Roldan dragged his attention back to the fight in time to avoid an expert flick and twist of the black-clad man's sword. He couldn't afford to let his thoughts wander like that, and yet as their blades met again, his gaze shot upwards once more. The clouds were boiling, as if something was struggling to emerge. A yawning pit opened in Roldan's stomach. Wrongness battered at him just as before.

He wrenched his eyes back to the man in front of him, whose face had gone strangely slack. The enemy blinked and shook his head, and the alertness returned to his expression, but in his momentary distraction the tip of his weapon had lowered—only a fraction, but enough. For the first time, there was an opening in his defence, a chance for a killing strike.

Roldan didn't take it.

FIFTY-SIX

Cahira

Ferdy's face was congested. Blood trickled from both nostrils now. He swayed on the spot, his chest heaving. Cahira's own breath was ragged, and her throat was on fire. Kolos whispered in her mind until she felt she'd go mad. Somehow, she held on and kept singing the counterpoint.

And it was working. Down below, her countrymen had rallied and were engaging the Bregians again. But she couldn't keep it up forever. She was making too many mistakes, and in constant danger of losing the thread of her melody.

A cry cut through the insanity around and inside her. One she'd heard before. She turned her face to the boiling sky, to the purple-black cloud with its murky tentacles that were becoming more solid by the second. Tiny by comparison and almost blindingly white, a seabird soared and dived, calling as it flew. The flexible limbs reached for it, but it eluded their grasp. The call came again, high and pure: *aah... aah.*

Cahira's fractured thoughts latched onto that clear note and used it as a focus to weave her counterpoint afresh. The bird kept crying, louder and louder, and she sang with it, feeling hope rise.

But as she looked to the battlefield, she saw the knots of fighting unravelling. The defenders were slowing and faltering once more. Tears sprang to her eyes. Despite all her efforts, it was happening again. Bitterness filled her mouth.

But something was different this time. It wasn't only the Algarthans who were affected, but the Bregians, too. Within minutes, all movement down there had ceased. What could it mean?

FIFTY-SEVEN

Niall

In the midst of the fight, something broke Niall's concentration. His sword tip dropped of its own accord, giving the Bregian his first chance to go on the offensive. But the man stepped away, lowering his own weapon as if it had grown heavy. Niall stared, wondering why he wasn't already dead.

The Bregian raised his other hand and gestured urgently towards the rock shelf where the three figures stood. The message was clear: he wanted Niall to go up there. It made no sense, but the man's motives didn't matter.

His boots tangled themselves together as he turned, almost sending him to the ground. He recovered with an effort and headed for the grassy slope. But whatever had caused him to stumble continued to affect him. With every step, his feet grew heavier, his gait clumsier.

Stopping yet again to regain his balance, he peered upwards. Cahira was still too far away for her face to be anything but a small, vague smudge above the sapphire cloak. He mocked himself for his certainty back at the tower that the tiny figure was her at all. It could be anyone standing up there. She didn't own the only blue cloak in the world. But no matter what he told himself, his heart knew what it knew. It was her. And he had to reach her, even though his legs seemed encased in lead.

He should check to see if he'd been followed. Long seconds passed before he managed to twist his head around. When he did, he felt the hairs rise on the back of his neck. The combatants, Bregians and Algarthans alike, were moving as if they were wading through chest-high water. Some had ceased their efforts altogether and were standing like statues. As for Niall, his entire body was fighting his desire to resume walking, demanding that he stay here and rest instead. Even turning to face the slope took an enormous effort of will.

The familiar, comfortable presence of equine minds, not too far away, intruded on his struggle. He couldn't see them from here, but they were up ahead, at the junction where grass met rock. They were calm and not in any distress, unaffected by whatever was holding him back, and one of them was the black stallion from Virtue Farm, the animal he'd been trying to help when he'd been attacked in the stable.

An idea came to him, born of his first memories of exploring his skal, when he'd been on the road with only Sienna for company. He'd never attempted it with any other horse, but it could be exactly what he needed right now. He focused on the stallion's mind and joined himself with it, sinking deeply into its awareness.

The complexities of humanity fell away, replaced by the rich sensations, simple thoughts, and unambiguous emotions that the animal was experiencing. His muscles loosened. It was working. He took one step, then another. It wasn't easy, but as long as he stayed linked to the stallion, he could do it.

A dozen steps. A dozen more. He stopped counting, kept going. Almost there now. And then, without warning, whatever was restraining him fell away completely. Surprise drove him back into his own mind. Maintaining a light bond with the horse in case he needed it again, he dashed for the rocks.

FIFTY-EIGHT

Cahira

It's the bird, she thought. *It must be.* In some way she didn't understand, the seabird's call, woven into her song, had halted all the fighters.

Before she could decide if this was a good thing, a scream blasted through her mind. It silenced her, scattered her concentration to the winds. She lifted her gaze to Ferdy, afraid of what she might see. But he was still on his feet, staring back at her, with his own song abruptly ended.

A second screech shattered Cahira's thoughts. It was coming from Fadra, but it didn't sound like anything human. The older woman's face was distorted out of all recognition. Her mouth gaped red, and her eyes were black pools. But even as Cahira watched, the darkness drained away, leaving Fadra's natural brown behind.

"No!" The Disciple wailed, her hand sliding from Ferdy's shoulder. She raised her face to the sky. "I have served you." Her voice wavered, broke. "You owe me…"

Her whole body stiffened. And then her head arched towards her heels, her spine curving more and more until it seemed it must break. She lifted shaking hands, gave a single choked cry, and toppled backwards. She came down hard, sprawling full length, with her upper back striking the sharp, seaward edge of the rock. Her long hair hung down over empty air. Cahira stared in shock. Was she dead? No, she was still breathing, but she must be badly hurt.

A low *crunch* broke the silence, followed by the harsh grating of stone against stone. A cry burst from Cahira, and she stretched out an involuntary hand. Fadra wailed once more, a sound devoid of hope. Then the thin layer of rock beneath her gave a sharp *crack* and snapped off, carrying her headfirst over the edge. She disappeared from sight in a shower of chips and flakes.

Cahira shuddered and turned her face away. Ferdy was swaying, with his eyes closed and blood still dripping from his nose. Above and behind, the chaotic sky was shifting from purple to green and back again. Something huge appeared, fading in and out of view. An enormous, blind head, its black mouth gaping like the entrance to a pit.

Ferdy stirred and opened his eyes, revealing inky swirls. Kolos had used Fadra up and discarded her, then turned callously to another vessel. But Ferdy was no Disciple—not yet, anyway—and never would be if Cahira could help it.

"*No!*" she shouted. She grabbed his arm in an iron grip and shook it. "Ferdy, fight it!"

He blinked, and his eyes cleared. "Cahira?"

She pointed upwards. "It's trying to control you, make you sing its song. If you give in, you'll die, like Fadra."

"There's a voice." He lifted a hand to his head. "In here."

She shook him again, hard. "Don't listen! Look at me. Sing with me. We can beat it together."

She held her breath as he stared mutely at her. She couldn't hear Kolos at all—it must be concentrating on Ferdy—but she remembered all too well how powerful, how seductive, its urgings had been.

"Please, Ferdy. I'm so sorry I hurt you, but it will harm so many more people if we let it. All it cares about is power. We can't give it any more."

He shot another glance upwards and his whole body began to shake. "Aal help me."

He looked so young, and as pale as when he'd lain in the cave, still as death. Shame smote Cahira. He was only a child. She should be protecting him, not pressuring him again. She took him gently by the shoulders. "Forget about singing with me. I'll do it. Just don't make a sound, all right?"

"I'm as strong as you." A flash of the old bravado there, and it warmed her, but she couldn't let him take the risk.

"I know you are. It's not about that. But I couldn't stand it if you were hurt again. Can you resist the voice? Can you stay silent?"

He stared at her for a long moment, then bowed his head. When he raised it, his eyes were still that honest hazel. Jaw tight with determination, he nodded. Cahira could have collapsed in relief. But there was no time. It was up to her now.

She planted her feet, tipped up her chin, and began. It wasn't Kolos' song, or the song of the white bird. It was hers: her cry of resistance to the monster and everything it stood for. She composed it from anger and grief, desperation and regret, and blasted it into the heart of the evil swirling above.

She felt the power flowing from her, greater than any she'd ever accessed before. But the mouth only gaped wider and wider, as if welcoming the hatred she fed it. The head swelled and grew. The tentacles lengthened and solidified, stretching out and out. An enormous voice boomed laughter into her brain.

She wasn't weakening it. She was making everything worse. Her song echoed off the rock all around, threatening to deafen her. She tried to pull back, but the mouth was a black whirlpool, sucking the music from her and expelling it at hideous volume. She couldn't break off. Couldn't change the song. Couldn't do anything at all.

FIFTY-NINE

Niall

He had almost reached the rocks where the horses waited when an appalling noise arose. He stopped and pressed his hands against his ears, but it didn't seem to make any difference. And now a whispering scratched at his brain: *Give up. You can't win.*

He gritted his teeth and peered up to the mass of storm clouds over the headland. But they were the wrong shape, and moving strangely. They looked like writhing limbs. And in the midst of them, a black hole yawned, as if eager to swallow the slender blue-cloaked figure beneath.

Niall shuddered violently and tore his eyes away. He couldn't help her from down here. Burrowing deep into the stallion's mind, he filled his thoughts with its immediate physical sensations. It was standing at rest, pleasantly sheltered from the stiff wind, pulling up tough strands of dried grass and thinking of nothing. Its docility surprised him. From the encounter at the farm, he'd assumed this was a fiery, intelligent animal. The stable hand had even called it a 'vicious devil.' But now it was almost comatose. It was barely aware of the noise and completely oblivious to the whisper. While Niall could still hear both, he was less affected than before.

He continued forward, one slow, heavy step at a time, his breath short and his thigh muscles burning. But it was Cahira up there with that hideous vision looming over her, and nothing was going to stop him, no matter how long it took.

He allowed himself another moment of rest as the grass finally gave way to rock. He stood doubled-over, heaving for air, and then straightened up and looked for the horses. There were six of them altogether, hidden off to one side behind a cluster of head-high rocks. This close, it took barely any of his attention to stay in contact with the stallion. It was still calm—unnaturally so, he thought—but its companions were jittery, distressed by the cacophony raging around them. Normally, he would have taken time to reassure them. But he'd need all his energy for the climb ahead.

From this angle, the steep slope hid Cahira from view. The footing looked treacherous, but a cleared path threaded a narrow, looping way through the broken stones. It must have been made by Oren's Guards, heading up to do lookout duty. *Thank you kindly, gentlemen*, he thought, and started out.

He was focusing on his link with the stallion, worrying about Cahira, and trying to ignore the noise. All of which explained why he didn't hear them coming.

A weight slammed into him from behind, smashing him down onto the path, knocking the air out of him. His arms were pinned beneath him so he couldn't reach his sword or knives. He heaved upward with everything he had and felt the burden slide off. He flipped over, bracing himself against the ground with one hand and feeling for a knife with the other. His fingers found the hilt and tugged it out, but he still couldn't get a breath. Spots swam before his eyes, blurring the figure that sprang up before him.

With a mighty effort, Niall sucked in air. His head pounded, but his vision cleared. Two men faced him on the path. In front, a muscular, dark-haired stranger. Behind him, the white-headed traitor, Jak. The brown-haired man flicked his fingers, and the wire-bound knife handle turned in Niall's grip. Small silver globules appeared along the honed edges of the blade. The hilt grew strangely warm, almost hot. Then the drops slid down towards his unprotected flesh, and Niall finally recognised what was happening.

He cried out hoarsely and threw the ruined weapon as far from him as he could. But he was too slow. His hand burned with agony. The molten wire had carved lines of fire into his palm, and the skin that hadn't been torn away with the knife was blackened and blistered.

The dark-haired man—the Metal Shaper, as Niall had realised too late—bent and grabbed his shirt front and hauled him to his feet. Niall struggled to break free as the Shaper drew back a solid-looking fist.

A scream from below froze them both. The link with the stallion worked both ways, and Niall's pain, anger, and desperation had finally got through to the horse. Wrath was blooming like a gout of flame in response. Here was the animal he'd tried to rescue at Virtue Farm. It trumpeted again, and Niall discovered his muscles had been liberated.

He pulled free of the Shaper's loosened grasp, ducked beneath the raised arm, and went straight for Jak. The force of his charge carried the traitor off the path to the shard-littered ground. He banged the white head on the sharp rocks, then leapt up and over the prone form and back to the track.

The scrape of a boot spun him around. That cursed Metal Shaper was almost on him again. He ducked and rolled between the widely spaced legs. The man might be talented, but at least he wasn't fast. By the time he'd twisted, Niall was on his feet, with the second knife in his uninjured hand. He sent it flying, but his haste to act before the Shaper could melt it spoiled his aim. Only the flat of the blade struck, bouncing off the man's chest and falling harmlessly to the ground.

Nothing left now but the sword, and the Shaper's fingers were moving as he advanced. Cursing the man to hell and back, Niall dropped his last weapon. It hit the rock with a dull clang, the metal already slumping. He backed up, trying to stay on the track, but the stallion had stopped screaming, and the other noise intruded on his attention again. It pounded through his head, slowing his reflexes, making it hard to think. And the man was still coming.

One miscalculation. Only a small one, but it sent his foot lurching sideways off the path. Even then, he might have saved himself, but a loose stone cracked under his boot, shifting his weight further onto the wrong leg. A second later, he was flat on his back, sliding feet first down the slope. Out of control, he rode a jagged flood of flints and shards until he was brought to a stop by the pile of slate that had built up against the soles of his boots. He lay still for a moment, wincing at the pains emanating from multiple body parts. At least nothing seemed broken, only bruised and tender. Luck of a sort, he supposed, and if that was the best on offer, he'd take it.

He twisted around, hoping the Shaper had lost his footing too, but fortune hadn't been that generous. The wretched man was standing squarely on the path above him, his sword intact and his gaze fixed on his quarry. He had the advantage of both terrain and weapon, not to mention two usable hands. Barring a miracle, there was no way to get past him. And Niall put no faith in miracles. Luck, yes. Miracles, no.

He pounded his undamaged fist on the ground in frustration. He'd already wasted too much time here. Anything could have happened to Cahira by now. He stared up into the man's eyes, abruptly consumed by hatred.

Another scream pierced through the clamour, and a black mass of muscled fury thundered up the path towards the Metal Shaper like an avenging angel. He turned and flung up his arms, waving the sword wildly. But the horse was already rearing, overshadowing the puny human. Niall hadn't called the stallion, but it had come to his rescue. Maybe it was time to start believing in miracles, after all. For one breathless moment, the powerful forelegs seemed to hang in the air, and then they drove downwards. The hoofs descended like twin hammers on an anvil, and both sword and man crumpled beneath them.

Protecting his injured hand as best he could, Niall crawled carefully up to the path and pushed himself to his feet on shaking legs. He drew a tentative breath, then another. He definitely had a couple of bruised ribs, not to mention the many cuts and scrapes that were going to hurt even more tomorrow, assuming he survived that long. But he could continue.

He hadn't forgotten there'd been six horses down below, with only five riders accounted for so far: Cahira and the other two above, the Metal Shaper, and Jak. He spared a single glance for the latter, saw him stretched out on the ground, unmoving. The Shaper was probably dead, but that still left Niall badly outnumbered, even if he refused to count

Cahira among the hostiles, which he did. He was unarmed, and in no shape to fight off one able-bodied enemy, let alone three.

As if to remind him he had an ally, the stallion stepped up and lowered its noble head. Its mind was calm again, but alert, sharply aware of everything. And yes, intelligent. Maybe even cleverer than his beloved Sienna. The dull-witted beast from down below had vanished. *Drugged*, Niall thought suddenly, knowing he was right. *It was drugged.* Fadra had been riding it, and she'd given it something to force its obedience. And now, aided by the potent emotions coming through the link, it had thrown the sedative off.

Holding a tight rein on his temper lest he reawaken the horse's fury, Niall stroked its neck and assured it he would never let it be compelled again. It snorted and bumped him under the chin, telling him to stop wasting time and get moving. It was right—Cahira needed him. With a last, friendly slap on the glossy shoulder, he started laboriously up the path.

The noise blasted from every side, and a wall of resistance seemed to tower in front of him, but he concentrated on his bond with the animal and pushed forward one slow step at a time. His companion followed, its willing presence easing his heart. Whatever awaited him at the top, he wouldn't be facing it alone.

SIXTY

Cahira

The world tilted beneath her feet. The sky rolled. Or was it she who was moving? She had no anchor, no way to tell. Dizziness assailed her. Her head snapped back, then forward again, wrenching her neck and forcing her teeth together. Her tongue was trapped between them. Sharp pain. The taste of blood. Swirls of ink before her eyes. She'd fought her hardest, used up all of her strength, and it hadn't been enough. Her defiance of Kolos had only added to its power. She was still feeding it, and she couldn't stop.

"Cahira!"

Blindly, she thrust out her hands, desperate for something real to cling to.

"Cahira!"

Warmth, softness. She grasped them, held on tight. The wheeling stopped, but the wrenching continued. A pink blur replaced the swirling ink. It was Ferdy's face, only inches away. His eyes were wide, his mouth moving. His voice seemed to come from a great distance. *"Cahira! Stop singing!"*

What did he think she was trying to do? It wasn't that easy, especially with him shaking her hard enough to jar her brain loose. She was going to be sick. Fingers still tangled in his shirt, she tried to push him away. "No, don't…" Her heart jolted as she realised she'd spoken the plea, not sung it. She had control over her voice again.

He released her shoulders and peered into her eyes. "Are you all right?"

How could she be all right? And yet, gazing back into that blessedly normal, freckled face, for a moment she was. Breathing hard, she nodded and let go of him.

He took a step away and pointed upwards. "Look."

Cahira flinched. She knew only too well what was lurking there, and the power it had over her. She didn't need to see it again. Her eyes flicked instead to the plateau of stone that stretched below. The long expanse was empty, but a dark shape had appeared at the far edge—a head and shoulders. Someone was climbing up from the path. Her breath hitched. Aidan? Or the other one she'd left unconscious near the boulders? But as the whole figure came into view, she saw the horse following, its coat as black as the man's clothing. Understanding swept over her.

Caught between relief and wonder, she breathed again, but she couldn't utter a sound. As if he felt her gaze, Niall lifted his head. He broke into a run, trailed by the animal. She recognised it now—Fadra's magnificent stallion. They'd crossed about a quarter of the distance when Niall stopped dead, turning aside. Perhaps he was talking to the horse. But then he spun on his heel to face the way he'd come.

Her heart stuttered as she saw what had snatched his attention away. A man climbed onto the platform and started across, followed by three more. The first was Aidan, and the second unmistakably Jon. So, she hadn't killed him. Just another of Fadra's lies. She thought the next might be Aidan's earlier companion, but she wasn't sure. The fourth man carried a staff.

The Metal Shaper was weaving a little from side to side, and she could see dark stains, like blood, on his head and tunic, but they weren't slowing him down. The light glinted wickedly off a raised blade as he headed for Niall at a run.

Cahira screamed silently and started forward, but the stallion was already there, positioning its muscled bulk between Niall and the newcomers. As Aidan came within range, it reared and squealed, its massive hooves thrashing the air. Aidan threw himself to one side, slashing wildly at the stallion's legs as he rolled. Cahira gasped, but the horse snorted and tossed its head, uninjured. Niall hadn't even tried to come to the animal's aid. He must be unarmed, maybe wounded. He needed her, but she was still mute.

If she could get her voice working again, it would only take seconds. She could blind the attackers, or terrify them and make them crawl. But anything she sang might affect Niall too, and her whole being rebelled at the thought of harming him.

Aidan was up again. All four were closing in, forming a circle around Niall and the horse. The stallion responded like a mad thing. Neck stretched and teeth bared, it dashed at each of them in turn. As they scrambled back in disarray, Niall darted forward and snatched something off the ground. He straightened and planted his feet. A long piece of wood swept through the air in front of him. It was the staff, dropped in the haste to avoid the stallion's attack.

The aggressors drew away to one side, as if considering their options, and Cahira relaxed slightly. Then Jon's head lifted and swivelled in her direction. He stiffened, and she felt the force of his malice. He nudged Aidan and spoke. Soon, every eye in the group was turned on her.

Pressure pulsed in her mind, an urging to go forward and meet them, join with them. It was what she'd felt at Eder Ford, both an invitation and a threat. The invitation held no appeal, but the threat grew stronger every moment. She didn't need to see the colour of the Mind Wender's eyes to know where he was getting his power. Kolos had been biding its time, but now it had decided to act. She clutched Ferdy's arm, scared he might be tempted too, but he was standing steady as a rock, his boyish face twisted with scorn as he stared at Jon.

Forgotten by his attackers, Niall sprang to the horse's back. He raised the staff in one hand as they plunged forward, and Cahira heard the sickening smack of the wood connecting with Jon's head. He dropped like a stone. The stallion rode one man down without slowing, then wheeled to block Aidan and the other. With Niall swinging and the animal kicking and biting, they forced the two men to the far edge of the platform.

Jon was down, but the pressure on Cahira's mind only increased. The thin veneer of fellowship was stripped away, leaving only the naked threat. It was coming directly from Kolos now. Even though she refused to look up, she felt its presence like a great clammy blanket, suspended a hair's width above her head, ready to stifle and suffocate her. It pressed down, and down, until she could barely breathe for terror. It was taking every speck of her courage and determination just to stand upright for one more second, then another.

You are nothing. A maggot. A worm. Down on your belly in the dirt, where you belong.

She had no attention to spare for Niall. She was fighting for her life and her sanity. Her soul, if she still had such a thing, stained as she was by that foul ink.

"Cahira, listen." It was Ferdy, staring into her face again. For a moment, she thought he'd been taken over, and was telling her to obey the monster. But his eyes were clear.

"Listen," he repeated softly.

Finally, she heard it too. From somewhere high above, the seabird was calling, its voice slicing cleanly through the vile hissing invading her mind. She focused her attention on each cry as if it was the only sound in the world. The pressure eased a little. Perhaps she was imagining it, but she thought the bird wasn't crying *"aah, aah,"* but rather *"aal, aal,"* like the name of the god. The words of the Healer in the garrison came back to her: *Aal, we invoke your protection over this precious soul.*

She was no holy woman, and she didn't know what she believed any more, except that she hated Kolos and everything it stood for. The prayer to Aal had seemed to dispel its influence over her, at least for a while. She had nothing to lose by trying. But her throat was still closed. She pushed harder, to no avail. She sent out a thought instead, putting as much hope into it as she could. *Aal, if you're there, if you care about us at all, give me the strength to keep fighting.*

The bird's call changed from a single note to a rising sequence. A melody sprang into Cahira's mind—wordless, beautiful, gaining in complexity moment by moment. Effortlessly, she grasped the flow of it, how it dipped and soared, ebbed and surged. She was enthralled, enraptured. In all the world, there was nothing but this. Her chest heaved. She felt wetness on her cheeks. She couldn't tell if she was laughing or crying. It didn't matter. It was all the same.

The song was perfect, like an exquisite tapestry, and yet she began to see that there was room for one more thread. She could feel exactly where it needed to go, how it would weave through the rest, and she knew it was hers to sing, hers alone. Her heart leapt, but the gladness was swiftly followed by terror that she might get it wrong, ruin the entire thing.

A vast reassurance flooded through her. She couldn't spoil it, as long as she sang with her whole heart. Because the thread wasn't just a melody. It was her: Cahira Gelt. Not only who she'd been and who she was now, but who she might become. Something inside her released. Her throat unclenched. She drank in a draught of free air and let it flow out in song.

Light flared. A warm, golden glow lit the grey rock all around. For the first time, she dared to glance up. Over the strait, the sun was breaking through the murk, setting the sea sparkling. But directly above, tentacles thrashed within a cloud of indigo and green.

Crawl before me.

The horrible pressure descended again. Stronger than before. Irresistible.

And then there was no need for resistance, because Cahira was snatched away, sent far out over the tossing, sunlit waves. She rode the freshening air on long white wings. Fierce joy thrilled through her as she sang. She banked and turned, her sharp eyes taking in every detail of the scene below the castle.

Freed from the despair of Ferdy's song and the strange paralysis caused by the bird's, the Algarthans had rallied once more, but they were scattered and outnumbered. The fighting was fierce and bloody. Innocent lives were being sacrificed. She had to stop it. And now she could. In answer to her prayer, she'd been given the chance to turn the tide. Up here, her mind was free. Kolos couldn't touch her. She'd sing strength and courage into her people, and dismay into the hearts of the enemy. She knew exactly how to do it.

She broke off her thread of the tapestry, ignoring the small pang of loss that pierced her like a needle, and brought the battle song to mind, the one she'd performed at Virtue Farm. She'd vowed never to sing it again, but now it was just what she needed. She'd rouse the defenders to greater effort and make the enemy quail before them.

Abruptly, she was standing on the headland once more, earthbound, her wings stripped away. She screamed in frustration and fury. But she wouldn't give in. She could still do this. The golden light shone all around, and Kolos seemed to have given up trying to attack her. She felt no downward pressure, heard no hissing voice.

Across the plateau, Niall and the stallion were keeping Aidan and the other man from her so she could do what she needed. She fixed her eyes on the knots of fighting below the garrison, let the coarse, thumping rhythm of the song fill her mind, then began.

Stout-hearted and strong, to battle we go
Full wrathful and righteous, we face down the foe
Their numbers we deem not, their doom is at hand
For greatness, for glory, for lord and for land!

"Daughter." Sadness infused the single word that chimed all around her, as if the golden light itself was speaking.

Cahira stuttered to a stop. That hadn't been Kolos. She knew its voice only too well. Could it be Aal? She was grateful for the god's help, but she couldn't afford any distraction now. She started once more from the beginning:

Stout-hearted and strong—

"Daughter."

Cahira grimaced, annoyed that she'd allowed herself to be sidetracked again. "They're dying down there! Don't you care?"

"More than you can imagine. But this is not the way."

"What other way is there?" she snapped, striving in vain to bring the song back to her mind.

"Only sing."

"I was singing! You stopped me! And Adric could be down there!"

"Is he more important than the others, then?"

The gentle question roused her to fury. "He is to me!"

Silence.

"No," she said finally, grudgingly, "I don't mean that. They're all important." Fear hollowed her stomach. "That's why I have to help them!"

"Yes, they are all important. All precious, unique lives."

"Then tell me how to save them!"

As if in answer, the tapestry song flowed into her mind. Beautiful, perfect, and yet with space for one more thread.

"Trust me. Join your voice again to mine. This is my fight. It always was."

"Your fight? Who are you?"

"I am."

A pause.

"Are you Aal?"

"That is what your people call me."

She wavered. The tapestry melody beckoned, but suddenly the battle song was accessible too, every word and note. She felt nothing like the compulsions that Jon or Kolos had attempted to force on her. She knew, somehow, that whichever piece she sang, she would be allowed to continue. Aal was offering her a free choice, a genuine invitation. It was up to her to accept or reject it.

Time stretched out while she considered. She searched her heart, her mind, her memories. She tested her emotions against what she knew to be true, and her knowledge against her feelings and instincts. Her pulse beat slowly—once, twice. She drew a breath. She chose.

Her soul flew on the wind, wheeled, and swooped over the castle. She and the bird cried, in one voice, to all those locked in battle below. They sang of hope, of peace, of freedom. Of life.

One by one, the combatants raised their heads. Their bodies stilled. They stood listening, with faces upturned and arms fallen to their sides.

SIXTY-ONE

Roldan

With his lifeblood seeping into the soil of a foreign land, Roldan lay on his back and watched white wings soaring through a doom-laden sky. His thoughts travelled to another bird, a different storm.

He was a freshly minted junior officer, proud to be assigned his first tour on a real sea-faring ship. He'd acquitted himself well, helping to capture a crew of smugglers who'd been a thorn in the side of legitimate traders for some time, and was looking forward to dry land and an approving visit from his parents, when the massive storm-wind hit.

The first ferocious gust snapped the mast and brought the heavy sail crashing down in a mess of ropes and spars. Something struck Roldan on the forehead and knocked him backwards to the deck, where he lay dazed and winded, unable to rise. The ship tossed beneath him, all headway lost. Waves washed over the sides and flooded across the boards.

As he stared upwards, drenched and breathless, expecting only death, white wings caught his eye, stark against the charcoal clouds. The sea pounded, the wind roared, and yet the seabird glided, serene and free, seemingly untouched by the storm. Roldan's heart beat faster, as if it yearned to be up there, too, flying high above the little world of men and ships. *Even dying might not be so bad*, he thought, *if I could believe in something like that on the other side.*

But death hadn't claimed that young sailor. Against the odds, the ship had weathered the storm and come safely to port, and Roldan's injuries had been tended. In the busy years that followed, he had almost forgotten about the bird and the comfort it brought him as he lay on that wave-tossed deck.

This couldn't be the same creature. The very idea was absurd. And yet, his heart told him that it was. It called just as before, enticing him upwards, and something deep within him responded with a thrill, began to rise. An instant later, the leaden weight of pain dragged him back into the broken shell that was his body.

Three of his soldiers had seen him spare the life of the man in black. They had rushed towards him, and Roldan had recognised his own imminent death in their eyes. But just as they reached him, their bodies slowed to a stop. Roldan's limbs were frozen, too, only his mind still active and wondering. As soon as the strange compulsion passed, they surrounded him, shouting ugly names: *traitor, turncoat, vermin.* The words cut deeper than the blades they thrust into his flesh. And yet, he couldn't find it in himself to blame them. From their point of view, he was exactly what they called him. He refused to turn his own sword against them, but stood and accepted every blow as his due, until he could no longer remain on his feet. He fell then, expecting nothing but a quick death.

But his soldiers had scorned to grant him a merciful end. After wounding him fatally, they'd abandoned him. And so, he still breathed, even if only for a little while more. The battle seemed to have moved away, too, the clamour retreating from his awareness.

Only one sound, one voice, reached his ears. The seabird called over and over, its wordless cries speaking to his heart. In his dying delirium, he believed he understood what it was saying. It sang of a higher purpose than soldiering, a greater joy than victory for his nation, and a future that lay waiting beyond his imagining. He was filled with a strange hope, even though he knew there was no future of any kind for him.

He wished he could see Bidi one last time. If only he could explain it to her, she would understand. She would never blame him for the choice he'd made: light over darkness, a clean death over a life mired in dishonour and evil. Disciple Hellin's evil, being conjured up there on the rocks. It was the reason he'd let the man in black go, in the sudden, illogical hope he might stop it.

But if that had been the man's intention, he had failed. For a nightmare was breaking free of the cloud above the headland: a many-tentacled horror with a bottomless pit for a mouth. In allying with this thing, the homeland that Roldan loved had taken a wrong turn, a crooked path. He was glad he'd not be alive to see how it ended.

It was getting harder to breathe. Blood must be filling his lungs. Not long now. He turned his gaze from the monster and found the bird again. It circled lower and swooped over him, its beak open, still calling even though he could no longer hear it. He closed his eyes and imagined himself up there with it, soaring free above all the mess of this flawed and broken world.

SIXTY-TWO

Cahira

An immense grief flooded over her, even as she sang of joy and peace. Her own deep longing for Bram and everything she'd lost was part of it, but only a tiny part. This sadness, this yearning, was enormous. It encompassed not only the embattled forces from the garrison, but all the fallen dead and dying, and every human being still engaged in the fighting, Algarthan and Bregian alike. Pain and love, mourning and hope, wove together until Cahira thought she could hardly bear to feel anything more. She wept as she flew.

And in that moment it came, boiling across the brightening sky, dragging darkness and despair in its wake. Wrapped in Aal's song, Cahira knew she was beyond harm, but the livid hideousness that was Kolos descended low over the battlefield, and men cried out in terror from beneath its weight.

"Now is the time. Sing, daughter!"

She understood the god's meaning instantly. This was the moment to bring her whole skal to bear. She braided multiple voices and harmonies, more than ever before, and sensed her thread growing thicker, stronger. An image of it appeared in her mind, as sharp and clear as if she were seeing it with her physical eyes. Surprise and delight filled her, followed by a deep sense of rightness. *Of course*, she thought. *What other colour could it possibly be?* She gazed at the vibrant sapphire blue and felt laughter bubble up.

This new inner vision expanded rapidly to encompass much more than her own thread. Soon, the entire tapestry stretched before her. It was immense—bigger than the world—and yet she could see it all. To her amazement, people and objects were moving within it, riding strands of every hue and texture.

Over there, a familiar dark-skinned man stood on the deck of a ship running before the wind. A ribbon of translucent emerald, like the sea on a summer day, flowed beneath the hull. But Captain Mundar had told her he'd left the life of a sailor behind. Perhaps it was his past she was seeing.

A different thread caught her attention: a knobbly brown string, full of knots. It looped over and over, snarling and doubling back on itself, before wrapping tightly around a scowling, bearded man, gesticulating in front of a faceless crowd—Berek, the Seeker of Virtue. For the first time, Cahira felt pity for him, wished he could be as free and unentangled as she was.

A brightly painted box on wheels moved steadily along a strong-looking, golden fillet. On another of the same colour nearby, a small figure in a battered hat was riding a mule, leading a fine-boned black horse behind him.

A double-braided cord—red twined with charcoal—ran straight and true for a long way, then split into two forks. A man, wearing a dark grey uniform splattered with patches of blood, lay across the exact place the thread divided: charcoal in one direction, scarlet in the other.

A thin length of some fragile, almost colourless fibre, as cramped and bunched-up as Berek's muddy string, suddenly flashed to gleaming silver. It unravelled and stretched out, growing broad and straight. Running along it, her brown skirts lifted and her bare feet almost skipping, was Perna. Cahira gazed in wonder and bewilderment. What did it mean?

Further away, a shining copper filament caught the light, its path rising and falling like waves on the ocean. Squinting, she could just make out a figure, too small to reveal any details. A brief glint of the same warm, metallic colour winked out from it as it strode forward.

So many threads. Hundreds, thousands. Impossible to follow them all. They jumbled in her head, filling it with colour and movement.

But in the very centre of the tapestry there was a space, clear of threads but not empty. A human figure stood there—male or female, she couldn't tell. A golden glow emanated from it, shining brighter and brighter, until she had to look away or be blinded.

Her eyes opened again to the world outside, where the same light was gilding sky, water, and land. It touched Kolos, and for a moment Cahira thought the monster might flinch from it. But the huge black maw only gaped wider and wider. Its intention was clear. It wanted to suck in all the surrounding brightness, to gorge itself on it, the way it had fed on Cahira's song.

As if in response to Kolos' desire, some of the light coalesced, forming a kind of whirlpool above the enormous head. A single gleaming thread separated from the whole, and was drawn towards the hungry mouth. The lower end descended into blackness, and the whirlpool, to which it was attached, spun faster, drawing in more radiance from around it.

The sky dimmed. The maelstrom grew. Soon, a broad stream of gold was swirling into the waiting gullet. The bloated monster swelled to fill Cahira's vision. She could no longer tell if she was on the land or in the sky, couldn't feel the air, see the tapestry, or hear Aal's voice. If the bird called, she was deaf to its song. She didn't know if she herself was singing, or if she'd fallen silent. She saw only Kolos, felt only the horror of its presence, and knew that she'd failed. Even joining with Aal hadn't been enough.

As the very last of the light slipped down inside the monster, it roared in triumph. Its inky tentacles stretched across the charcoal sky from horizon to horizon, every trace of green expunged. Beneath, the world was fuzzy and dim, as if shrouded in dirty fog.

Black, Cahira thought numbly. *Indigo. Grey.* No colours existed but these. And the only sound in the universe was that unbearable roaring. Light and music were gone, extinguished forever. Beauty and joy were less than a memory, barely a fading dream. Horror, fear, and regret were all that remained. All that would ever be.

Long ages passed.

A single bright dot, unimaginably small, appeared on the surface of one immense tentacle. Cahira stared. Her bruised mind was playing tricks on her. How could any light exist here?

But now a second point flared into life, and then a third. A thin scatter of them sprayed itself across the head. A glowing rash erupted along a different tentacle. And as they multiplied, they grew in size and brilliance. Soon, entire constellations were shining out of the darkness. And they were not golden, like the light that Kolos had swallowed, but blinding white.

The monster broke off its roaring. In the sudden quiet, Cahira found she was still singing after all. Music was pouring from her throat, familiar and beautiful. It was the song of the bird, the radiance, the tapestry. The song of her life. The song of Aal.

Kolos moaned and writhed, its pierced limbs bleeding fine white trails, like lines of chalk, across the grey sky. Suddenly, it screamed, high and terrible. Its mouth convulsed and vomited a gout of light onto the sea below. The tentacles jerked, curling and straightening repeatedly like the legs of a spider in its death throes. It screeched again. Flailing wildly now, it pulled the tentacles in and whipped them around its head, where they coiled up and squeezed together. The top of the head bulged above them as they tightened. Kolos was trying to crush out the sparks and hold onto all the shining power it had consumed.

But the brightness would not be contained. It burned its way through a hundred glowing pores, then a thousand, then a million. Fine rays shot in every direction, broadening out as the unbearable light corroded the monster's blackening flesh. Great swathes of colour, like paint flooding from the brush of a gigantic artist, swept across sky and land.

As the radiance abandoned it, Kolos' screaming grew thin and weak. The bulging head, its surface now a dull ebony, wrinkled and collapsed. It slowly sank in on itself, disappearing inside the coiled tentacles. But they were transforming, too. Before Cahira's wondering eyes, they shrank and faded, withering and curling like dry leaves. One grey wisp detached itself and dropped away, dissolving to nothing as it fell. The others followed until only a shapeless husk—all that was left of the head—remained.

The last dark remnant of Kolos hovered in place for a moment, its edges fraying like an unravelling garment. Then it fled inland.

As it went, the wind shredded it further. It passed over the castle as a few tattered scraps of black and a low moaning on the breeze. By the time it reached the sky above the city, all Cahira could discern was a slight darkening in the air, sinking downwards, and a faint wailing that trailed away to a whisper. And then every trace of it was gone.

She stood on the headland in blazing sunlight beneath an azure sky, quietly singing. Her eyes travelled over the garrison to the fighters. Those still on their feet were motionless, with heads bowed. They began to stir, and for a moment Cahira was afraid they would take up the battle again. But they only bent to lay their weapons on the ground, then turned and walked away, some to the castle and others down to the docks, where they streamed onto the Bregian ships.

The wind shifted, pressing against Cahira's back. Sails rode up the masts, flapping in the stiff offshore breeze. One by one, the vessels slipped their moorings and glided through the sun-spangled water, out of the harbour and north across the strait.

Cahira sang one last note, pure and true, then drew a deep breath and closed her lips gently. She must have been singing for many hours, and yet her throat wasn't the least sore. She didn't even feel tired. She was alone in her mind again, and the only sounds were the waves breaking on the rocks far below and the wind rushing through the grass of the headland.

Above her, white wings soared. They swooped low over Ferdy, whose glowing face was upturned. They glided over Niall and the stallion, standing close together with the horse's head on the man's shoulder, their enemies nowhere in sight. The bird flew on, circling the garrison once before continuing south. Cahira watched until it was nothing but a distant speck in the vast blueness of the sky, then turned to her young companion, who was grinning at her.

Feeling a rush of affection, she ruffled his springy hair. Then she huffed out a breath that was almost a laugh, felt a sudden, bone-numbing exhaustion flood over her, and sank down onto the sun-warmed rock to wait for Niall.

SIXTY-THREE

Roldan

My son, it is not your time.
The words rolled through Roldan's mind, as golden light bloomed around him. His pain vanished, replaced by an all-encompassing warmth.

There is more for you to do.

The voice was intimate, familiar, yet he couldn't place it. *My son*, it had called him. Was it the spirit of his father? His mother? Perhaps it was nothing but the random thoughts of a dying brain. A moment ago, he had been content to die—more than content—but now he wished to know, to understand.

"Who are you?"

Something descended onto Roldan's broken body like a heavy, smothering blanket, blotting out the light. Pain flooded back, even stronger than before. His voice rang out briefly, mingling with the terrified cries of others. Then he had no more breath to spare. He lay in utter blackness, slowly suffocating as the enormous weight pressed down and down. Soon it must crush the life from him. Then he would be taken from here and put in the cold, dank earth. Worms and blind, nameless things would strip his flesh away, until nothing remained of him but bones and rags. That was the truth of it. That had always been the truth of it. Darkness was more powerful than light, and death stronger than life.

It is not so. It shall not be so. Look up, my son.

Roldan's eyes strained to pierce the shadow over him. High above, a tiny spark kindled. The pain was intense, and he could barely breathe, but he fixed his sight on the small, bright point. He wouldn't give up hope, not while that single light lived.

Who are you? he asked the voice again.

I am.

It wasn't an answer, but it brought him a strange kind of peace.

He must have lost consciousness then. The next time he opened his eyes, he was gazing up into a cloudless blue sky. A great silence lay all around. He propped himself on one elbow, grunting and wheezing, and twisted his head this way and that. He was alone, except for the fallen dead that shared the ground.

He sat up higher, craning his neck. The downhill road was also deserted. His eyes roamed over the docks below and stopped. He stared at the empty water where his ships should have been moored. He could think of only one explanation for everything he was seeing. His people had abandoned the assault on the garrison and sailed back to Bregia without him. Something decisive had occurred while he'd been unconscious, but he couldn't imagine what it might be.

With nowhere to go, he stayed where he was, panting shallowly against the pain and tightness in his chest, wondering what would happen next.

Not long afterwards, a figure in a long cream robe came into view: a woman with steely hair cropped like a man's. She knelt beside him and pressed firm hands to his heart. "Lie back while I ease your breathing."

He let her push him down.

"There is much damage, although the worst has already been dealt with." Grey eyes held his gaze. "Even so, this will not be a simple Healing for me, or an easy recovery for you."

She was Algarthan—she must be—and from his uniform she already knew he was Bregian, and a soldier besides.

"Why help me?" he rasped.

"I was sent," she said briskly. "Please stop talking. I need to concentrate."

After a while, the discomfort and pressure in his chest eased a little. He took an incautiously deeper breath, and winced as fresh pain stabbed at him.

"There," she sat back on her heels. "You'll do for now. I'll find someone to carry you into the garrison." Back on her feet, she fixed him with a stern eye. "Don't try to move. If you start that bleeding again while I'm gone, I won't be responsible."

It seemed that the voice, the one who had called him *son*, had spoken the truth; Roldan would survive these injuries. But his salvation had come at a heavy cost. His countrymen had disowned him and left him to die, and there would be no going back. He was a prisoner, at the mercy of the very people he had tried to conquer.

Somehow, that knowledge didn't feel nearly as disturbing as he thought it should.

SIXTY-FOUR

Perna

The sun streamed into the room, stirring Perna awake. She lay still for a few moments, savouring the memory of her conversation with Adric last night, then sat up to look for him.

He was stretched out on the floor a few lengths from her, breathing deeply and steadily. She allowed herself the luxury of drinking in the sight of him to her heart's content, before slipping from her blankets. She felt stiff and tired, but surprisingly cheerful. And hungry.

She wove her way between the other patients, briefly checking each one as she went. Some were asleep, like Adric. Others responded softly to her greeting. None of them seemed to be in immediate danger.

The kitchen was empty, but there was some thick porridge in the bottom of the pot, the heavy iron retaining enough heat to keep it warm. They'd run out of milk days ago, but she found honey and some dried raisins. She served herself a big bowl and sat at the table.

As she stirred in the sweetener and the fruit, she reflected on all the meals she'd been denying herself over the past months. She'd been so stupid. Why had she thought that starving herself, weakening her body, would be pleasing to Aal? The god had given her the gift of Healing. If she made herself sick, how could she help others? She spooned up the porridge and felt her energy level rise. Whatever happened today, she'd be ready for it.

She spent the next hour bathing wounds, changing dressings, and checking on Adric to see if he'd woken up. When he finally did, they went out into the sunshine and sat on the top step of the dilapidated porch, surveying the blessedly empty street and talking quietly. The fighting seemed to have ceased, or at least moved away from the area around the House.

After he'd finished his own portion of porridge, his slight grimace at the taste bringing a smile to Perna's lips, Adric sprang up. He wanted to explore further and find out what was happening.

Perna bit back the impulse to tell him to be careful. She wasn't his mother or his wife. She wasn't sure what she was, not yet. A friend, at least. And she knew that prioritising his own safety wasn't part of Adric's nature. Remembering her reckless exploit at the waterfront in Welsea, she considered that perhaps this was something they had in common. It was a brand-new thought, and it pleased her enormously.

She sat alone for a while, enjoying the sunshine and the silence, until Tabia came out and joined her, lowering herself with a grunt of discomfort.

Perna hesitated, unsure if the Elder wanted to talk about her disability. But the wrinkles around Tabia's eyes had tightened in pain, so she plunged in. "Is your leg bothering you?"

"It's giving me a bit of trouble."

"Can't it be fixed?"

Tabia shook her head. "I broke it falling down the stairs when I was six years old. No Healer in my family, no money to pay for one." She shrugged. "It mended crooked. Nothing to be done about it."

Perna was all Healer now. "Is it always this painful?"

Tabia wrinkled her nose. "Only when I'm awake."

Perna reached out a hand instinctively, then stopped. "May I?"

Tabia nodded. A few more coils of hair came loose from the pins and fell onto her forehead. She pushed them back with impatient fingers. "Go ahead. If you can do anything, I'd be grateful."

Perna gently touched the red, swollen place just below the knee. The pain struck her, hot and sharp, and she marvelled that Tabia had been enduring this, day after day, without complaint. Healers couldn't use their skal on themselves, but the Elder had been living in a community of them. They might not be able to straighten the leg, but they could have drawn off the discomfort. Why hadn't she called on them?

"Wasn't always as bad as this," Tabia said, doing that trick she had of knowing what Perna was thinking. "Been getting worse the past few weeks."

And you didn't want to ask for relief because that could have meant another patient suffering, maybe dying, Perna thought. *We've all been stretched to our limits trying to keep the wounded alive.* But right now, she had time and energy to spare. She concentrated, siphoning off the pain, relaxing the tendons and muscles, quietening the nerves.

Tabia gave a deep sigh and touched her hand. "Thank you."

A question had been gently nagging at Perna ever since the Elder had arrived. It was embarrassing after their last conversation, but it felt important. She swallowed her pride. "How is the girl, the thief?"

"Not so well. She's Healed, far as I can tell, but she won't get up, or eat anything. Did you notice her throat?"

Perna shook her head. It had been her own neck she'd been thinking about.

"It was covered in bruises. Someone half strangled that child, and probably not for the first time. Her voice is permanently affected."

Horror and remorse flooded Perna. She'd assumed the hoarse tones were due to some minor illness. She'd assumed so many things.

"Can I see her?"

Tabia's eyes searched her face for a moment, then she nodded. "She seems scared stiff of everyone, so I put her on her own. Second floor, the first room on the left. Perna?"

Already on her feet, Perna paused. "Yes?"

"Her name is Lila."

A few minutes later, Perna stood in the open doorway. The blanket-wrapped figure in the bed looked so small, almost like a child. She hadn't remembered the thief—Lila—being this tiny.

But the face that turned towards her in alarm was the same one, the skin pale between the patches of grime. And the terrified eyes were the same too, staring out from under the shock of dirty blond hair. The girl shrank against the wall, trying to get as far away as she could. She was helpless, and afraid of what Perna might do to her.

Deep shame heated Perna's cheeks. She'd been arrogant and cruel. Who was she to decide if someone deserved her help? She'd given all her energy to those wounded soldiers yesterday, without considering what sort of people they were. How did she know they hadn't done worse things in their lives than this poor child? And what about Perna herself? She'd condemned Lila for giving her a minor cut, when she'd killed a man by slitting his throat.

The girl was still staring at her with wide, frightened eyes. Where Perna had imagined evil, all she saw now was a desperate need for reassurance.

"No one's going to hurt you here, I promise," she said softly. Careful not to make any sudden moves, she lowered herself onto the chair beside the bed and folded her hands in her lap. She struggled to find the right words. "I'm sorry I haven't visited you before, Lila. How are you feeling?"

The scared look was replaced by a frown, as if the girl was confused by Perna's gentleness. She didn't reply.

"Is your head still hurting?"

"What do you want from me?" The croak burst out with a bravado that drew Perna's admiration. Despite all that had happened to her, Lila's spirit hadn't been broken, just bruised a little.

"Nothing. Just to help."

Lila glared balefully at her for a moment, before rolling over to face the wall.

Well, Perna thought wryly, *at least she's not scared of me anymore.* Lila clearly didn't want her here, but leaving didn't feel right, either. Not knowing what else to do, she stayed where she was and prayed a silent blessing over the figure huddled in the bed.

She'd watched Elder Meril say the same words over a sick child, and then spent a long time secretly memorising them, practising to get the Elder's intonation exactly right. She'd used them once herself in the presence of another Aaldan, feeling proud of how well she'd learned.

But until now, she'd never truly *prayed* them, never understood what it meant to bless someone. This wasn't about the words, or any kind of performance. It was all about Lila, and asking Aal to help her. Again, Perna felt that warm, reassuring touch on her shoulder, and this time, she understood it. The god had heard her.

Something brought her out of her prayers. She sniffed. Smoke. Her first thought was for the chimney. The logs in the fireplace were burning with a bright, clear flame, but the acrid stink was definitely growing stronger. The window was closed. It must be coming from the hallway.

As soon as she pulled open the door, a grey choking cloud enveloped her. Coughing and gasping, she slammed it shut again, ran to the bed and grasped the blanket-covered shoulder. "We've got to go!"

The girl reared up and twisted to face her, small fists raised to defend herself.

Perna retreated a step. "The house is on fire!"

Lila just stared at her.

"Come *on!*" Perna grabbed one thin wrist and tugged. Lila resisted for a moment, but then she must have smelled the smoke, because she sprang to her feet. Shrugging off Perna's grip, she headed for the door.

"No! The fire's out there!" Perna looked around wildly. "The window!"

The girl put a hand to the door, held it there for a few seconds, and then snatched it away. Shaking it, she came back.

The window was closed with a simple arrangement, an iron ring in the sill that captured a hook attached to the bottom of the wooden frame. Perna unlatched it and swung it open. The street below was empty, except for the ginger-haired man from yesterday. He was standing on the other side of the road, above the gutter where his son had died.

Perna waved her arms. "Get water, the house is on fire!"

He stared up at her for a few seconds, then his mouth twisted into a smile. Putting his hands into his pockets, he strolled away.

Perna shouted for help as loudly as she could, but when no one else appeared, she turned back to the room. The smell was stronger, and her eyes smarted. Wisps of smoke were coiling through the cracks around the door.

It was a long way down to the street, and a hard landing at the bottom, but they had no choice. She addressed the girl standing by the bed. "We have to jump."

Ignoring her, Lila snatched up the blanket and sheet and began knotting two corners together. Perna was impressed with her quick thinking. The makeshift rope wouldn't reach the ground, but it might be the difference between risking death and just getting a few bruises.

The first tendrils of smoke had almost reached them now. Tears streamed down Perna's cheeks as she coughed. Lila's face had turned red; she must be holding her breath. Heaving her handiwork onto the window sill, she tied one end to the ring, throwing a belligerent glance at Perna, who hastily moved aside. Lila climbed into the opening, took hold of the blanket, and started lowering herself.

Eyes squeezed to slits, Perna stuck her head out to reach fresher air. She sucked it in between fits of coughing, waiting for Lila to get far enough down for her to begin the descent. The smoke reached the window. Suddenly, there was no more clean air to be had. And Lila seemed to be crawling. Her head was barely below the sill. Perna tried holding her breath, but a cough forced it out again. Against her will, her body drew in another smoky lungful. Gagging, she peered down desperately. Thank Aal, Lila was onto the sheet. Perna clambered up and grasped the ring.

It tilted under her hand. She squinted at it in alarm. It was joined to an iron spike that had been driven deep into the sill, and part of this was now sticking out at an angle. The surrounding wood was freshly splintered. Even as Perna watched, the rusted metal slid out another notch. Lila's weight was pulling out the ring. When it tore completely free, she would fall. She was so physically frail, the landing could kill her.

No, Perna thought savagely, *not this one*. Not if I can help it. She grabbed the bulky blanket in both hands. Still fighting the urge to breathe in more smoke, she lowered herself to the floor. She placed the sole of one sturdy shoe against the wall and the other beside it. Bracing her legs and pushing hard into her heels, she took up the strain and leaned back as far as she could. Fortunately, she weighed more than Lila.

Her arms were being pulled from their sockets, but she was rewarded by the blurry sight of the spike slowly straightening up. Please Aal, she could keep holding on until Lila reached the end of the rope.

Her lungs were bursting. Her heart was pounding like a funeral drum. Her shoulders were burning. Her eyes were blind. Her head swam. She was going to die here. If only she could be sure of saving Lila, it would be worth it.

But she felt sad she'd never see Adric again.

A crash, followed by a thundering across the floor. She was grabbed around the waist and lifted off her feet.

"*No!*" she croaked, trying to squirm free without letting go of the precious lifeline. "*She'll fall!*"

She broke into another fit of coughing, gasped in air, and found it breathable.

"She's safe," Adric's voice said in her ear.

Could she believe him?

"I can see her." He sounded hoarse, too. "You saved her. And the fire's almost out."

Something in his tone convinced her. She stopped struggling and unclenched her hands from the limp blanket. She drew in another painful breath, feeling unutterably thankful, and let him carry her away.

SIXTY-FIVE

Cahira

One month later

The first sign that Virtue Farm had changed for the better were the unguarded gates, standing wide in invitation. The name board was gone, too. Cahira leaned forward and gave Blackbird an affectionate pat on the neck as they passed between the posts. After the ambush by Dostig and his men, she'd thought the mare lost to her forever. But on her return home her father had taken her arm, saying he had something to show her. The sight of the beautiful black horse, grazing placidly with the stud herd, had rendered Cahira speechless.

Da had smiled at the success of his surprise. "Horses are wiser than people give them credit for, pet. They'll find their path to the right place from many reaches away, even if it takes weeks to get there."

But Cahira had remembered the old man in Aal's tapestry, riding a mule and leading a fine-looking black mare. Perhaps Blackbird hadn't come home on her own, despite what Da believed. Either way, Cahira was grateful to have her back.

Niall followed her through the farm gateway, mounted on the stallion that had saved his life. The two of them seemed to have claimed each other, much to Sienna's disgust. When they'd left the stable this morning, the mare had wrinkled her top lip, like a lady smelling something unpleasant, and then given the stallion a spiteful nip, which it had loftily ignored. She would come around eventually, Cahira thought. No equine could resist Niall's charm forever, and they'd been together for a long time. Love couldn't be so easily set aside, even when things changed.

They dismounted outside the main house where Bett and Mara were waiting. Mara coolly held out her hand as she bade Niall welcome, but Bett flung herself on Cahira and hugged her tightly. They'd been invited to stay the night, and Cahira hoped to spend more time with Bett while she was here.

Looking around, she spotted a small grey horse in the adjacent field. She gaped as Dove trotted over to the fence. "Where did you come from?"

"She turned up a few days ago," Bett said. "Do you know her?"

Cahira still felt dazed. "She was lent to me, but her owner…" She swallowed. "Her former owner's gone now."

"Some of the children have been riding her," Mara said. "She's very gentle with them. But if she's yours, please take her."

Cahira gazed into the little mare's liquid eyes and shook her head. "No, somehow I think she found her path to the right place." Dove nickered as if in agreement.

As they approached the dining hall, the sound of lively chatter reached them. Another improvement over her last visit. The room was crowded with women and children, but Mara led them to a long table where Adric and Mundar were seated, with Perna between them.

The meal of soup and bread was substantial and delicious, and went on for some time. Cahira enjoyed the food and the warm atmosphere of festivity, but the noise made it difficult to hold a conversation with anyone but Bett and Niall, her immediate neighbours. When the room finally emptied, Mara fetched more ale and another pot of tea. Bett handed cheese and little honey cakes around, and the seven of them settled down to catch up on each other's news.

Mundar told them that Berek and Ruston had both been confirmed dead, killed in Eorna, along with most of the men who'd followed them. Some survivors had been captured early and were being held in the garrison awaiting trial, but no one knew how many had simply disappeared into the general population of the city or fled into the countryside.

What was certain was that none had returned here, and Mara, who had somehow become mistress of the community, was resolved to evict any who tried it. Adric offered to send a few Guards to assist her.

Mara shook her head. "Thank you, but we can defend our home without help. We have all faced harder challenges than that."

Seeing her determined expression, Cahira believed her.

A handful of men had remained on the farm, but they were all elderly and frail, like Berek's Uncle Petir. "They were never Seekers," Mara said. "Younger family members brought them here, and they have nowhere else to go. Besides, it's good for the children, especially the boys, to be around men who are different to Berek and his followers."

She sounded comfortable in her new role, but Cahira didn't understand how the change of leadership had happened so quickly and smoothly. Surely someone must have objected to Mara—a woman who had been a cook only a few weeks ago—seizing control like this? Waiting until Mara was deep in conversation with Mundar further along the table, she turned to Bett, keeping her voice low. "Who owns this place now that Berek's gone? And how do they feel about Mara taking charge?"

"That's the best bit," Bett whispered back. "Would you believe, that rat Berek never owned the farm at all?" She paused, then nodded at Cahira's surprised expression. "Guess who it belongs to." A mischievous smile played around her lips.

Cahira raised her eyebrows. "Who?"

"*Uncle Petir!*"

Bett nodded again, satisfied at the effect of her words, and rushed back into speech. "It's true! When he got too weak to work the farm, he sent word to Berek, askin' him to help out, like. An' then Berek brings his followers here and takes over the whole place."

She stopped to draw breath, then went on just as fast. "It all came out when Mara told him his nephew was dead. Petir's a sweet old man, an' he had no idea what was happenin' here. Now he knows what Berek was up to, he's as angry as a turkey cock. He's got the papers to show he's the owner, an' he's put Mara in charge. *An'* he made a will leavin' everythin' to her when he dies."

Still processing this startling news, Cahira stared up at the head of the table, where Mara was sitting with her back straight and her chin lifted. Her long hair was braided on both sides. The shiny pink burn scars, out in the open for all to see, suddenly seemed more a badge of honour than a disfigurement.

As if sensing the interest in her, Mara broke off her conversation with Mundar and smiled at Cahira. She raised her voice. "So, how do you like Abundance Farm?"

"Is that what you're calling it now?"

"Not me. It's the name on the title deed. *Virtue Farm* was Berek's idea, about as sensible as most of his others. Abundance Farm is better, don't you think?"

Cahira agreed. "So, will you all stay here and work the land yourselves?"

"Most of us, at least the single women and the widows. Some of the wives have already gone searching for their husbands, mainly the ones who went along with Berek's nonsense themselves. Good riddance to them. But the rest are just relieved it's all over, even if they're grieving. It will be a long road for them, but we'll give them purpose and support them, and they'll come through."

"Our House is going to help," Perna said. Like Mara, something had changed in her. The pinched, sour look was gone from her mouth, and her eyes sparkled. "Berek was wrong about a lot, but he got one thing right. There are so many women in need in the city, women with nowhere to go. We see them all the time in Dyers Lane, with bruises, broken bones, and worse, or practically starving. And now we can offer them a real home when they've been Healed, if they want it." A smile animated her whole face, reminding Cahira of the vision of her skipping along the gleaming silver thread. It had made no sense back then, but she could imagine this new Perna doing exactly that.

"One of them, Lila, is here already, working in the stables," Perna continued. "She loves it. She told me she hopes to be a Beast Speaker or Beast Healer when her skal comes in. Isn't that wonderful?"

"Thanks to you," Adric said gruffly. "She'd be dead if you hadn't risked your life to save her." The strange mix of admiration and pride in his expression as he gazed down on Perna turned Cahira's thoughts in a new and astonishing direction. Adric was smitten, and with a novice Aaldan, of all people.

Perna lifted her eyes to meet his. "And I'd be dead if you hadn't risked yours to save me." The soft, intimate tone made her own feelings clear.

It seemed like a very strange match, but people were full of surprises, no matter how well you thought you knew them. Cahira suspected this particular couple might have an interesting road ahead, to say the least.

"Does this mean you're staying in Eorna, Mistress Perna?" Niall asked cheerfully.

"Oh yes, I couldn't leave Dyers Lane now. I'm still learning so much, and not just about Healing."

"And you, Adric? What are your plans?" Niall's bland expression was innocence itself.

The tips of Adric's ears went red. "I'm staying on in Eorna too. Um, in the garrison." He seemed at a loss for any more words.

Niall, of course, was never at a loss when it came to amusing himself. "Let me see, that's not too far from Dyers Lane, is it?" Despite being only three years older than Adric, he beamed across the table like a fond uncle. "What a lucky coincidence! Why, I'm sure you haven't even thought about it, but you could visit Perna sometimes on your day off, give the poor girl a bit of a break from all that work and learning. There, how's that for an idea?"

Adric's cheeks were scarlet now, but Perna merely laid a small, proprietary hand on his arm and bestowed a serene smile upon Niall.

Out of sight beneath the table, Cahira nudged her friend with her knee. "Stop it," she murmured, fighting a strong urge to giggle. He stared at her with one black eyebrow raised in surprise, as if he couldn't imagine what she might mean.

Cahira desperately bit down on her bottom lip until she had her feelings under control. Refusing to look at Niall again, she distracted herself by raising her voice to address Mundar. "I suppose you're staying in the garrison too, Captain?"

But he shook his head. "No, I've left the Guards. I have my navigator's ticket and I've signed on with a trading ship, sailing in a few days. There should be plenty of opportunities for us, now that the Council have hammered out a new trade deal with Bregia."

Cahira was surprised. Mundar had told her at the docks that the shipboard life of his Trader family wasn't for him. What had changed his mind? The image of him in the tapestry, standing on a tossing deck, came back to her. Perhaps it was his future she'd seen after all.

"I don't know why we're dealin' with them Bregians at all," Bett burst out, "when they attacked us that way. We should go an' invade them, see how they likes it."

Niall shook his head, his eyes wide and guileless. "But, haven't you heard, Mistress Bett? The rulers of our dear neighbour across the strait knew nothing about any invasion plan. The Imperator is deeply distressed that a group of war hawks high up in the military *dared* to act alone, *completely* without his authorisation. The Bregian delegate to the Council was extremely apologetic."

Bett snorted. Niall clasped his hands together on the table and plastered an ingratiating expression on his sharp features. His voice rose half an octave and took on a simpering tone that had Cahira biting her lip again.

"A truly *shocking* act of insubordination, honourable councillors, that will be dealt with *most* severely. It is to be hoped that this *unfortunate incident* will not be allowed to sour the friendly and *mutually beneficial* relationship between our two great nations."

"And how did he explain the appearance of that thing in the sky above the harbour, and the effect it had on everyone?" Mundar asked, his voice and expression too neutral for Cahira to guess at his true feelings on the matter.

Niall dropped the mimicry and reverted to his usual drawl. "Why, a mass hallucination, my dear chap, deliberately brought on by a small group of religious fanatics. Drugged smoke is the current theory, I believe, blown from the top of the headland over the fighters below."

Cahira's whole body stiffened. The memories swept over her, and any temptation to laugh at Niall's nonsense fled. She wasn't ready to joke about Kolos. Maybe she never would be. The monster had come so close to destroying not only her, but everyone and everything she cared about. She shuddered at the memory of tentacles sliding through her brain, taking over her thoughts. She clenched her hands under the table, resisting the sudden urge to check them for traces of indigo rivulets flowing beneath the skin.

Niall sent a sidelong glance her way and rushed back into speech. "Anyway, the upshot is, Logen has secured very favourable trading terms with the Bregians."

"Huh," Bett huffed, "well that's good, I guess, but I still don't trust 'em."

"Oren will have people keeping an eye out, both here and in Bregia," Mundar said. "Trade and free travel create many opportunities, not all of them financial."

He said no more, but Cahira believed she knew why he'd abandoned the Guards and returned to shipboard life. He was still secretly working for Oren, in a job where his ability to hide his thoughts and feelings behind a mask of neutrality would be a distinct advantage.

"And what about you, Cahira?" Mara asked. "What are your plans?"

Before she could answer, a commotion arose outside the room.

"Let me in!"

A brief scuffling, a grunt, and a gruff "None of that!", and a blond head poked in through the doorway. "Mara, there's a young man here, says he wants to see Cahira."

Cahira rose in surprise. From the corner of her eye, she saw Niall do the same. Her mind flashed first to Ferdy, but it hadn't sounded like him. Besides, Ferdy was safely installed at the Academy. She'd taken him there herself and left him in the care of her old teacher, Adara Domben. Adara was Head Scholar of the Academy now, and she'd been delighted to sponsor the talented Skalsinger. But what other young man would be asking to see Cahira?

"Bring him in, Dana," Mara said. "She's very protective," she added in an aside.

Two well-built, muscular women entered the room, with an even taller figure held fast between them. Red-haired, but not Ferdy. For a moment, Cahira thought she was looking at a stranger, until Niall exclaimed, "Kelan!"

He was right. The intruder was lankier than the last time she'd seen him, but it was the teenager Bram had saved at Fortune Creek.

Cahira had spent more than a few sleepless hours since then thinking hard thoughts about Kelan, wondering if things would have turned out differently if the inexperienced boy had just stayed under the table with his mother, instead of trying to help fight off the Guards. But that was unfair. He'd only been wanting to do his best, like the rest of them.

And, according to Niall, the newly-skalled Charm Shaper had already invented something that had helped the defenders' arrows fly true at Eder Ford. But it was a month into winter now, and Kelan should be in class. What was he doing here, looking for her?

His eyes met hers, then flicked around the table, widening as they alighted on Niall and Adric. "Thank Aal you're all here! Tell them to let me go! I've got news you need to hear, right now."

"It's fine," Cahira said to Mara. "He's a friend."

Mara waved a hand. The women released Kelan's arms and stepped back.

Kelan strode up to the table. "Cahira, you have to come to Eorna," he blurted. "There's something wrong in the city. And it's to do with Kolos."

Cahira's mouth went dry. All the pleasure of this reunion drained out of her.

"Kolos is dead," Niall said harshly.

Kelan shook his head. "I know we all thought that, but this has been turning up in the Academy, and lots of other places, and people are acting weird." He pulled a rolled parchment from inside his jacket and thrust it into Niall's hands. Cahira peered down as her friend spread it out on the table.

It was a simple ink drawing, like something done by a child, but even so, its subject was unmistakable. It was all there: the blind, bulging head, the black hole of a mouth, the tentacles. Cahira sucked in a sharp breath and backed away, as if she might be contaminated by standing too close.

Niall released the vile sketch, which rolled itself up. The crackling of the parchment was loud in the sudden silence. Niall wiped his fingers on his cloak.

"You beat it once," Kelan said, green eyes pleading with Cahira. "You can do it again."

She mutely shook her head, desperate to be anywhere but here. She couldn't go through all that a second time. She wouldn't.

"Leave her alone," Niall said flatly, his tone deadly serious.

Kelan backed off a step, but then that stubborn determination Cahira remembered stamped itself on his features. "I can't. We need her."

"I'll come with you," Niall said, "but she's done enough."

"Me too," Adric said, pushing his chair back. "I'm reporting to the garrison today, anyway. Don't worry, Kelan. It's probably just some idiot's idea of a joke. We'll sort it out."

Mundar stood without a word.

But now that the three of them had given her a way out, something tugged perversely at Cahira, urging her to reconsider. No matter what Adric said, she had known at first glance that this was serious. Did she really want to return tamely to her parents' estate and let her friends go into danger alone? She didn't. Yet how could she endure that nightmare again? She hesitated, miserably balanced on a knife edge between two very different paths.

In the silence, Perna also left her seat. But instead of offering her help, she leaned across the table, snatched up the parchment, and whirled to face the fireplace. She took a couple of quick steps forward and drew back her arm. Then, in one fluid movement, she flung the rolled-up drawing straight into the centre of the blaze and bowed her head.

"No!" Cahira choked out.

The fire roared up fiercely, as if eager to consume what Perna had fed it. Cahira stared in dismay as the red tongues of flame flared a familiar, murky green. They grew taller and taller, their purplish tips licking up into the chimney. And then, the whole conflagration flashed to a white so brilliant that she was forced to shade her eyes. When she could see again, the parchment was gone. Not even flakes of ash remained. The logs burned sedately with clear yellow flames.

Perna wiped her hands together matter-of-factly and turned to face the silent table once more. Her small face was untroubled.

"Wh—" Cahira swallowed in a dry throat and tried again. "What have you done?"

The novice drew herself to her full, diminutive height. Wide russet eyes pinned Cahira with a level gaze.

"Courage," Perna said.

SIXTY-SIX

Cahira

The word echoed through her head as she trudged up the hill. Brittle frost crunched beneath her boots with every step, and the syllables kept the beat: *cou-rage, cou-rage, cou-rage.* By the time she gained the rounded summit, the sounds had almost lost their meaning. Almost.

Below, the world lay still and frozen. There wasn't the whisper of a breeze. Cahira drew a breath of cold air right down to the bottom of her lungs, released it. Warmed and moistened, it danced before her eyes in misty swirls, as pale as ghosts against the slate-grey sky. She waved them away irritably.

Even up here, the word wouldn't leave her alone. The hot resentment came rushing back. *Haven't I done enough?* she fumed. *Haven't I proved myself? What more do you want from me?* She'd risked her life and her sanity. She'd stood up to an attacking bear, an evil Mind Wender, a treacherous sorceress, and finally a monster out of a nightmare. Who was Perna, to look at her so solemnly and suggest that she needed more courage?

Cahira indulged her indignation for a few moments, then set it aside with a sigh and watched the misty ghosts rise again, this time unhindered. She hadn't come to this place she'd avoided for so long to hide from the truth dredged up by Perna's calm voice, but to face it squarely.

It hadn't been courage that had led her to tackle those dangers. She'd been driven by a myriad of emotions—fear, rage, revenge or sheer desperation. But behind them all lurked something that she'd refused to look at. Like a child hiding her head under the bedclothes and clenching her eyes shut against the darkness.

Niall had recognised it months ago, on the way to Mirston. He'd spoken with so much anger, so much hurt, but she'd turned away from his words, afraid to even consider them.

"He's gone, Cahira, and nothing is going to bring him back. Not this obsessive search for Adric, not ignoring your own health, not putting yourself in danger, nothing."

She'd replied hotly that he didn't understand. And he'd come right back at her with equal passion: *"I understand this is no way to grieve."*

And then the final shot, piercing her like an arrow: *"Have you even let yourself shed a tear for him, your beloved husband?"*

Not a single one, she thought. *Not back then.* She'd been too busy, hadn't she? Striking out in all directions. Following every lead. Keeping on the move at any cost. Staying ahead of the horror that lay close behind, threatening to swallow her whole if she stopped for a second—the black, bottomless well of her grief. She had looked into it briefly in the caves, but then sealed it up tightly again, thinking that was the only way forward.

But two weeks ago, in the dead of night, hours after Perna had delivered her brief, offensive message, Cahira had woken with a start and shot upright. Her heart was thumping, and Niall's words were breaking over her like waves crashing onto a seashore, obliterating her defences as if they were made of sand. She had wept for a long time, alone in the dark, and then she had done some hard thinking.

And so, when the others had set out with Kelan next morning to investigate the mystery of the drawings, she'd turned Blackbird towards her parents' estate after all. Only the day before, the chance of meeting Kolos again had horrified her almost beyond measure, but she already knew, even as she rode away, that in some ways it would have been the easier path to tread.

Because true courage required her to do something infinitely harder. To return home alone, climb this low, quiet hillside, and face what awaited her here: her own heart, ripped from her body and buried beneath the ground, weighed down by a heavy, grey stone.

Even after she'd made the decision, it had taken twelve days, setting out from the house in the dimness before sunrise, to walk all the way to the top without buckling and turning back.

She tugged off a glove, then knelt and brushed shaking fingers over the incised letters:

IN LOVING MEMORY OF BRAMLEY GELT
BELOVED SON, BROTHER, HUSBAND, AND FRIEND
GIFTED GREENHAELAN AND BEST OF MEN

Rest you now in peace
All strife ended
All struggles ceased
All hurts mended.

Sobs shook her. Twin rivers of tears flowed down her face and dripped onto the frosted ground. An enormous ache filled her entire being. And yet, she was not destroyed, not swallowed up and lost. She remained herself, Cahira. She traced the letters of his name and felt only sorrow and love.

Her blurred eyes went to the dedication again. She had taken no part in erecting the stone, had bitterly refused to be involved, but both the location and the words struck her as good. She should make a point of thanking her mother, who had loved Bram too, and had organised it all.

A breeze was drying the wetness from her cheeks. She took a breath and felt as if some binding cord, deep inside her chest, slowly parted and dissolved. She read the last three words again: *All hurts mended.*

Well, her hurts weren't all mended, not even close, but there'd been times this past week when she'd been truly glad to think that Bram's might be. She hadn't seen him in Aal's tapestry, but she was suddenly certain that he was there, walking forward with his steady, long-legged stride. His thread, she thought, would be a smooth, warm brown, with no tangles or knots.

There had also been sleepless nights when she'd soaked her pillow with bitter tears. And days when she'd ridden out of earshot of the house to scream aloud at the agony of having to live without him, minute after minute, day after day, for the rest of her life. She knew there'd be more of both to come. But it would be worse to lock up her heart and refuse to think of him at all. Because that would be killing him a second time.

The light grew, casting a delicate blush onto the back of her hand, still touching the stone. No drop of ink, real or imagined, remained. She was as sure of that as she was of anything. Every trace of Kolos had fled from her as she sang on the headland. She remembered nothing of that glorious song now: not a word, not a note. Only the feeling had stayed with her.

That was a kind of grief too, but one that contained a piercing sweetness. As if heartbreak and joy were inseparable, each somehow less without the other. Like the misery of going on without Bram, and the pleasure of remembering their time together. Two sides of the same coin. Or two halves of the same heart. Fresh tears traced warm rivulets down her frozen cheeks.

A fluttering startled her. She snatched back her hand with a jerk. A robin landed on top of the grave marker in a flurry of wings, cocking its head and fixing her with a gleaming eye. The sight brought a small smile to her lips.

"Well, hello," she said. "You're a fine fellow, aren't you?"

The bird chirped and puffed out its red-badged chest, as if it understood the compliment and agreed with it. Cahira laughed. It felt good.

One last thing to do here. She fished the sky stone from her pocket and held it up to catch the light. Faint wisps of pure white that she'd never noticed before gleamed between the streaks that had always reminded her of storm clouds.

Not so dark after all, she thought.

The robin watched with bright eyes as she laid the token gently on top of the gravestone and stood to leave.

When she reached the bottom of the hill, she whistled the two notes Niall had taught her long ago. Blackbird lifted her head from where she'd been picking at the sparse, frozen blades of grass. Cahira gazed back fondly as the mare trotted up, then stroked the warm, velvety neck for a few moments before mounting.

She had formed no plan for the future, beyond reaching Bram's resting place. Even a day ago, that had seemed enough of a challenge. But as she settled into the saddle, a new course suddenly opened to her, written on her mind as clearly as if it, too, was engraved in stone.

Ever since she'd seen the drawing on the scroll, she'd been sure of one thing: Kolos might or might not be dead, but its influence was very much alive. The battle had been won, but not the war. And now she knew what her next role in the struggle was to be. It wasn't anything she would have predicted for herself, but it felt absolutely *right*, and she was already working out how to make it happen.

She ticked the steps off on her fingers. First, she'd talk to her parents. They'd been worried about her, and they would be glad she had a purpose again. She must remember to thank them for everything, too.

Then she'd pack and enjoy one more night's sleep in a familiar bed, and leave early tomorrow. It was a tradition that any Master Skalsinger could claim a set of rooms at the Academy in exchange for a little teaching. She'd never intended to use the privilege, but it would come in handy now. She'd ask about Ferdy, too, and make sure he was doing well.

Sixth finger: she'd arrange to meet Niall and Adric to find out what they'd discovered about the drawings so far. She could invite Logen and Bella, too, and get the latest news from the Council and the tavern keeper's network.

Armed with all this information from the present, she'd begin her real task: delving into the past. She'd ask Adara Domben for permission to explore the Archives in the ancient tunnels beneath the Academy, the ones that had lain untouched for at least eighty years. Adara was an intelligent woman and a friend. She'd help in any way she could.

Important answers lay down there, Cahira knew it. There would be songs, poems, journals, historical accounts—all manner of things— going back centuries. Somewhere among them must be long-forgotten writings about Kolos and its Disciples. And any difficulties translating the oldest texts could be dealt with by the Academy's history and languages faculties, also under the charge of Cahira's former mentor. It was perfect.

And while she was there, she'd do some searching on her own behalf, about Aal. The encounter on the headland couldn't be ignored. Or rather, she didn't want to ignore it. Oh, and she'd find out if Elder Meril was still in Eorna and ask her some questions, too.

The whole enterprise would need patience and attention to detail, not Cahira's strongest traits. But her curiosity had always been intense, and it was that side of her personality she'd be following now. Who knew what buried secrets she'd discover, what strange mysteries she might solve? *I'll be digging for long lost treasure*, she thought, and a fizz of excitement filled her.

She had run out of fingers. There was a lot to do, and she couldn't wait to get started. But not because she was fleeing from anything—not this time. She wouldn't avoid thoughts of Bram, no matter how painful they were. She'd carry her love and her memories with her, nestled in her heart alongside her grief.

A rapid series of notes swelled from somewhere above. She peered up, searching for the source. Perched on top of Bram's stone, bathed in rosy light, the little robin poured out its dawn salutation, like joy made audible. As if summoned by the bird, the sun breasted the horizon, its low rays setting the frosted grass afire with golden sparks. An irrepressible smile twitched Cahira's lips as she pressed her heels to Blackbird's flanks. The mare moved off into the glittering new day.

Still listening to the robin, Cahira drew in a generous portion of air, held it for a moment, then sent it forth in a gentle hum. In her mind, the threads of a winter song wove themselves together.

END

ABOUT THE AUTHOR

L.A. Webster (Lyn) is a retired teacher who writes speculative fiction, mainly adult fantasy. After spending a considerable portion of her life exploring imaginary places in books written by other people, she finally took her courage in her hands and set out in search of a fantasy world of her own.

After a few wrong turns, she found herself mysteriously transported to the magical island of Algarth, where she's been spending most of her fictional time ever since.

In the mundane world, Lyn lives, writes and gardens in regional Australia (another strange and wondrous land) with her husband and a small enthusiastic dog.

You can find Lyn at her website **LynWebster.com**
Or catch up with her on Twitter **@TwoBooksBlog**

www.ingramcontent.com/pod-product-compliance
Lightning Source LLC
Chambersburg PA
CBHW020008120726

47903CB00004B/1195